BLOODSTOCK

Simon Ellice. Si. The good-looking, confident boy who could swim faster, tackle harder and box better than any of the others. The first to have sex, the first to steal a car, still the only one to climb the front of School House.

I wanted to hate him, but I couldn't help liking him. Always having fun, always doing something no one else would think of, or dare to do. Good with horses, good with guns and when it came to it, good with me.

Trouble to have around, but when trouble came, the one I needed.

Melissa Franklin

BLOODSTOCK

ROD HUMPHRIS

a Simon Ellice story

First published in Great Britain in 2020 by Rat's Tales

Rat's Tales Ltd 6-7 Queen Street Bath, BA1 1HE

Copyright © Rod Humphris, 2020

The moral right of Rod Humphris to be identified as the Author of this work has been asserted

This is a work of fiction. Names, characters, businesses, places, events, locales, and incidents are either the products of the author's imagination or used in a fictitious manner. Any resemblance to actual persons, living or dead, or actual events is purely coincidental.

10 9 8 7 6 5 4 3 2 1

Typesetting by sheerdesignandtypesetting.com
Printed and bound in Great Britain by T J Books Limited

Illustrations by Laura Molnar

A CIP catalogue record for this book is available from the British Library

ISBN: 978-1-9996517-2-5

All rights reserved. No part of this publication may be reproduced, distributed, or transmitted in any form or by any means, including photocopying, recording, or other electronic or mechanical methods, without the prior written permission of the copyright owner and the publisher of this book.

The paper this book is printed on is certified by the (c) 1996 Forest Stewardship Council A.C. (FSC). It is ancient-forest friendly. The printer holds FSC chain of custody SGS-COC-2061

CONTENTS

1	An Inexpensive Woman	9
2	The Smell of Hay	32
3	Thomas Wild	50
4	Harmless, if not Cute	61
5	Apollo in the Shades	78
6	The Gun Room	90
7	Some Strands of Hair	105
8	An Expensive Woman	120
9	Undone	140
10	A Can of Worms	157
11	Let it Snow	174
12	Knock Out	191
13	Live Bait	200
14	Residue	216
15	Nutters	228
16	A Screaming Peacock	241
17	Faces of Desire	251
18	The White Wood	265

19	Hare's Ears	278
20	Bacchus Est Deus	294
21	The Goddess of the Sanctuary	318
22	Let it Rain	337
23	In which Case, Aphrodite	351
24	Under the Influence	366
25	Return of the Native	375
26	A Diving Eagle	390
27	Thunder Clouds	408
28	A Wounded Bird	424
29	Here, Boy, Pass Me My Assagai	434
30	A Rabbit on a Green Field	450
31	The Greens	464
32	Stoat's Nest	472
33	Good Evening, My Lady	485
34	In the Hands of Women	491
35	Soup's Off	495

To Domnita

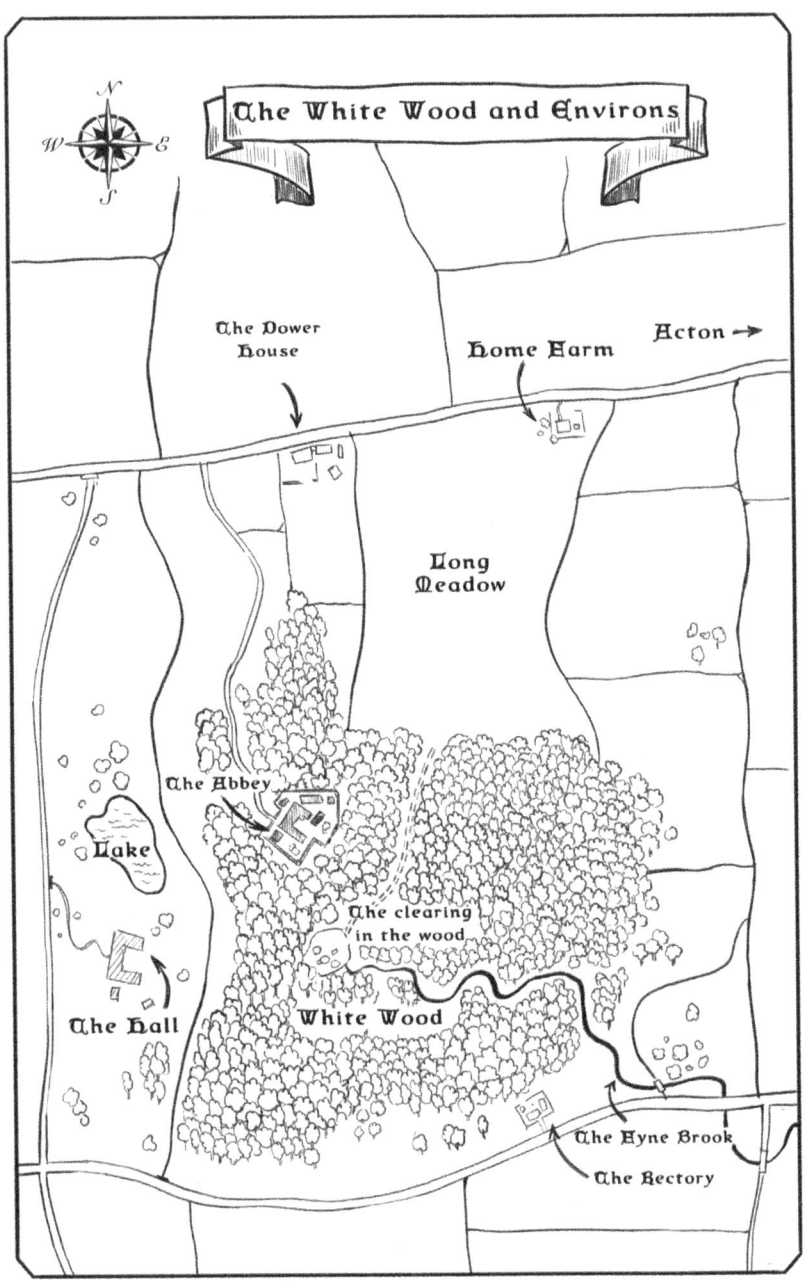

1

AN INEXPENSIVE WOMAN

I saw her and wanted her. What can I say; I'm a man, and it had been a while. She was leaning on the rail, looking across the water at Polly, and I was certain she was alone. I went over to her and said, "She looks like a swan in the company of pigs, doesn't she?" It was the best I could think of at the time.

"She?" she said, in a Russian accent. She didn't move her head, but kept right on looking at Polly.

"All boats are female," I said.

"Boat go anywhere," she said.

"You can. From shore to shining shore. She has swum the coral main and braced the foaming seas of faery lands forlorn."

"Boat yours?" She turned to me now. Her face was lovely in that pale, high cheek-boned way. Her widely spaced eyes were as blue, in their heavily shadowed orbits, as the winter skies over the caucasus. Or so it seemed to me.

"She's mine, or I'm hers," I said.

"What mean?"

"She's my companion and my home."

"You talk like woman, but thing."

"I feel about her like she's a woman. More or less."

"More. For you, women thing. Boat more expensive than woman."

"Did I wrong you in a previous life?"

"You man."

"Sorry about that. I haven't been in the habit of seeing that as a problem, but I could be wrong."

"Never do."

"Us men, you mean?"

"Rich boat. You very rich."

"I stole her."

"Da. Rich steal. You have woman clean boat."

"No, I clean her myself and I have no woman."

"Da. You want sex."

"Ah. Sorry about that; I didn't mean to be so obvious."

"You man." She shrugged.

"So it seems. I don't mean to rule sex out, but can I buy you a drink while we talk about my shortcomings?"

"Nyet."

"To be fair to me, the drink is just a drink. I want one myself and I'll enjoy it more in your company, but I won't think I'm buying you with it."

"Nyet. I woman you buy, not buy drink."

I had to think about that for a moment.

"Ah. Sorry, I didn't realise."

"Now you not buy, or buy drink."

"No, I'm enjoying your company and I definitely want to buy you a drink. What you do for a living is none of my business."

"Nyet. I rude to you. You go away."

An Inexpensive Woman

"I know, but I like it. You can carry on being rude to me if you like, but let's do it with glasses in our hands."

"Maybe you buy drink," she shrugged, "cost same."

"Okay, what the hell. How much?" I got a roll of notes out of my pocket.

"Nyet. Man there." She indicated a nearby bar called the *Sea Hare* with her head.

"Oh." I put the notes back in my pocket.

"Da?"

"My pride is being a problem."

"You man." She shrugged again.

"So it seems. I don't want to give another man money for you. Does he really own you, this man?"

"More women."

"I can't see any," I said, and looked about. There were some other women in the vicinity but none of them as beautiful as she; not nearly.

"You go now," she said.

"Can I buy you from this man and set you free so that you can have a drink with me? But only if you want to."

"You romantic, Mr Rich Man." She said it like it was a bad thing.

"Call me Si and let me set you free. Don't you want to be free?"

"Not free."

"Why can't you be free?"

"Not game. You go now." She glanced in the direction of the club.

"How much do you think you would cost?" I said. "To be free of him, whoever he is."

"Nyet. You go now."

"I don't want to do that either."

"You always getting you want."

"People have said that about me."

11

I looked at Polly sitting on the narrow bit of water inside the big, dirty city and wondered what I wanted. Apart from the woman. Well, the woman would be a good start. And a drink.

"Da?" she said.

"I was thinking that I had never bought a woman before, but perhaps that isn't really true," I said. "Men and women and money and power are complicated subjects."

"True. You stay in safe, rich, Mr. Is better for you."

"I'm bored of my safe, rich world. Why don't we take the boat and go? Right now. We could steal you from him. Then you would be free. Where would you like to go?"

"Nyet. Not free. Not go."

"Yes you can. You were looking at her a moment ago thinking of sailing away on her. I could see you were. Say yes, and we'll go now. Right now. Anywhere you like."

"Nyet." Her eyes were troubled. She looked at me, measuring me.

"Why not? I don't really want to be here and you don't either. Let's go somewhere else." I let her see that I was serious, and as a matter of fact, I was.

"You will get hurt."

"Will I? Who will hurt me?"

"Stupid." She looked towards the *Sea Hare*

"Someone inside there is going to hurt me for talking to you?"

"Da."

"Even if I buy you?"

"Probably I buy already." She shrugged again.

"Then I will pay more."

On cue a man came out of the restaurant and walked towards us. He didn't look happy to see me talking to the woman.

"I need you, now," he said to her.

"Da," she said, and her voice wasn't the voice she'd been talking to me with.

"Excuse me…" I said.

"On your way, chum," he said to me.

"I beg your pardon," I said.

"You heard me," he said.

"Is nothing," she said. "Is no one."

She stepped forward and he took her arm between his fingers and began taking her away. It was nothing to do with me and I wasn't going to do anything, but then I did anyway.

"Forgive me interrupting," I said, stepping forward quickly and getting in front of them, "but I want to speak to you."

"Not interested, mate. Now fuck off," he said, jerking a thumb.

"No." I said.

"Look, don't be a stupid prick. I'm busy, so go away before I have to hurt you."

I looked at him, measuring his intent. There was quite a bit of him and he had a stupid, brutal kind of face.

"No, I think I'd rather not," I said, smiling in spite of myself.

"Fuck. Okay, if that's the way you want it."

He let go of the girl and absentmindedly turned the ring on the little finger of his left hand round so that the stone was on the inside. I watched him do it, feeling time slow down and everything come into focus, the way it does in such circumstances.

When he came at me, I let him take the first swing. It was a wild blow but powerful; his bigness wasn't just for show. I moved my head out of the way and, as his arm swung through, punched him on the nose over it. I could feel myself grinning.

Bright blood ran down onto his white shirt and he bellowed something and came at me again with both arms swinging fast; the hard, professional blows of a man who has boxed. He drove me back, meaning to overwhelm me with his slugging. I went back, blocking and ducking until I began to run out of space, then

I stopped going back and punched through, connecting with his nose again. This time I felt it break. It was an excellent feeling.

He stopped trying to hit me and held his face, feeling his nose with his fingers. He was done for the moment, so I left him and went back to the girl.

"Sorry about that," I said.

"Nyet," she said, shaking her head.

"Okay, I'm not really sorry, but I mean to be sorry," I said.

"Trouble now," she said, looking towards the man.

"You were in trouble anyway," I said.

"Now he hit me."

"So come with me and then he won't."

"Nyet."

"Why not?"

"Nyet."

"Tell me why."

"Nyet."

"There must be a reason?"

"Dochka," she said, and there was a longing and a grief in her voice that finally got my attention. "Irena. Dochka."

"Dochka? Daughter?" I said. "Ah, fuck. I'm sorry, I've been very stupid."

She looked at me with pain and no hope and I saw that her attitude before had been an act of courage and that by offering her things she couldn't have, I'd been unkind.

Her eyes moved past me to the man and were full of fear. I turned to look at him too. He'd stopped holding his nose and was looking at me with hatred. He looked back towards the bar and then put his eyes on me and took his phone out of his trouser pocket.

When he looked down to use it, I closed the distance between us in two silent strides, plucked it out of his hand and tossed it into the water. It made a surprisingly loud splash.

"More?" I said, meeting his eye.

He saw that I wanted it but he didn't want it.

"Later," he said and turned away and went into the *Sea Hare*.

The people around had stopped to watch. Some of them looked interested and some of them looked embarrassed. I ignored them and went to the girl again.

"Sorry," I said, again.

"Sorry no good," she said.

"What're you going to do?" I said.

She shook her head without speaking.

"Would some money help?"

She looked at the ground and gave her head another little shake. "Nyet."

"Here," I pulled out my bundle of notes, peeled off a few and held them out, "You could hide some and give them the rest. Tell them I gave it to you."

"Nyet," she said, raising her head and looking at me. The way she did it didn't make me feel good at all.

"So, what would help?" I said, meeting her eye and taking what she was giving out, which was only fair.

"Dochka," she said. "Irena dochka."

"Ah," I said.

"Da?"

"I don't know," I said.

"Trakhat tebya," she said, and then she stepped past me and walked across the space and into the *Sea Hare*.

Seeing that the entertainment was over, the crowd went back to doing other things and so did I. I went and leant on the rail where she had been, looked at Polly and thought about the beautiful, hard, brave, Russian woman.

Polly, Wise Policy, the beautiful sailing yacht that I'd stolen from my father and was now my home, was still lovely, sitting slack at her mooring in the company of fakers and cheats, but nothing else was any good. I could take the next tide and go back down river. Back to the wide blue sea and the lithe, tanned party girls of the Mediterranean yachting scene. Back to the empty bloody sea and the empty-headed bloody girls of the pointless, boring Mediterranean yachting scene. I remembered that I'd been about to go and find a drink and decided that that was probably a good idea. Or at least, the best one I could think of under the circumstances.

"Excuse me, sir," a voice from behind me said, in that unmistakeable way.

"Yes, officer?" I said, turning round.

"I believe you've been involved in an affray, sir."

He was black, under thirty, not excessively tall and bulky in a vest which seemed to contain enough equipment to go camping.

"I suppose you could say that," I said.

"I believe you started it. Is that correct, sir?"

"Don't they say it's our oldest profession? No, I didn't start it, officer. Not by a long, long way."

"I see, sir. If you would just tell me your side of the story before I decide whether I need to take the matter further." He was looking at me as if I might be trouble. He may have been right.

Behind him, the man I'd hit and two others appeared in the doorway of the bar. They eyed us balefully. I gave them a smile. They hesitated and then turned away.

"I can't say I will," I said.

"I beg your pardon, sir?" the policeman said.

"Look, it wasn't anything much. Can't we just not bother? I want to go and have a drink," I said.

"Now, look here, sir…"

"Don't tell me you're in trouble already, Si?" A lean man in a bad suit and thick-rimmed glasses joined us.

An Inexpensive Woman

"I don't think so, Bill," I said, holding out my hand.

"Well, thank fuck for that." He took my hand and stood there looking at me. The sardonic bastard looked nearly as tired as when I'd seen him last but the keen, hawk-like toughness was still there. Seeing him made me feel better. A bit.

"This gentleman is inquiring into a minor affray," I said.

"Only minor?" Bill said.

"Excuse me, sir. I'm in the middle of questioning this gentleman. If you wouldn't mind stepping back," the officer said.

"At ease, constable. I can vouch for this man." Bill extracted his warrant card, flipped it open and held it out for the man to see.

"I see, sir," he said, and it was a very different kind of 'sir'.

"Someone tell me what happened, then," Bill said.

"Report of a BOP, sir. Two IC1 males. One IC1 female involved, sir," the constable said.

"Someone was being nasty to a hooker," I said.

"So, you hit him?" Bill said.

"Yes."

"And what do you think he's going to do to her?"

"Okay, it was stupid. It's being in the city; I feel hemmed in," I said.

"So, you took it out on some poor chap who was just minding his own business making a living from the suffering of others," Bill said.

"I suppose I did."

"Fair enough. On your way, constable. Nothing to do here."

"Very good, sir. If you say so. Goodnight, sir." He nodded to me and went away.

"Was she pretty?" Bill said.

"Very," I said.

"You look well," he said.

"You look knackered," I said.

"I expect I do. How're you finding London? Or shouldn't I ask?" He grinned at me.

"Who says I'm even here," I said. "Are you drinking by the way? Or are you on duty or something?"

"Don't give me that crap."

We went further along and sat at the bar of a pizza restaurant. There seemed to be a choice of more or less pretentious lagers. I had what Bill chose and it wasn't too bad.

"It's good to see you, Si," he said.

"It's good to see you too, Bill," I said.

"But you're not unreservedly happy to be here in this wonderful city then?"

"You've a funny idea of wonderful. I can see the point of civilisation, but that doesn't mean I have to like it. There are millions of people round here pushing bits of paper from one side of their desks to the other for no particular reason. It scares me and I don't mind admitting it."

"Don't worry, no one's going to make you join them."

"I'd like to see them try."

"Have you been to see your folks yet?"

"No. I'll do that tomorrow."

"Fair enough. Mud in your eye." He lowered the level of his glass considerably and put it down.

"Likewise," I said.

We looked at each other. What we'd done together in Morocco the summer before was still there between us and I was glad I hadn't killed the bastard. Perhaps he was glad he hadn't tried to arrest me. I hoped so.

"You've got glasses," I said.

"So it seems," he said.

"And I take it you're still vainly trying to make the world a better place?"

An Inexpensive Woman

"Unlike you."

"What would you have? I am what I am."

"Nothing; I'll take you just you are you are, old thing."

"That's all there is. Who've I pissed off, by the way?"

"It's probably a long list…"

"I mean the man I just hit. From that bar." I nodded towards the *Sea Hare*.

"Oh…" he tapped his teeth with one finger, "…no idea. Probably just a freelancer with her minder. Don't worry about it."

"I don't think so. She said they had her daughter."

"Ah, the nasty side of it."

"It has a nice side?"

"That's a point of view. For some girls, it's pretty much a career choice. They put themselves through college or whatever. You could say that they're pressured into it by poverty or you could say it's their choice. Like I say, it depends on your point of view."

"She didn't know about the money they charge for her either."

"Then that's the gangs. Slavery by any other name. They buy the girl and then feed and house her but after that it's all profit. Same with the sweatshops, seasonal labour, begging, thieving, all that. We'll be having people brought in for their organs next, if we aren't already. Didn't know that place was anything to do with it though."

"I thought I'd left all that sort of thing behind in Africa."

"Not a bit of it, old son; crime is a universal feature of mankind. Didn't you know?"

"You're not expecting to run out of work then?"

"No." He gave me a weary grin, "I'm not. But what about you? You miss it, don't you?"

"Miss what? Crime?"

"You know perfectly well. Being involved. Being a player. Having something to do. You're a man with a very low boredom threshold."

"He said, 'later,'" I said. "The man I hit."

"And you're hoping he wants a return match?"

"I don't know."

"Oh yes you do."

"Okay, maybe I do."

"You want to have a good fight and get the girl, don't you? It's amazing you've lived this long."

"I did like the feeling of his nose breaking."

"Go on, admit it: you're bored."

"Possibly. Slightly."

"Well, let's hope that whatever you do about it this time, is more sensible than last time," he said.

"Let's not hope for too much," I said.

"Fair enough. I'm glad you phoned. I was hoping you would."

"Pleased to see me then?"

"Didn't I say so?"

"Sort of. But you've other reasons?"

"Why did you?"

"Phone? Soumy told me to."

"Your girl? The Moroccan one, I mean?"

"Not my girl. She says she loves me but that I'd make a really bad husband. She's probably right."

"I'm sure she is."

"Thanks. She told me to go home and start my life again. I said I would; she's more likely to be right about that kind of thing than I am. She said I should find you and ask you what you meant by a job, so here I am."

"She's a very clever girl."

"Yes, she is. So, stop trying to wind me up, and tell me what you meant by a job."

"Ah, well, yes. I just said that. I do that sometimes, have an idea in the moment." He looked into his beer. "Sometimes they come to something, and sometimes they don't."

"Yes, and…?"

"What're you doing now?"

"Right now?"

"Could you eat something?"

"I can always eat something, you know that."

"Well, come on then."

We walked up to Tower Bridge and Bill led the way to a taxi parked on double yellow lines not far away. It had a parking ticket stuck to the windscreen. Bill pulled it off, got in the front and added it to a raft of them stuck to the underside of the glove box.

"Get in the back. You can be my passenger," he said.

"Did you steal this, Bill?" I said.

"Confiscated it. The parking fines are going to the address of a small-time crook I'm trying to piss off."

"Why?"

"So that he does something stupid."

"Like what?"

"I don't know, try to have me killed perhaps."

He indicated and we were let out into the stream of cars by another taxi. There was a lot of traffic and we abandoned the taxi somewhere on Camden Road and went a few stops up the Piccadilly line.

"This is a bit overkill just to have supper in some bistro, isn't it?" I said, walking with him up a quiet residential street in Finsbury Park. "Not that there seem to be any."

"Actually, there's a nice one round the corner, but that's not where we're going, this is." He took a key out of his pocket, opened the front door of number 114, and stepped into the hall. "Come on in. Hi, honey, I'm home."

A slim, dark woman in a paint spattered smock came tripping lightly down the stairs and looked at me over her glasses.

"You must be Simon," she said.

"Simon. Natalie, my wife," Bill said.

She wiped a hand on her smock and offered it to me.

"Bloody hell, Bill," I said. "Nice to meet you, Natalie." I took her hand. There was still some paint on it.

"Bill's told me all about you," she said. "You're staying for supper." It wasn't a question.

"Nat's my sanity," Bill said.

"And he's mine, aren't you, darling?" they kissed hello and she carefully took his glasses off and put them on the hall table. "That's better. I've got an exhibition coming up and I'm behind as usual," she said.

"You carry on, darling. We'll make supper. I'll call you when it's ready."

"That's very sweet of you. There's chicken in the fridge."

"This way, Si. You can wash that off in the sink," Bill said, leading the way into a cluttered and homely kitchen-come-dining room.

Almost all the available wall space was taken up with oils. Mainly wood and stone, water and light, but some portraits too. There was also a stack of them on the floor leaning against the wall.

"You'll find a bottle of wine in the fridge and an opener in the drawer. I'll be back in a moment. Make yourself at home." Bill took off his shoes and put them in a rack by the door to the small back garden and disappeared upstairs.

When he came down again, wearing an old jersey and loose cotton trousers, I'd washed my hands, got the bottle open, helped myself and him and taken my own shoes off.

"I had no idea, Bill," I said.

"That I was married?" he said.

"What on earth does she see in you?"

"Don't ask me," he said, and I envied him his smile as he said it. "How are you on garlic and chilli, by the way?"

"I'm entirely positive about garlic and chilli."

"Thought you would be. I've been pretty busy since you skipped out on me, by the way. There was all the clearing up to do and…"

Bill clearly wasn't ready to get to the subject in hand yet, so we talked about the past and this and that while he cooked and I laid the table under his direction. I'd done a bit of drug-running from Morocco to Spain, and he'd come out there to catch me, and my parents had turned up and… well, it got complicated. But we'd ended up as friends. Sort of.

When there were good smells coming from under the grill, he said, "Right, you watch that and I'll go and call Nat."

While he was gone, I kept one eye on the chicken and had a proper look at the paintings. They came back down together and Nat had taken off her smock and replaced it with a comfortable, but flattering, blouse and got almost all the paint off her hands. I poured her a glass of wine and topped up mine and Bill's.

"Thanks, Simon," she said, taking a sip and then peering under the grill. "That smells good, darling. I'm ravenous."

"Sit down you two. I'll serve," Bill said, taking off his apron and putting it away.

We ate grilled chicken with garlic and chilli, new potatoes, roast peppers and salad. It was excellent. We also opened another bottle of wine.

I asked Nat about her work and she told me, shyly, about her struggle to be good enough, and to believe that she was good enough, and then to begin to deal with galleries. If I'd had a house to hang pictures in, I would've bought some of hers, and I told her so, pointing out which ones I liked and why. Bill didn't say anything but he looked like he might burst with pride.

"I think you're very lucky to have a vocation, Nat," I said. "And you, Bill, with your insane desire to save the world."

"It's not insane," Nat said. "He saves peoples' lives. Sometimes. It's far more important than what I do. Pictures don't really matter. Not compared to what he does."

"You're wrong," I said. "Your paintings, and the love and commitment that goes into them, is the weight on the other side of the scales from the nastiness that he deals with every day. It makes it worth doing for him and helps him not to drown in it."

They both looked at me.

"What?" I said.

"You understand that and express it so clearly," Nat said, reaching out and putting her hand over mine.

"And yet he doesn't feel it," Bill said.

"Don't be nasty. This is the man who saved your life, remember," she said.

"Only because he wanted to talk to me. Right after that he told me he was going to feed me to the fish, and I believed him."

"That's perfectly true," I said.

"Well, as we're being serious, when you saved his life, you also saved mine, Simon. So, thank you," Nat said.

"If you're going to say things like that to me, Nat, I think you should call me Si," I said.

"Okay, Si, I will."

"And if I'd known Nat was at home worrying about you, Bill, I'd have locked you up in one of the dungeons of the Riby for your own safety."

They exchanged a look.

"What have I said now?" I said.

"Would you like some pudding?" Nat said.

We shared a pavlova with raspberries and cream and then Bill made coffee.

"I'm going to take mine upstairs and leave you two alone," Nat said. "You can leave the washing up."

"Okay, darling. Thanks," Bill said.

He stacked enough of the supper things on the draining board so that there was a clear space on the table and sat down.

"Now then, Bill. It's been a lovely evening and I'm touched that you've brought me home to meet Nat, but if you don't start talking, I'm going to load you into that dishwasher and put you on an intensive wash," I said.

"Okay, but before we talk about the job, there's something else I have to say."

"So, say it."

"Well, actually, it's *the* thing."

"*The* thing?"

"Yes…"

"You've gone funny again, Bill. Spit it out, man."

"Okay. I wouldn't say this to most of my colleagues. Actually, to any of them. But I have to be okay with myself. In life, I mean."

"In life?"

"Yes. And, for me, that means I have to get up everyday and do something useful. Something that has meaning for me, something I care about."

"You poor thing."

"I may look knackered. I may be knackered. And I know the job will never be done, but I'm here and it's here and I have to do it. And that's satisfying. It makes me happy."

"Fine. Did I not just say that I envied you and Nat having vocations? What's your point, exactly?"

"I heard you. You don't care about money, do you?"

"Not as long as I've got some, no."

"And you clearly don't care about what anyone else thinks of you, do you?"

"Why the fuck would I?"

"Exactly. So, what do you care about?"

"What do I care about?"

"You know what I mean."

"No, I don't. Well, I do in an intellectual way, but not like you do."

"Then, it's time you did. I'm asking you to start helping. Just because you can. And see if it works for you. Do you understand?"

"Possibly. Are you giving me a lecture on morality?"

"Yes." He looked at me; self-conscious and vulnerable and determined.

"Are you trying to save me, Bill?"

"Yes. I'm sorry, but I am. In your own way, you're a remarkable young man. I want you on my side. I want you to stop fucking about and take something seriously, before it's too late. Before what you did in Morocco becomes your reality."

"That's rather sweet." I gave him a grin. "But don't worry about it, I've done that, I'm not going to do it again."

"Bastard." He shook his head and then took a drink of coffee and put his cup down. "Why the fuck do I bother."

"It's in your nature. Now, Bill, stop distressing yourself and just tell me what you want me to do."

"Okay. This job we've been talking about."

"Or rather, not talking about."

"I just want you to be yourself really. But for the right reasons."

"Bill, you're being evasive. Lay it out for fuck's sake. Specifically, what?"

"Okay. You were right when you said I took some stupid chances in Nador. I shouldn't have done that. It's not what I'm good at. In the company of crooks, I look like what I am."

"A policeman."

"Yes. I've promised Nat not to do anything like that again."

"So, the thing with the taxi?"

"Oh, quite different."

"If you say so. But why me? Why not someone like, for example, Freddy."

"Ah, that is very much to the point. I won't tell you, I'll do better, I'll show you."

An Inexpensive Woman

He picked up his iPhone, passed it to me and got me to take a photo of him with it. He took the phone back and then played about with it for a bit. I drank my coffee and waited.

"We'll just give it a minute," he said, putting it down on the table, "ah, hang on, it's cooked. Look."

He passed it over to me. There on the little screen was his face and the words 'William Henry Smith, 98% probability'. Below that were multiple entries in Facebook, Youtube and other places.

"Facial recognition software?" I said.

"Yes. It's not a widely known fact, but undercover police-work has become more than a tad difficult of late. Almost impossible in fact. Any photo on any social media site, or CCTV image, and more and more of that is becoming available online, can establish a connection or even just a co-location with the wrong person and the outcome is a concrete overcoat."

"Hence the funny glasses?" I said.

"Yup. They've got infrared and stuff in them. I don't want you connected to me in any way. It's a technological arms race and we're losing it. This phone isn't registered to me or the Met, by the way, and this one," he put another one on the table, "which is, is turned off. And this one," he pulled out yet another phone, "is encrypted and hardened and…"

"A bit like this one?" I said, putting mine on the table.

"Oh. Yes. Anyway, that's for you." He gave me the phone.

"Thanks. Yes, I get the general idea."

"We've started a training program that looks for prospective undercover operatives and tries to recruit them before they've picked up associations that may later get them killed. It's only in its early days but we'll get there. We're also learning to hide a person's real associations under layers of disinformation. It's more of a workaround than a solution but it can work for less sophisticated targets. Now let's try you."

He took a photo of me and set the software running. It found me without any trouble and a few seconds later I was looking at a photo of a dusty yard outside an ugly concrete building on Romeo Harrak's Facebook page. Standing in the sunlight in front our dealing table was me and Happy and Karim. I was clearly giving orders and I didn't look pleased. There was about a block and a half of hash on the table.

"The stupid fuck," I said.

"You didn't even know he took that photo, did you?" Bill said. "There's an indellible record of you working for one of Morocco's most violent and sucessful hash dealers, and that is how the world will see you. Like it, or not."

"It wouldn't exist if I had," I said.

"You realise that's there forever now. No power on earth can get rid of it."

"Shit."

"Keep looking."

I did. There were photos of me on Nottambulo and, on Zara's page, photos of me and Guy by his pool. The old bastard was giving the camera a nasty leer.

"So, my plan to get away and put some distance between me and all that..." I said.

"Let's just say it was a bit naïve, shall we?" Bill said.

"Fuck."

"You may think that's in your past, but it may not be that simple. Have you considered how you're going to explain yourself to the inland revenue?"

"I didn't know I was going to bother. Why should I?"

"You just try buying a house and see what happens. Or even a car. Is Polly registered to you, by the way?"

"You know she isn't."

"So, if someone else took possession of her, what could you actually do about it?"

"I'd shoot the fucker for a start."

"That might possibly work in Nador, but in London, or Nice, or Barcelona?"

"Are you threatening me? I hope you're not." I looked at him carefully.

"No, I'm not. I'm really not. I'm just telling you, you're out on a limb and you haven't even noticed."

"I see."

"Don't worry, those of us who enforce the law also know how to get round it. None of this is unfixable."

"If I join your gang?"

"Yes. Don't be down-hearted, old son. All this just means you're super-qualified for undercover police-work, that's all."

"That sounds mean and grubby."

Bill took the phone from me and scrolled until he found the photo of me by the dealing table.

"And this wasn't?" he said.

"It didn't seem like it at the time," I said.

"And I have a theory," he said.

"Oh, do you? About what?"

"About you. I call it my smelly fish theory. Do you know what the biggest threat to a crook is?"

"Presumably, a bigger crook."

"Exactly. Sadly, not us. I'm willing to bet that if you put a crook in a room with a hundred other people the first person to notice that he's a crook will be the other crook in the room."

"Because the innocent lambs of the world don't think like that and aren't looking for it?"

"No, they don't. And you, old thing, stink like a dead haddock that's been out in the sun for a week. I bet that in any given group of people, the one I'm going to be most interested in, will be the one who tries to recruit you or kill you."

"Great."

"Just trying to save you from yourself, old thing."

"Thanks. And I don't like London. You want me to hang about with city gangs and inform on them?"

"Not particularly. I'm not interested in geography. Or gangs as such. I was just using that as an example."

"But you're the Met; you know, 'metropolitan'. As in, the city of London?"

"Heard of globalisation, have you? Think it doesn't apply to crime for some reason?"

"You mean abroad? You don't have jurisdiction."

"What makes you think I care? We met in Morocco, or have you forgotten?"

"Fair point. So, what is it you want me to do exactly?"

"Look into things, mainly. Track things down. Be a lightening conductor for interesting shit. Like I said, be yourself."

"Yes, but what kind of things?"

"Well…"

"You mean, you don't know?"

"Yes, I do… out-of-pattern things."

"What do you mean?"

"Things come up that don't necessarily fit into the pattern. Except sometimes much later when it's too late."

"What pattern?"

"The pattern the usual shit makes; you know. I'm not going to bother you with the routine stuff. I mean the odd things. Things that I can't justify resources for, but that are interesting. Or might be. Also, things that would ring alarm bells with the powers that be and get me shut down. Remember, we don't know each other."

"I see. Or I think I see."

"And there's another thing."

"What?"

"Why didn't Guy kill you?"

"Because I killed him first."

"Yes, but why?"

"I'm assuming it's because I'm a bit cleverer, or do you disagree?"

"He underestimated you, didn't he?"

"I suppose so…"

"But you don't realise why, do you?"

"Apparently, you're about to tell me."

"You have a certain boyish charm. People get misled by it. They mistake you for the easy-going chap you appear to be. Even when they should know better. Don't they?"

"I suppose so. Sometimes."

"I've seen it happen. You did it to Freddy. You did it to me for fuck's sake. And that was after you'd saved me from Major Grant and then frightened the crap out of me. See what I mean?"

"What can I say…" I said, giving him a grin, "it's a talent."

"There you go. You look like an easy-going, good-natured young man with no discernible morals, and people so often just don't get what a tricky, ruthless bastard you really are, until it's too late."

"What do you mean, too late?"

"Would you like a little brandy? I've got a nice Armagnac in the cupboard."

"Yes. What do you mean, too late?

"Ah, well. That depends."

"Oh, I see," I said. What he wasn't saying was finally starting to make sense to me.

"Do you?" he said, looking a mite apprehensive.

"You're planning to revive Scitan, aren't you?"

"Not really."

"Not really?"

"Well, okay. Maybe a bit."

2

THE SMELL OF HAY

The next morning I took myself off to the café nearest to Polly and ordered the full English and coffee and looked at the world and the people passing. Most of them, I supposed, were passing with the intention of going somewhere to do something.

"You look thoughtful, sir," my waiter said.

"I'm wondering if I should take a job," I said.

"Is it well paid, sir?"

"I didn't ask."

He looked at me as if I was a strange kind of fish.

"In which case, is it your vocation, sir? Are you called to it? Does it call to you?"

"I don't know that either. It is a good question though," I said, and gave him some more of my attention.

"I cannot advise you, sir. Perhaps you should toss a coin."

"Do you have a vocation…?"

"Henriques, sir. Yes, I'm an actor."

"Ah. I was starting to think you weren't really a waiter."

"More coffee, sir?"

"Thank you."

He wandered off about his occasions and I did a thorough job of clearing my plate and thought about the beautiful Russian woman; what she would be doing and where she might be.

Henriques wandered back and topped up my coffee cup and failed to depart. I looked at him and raised an eyebrow.

"It's none of my business, sir…"

"Go on."

"Will you be staying long?" he looked at Polly and then back at me.

"I don't know. Why?"

"It's just that Tony… Let's say, he knows how to bear a grudge."

"Tony? Ah, the thug from last night. You were working? You know him?"

"An apt description, sir. Yes, I watched the incident with interest. I would predict that he will lie in wait for you with some friends. Probably tonight, sir."

"Very good of you to point that out, Henriques. It'd slipped my mind."

"You're welcome, sir."

"This Tony, who is he? Who does he work for?"

"I couldn't possibly say, sir."

"No?"

"No, sir."

"Fair enough."

He left me to my musings and not long after that, I decided that it was time I went to see my parents. That meant getting to a small village in rural Hampshire and I didn't have a car, so I packed a few things in a bag, locked Polly and walked up onto Tower Bridge to find a taxi.

The big, dirty river was sweeping past the boats moored below Butler's Wharf. There was a profusion of plants on many of them, and together they looked like a floating garden that at any moment might break free and be swept down to the sea. I stopped looking at the view and concentrated on the road. A cabby responded to my upraised hand, pulled in beside me and put his window down.

"I need to get to Hampshire," I said.

"You want Waterloo, mate," the driver said. "'Op in."

"Actually, I was hoping you'd take me," I said.

"To 'ampshire?"

"Yes."

"Whereabouts in 'ampshire?"

"Aldermark. It's a bit west of Stockbridge."

"Go on then, I don't mind."

I got in and we moved off into the traffic, crossed the bridge and headed towards the M3 through the bustling city. It was nice to be moving, even though it would've been nicer if everyone else got out of the way. Clapham High Street was a bit of a nightmare but it got better after Battersea and soon we were driving past Richmond Park. Not the countryside, but an improvement on the city. The A3 became the M3. I put the window down a bit and decided that the air was more like air, and less like whatever they have in London.

"You took me back there a bit, mate," my driver said. "But now I'm startin' to think it's rather nice to get out of the city for a change."

"You sound like you're a Londoner," I said.

"Do you think so?" he said, grinning. "I've never lived anywhere else. Not my 'ole life. Nor worked anywhere else, neither. Why would you, that's what I say. Best place on earth."

"So, not for you, your own piece of the rural idyll? No soft-ploughed acre of this other eden? No bank where the wild thyme blows, the oxlips and the nodding violet grows?" I said.

"Eh?" he said.

The Smell of Hay

"Lots of people have a thing about living in the country, don't they? A rose covered cottage with a garden. The British, I mean. We're known for it, aren't we?"

"Ah. I thought you wus taking the piss there for a minute. No, not where I come from, mate. We like ol' Lun'n tahn. It's where things happen. It's the nexus of the whole world, is London."

"The nexus of the world?"

"That's what I'm saying. If it 'appens anywhere, it has repercussions and connections with London. If a camel farts in Katmandu, someone in London will make a penny or lose a penny. I bet you."

"The cesspit into which all the loungers and idlers of the empire are irresistibly drained," I said.

"That too. If we still 'ad an empire. What's your game then, guvnor? I'm usually a good hand at guessing my customer's occupations but I can't quite put my finger on you."

"I'm wondering that myself. I suppose you could call me unemployed."

"But not skint, I'm hoping…?"

"Don't worry, I'll manage to pay the fare."

"I thought so. Well, if you'll take my advice, find something to do. In my experience men go off if they have money and nothing to do. It rots them. Something you like, I mean. Something that gets you up in the morning."

"D'you like being a cabby?"

"It's okay. I'm not saying it isn't, but it's not the same; I have to, but apparently, you don't. What're you good at then?"

I told him what I thought I was good at, and a bit of what I'd done, and we spent a while trying to think of a job for me. We didn't reach any conclusions but it was fun.

When we got onto the old 303 the countryside began to be countryside, not suburbia. I had a feeling for seeing more of it, so when we crossed the Test, I directed us to follow the beautiful river down its valley. At Stockbridge, we turned into lanes that were both familiar and somehow out of perspective, as if the brief intervening years had subtly rearranged them, and then, before I was expecting it, we were in the village of Aldermark.

It was, as villages are supposed to be, quiet with little sign of modernity, apart from the cars and street signs. The farms that had brought it into being were just houses now and there wasn't even any horse shit on the road. It seemed clean and tame, and smaller than it ought to be.

My bag wasn't heavy so I decided I'd walk the last bit and made the cabby drop me in the village square.

"Think you can find your way back to the smoke?" I said, unwrapping a bundle of notes for him.

"Ta, mate. Don't you worry, I'll find my way home. Just you watch me go."

"Thanks for the conversation."

"Anytime. Hope you keep out of the kitchen."

"Kitchen?"

"Kitchen sink."

"Ah, clink. Thanks."

I watched him turn and drive away and it struck me that the black cab looked as out of place here as its owner probably felt. Same country; different worlds.

I shouldered my bag and walked west, past the row of workmen's cottages and the vet's house towards Watery Lane. Two women and two labradors passed me. One of the dogs looked at me with a little interest but the women carried on talking to each other without saying hello. I came to the lane and turned down it. The edges of it were high with summer growth and there were hoverflies zooming about amongst the cow parsley and red campion.

The smell of the countryside, the sun on my face and the exercise worked on me and I found myself in a better frame of mind than I expected when I arrived at the brick and flint house that is the Ellice family home.

I walked over the gravel drive and opened the kitchen door. Mum was washing up and Dad was reading the paper at the table.

They made me welcome in a warm, confused sort of way. I seemed to be confused too. We were new people in an old setting and none of us knew the rules. Mum did the natural thing in such circumstances and put the kettle on to make tea.

We talked in a slightly forced way about what I'd been up to since I'd last seen them six months ago. I told them about sailing and the Caribbean and when I asked him, Dad told me about his recovery from the wound to his knee and the subsequent operation. When he got up to get more milk from the fridge I could see that he wasn't as strong as he had been before, but his limp wasn't too bad.

He didn't tell me what I should've done once. I didn't even feel that he was silently disapproving of me either. It was strange and it left me with all my old defences cluttering up my mind uselessly.

Mum was equally confusing in a different way. She seemed to have gone from being maddeningly carefree and irresponsible, to caring and worried. It was disconcerting. Coming home was turning out to be hard work.

"Are you going to mow the lawn then, Ed?" Mum said, after a bit.

"I said I would," he said.

"Well go and do it now. I'll send Si to get you when lunch is ready."

"Of course. I'll go and do that," he said and fetched his boots and put them on and then went off out of the back door.

"He doesn't quite know what to say to you, poor lamb," she said, coming to sit next to me and taking my hand and looking at me.

"Me neither," I said.

"I know. I'm so sorry," she said. "We're both so sorry. For what we did. It was very selfish and thoughtless."

"It's okay, Mum," I said.

"Are you sure, darling?" she said.

"Yes. Don't worry."

"If you say so."

"I do." I put my arms around her and she rested her head against my shoulder and gave a big sigh. When she lifted her head up there were the tracks of a few gentle tears on her cheeks.

"It's so nice to have you back, darling," she said.

After that we sat together more comfortably, drinking tea and talking of this and that, and then she started getting things out for lunch.

"So, what're your plans then, darling?" she said.

"For the day or the week?"

"If you like." She looked at me with a cheeky smile, which was a thing I'd not seen before. "Or for life."

"Life?"

"You know. Somewhere to live, something to do. I don't mean a job exactly but… you know."

"You don't think I should spend the rest of my life sailing Polly then?"

"I think you'd get bored, darling. Don't you?"

"I could go back to smuggling."

"Darling!"

"It's okay, Mum. I'm only joking. I've done that, anyway. What do you think I should do?"

"Take the job, of course."

"Oh, what job is that?" I raised an eyebrow.

"Your dad tells me everything now, darling. Don't look at me like that; it's not the same. No one's going to try to make you do anything you don't want to again."

"They'd better not."

"What I really want you to do is take some nice safe job where I won't have to worry about you, settle down with a nice girl and give me some grandchildren to look after. But I have to face facts, and so do you. Don't you?"

"Since when?"

"Since now. It'll suit you, and Bill's a good man."

"I'm thinking about it."

"It's okay, darling. We just don't want to lose you again, that's all. I know you'll always be restless. You're like your grandfather in that way and it can't be helped. We won't try to make you into something you're not."

"D'you know something, Mum?"

"No, what?"

"You remind me of someone called Soumy."

"Oh. Is that a good thing?"

"Yes."

"I'm glad. Will you go and find your father for me?"

"Yes."

I walked across the lawn and through the gate into the orchard. Dad was tooling the sit-on mower about under the trees. I stood there, looking at the familiar place and smelling the smell of cut grass. He saw me, stopped the mower and walked over.

"Is it time for lunch?" he said.

"Yes," I said.

"Is it good to be back?"

"The grass smells good."

"Doesn't it."

We ate at the kitchen table; bread and cheese and apples and chutney and Dad and I drank some of his light home-made beer. Mum smiled when I helped myself to more food. After that there was fruit cake and more tea.

Conversation turned to people of the village, old family friends and relatives. I recognised that Mum was gently catching me up with the world I'd left, or at least not been a part of, for years. There were some births, some marriages and some deaths. And quite a lot of no particular change at all. The smell of the wisteria and the quietness of the countryside drifted in through the open window.

After lunch Dad went into the conservatory with the papers, which I guessed was a nap by any other name. He had the strained look of chronic pain and I guessed that his injury still had its grip on him.

"Well, darling," Mum said, "I'm going to go the village shop for supplies and I've promised to call in on Mrs Hodgson. You remember Mrs Hodgson? No? Well, you can come with me, if you like?"

I may have pulled a face.

"I didn't think so. Why don't you go and say hello to Grace. She always asks after you."

"That's a good idea, Mum. How are they?"

"Henry died, darling. More than a couple of years ago now. She's in the Dower house with Giles."

"Oh. In which case I must go and see her. What happened?"

"It was a stroke. They found him by the river with Hermes lying beside him."

"Bloody hell."

"Quick is good."

"I suppose it is."

"Take the car. You can drop me in the village and I'll walk back."

"That's okay, Mum. I think I'll cycle. If my bike's still here?"

"Of course, darling. Where else would it be?"

My old bicycle was hanging up at the back of the garage and the tyres responded to the pump, so I was soon whizzing through the lanes like I used to when I was a boy. There was no denying that it was nice to be in the countryside. My countryside, I mean. Its soft, summer sweetness was charming and friendly, and achingly familiar.

The bike turned the corners as if it knew the way and I pushed at the pedals like a demon until I began to be out of breath. As always,

The Smell of Hay

it was great to be physical; exercise puts me in a saner place every time. The tyres scuffed against the worn road surface pleasantly and almost every field, farmyard or wood held memories, not all of them happy, but all of them mellowed by time and poignant on this day.

At the edge of the estate I put my bike behind the hedge, where I used to put it, and started walking through one of the fields that skirted the White Wood. The Hall itself was half a mile west of me but the Dower House was on the outskirts of the village of Acton, not far away. Crossing a few fields and the Fyne brook would take me to its back garden.

A couple of bunnies stopped cropping the turf and scuttled for the cover of the brambles at the edge of the wood. In my mind, I swung a gun at them reflexively. The sun was quite strong and I was warm from cycling so I stepped into the dappled shade of the trees at the edge of the wood. I walked along quietly, keeping an eye out for any deer that might be there.

The turf was soft and springy and the horses came almost faster than the sound of their coming. Two of them, racing each other and the turning earth. I faced them and stood still, letting them decide how to miss me. It was a man and a woman; a young woman, pale skinned but sparkling alive with a mane of flying red hair.

At the sight of me, the man checked slightly and rose a little in the stirrups, but the girl kept her hands down, leaning into the gallop, willing her horse on. She grinned at me as they passed like a wave breaking, one on either side.

I watch them go, taking their drum-beat with them and leaving scars in the turf. The girl was in the lead now because she'd gained by not checking. Before I had had enough of looking at them, the curve of the wood had taken them out of sight. I wished I was riding with them, whoever they were. I walked on after them and at the gate into the next field I read their prints in the ground and saw that they had jumped it.

The brook, when I came to it, was low and weed-bound. A shoal of sticklebacks hung in the sunny piece of water above the ford, ready to flee into cover at the slightest sign of trouble. I stepped into the shadow of the thick hazel just there and watched them, as a fisherman will naturally be drawn to watch fish, however small. Occasionally they would reorganise themselves; one at the front sliding back and the others jockeying for position, and then settling down again. It was nice and my mind drifted back to boyhood summers past.

The two riders returned; this time leading their horses to drink and cool off in the river. They didn't see me standing motionless and silent in the shadow of the leaves, and were in their own private world.

The man was talking, "…asking about cell-memory. I think you should add psychometrics and… in you go, boy." He flicked the reins over the horse's head and let it go down into the water by itself.

"Why don't I just include favourite colour and taste in men?" the girl said, doing the same. "You'd think… hello…" She spotted me. "Who are you?"

"Hello. I'm the man you didn't run over," I said.

"So you are. Don't worry, you weren't in any danger," she said, coming nearer and having a closer look at me.

"He didn't think so," I said, stepping out of the shade to join her.

"That's because he's really just a great big wendy," she said. "And a loser. You have a name?"

"Yes. You?" She had clear green eyes as well as flaming red hair.

"Dutton. I'm Julius and she's Jessica respectively," the man said, joining us. "Sorry about that earlier. We weren't expecting anyone to be lurking in the purlieus." He was a red-head too; heavier built than she. We shook hands.

"Simon Ellice."

"Yes, why were you lurking in the said purlieus, Mr Simon Ellice," the girl said. "And indeed, here by the brook. Explain yourself." She was quite tall, glowing from the exercise and those clear green eyes were looking at me with interest. It was a look that I was happy to return.

"Easy, sister. I'm sure the man has a perfect right…" her brother said.

"He may be a poacher," she said. "Are you a poacher, Mr Ellice? You do look as if you might be."

"I used to be," I said. "I may get back to it, who knows."

"I see," she said. "Or rather, I don't. Ellice; I know that name."

"I'm sorry, Mr Ellice," the man said, "She can't help herself. Ignore her, I would. She'll probably go away in a minute."

"No I won't," she said, maintaining her direct appraisal. "I want to know what manner of creature this is, loitering here in the shape of a man."

"Just a man," I said, smiling into those green eyes. "I don't suppose you'd care to lend me your mount? I'm not going far and I haven't been on horseback for ages."

"Definitely not," she said. "But fair play for asking. Going where? Exactly and specifically; no evasions now."

"Wouldn't dream of it. I'm headed over yonder to a bank where the wild thyme blows and where oxlips and the nodding…"

"…violet grows. Does Titania live in the White Wood then?" she said, laughing.

"You seem to have met your match, sister," the man said. "Well said, Simon. Take no nonsense from the trollop, she has no business…"

"Quiet, brother. So, Puck," she said. "You've come with the juice of a flower pierced by cupid's arrow, have you? You're here chasing some piece of local skirt? That seems quite likely."

"Not exactly…"

"Jess! For goodness sake leave the man alone," the man said. "Come on now, the horses are watered and cool. We've things to be doing." He stepped into the shallow stream and led out the horses.

"Poor man, my arse," she said, still looking at me. "For all he's dressed like a poacher."

"Don't swear at him, sister mine. Sorry, Simon; she was dropped on her head as a baby," Julius said, passing her the reins of her horse and easily mounting his.

"I don't mind in the least," I said, grinning.

"No, he clearly, doesn't," she said. "I can't place this under-dressed and over-educated bedlamite and it bothers me."

"Okay, I'll wager you a race," I said. "If you win, I promise to be an open book to you. And if I win… well, it looks like it would do you good to be beaten a bit."

"Would it by God," she said.

"It certainly would," her brother said, laughing.

"Very well. I will lend you my brother's horse and we will see. Seek me out another day, if you dare."

"Oh, I expect he dares," the man said. "You'll find her at…"

"Don't tell him," she said. "If he can't…"

"… find you then I don't deserve to. I quite agree. Don't worry, I will find you, Jessica Dutton. When I want to," I said.

"Bloody hell," she said, remounting in one lithe movement and gathering the horse into readiness. "You just never know what you'll find lurking in the undergrowth round here. Race you to the gate, loser."

And she was gone, waking the lovely chestnut into a full gallop in the first few strides, her brother a length behind her.

I watched them go again and then crossed the ford, enjoying the cool water soaking my feet and ankles. The path led into the long meadow that belonged to Home Farm. Straight ahead of me across the field I could see the shape of the Dower House sitting in its gardens. The grass was high, so, rather than going straight across, I followed the track up beside the hedge towards the farm. It wasn't called long meadow for nothing, so this took a while.

When I got to the top, I could have taken the path that led towards the house but my idle and careless feet, and my remembering nose, took me through a gate in a hedge which was alive with finches, and into the outer farmyard.

The place looked great; used and organised and untidy, and had dirt and dried mud and nettles growing in the un-trodden areas. There was a more modern hay barn at the back but the old stone buildings were all in use too. There were chickens running about and a row of pigsties with a sow and little ones in one and six young weaners in another. I scratched their heads, replied to their squeals that I had nothing to give them and wandered further in. I could hear sounds of movement in the hay barn so I headed that way.

The place smelt wonderfully of the big steaming muck-heap at one side; there were starlings busy on the ground; a swallow shot past me and disappeared under the eaves of the roof; then another. I walked in and looked up at their nests clinging to the steel beams. There were about twenty of them. I stood by the wall of hay and pushed my hand in between two of the bales. It was warm and moist in there, but not too much.

Someone had backed a big hay trailer into one bay with an old Fergy 35. Perhaps the man standing on the hay on the trailer. I patted the old thing's bonnet and went in to see what he was doing.

The trailer was more than half full of small bale hay. You don't see so much of that nowadays and one of the reasons is that you still tend to have to move it about by hand. This was what he was up to, pitching it up to the stack in the next bay. The stack he was pitching it up to was considerably higher than the level of the trailer, heading up into the eaves of the building. I watched as he sent one up, failed to get it over the edge and had to duck as it came back down at him.

He swore and attacked it with his fork with personal fury. He was a small, bandy legged chap. Not old but a little stooped. He had a width about his person that was all lower down. I'm not saying he was fat, he wasn't, but he tapered rather and his shoulders weren't a lot wider then his head.

He heaved, got the bale up, teetering over him, got it balanced a bit and made to send it up. Through some fluke, it touched the rim of the stack and paused there. Hands grabbed it and pulled it over. He stabbed the next bale and paused to wipe his face with a red, spotted handkerchief, sweeping his fine pale hair back from his face.

I like hay, always have, so I hopped up onto the trailer and took hold of the fork. He finished wiping his face and looked at me as if I'd just materialised from nowhere, which I suppose I had.

"Mind if I do a few?" I said.

"Fuck me, no," he said, and sat down on a bale. "Whoever you be."

I pulled out the fork. It was a small-headed pitching fork, the kind that will grip a bale and lift it well, but also, if you give it a tweak and get the angles right, release it cleanly too. I reinserted it into the bale and had an experimental lift. It was sufficiently well balanced to go, so I put my shoulders into it and sent it up, letting my arms go up with the fork and jerking clear at the last instant. The bale sang on up and over. It was a good feeling.

As with all such work, the trick is to find your rhythm. Doing one is nothing, it's getting into the groove and pushing on that gets the job done. I took my next bale, sent it up in a more fluid movement, selecting the next as I did so, so that the fork came down into it, swinging my shoulders round and pitching up. That was good so I pushed on a bit, going a little slower than I could, so that I didn't over-reach, and seeing to it that no movement was wasted, building a rhythm.

The catcher above seemed caught a little off guard and I had to space them along the edge but that was no bad thing. Should be more efficient for him to take them and lay them into the stack. It was

The Smell of Hay

happening naturally anyway as I went into the pack. I worked along the inside of the trailer, laying them along the edge of the stack above and then went back to the other end and starting again. Whoever was up there had cottoned on and was taking them quickly now.

The two of us, unknown to each other, linked by the constantly flying bales worked through the stack at a good pace. I got properly warmed up and started to sweat so the stalks of hay falling back on me stuck in my hair and on my face. I didn't mind though; hay is an element and when you are working with it, the only thing to do is dive in and swim.

My friend with the handkerchief got up and made way as I speared the last bale instead of him and grinned an ecstasy as I sent it up.

I passed him back the fork and he took it as if it was a strange object. He held it and I brushed the worst of the hay off my head and we both looked up at the, now smaller, dark space above the stack.

"What the fuck are you on, Cal?" a pale face, framed in black, disordered curls and wisps of hay looked at us over the edge of the bales.

"Is 'im," he said, giving me back the fork and stepping away from me.

"Hi," I said giving her a wave, for she was a girl, and though it was hard to tell, quite possibly, a pretty one.

"Who're you?" she said.

"Call me Si," I said. "I was just passing."

"Well, thank you, Si."

She swung her legs over and started stepping neatly down the ladder at the end of the stack. She was wearing what was left of a pair of jeans and an old smock. When she was far enough down she jumped off the ladder onto the bed of the trailer and came over to me. She was a head shorter than me and slim, but all alive and on her toes.

She cocked a hip, put her head slightly on one side and looked at me. I might have been a horse she was considering buying.

"Would you like a drop of cider?" she said.

"Yes please," I said.

"Follow me then. And you, Cal. That's it for now." She jumped cleanly down from the high bed of the trailer and walked off towards the other yard and the farmhouse without a backward look.

"Thank fuck for that," Cal said, dropping awkwardly down from the trailer.

I jumped down too and caught her up.

"Just passing, then?" she said to me as we walked through into the inner yard by the farmhouse. It was roughly cobbled. Some of the buildings and the farmhouse itself were swaybacked and ancient. The swallows were catching insects in the still air between the buildings.

"I'm on my way to visit Grace."

"Lady Beresford?"

"That's the one."

"You're a relative of hers then?" she said, looking at me again.

"No, I'm a commoner, but I grew up over at Aldermark and my parents were friends with Henry and Grace since forever."

"I see. Have a seat, I'll be back in a sec."

She went inside and Cal and I sat down at the outside table. I idly pulled some of the bits of hay off my clothes and the ginger cat lying in the sun on the top of the mounting block washed his face with his paw. He was doing a better job than I was.

"I'm Cal," Cal said.

"Pleased to meet you, Cal," I said. "I'm Si. Who's she?" I nodded my head towards the house.

"'er name is Lizabeth but most calls 'er Lizzy," he said. "She's the boss here."

"Ah," I said.

The Smell of Hay

A woman came into the yard from the other side through an arched doorway in the wall. She was in her early thirties and wore loose dungarees and possibly not a great deal else. She had a good-sized bunch of cut flowers in one hand and secateurs in the other. She came over to the table, put the flowers and the secateurs down, sat down, looked at me and said, "Hello. Who're you then?"

"Call me Si," I said.

"You've got hay on you," she said.

"So's he," I said, indicating Cal.

"He's got a lot worse than hay on him, trust me," she said.

The girl, Lizzy, came out of the house with a tray with glasses and a plastic container of orangey liquid.

"Hey, Julie," she said.

"Hey, Liz. How's it?" Julie said.

"Done is what it is," she said.

"Really?" Julie said.

"Yes. Thanks to this wandering hay-chucker."

She poured liquid into glasses and the smell of cider joined the other smells of the summer's afternoon in the countryside. And whatever else was on Cal's overalls.

"'e's not bad with a fork," Cal said, indicating me with a thumb.

"I'm Julie, by the way," Julie said offering me a hand that was strong and rough from gardening.

"Hi, Julie. I guessed," I said.

The cider was rough and strong too and the smell and taste of it took away the intervening years. I followed the swallows with my eyes as they went flicking left at the house then up over the wall, up into the air, banking round and back down to flash across the warm tiles of the roof and turn again.

"You look thoughtful," Lizzy said.

"He looks like he's never seen a swallow before," Julie said.

"It's a funny thing," I said, "but I feel like I've come home."

3

THOMAS WILD

Julie gave me a cardboard box full of vegetables and salad and I walked back through the outer yard and followed the path across the top of the field to the garden gate of the Dower House.

It sat looking pretty and comfortable, swathed in wisteria and lapped round by lovely gardens. I crossed the lawn and saw that the doors to the orangery were open so I went in that way. The two Great Danes, Hermes and Apollo, were lying on huge cushions near the door. Apollo gave a low growl before he bothered to raise his head, then, seeing that it was me, gave a perfunctory wag of his tail, slapping the flag-stones briefly with it, before letting his head back down and closing his eyes. Hermes continued with his dream and didn't bother to wake.

Her ladyship was drinking tea at a table under a pale blue Hoya. She put down an iPad as I came in.

"Simon, how lovely to see you." She got up to kiss me hello and then sat back down, motioning me to take the wicker chair opposite her. I put the box on another seat and did so.

"It's good to see you too," I said. "You look…"

"Alive?" she said.

"I was going to say, very well."

It was true, although she must have been in her seventies, her white hair was thick, her skin as firm as someone a lot younger, and her eye as sharp as a magpie's.

"I am, as it happens. You don't look too bad yourself," she said, picking up a small silver bell and giving it a shake.

"I'm pretty fit. Been sailing a lot."

Giles, her ladyship's butler, appeared and said, "Shall I refresh the pot, your ladyship?"

"Yes please, Giles," she said.

"Hi Giles, how are you?" I said.

"Very well thank you, master Ellice."

He removed the box, brought another cup and saucer and topped up the teapot from a kettle. I swished it about a bit and poured for myself and topped up Grace's cup. It was Indian, good and strong. I added some thick, creamy milk from the jug on the table.

"I just heard about Henry," I said.

"It happens to us all. He had a good life and a long one," she said.

There didn't seem to be anything to say to that, that wasn't either trite or insensitive so I just raised my teacup in silent tribute to the man. Grace nodded and we both took a sip of tea.

"So, Berry is…" I said.

"The tenth earl, God help us. Yes."

"Has he, er… settled into the role?"

"Possibly. Well, perhaps his idea of it, anyway. He's an urban creature at heart but he has made some effort with the estate. I've moved out of the Hall to give him space."

That made me smile inwardly; the Hall wasn't what you'd call short of space. I wondered how he'd managed to pay the death duties, but decided not to ask.

"So, I'd find him in London?"

"Usually. And I'm certain he'll be delighted to see you. Giles will give you his number."

"Thank you. I don't suppose I'll linger in the city, but while I'm there…"

"You might as well sample its delights?"

"I expect he could show me around a bit."

"Yes, I expect he probably could."

We contemplated the enormity of that understatement for a moment and then I said, "I stopped in at Home Farm on the way and lent a hand with the hay. I'd forgotten how much I used to like haymaking.

"They will have been grateful. They had another man, a Pole, but he disappeared a couple of weeks ago. Cal is neither strong in the body, nor the brains. It's a lot for two women on their own."

"They gave me a glass of rather good cider and I sat in their yard and watched the swallows for a bit. I'd forgotten how lovely it can be here." I picked up a twig from an oak tree that was lying on the table. It had a couple of small, fat, nascent acorns attached.

"This land is precious and always will be, but, God willing, it will be here long after we, and all our silly toys, are dust." She took the bit of greenery from me and put it in a vase that was on the pedestal beside her.

"When I was a boy I always wanted to be somewhere more exciting, but now that I've had some excitement I seem to be appreciating it anew. I'm glad it's in good hands."

"I didn't say that. Berry was the child of our relatively late age, and we didn't perhaps share our passion for the place with him as we could have. He may grow into it though; people sometimes do. You come from here too, but I don't suppose you intend to live here and help care for it either, do you, young man?"

"What would I do?"

"Indeed. And what will you do? Now that you've had some excitement."

"Go and find some more excitement I expect," I said, giving her a grin.

"You didn't have enough of that working for Guy Wealden in Morocco then?" she said, her keen eye twinkling.

"How can you possibly know about that?" I said.

"I am old, but not unconnected. How did he die?"

"You knew him?"

"Oh, my dear boy, we all knew Guy. A bastard but a charming one. He and your dad were quite close as I remember. How's his leg?"

I looked at her and wondered how much she knew and how much she guessed.

"Mending quite well I think. Mum seems to be enjoying looking after him."

"Really?"

"Yes. I've never seen them closer," I said.

"Well I never. Still, you never know what may happen in a marriage. Give them my love, will you, when you see them."

"I will, and they send theirs."

"I didn't gather what the problem was?"

"Oh."

"But I won't be offended if you don't care to tell me."

"He took a bullet in the knee."

"In Whitehall?"

"In the line of duty," I said.

"Very good. All right, I won't ask again. Tell me what you intend to do now instead."

"I'm not completely sure. I expect something will turn up."

"I imagine something already has."

"Why do you say that?"

"Because I've known you for a long time, Simon. But it's a good habit to keep things to yourself. Bertie was the same and you and he are a lot alike. That reminds me…" she rang the bell again and we waited for Giles to appear.

When he did, she said, "Giles, the Thomas Wild."

"I have it ready, your ladyship," he said.

"Well, why didn't you bring it in then?"

"I will do so now," he said, gravely, and turned on his heel.

"Your grandfather left something for you," Grace said. "Or rather I know he wanted you to have it, so here it is."

Giles came back in carrying a beautiful old English shotgun.

"Give it to Simon, Giles."

"Yes, your ladyship." He held it out and I lifted it from his hands.

It was heavy and smooth with many decades of handling. The metal had the deep, subtle patina of age and the walnut stock glowed from endless contact with skin and clothing. Not an aristocrat of guns but a yeoman; a good working gun.

I turned a little sideways and mounted the gun towards the open door. It rose to my shoulder so sweetly that there was no consciousness in the movement, it was just a thought made manifest.

"That looks right. She's a little long for most but not for you," Grace said.

"She's nice," I said. I lowered her and thumbed the lever. She dropped open easily and I studied the inside of the barrels.

"Well in proof and straight and clean," she said.

She was right. There was no pitting in the barrel, no ripples, just bright, oiled metal reflecting the light in kaleidoscopic patterns.

"What is she? A century or more?" I said.

"Eighteen ninety-eight."

"Funny I don't remember her. I thought I knew all his guns."

"It's a spare he kept with us in case he wanted to walk round if he called in."

"He didn't bring his Hollands?"

"Not always."

"I see."

I looked at the old but still handsome woman and thought about my deeply amoral grandfather calling in to see Grace and Henry. Maybe not so much Henry.

"Don't look at me like that, young man," she said.

"Sorry, Grace," I said.

I laid it on my knees.

"You will care for it." It was a statement and a command.

"I will. Thank you very much," I said. "I really appreciate it."

She didn't say anything to that but just carried on looking at me so I sat and sipped my tea with my grandfather's gun resting on my legs and looked at her.

"I used to call him Avus and he would call me Nepo," I said.

"I know. You were lucky to have known him the way you did. And so was he you."

"I miss him."

"So do I. The bastards will die," she said.

"I'm sorry," I said.

"So am I, but it can't be helped."

We were quiet again, thinking of the men who were not in the room and never now would be. In her presence, I felt like I was a boy again, and sharing her grief I also felt like a grown man. Things fall apart, but they also come together.

"I'll tell you the story, Grace," I said. "About Guy, I mean. If you would like."

"Thank you. I don't completely live in the past yet but I like to know the end of a story when I can get it."

I told her about my time in Morocco and it was easy to do so; she was a woman who understood such things. I didn't tell her about Guy and Ed. Or about Guy and Mum, but I could see that I didn't need to.

"Thank you," she said. "I will keep what you have told me to myself. And what you haven't told me."

"Avus said you were good at keeping secrets. I'd forgotten."

"I am. He told me that you would be good to call on if I were in trouble and trouble to have around if not. He knew I would outlive him."

"Are you in trouble?"

"Not in the slightest. Are you?"

"Not that I know of."

"I imagine you soon will be."

"Do you? Why?"

"It is your nature. As it was his."

I thought about that for a moment and gently thumbed back one of the hammers and then let it back down. It felt fine.

"I would have talked to Avus, but he is dead so you will have to do," I said.

"That is a wise decision and I shall choose to take it as a compliment."

"I mean it that way. I've been offered a job and I'm trying to decide whether to take it. You can help me."

"Certainly. If I can. What does it entail?"

"Unless I'm mistaken, hunting and probably killing. But for the common good. Or at least one idea of it."

"You are a hunter by nature and training. And I imagine killing doesn't bother you unduly."

"I'm not saying I like it, but…" I shrugged.

"Quite. And you would be, at least to some extent, on the right side of the law?"

"In an illegal way, yes."

"Then I think you should take it and be grateful."

"Do you?"

"Yes, I do. You're made the way you are, just as they are," she indicated the two sleeping Great Danes, "and your greatest enemy is boredom."

"Hm." Looking at her, it occurred to me that I couldn't think of any other silver-haired old women who were quite like Lady Grace Beresford.

"It's been suggested to me that if I don't work for them, I'll end up permanently on the wrong side of the fence."

"As Guy did. Yes, if you don't find something useful to do with yourself, something will find you, and whatever it is, may not be good for you. You remember all the stories Bertie used to tell you about his trips abroad?"

"Yes." I looked at her, wondering.

"Did he tell you why he was wherever he was?"

"Yes. No, not always. Not directly. I got into the habit of not asking. Why?"

"Do you think you are the first member of your family to face this dilemma?"

"Avus?"

"Think about it."

I thought about it and then said, "Bloody hell."

"He never actually ended up in court, did he?"

"No."

"What would he say?"

"About the job? I believe he would've said much as you have."

"So do I. And, this job, will it be reciprocal? They will call on you, will you be able to call on them?"

"How do you mean?"

"In case of trouble. Or in case you want something done. You're more given to giving orders than taking them."

"That's a very good point. I hadn't thought of it. You think I'm likely to want to take charge of things, on occasion?"

"Isn't that what usually happens?"

"It has been remarked upon, I believe." I smiled.

"Has it now." Her eyes twinkled at me.

"I was wise to talk to you, wasn't I?"

"Yes, you were. Now, Simon, it's been very nice to see you, but I have things to do."

Apparently I was dismissed.

"Okay, Grace. Thank you. I will give it serious thought. May I leave this with you for now and come again and walk around the estate with it?" I lifted the old shotgun feeling the balance of it once more.

"Yes, as it's a family tradition, you may. And it will be good to see you, and perhaps hear your tales. Come again when you like."

I kissed her goodbye, stepped over the sleeping Great Danes, and let myself back out through the garden gate into the field and started trotting back the way I'd come.

Mum and Dad were sitting side by side on the bench by the table on the lawn when I got home. I can't swear to it, but they may have been holding hands.

"Ah, there you are," Mum said, getting up. "What would you like to drink?"

"Don't move, Mum. I'll get it," I said.

"No you don't. Come and sit down. That's an order. I have to go and look in the oven anyway."

"Oh, okay. A beer would be nice."

"Coming right up," she said, and left me with Dad.

The air was sharpening slightly but I was warm from cycling. The light on the field was moving from gold towards amber and the stillness was lovely. Dad sat looking thoughtful and not saying anything. I was happy to do the same.

Mum brought a tray with bottles and glasses, put them on the table and went away again. I popped a cap and poured the liquid into a glass for me and then one for Dad. I passed him the glass and he took it.

He didn't drink but looked steadily at me. "I want to say I'm sorry," he said.

I looked at him and saw that he looked troubled and older than he'd seemed earlier.

"There's no need," I said.

"There is and I'm saying it," he said. "I'm sorry. Really sorry."

"Then, okay," I said. "It's okay. Really."

"Okay."

I held out my glass and he touched his to mine.

"Cheers, Dad."

"Cheers, Si."

We looked at the view and didn't speak for a bit.

Then I said, "So, this job then?"

He took a deep breath and said, "I'm working on a simple premise…"

"Which is?

"Given that you're pretty certain to be up to something you would describe as interesting…"

"By which you would mean, something that might get me into trouble?"

"That's what it usually means, isn't it?"

"I take your point."

"Well, it's the nature of my work …"

"… at the Home Office?" I said.

"As you say, at the Home Office," he smiled at me, "and sometimes Bill's, at the Met. So, I might as well get your help with them. Don't you think?"

"Possibly."

"And… I think I should be honest about this…"

"Yes, you probably should."

"And… if we're working together I may be in a position to know when you need help and be able to send it."

"I see."

"Which is not to say that this is in any way a made-up job. Let's say that I know you a bit better since we went for that drive in the desert. I'm taking a deep breath, ignoring all my instincts as a parent, and trusting you to carry on being the jammy bastard who's still alive when the smoke clears."

"Hm. In what circumstances, for example?"

"Okay. For example, there's something funny going on in the Pyrenees. We think it should be looked at."

"I like the Pyrenees. Funny, like what?"

"It's more Bill's thing than mine, but there's something up there that calls itself an intentional community. Bill thinks its intentions aren't as advertised."

"And he'd like me to go and find out?"

"Yes. And I would too."

"And if it's turns out to be just a bunch of hippies?"

"Then we'll owe you an apology. But I'd be very surprised."

"If you and Bill think it's funny, then I suppose I would be too."

"Anyway, I expect some of them are quite attractive. The girls, I mean."

"There are girls? Why didn't you say so?"

"What are you two looking so cheerful about?" Mum said, joining us.

"Apparently, I just started working for Dad," I said.

"Oh, did you," she said, complacently.

"I have to say, until quite recently, I would never have foreseen that," Dad said.

"Well, be that as it may, I foresee that supper will be ready in ten minutes," Mum said.

4

HARMLESS, IF NOT CUTE

That night I went to bed in my childhood bedroom for the first time in a long time. I slept well and woke naturally when it was still early.

I sat up and looked at the map of the world on the wall. Marked in red were the places where I'd been, though that was out of date now, and in blue and more numerous, where Avus had been. When I used to visit him, we would sit in his gunroom and he would tie flies and tell me stories. When I got home I would mark the locations on the map. Perhaps if I researched the dates and locations, I'd find stories; a man killed, or a man saved, stitches in the fabric of life; pulling it a little this way, or a little that way. It had never occurred to me consciously before, but I had known it. The wicked, clever old bastard.

Everything in the room seemed to be pretty much as I'd left it; fishing things, books, maps, climbing rope and harness, snares and rabbit nets, the cartridge case from my first stag on the window-sill. I'd thought that Mum would've packed it all away, but she hadn't.

The birds were chattering outside and the day looked fine so I put on some clothes and went downstairs. There was no one stirring, so I let myself quietly out of the house and went for a stroll down to the river.

The dew was wet and I left tracks. The river was sleepy with a hint of mist on its surface. I stood and looked at it for a bit, watching a trout rise under a willow on the far bank. An early buzzard climbed into the sky and made its plaintive mewing call.

For some reason the phone that Bill had given me was in my pocket. On a whim, I took it out and turned it on. As promised, it had one number stored in it. I put it back in my pocket and watched the bird begin quartering his patch, looking for his breakfast. I would almost certainly see Griffon Vultures and Lammergeier up in the Pyrenees. If I went.

My stomach was rumbling so I started walking back towards the house. Before I got to the garden gate, the phone rang.

"You're awake then," Bill's voice said.

"So are you, apparently," I said.

"You turned the phone on."

"I did."

"You in, then?"

"You realise there's a certain irony in you lecturing me on morality and then recruiting me for extra-judicial justice?"

"Only when necessary. Have I recruited you?"

"If I work for you, will you work for me? if I want it."

"What do you mean? Doing what?"

"I've no idea, but if I want you to do something for me, you will have to do it. I won't ask without a good reason."

"I see. No, I don't suppose you would."

There was silence for a bit, so I said, "Well?"

"It worries me, but I can't say no. Yes, okay."

"Good. So, the Pyrenees?"

Harmless, if not Cute

"You're in?"

"I'll go up a mountain for you and then we'll see. Fair enough? If I like it, I expect I'll be willing to do whatever you want after. If it's boring, you may have a problem."

"Yes, fair enough."

"Good. You can start by sorting out Polly and my finances, and all that too. When do you want me to leave?"

"Ah, yes. Give me a few days, and I'll…"

"Get your shit together. Fine, do what you have to do; I'm not in a vast hurry."

"I didn't know you were coming. I have to gather my facts and check some things, make a plan…"

"It's fine."

"What're you going to do in the meantime?"

"I expect I'll manage to entertain myself."

"Just don't get arrested doing it."

"How can I possibly get arrested? I work for you now, don't I?"

"Oh fuck."

Mum, in her dressing gown, was in the kitchen making tea.

"Morning, darling. You're up early," she said, warming the pot.

"But not out poaching," I said, smiling.

"I should hope not, at your age. What would you like for breakfast? Dad's on his way down. There's eggs and bacon."

"I expect I could manage some of that," I said.

Dad came in, also still in his dressing gown but looking rested and fresher than last night. He gave me a knowing smile but didn't say anything and we sat down to breakfast at the kitchen table.

"So, darling, what're you going to do today?" Mum said, when we'd made some progress through the meal. "You could take your rod off down the river if you like or…"

"I told Bill I'll go," I said.

"Oh," she said.

"Good," Dad said.

"Apparently he's got some work to do first," I said, looking at Dad.

"I expect he has."

"You can go and give him a hand," I said.

"Oh. Can I?"

"Yes. Why not?"

"You're right. Yes, I suppose I can."

"Good. While I'm waiting for you and Bill to do your thing, I'm going to spend a bit of time around here; shoot a few rabbits, probably. But first I'm going to go back to London and catch up with Berry. Hit the town a bit. So, you can give me a lift back; we'll leave at about eleven. Okay?"

They were both looking at me.

"Oh, darling," Mum said.

Mum came too and they dropped me somewhere in Notting Hill. I rode the tube back to the docks. Polly was still at her mooring, and still looking like the queen of the place, but the urge to get her out of there had subsided. By this time my breakfast had worn off too, so I sat down at a table outside the café for a spot of lunch.

"Did you find your vocation, sir?" the waiter, Henriques said, appearing with his order pad.

"Who knows," I said. "People have been telling me that I need one, but I'm not convinced."

"You surprise me, sir."

I looked at him to see if he was taking the piss. It was hard to tell.

"Lunch for one, sir?" he said.

"Do you see anyone else, Henriques?"

"No, sir."

"Henriques?"

"Sir?"

"This chap, Tony; are you really sure you don't know who he works for?"

"Tony? I'm not sure I know anyone by that name, sir."

"I see. Henriques…"

"Sir?"

"I'm feeling lonely. How would I go about getting some female company?"

He looked at me as if I'd disappointed him.

"It's possibly a bit early sir, but you can just walk up to Whitechapel and take your pick, sir," he said.

"Not a street girl. I'm thinking of something a little nicer and a little more expensive," I said.

"There's an app for that, sir. On your phone. You just look at the pictures and choose, sir."

"Henriques…"

"Sir?"

"Why don't we just pretend you're a waiter and you go and get me some food. Okay?"

"Let's do that, sir."

I ordered a few things to keep me alive and sat and stared into space and thought about the mountains and the rivers and the forests of Aragon, the Haute Garron and the Ariege. They're very nice, but they weren't going anywhere, and London was right here.

Then I looked about to see if I could see anyone interesting to talk to; preferably female. There were several walking past or, like me, having a late lunch at the cafes. Some with men, some with other women. A particularly striking girl, sitting alone at a table outside a café on the other side of the water, caught my eye. She had long raven-black hair flowing in soft waves down over her shoulders and the kind of build that is all woman. Not Athena, or Artemis, or Hestia, but Aphrodite, definitely Aphrodite. She was half turned in my direction, looking intently at her phone through dark glasses. She poked it a bit and then dropped it into her bag and raised her arms up and swept all that hair into her hands and curled it into an artistic bun, which she fixed in place with a long pin. The movement accentuating her magnificent breasts. My laggard brain put the pieces together and saw past the present goddess to recognise a skinnier, more angular version. I knew her and had known her since she and I were both children. She was Melissa Franklin. Bloody hell.

I got up and trotted round to her side of the basin at speed. She looked up at me, not really seeing me.

"Hi, Mel," I said.

"Who…"

"Si Ellice."

She sat there and looked at me for a bit.

"Fucking hell." There is some truth in the idea that the most beautiful women tend to swear a lot.

"You alright, Mel?"

"Si!"

"Hi, Mel." I gave her a grin.

"Where the fuck've you been?"

"I've been working abroad but I'm back. How're you, Mel?"

"Fuck, it is you. I'm completely fabulous, you bastard."

"I can see that." I sat down.

"What're you doing here?" she said.

"Nothing in particular."

"Fucking typical. What do you mean? Why? How? Have they just let you out of prison, or something?" She cast an eye over my, as usual, rather scruffy clothes.

"No. I'm just back from a cruise. You look fantastic, by the way. What're you up to?"

"Right now…" she looked at her watch, "fuck, I'm late. Right now, I'm off to work. Where're you staying?"

Harmless, if not Cute

"Here. In the marina. What're you doing this evening?"

"What am I doing this evening?"

"That's what I'm asking."

"You turn up after more than three years with not a fucking word, and ask me what I'm doing this evening?"

"Yes. I haven't seen you for ages."

"And who's fault is that? I'm working this evening."

"Okay, what're you doing tomorrow evening?"

"Tomorrow evening?"

"That's the one."

"Fuck. Give me your number."

"Sure." I accepted the pen she held out and scribbled on a napkin. "Now, about tomorrow evening…"

"I don't know. Oh, fuck. Now, stop holding me up; I'm late."

She got up, looked at me again, grabbed the pen, scooped up her bag and left. I watched her go and I wasn't the only one to do that.

I was about to return to the remains of my lunch at the other cafe when the waiter brought me her bill.

I considered going shopping and concluded that it wouldn't be wise, so I went back to Polly, put my feet up and closed my eyes for a bit instead. When next I was aware of myself, I was free climbing a rock face with Mel above me and the red-head on the horse below me. I couldn't seem to get near either of them, which was odd as I never remember Mel being much into that kind of thing, and you don't necessarily expect a horse to be much good on a rock-face. I rubbed my head a bit and sat up and took in the fact that I was where I was, and that I was, more or less, awake.

When I got up, I discovered that it was getting to be eveningish, so I wandered up to the café and sat on a barstool and sipped some scotch, watching the people and wondering what to do next. When in Rome and all that; I sent a text to the number Giles had given me for Berry.

Henriques, trotted back and forth a few times carrying food and I watched him do it. Next time he came within striking distance, I beckoned him to join me and he did.

"Hi, Henriques," I said.

"Good evening, sir," he said.

"Have you got a minute?" I said.

"Yes, sir."

"Good. Let's try this again; I want your help to finish something I've started."

"Your wish is my command, sir."

"I rather doubt that, but let's find out shall we. You can stop calling me sir and trot along to the *Sea Hare* for me." I thoughtfully folded and unfolded a few notes between my fingers.

"Really, sir?" he said, not taking his eyes off the money.

"Yes, really."

He looked at me with deep misgiving written all over his face. I added a few more notes.

"What... er, what exactly is it you want me to do there?" he said.

"Fetch me the girl. Russian, five feet nine, or thereabouts; Blue eyes; tawny blonde hair. Might be wearing a teal dress with a cute little jacket, or might not. Definitely stylish and chic. I expect you remember her, don't you?"

"You mean Anja, sir. *The* girl, sir."

"Her name is Anja? Good. Yes, *the* girl."

"You're going to get me into trouble, sir."

"No, I'm not, Henriques." I gave him a grin.

"I can't do it, sir."

"Yes, you can, Henriques," I said, holding the money out to him.

"Oh, shit. I suppose I can." He deftly plucked the notes out of my fingers and went.

I sat on my stool and thought about some of the many prostitutes I'd known in yacht clubs, hotels and back street bars. They

Harmless, if not Cute

were just there generally; cheerful and tough and good company. A fact of life, like the weather and beggars.

Twenty minutes later, a man and a woman walked into view along the walkway. I knew it was them by their body language: he the owner, she the owned. Luckily, he wasn't the man I'd hit. He parked her, on view, by the railings, just as she had been parked before. She had a great figure, and, although she was too far away to be certain, I was sure it was the same girl.

The man came into the café and looked for Henriques. Henriques, who had been avoiding me since our exchange, caught his eye and nodded towards me.

"You're looking for some company?" the man said, coming straight up to me and giving me a good look over. He wasn't as big as the one I'd hit, but seemed to be cut from the same kind of cloth; in his case Eastern European, rather than East-end.

"That's me," I said.

"There she is, very beautiful. Is three hundred for one hour, fifteen hundred all night, no rough stuff, understand?"

"Three hundred?"

"You want it or not?"

"Five hundred for two hours," I said.

"Two hours is six hundred," he said.

"No, five hundred," I said.

"Okay five hundred. No bruises."

"Okay." I peeled fifties off my roll and passed them over.

"Okay, she's yours. Where you go?"

"Right here. Bring her in."

"Here?"

"Yes, here."

"Your money," he said, shrugged, went out to her and led her to me. It was the girl.

I stood up to receive her and gave her an encouraging smile. She saw that it was me and I thought she might say something to the man but she didn't. She just looked at me and kept whatever she was feeling hidden.

"Okay," the man said. "Your time start now." He looked at his watch and backed away.

"Hello, my name is Simon but people generally call me Si," I said to the girl, offering her my hand. She didn't take it.

"Are we going to the boat?" she said.

"For sex?" I said.

She just looked at me.

"No," I said. "I decided to get over my pride and give the man money for you so that I could have a drink with you. Is that okay?"

"You don't want sex?"

"Actually, what I want is supper. Will you have supper with me? Please? Have you eaten?"

"What do you want?"

"I want to apologise for my stupidity the other day and I want your company. I don't mean you any harm. Would you like a drink? I'm not going to pick a fight with anyone or get you into trouble. I promise."

"You want company?"

"Yes."

"Not sex?"

"Yes." Not strictly true, but it's good to keep things simple sometimes.

"Okay."

"Excellent. Now, sit down and tell me what you'd like to drink."

We moved to a table and she took off her chic leather coat, put in on the back of her chair and sat down. I sat down too and waved over Henriques, who was hovering not far away.

"What you drink?" she said.

"I'm having what you're having," I said. "Tell the man what you want."

"Vodka," she said.

"Good. You heard her, Henriques. Vodka. The best you have and bring the bottle. And some food. Would you like some food?"

"I chose drink. You choose food," she said.

"Then Henriques will choose the food. Food please, Henriques. Whatever you decide. We will trust you."

"You're mad and I don't know who you are but I will choose the food," Henriques said. "But first I will get you the vodka." He gave us both an ambiguous smile and departed.

I looked at her and she looked at me.

"You speak quite good English, don't you?" I said.

"Nyet," she said.

"Well, you certainly understand it," I said.

She looked at me.

"Go on. Tell me you don't know a pronoun from a porcupine, I'll try to believe you."

"Fuck you," she said.

"That's better, now we can get to know each other a bit."

"Nyet."

"Da."

"Fuck you."

"No, we're only doing food and conversation tonight. Fucking will have to wait."

"Fuck you anyway."

"And you too."

Henriques reappeared with commendable speed, deposited two shot-glasses and heft two good slugs from a bottle into them. We both raised our glasses to that and drank.

"Thank you, Henriques," I said.

"Oh, yes," he said, pulled himself together, and went away.

"That man is a funny kind of waiter," she said.

"He's not really a waiter, he's an actor," I said.

"That explains it," she said.

"He said your name is Anja."

"My name is Anja."

"Hello, Anja. My name is Simon but people generally call me Si."

"You said."

"I'm sorry about the other day. I hope I didn't get you into too much trouble."

She shrugged her shoulders. "They prefer not to damage the merchandise."

"I see that. It wasn't very grown-up of me, but I'm trying to do better."

"You are a man," she said, and shrugged her shoulders. "What would you have done if it had been Tony who brought me?"

"I would've apologised and offered to pay twice. He wouldn't have wanted to start something in here and he would've wanted the money. He might still have wanted to hurt me, but probably a bit less."

"He will wait for you outside your boat."

"With a few of his friends, no doubt?"

"Yes, that is what they do. If someone bothers them," she said.

"I should probably move my boat anyway," I said. "She seems out of place here. Too far from the sea. She looks like a beautiful creature trapped in a hard and unforgiving world." I looked at her steadily, letting her know that I knew what I was saying but that I wouldn't make anything of it. Henriques reappeared and refilled our glasses, unnecessarily.

"Cheers," I said, raising mine.

"Vashee zda-ró-vye," she said, raising hers and then tossing the contents down the back of her throat in one practiced move. "To the beautiful creatures," she added with an ironic lift of one eyebrow.

"Thanks, Henriques," I said, taking the bottle from his hand and refilling the glasses again. He went, reluctantly.

"I think we are entertaining him," Anja said.

"I think we are," I said. "I hadn't thought of it before, but there are advantages to being ugly."

"He's not ugly."

"Hm."

"Okay, he's not *that* ugly."

"Beauty is truth and truth beauty, that is all we need to know," I said, looking at her.

"Only a man would have said that."

"True. It was a chap called…"

"Keats." She said it as if I was an idiot, which I clearly was.

"Ah, my mistake."

"'Where but to think is to be full of sorrow and leaden eyed despairs, and beauty cannot keep her lustrous eyes beyond tomorrow,'" she said, dipping her eyes delightfully.

"Who needs tomorrow anyway?" I said.

"Easy for you to say."

"Then let us say… 'Oh for a draught of vintage that hath been…' I forget how it goes on but…" I raised my glass, "cheers anyway."

"Za zhén-shsheen." She tossed hers back. "Which means, to the women."

"I can drink to that," I said, and refilled our glasses.

"As all men do," she said.

"Is there anything I can do to improve your opinion of my half of the species?"

"Yes. I told you what."

"Ah, yes. Go find your daughter and bring her back to you."

"Don't bother. You are no use to me."

"Because I'm a man?"

She didn't bother to answer that. Henriques brought whitebait and mayonnaise and bread.

"What about Henriques?" I said.

"What, about Henriques?" she said.

"He's a man too, is he not?"

"Yes, Henriques too," she said, considering him.

"What have I done wrong now?" he said.

"Breathing, I think," I said. "Having testicles and breathing, is about it."

"Oh. Then I will take my testicles and my breathing away," he said.

"Probably the safest thing to do," I said.

"I don't feel at all safe around you two," he said, and beetled off.

"Eunuchs are as bad," Anja said.

"And women?" I said.

"Worse."

"I thought so. Is this what you might call a Russian point of view? I mean, not unrelentingly cheerful."

As if by throwing a switch she changed her demeanour, becoming bright and cute and fluttering her eyes and said, "Oh, sir. It's so nice of you to spend your time with me and buy me this wonderful vodka. I'm *so* happy. You are *so* handsome. If there's anything I can do to make you happy it would make me *so* happy to do it for you." She put her hand on mine and looked coy.

I winced.

"Was that better, Mr Rich Man?" she said, returning to her normal self.

"I take it back," I said. "You go right on being as miserable as you want and I'll go right on pouring the vodka." I poured us some more vodka.

"Ya zhelayu vam gemorroy," she said, taking the shot.

"And the same to you, whatever it may mean," I said, downing mine.

"Let us stop talking shit and eat," she said.

"No argument from me on that," I said, breaking the bread and passing her some.

We ate the fish and the bread and I was happy to have the food and, I think, so was she. At the end, there was one whitebait left. She looked at it and then at me. I looked at it and then at her.

"Darling, have the last fish," I said, nudging it towards her.

"Fuck you," she said, and took it.

"Thanks," I said and poured us some more vodka.

Henriques appeared with a big, heavy bowl of something that contained fish and shellfish and beans. It smelt excellent.

"What is this, Henriques?" I said.

"It is called caldeirada de peixe," he said. "And I've taken the liberty of procuring you this, sir, madam."

He placed wine glasses before us and poured some into Anja's for her to taste. She did so and shrugged. "It tastes like wine," she said.

"Wine indeed!" he said, filling my glass. "It's a Douro."

"So it is," I said, tasting it. "And a very nice one. Thank you, Henriques."

"You're welcome. I think. Sir, madam."

We ate the food, which tasted as good as it smelt and I almost thought I detected a shade of genuine relaxation and enjoyment in her. Just for a fleeting moment.

"What are you?" she said, leaning back and looking at me.

"Apart from being a man?" I said.

"I cannot decide if you are one of them or not."

"One of the men who use women for profit?"

"I meant gangsters, but yes, to them we are... tovar... what's the word, a thing you buy and sell."

"A commodity."

"Yes. Less than human."

"No, I'm not that. I'm not saying I'm a fluffy little kitten, but I'm not that."

"A little cat…?"

"I mean harmless and cute. Well I might be a bit cute."

"Nyet. What is it you want? Why are you doing this?"

"Well…" I looked at her with appreciation and let her see it. And smiled.

"You can buy that," she said.

"Actually, I'm not so sure I can."

"Actually, you are right; you cannot buy that."

"You really are very beautiful indeed and I'm really enjoying your company."

"Even though I'm nasty to you?"

"Perhaps because you are."

She shrugged.

"I was bored, and now I'm not. Thank you."

"See, you are just using me."

"I've admitted to not being a kitten. By the way, where is your daughter?"

"Nyet."

"You won't tell me?"

"I don't trust you. And I don't know."

"Fair enough. I don't blame you. I just thought I'd ask."

"Why?"

"Why what?"

"Why would you help me?"

"Possibly, because it's something useful to do."

"But you aren't sure?"

"Let's say, I'm trying the idea out. People keep telling me I need to do something with my life."

"And you think the waiter is a funny man?"

"You may have a point there."

Harmless, if not Cute

We had ice-cream because that was what she wanted, and then coffee. I didn't press her to tell me anything but just enjoyed her company and let it all be whatever it was.

I didn't find out anything about her except that she was as clever and well-educated as me. And in the fractions of a second when she thought I wasn't watching, I could see that inside she was as sad and bleak as a long, long Russian winter.

All too soon her minder reappeared and stood there looking restless. I put notes on the dish and rose to my feet to help her on with her coat. We walked out onto the quayside and he went ahead of us, waiting for her to join him.

"Thank you, Anja. You've been great company," I said.

"You have been a man," she said, shrugging her shoulders and turning to go.

"A man, yes..." I kept hold of her arm for a moment.

"What?"

What the hell.

"Okay. What you said. I will if you want me to, I'll do it. I'm serious. I'll get your daughter back for you. I think I probably could."

She looked at me; troubled again. And then shook her head. "Nyet."

"Fair enough, but if you change your mind, you know where to find me." I let go of her.

"Perhaps you would like to hold your breath until I do?" she said.

"Thank you, darling," I said.

5

APOLLO IN THE SHADES

I wandered down Frith Street, Soho; crowded with places to eat and drink and a lot of people moving about, until I found a fine looking Georgian building with the legend, *Coma Club,* over the door. There was a queue of people waiting to get into it, so I joined them.

The elegantly dressed young woman at the rope was letting some people through and turning some away. It belatedly occurred to me that I should possibly have changed my clothes before I set out for the evening. I put my left hand over my right to hide my still bruised knuckles and looked at those around me to see if there was any chance of striking up a conversation and appearing to be part of a group.

The three girls in front of me were taking selfies and looking gorgeous, which they were. I was just about to offer to take a picture of all of them together when the lovely dragon guarding the door looked past us all, smiled a warm smile of greeting and moved to unclip the rope to let someone bypass the queue. We all turned to see who the privileged being was.

A tall man in his late thirties with a slim and ravishing blonde on his arm walked up from a departing Phantom. He wore his slightly curled black hair long and she had hers in a page-boy cut. He wore a sheer silk suit of plum and she a flapper dress in teal. They were a remarkably handsome couple. They walked up the line like royalty approaching their realm.

When they came level with me, I said, "Kimeridge Wentworth Thomas Leivre, earl of Beresford, good evening."

"Someone hails me?" he said, stopping.

"I do, my lord," I said.

"It can't be," he said.

"It is," I said.

"Well, fuck me, you found it," he said. "Si, how wonderful."

"Of course I found it, you idiot," I said.

He stepped forward, his arms out, and we embraced like long lost brothers. I thought he was carrying a little more weight than suited him, but he still looked athletic and he'd lost none of the power in his arms and shoulders.

"It's very nice to see you, you uncivilised beast. What on earth are you wearing?"

"And you too, you mad old peacock" I said. "These are just clothes, by the way. As opposed to whatever fancy-dress you seem to be wearing." I took the lapels of his suit in my hands and gave them a playful tug.

"This, dear heart, is the Da Vinci of couture and I'll have you know..."

"Berry, darling, stop talking about clothes and present me," the woman beside him said.

"Ah yes, sorry, my sweet, this is Simon Ellice, an ill-bred youth from the next village who used to steal our peasants. I think I mentioned that we might be meeting him."

"He means, poach his pheasants," I said. "More importantly, I'm the person who taught him to hold his liquor and keep his hands up."

"My God, you've got nerve," he said, standing back and looking at me with feigned awe.

"Don't trust yourself, old thing," I said. "You're getting old and I believe your brains are a little scrambled. My fault, I think."

"In your dreams, you little scrub. To think, when I dandled you on my knee and gave you your first sip of the life-giving elixir…"

"Berry, for goodness sake, stop drivelling and introduce me to this beautiful woman," I said.

"Ah yes, forgive me. This divine creature is Maisie."

"I am delighted to meet you, Maisie," I said, offering her my hand.

"Mr Ellice, how wonderful to meet you." She took my hand and looked up into my face with big, liquid eyes. "You look divine. I'm so glad." She reached up, put her hands round my neck, pulled my head down and kissed me firmly on the lips. "I'm Maisie, by the way."

"Hello, Maisie," I said, when she put me down.

She took my arm proprietorially, abandoning Berry, who seemed perfectly comfortable with the arrangement.

"Are you coming in, dear heart?" he said.

"If they'll let me," I said.

"Let you? Of course, they'll let you." He motioned us to proceed him and so we did, beamed upon by the dragon who deftly removed the rope for us and dropped a curtsy to my lord. I thought the watching throng would applaud.

The interior was impressive. It was a Georgian house with big rooms and high ceilings and the décor was complementary, but in a modern way. On the walls, there were huge, perfectly lit canvases of misty and fragmented industrial scenes, each one with a lone, and rather psychotic looking hare loping through it. The bar was a glittering but subtle masterpiece of glass and light. The furniture was comfortable and stylish, the clientele generally elegant and, unless I misjudged it, loaded. The whole gave a strong impression of sophisticated confidence and money.

We didn't arrive, we made an entrance. That was inevitable with Berry. Half the people in the room seemed to know him and want to be known by him. He deftly fielded the attention with a wave here and a kiss there and led us through the crowd to a group of sofas by one of the windows. A girl in what appeared to be pyjamas followed us and after a minute I realised that she was a waitress.

"Could I interest you in a cocktail, old thing?" he said to me.

"Consider me interested," I said.

"You know what to do, don't you, darling," he said to the waitress.

"I do, my lord," she said.

"Will you trust me, Si?" he said.

"With my life," I said.

"So be it," he said, and nodded. The girl gave a bow and departed.

"Well, my lord…" I said.

"Don't," he said.

"No?" I said, giving him a grin.

"It pleases them but I am above such tawdry baubles. Call me Berry like a gentleman or be prepared to give me satisfaction on the field of honour."

"Once more for old time's sake?" I said.

"No, I rather think not," he said, giving one of my biceps a thoughtful squeeze. "This time I think I really might get a kicking."

"What are you two talking about?" Maisie said. "Don't keep a girl in the dark now."

"Not for the world, my angel. This young bruiser used to run with the lads from the village; there was some disputation between the local yokels and their betters at the hall…"

"…by which you mean, you and two of the garden hands and a young footman. That's to say, your paid lackeys," I said.

"You put it so crudely."

"Local yokels?"

"Well anyway, there was a bit of good humoured rough-housing which, I'm ashamed to say, occasionally became quite physical. Good times. Good times. There was an occasion when this young hound got in a few good punches to yours truly's head. More by luck than science, you understand. Gave me a proper black eye and a fat lip."

"I was only fifteen," I said.

"Goodness, were you?" Maisie said.

"But somewhat overgrown," Berry said.

"You were in your full strength in those days," I said, looking him up and down.

"Are you saying I'm not now?"

"Far be it from me…"

"Insolent dog. Anyway, I've forgiven him his trespasses and am prepared to let bygones be bygones."

"Oh, Berry, I'm so glad," Maisie said, "So glad." She took his arm proudly and smiled at me.

"Very decent of you, Berry," I said, "but if you change your mind, I won't be offended." I flexed my fingers and gave him a smile.

"No, no, a Lievre never goes back on his word and that… ah, thank you, my dear… is something to drink to."

The waitress had returned with a tray bearing drinks. She put one in front of Berry and a similar one before me. They were long, dark drinks and had an oily sort of sheen on their surface. She gave something that might very well have been a martini to Maisie.

"Cheers, my dears," Berry said, raising his glass.

"Death to the French," I said, raising mine.

"May it always snow," Maisie said.

We drank and none of us choked. Whatever it was, was interesting.

"What is this?" I said, putting it down carefully.

"I call it the sixth earl," Berry said.

"Why?"

"Because the secret ingredient is elderberry," he said.

"As in the fruit?" I said, holding up the drink and looking at it doubtfully.

"Yes and no," he said, grinning.

"What do you mean?"

"Well, he was a fruit. The sixth earl. Had to get the butler of the day to do the necessary with her ladyship. Or, so they say."

"You're joking! You've dug him up and make drinks out of him? I don't believe it."

"Never buried him. We like to keep the ancestors close in my family. Don't tell anyone, but he's in that suit of armour in the banqueting hall. We chip a bit off now and then and grind it up. Adds a certain something, don't you think?"

"Don't listen to him," Maisie said, "he's teasing. It's only gunpowder."

"Whatever it is," I said, taking another sip, "it's growing on me."

"It will do that," Maisie said.

"The fifth is in the chest by the fireplace and the fourth is in the big urn by the main door," Berry said.

"Shut up, Berry. You're giving me the creeps," Maisie said.

"When my turn comes, I'm having the taxidermy. You can cut me up and sew me into the moose and that boar's head, and…"

"Ah, yes. Speaking of that," I said, "I was down yesterday and heard the news. I'm sorry, and sorry I didn't know before. I'll miss him."

"Thank you. As do I. But we all have to go, and so he went down to the river, and… Well, enough said."

"Yes. So, you've been… elevated?"

"Yes, I am indeed now the tenth earl. God help us all if there's ever an eleventh."

"Do your duty, man. For God and country," I said.

"Not on your life. But let's not go there. So, speaking of duty, what have you been doing since you got kicked out of the Rifles? That's what I want to know."

"I wasn't exactly kicked," I said, accepting the change of subject.

"You weren't exactly promoted either, I hear. I smell a story, now spill."

I gave them a moderately truthful account of my tour of duty in Afghanistan and then spun them a line about doing boat charter work in the Med and ending up in custody of Polly.

"So I've come back to the old country for a bit of recreation and to have a bit of a think about what I should do next," I said. "I thought I'd get out and about in town a bit and have some fun and sort of see what turns up. I had a feeling you might be able to help with that."

"Quite right. You're not actually short of the readies I take it?"

"I can probably manage to buy the odd drink here or there," I said.

"Good, good. The clothes then, are just...?" He looked at them quizzically.

"Just clothes, Berry," I said. "They're what I happened to be wearing when I got your text."

"As you say, just clothes. Well, I may possibly know some of the more hospitable establishments of the town, and if I can be of any small assistance in the matter of..." He looked at my attire again, speechless.

"I don't..." I started to say.

"...don't say it," Maisie said to me, putting her hand on my arm. "Berry is the last word. The razor's edge. You can trust him on this absolutely."

Apollo in the Shades

"I don't doubt you, Maisie," I said. "And I will do it. Berry, I'm in your hands. Take me in hand and make a man of me. Or at least a man about town of me."

"You won't regret it I promise you," Maisie said.

"Dear heart, your wish is my command," Berry said, considering my form thoughtfully. "I think a light suit from…"

"Berry, my saviour," I said. "Should we have another on the strength of it?"

"Another?" Maisie said.

"You'll do fine," Berry said.

"I'm so glad," Maisie said. "So glad."

We had another and Berry waved over a few people to introduce me to and soon there was a big group of us. Berry got up to circulate and Maisie held onto my arm as if she owned me while he was gone. I chatted with various people about this and that and the blessing of Berry and Maisie cast a glow over me that made me special and wonderful. Or that may partly have been the drink, whatever it was.

"You seem to know Berry rather well," Maisie said.

"Yes, don't mind us," I said. "It's village life, there tend to be limited opportunities for entertainment so you make the most of those there are. Berry and I both liked drinking and fighting. Though he was ahead of me in years, and other things."

"You seem to have managed to catch up. It's hard to imagine him growing up there. In the country, I mean."

"He hated it. I loved it, but we got on. At least most of the time. We developed a funny kind of friendship; a bit similar; a lot different, both under pressure in our different ways."

"I can see he really cares for you, and it's lovely to meet you," she said, and, leaning close to me, "sweetheart, could you oblige me?"

"Anything," I said.

"I want to powder my nose," she said.

"Do you want me to go with you?" I said.

"No silly, I want you to sort me out," she said holding her hand on my lap, palm up.

"Ah, slow of me. I'm sorry, Maisie, I don't happen to have any," I said. "I expect one of these gentlemen could oblige."

"Poor you. Never mind, I'll just go and feel up the old man," she said, and wriggled her way out. She slid up behind Berry who was talking to a couple of men not far away, casually extracted something from his jacket pocket and shimmied off through the crowd.

Another girl moved over to talk to me in her absence and I was on the point of asking her for her number when Maisie returned and stood over us.

"Darling, I want to dance," she said.

I looked at her and the girl looked at her.

"I think you'd better go and dance," the girl said.

"Then go and dance, I will," I said, rising. "Dear lady, may I have the honour?"

"I'm so glad," she said, "so glad," and took my hand and led me through an archway.

The *Coma Club* wasn't particularly a dance club but it had an exquisite dance floor. They'd laid a circle of parquet into the thick green carpet of the adjoining room and hung the walls with rich, medieval tapestries, and the windows were dressed with thick curtains. Purpose-made sofas in dark green and gold echoed the curve of the dance-floor. Subtle lighting made the space mysterious and penumbral. I couldn't tell you where the speakers were, but they must've been good ones.

I handed Maisie ceremonially onto the dance floor and she began to wiggle and bounce, buzzed up on cocaine. I joined her in dancing and discovered that I was enjoying myself. The music was good and dancing was good. Being alive wasn't so bad either.

Later someone cannoned into me. I caught her and she tried to slap me, but missed; out of her skull and sweating; no longer there. A man and another girl appeared beside her and led her away. Maisie shrugged and said, "Some people can't handle it, poor things," and took the opportunity to go and refresh herself. I left her to it and returned to the group in the other room and my own mysterious glass of poison.

"How do you find yourself, Si?" Berry said, joining me.

"Berry, I find myself enjoying myself, that is how I find myself. This was a fine idea."

"As Maisie would say, I'm glad. I have another idea. Do you fancy a bite to eat. I believe it's going on for supper time. Do you think you could manage something?"

"When could I not?"

"A point well made. Will you join me in an oyster? Perhaps two? I'm a trifle peckish."

"Berry, you do know how to live, you know that?"

"I do my best. I do my best."

The Phantom appeared out of the traffic and swept us away. I lay back in the soft leather and noticed that the lights of the passing lights had a weaving sort of effect on my eyeballs. I watched them with interest until they turned blue and then red and then blue and took on a familiar shape.

"Berry," I said.

"Dear heart?" he said.

"Is that large blue thing Tower Bridge?"

"I do believe it is."

"Where exactly are we going?"

"The briny ogin. The docks of Katherine. Place called the *Sea Hare*. Best oysters in London, and therefore, the world."

"Oh. Okay."

Berry and Maisie swept in and, I of course, swept with them. It was all very chic in a kind of faux nautical way. And also very busy, and Berry moved through the throng like a man utterly in his element;

knowing everyone, known by everyone. He was a king and we, his subjects, followed him gladly. The best table appeared and, some oysters, which if not necessarily the best in the world, were at least as good as I deserved at that moment. I cleaned my pallet with champagne and addressed them with as much sober attention as I was capable of; each one arriving and sliding down like a mermaid's kiss.

When they were gone, Berry excused himself to attend to his apparently endless acquaintance and Maisie slipped away to pick herself up with a little white dust up her nose. While they were away, I sat and watched beautiful pyjama-clad women gliding about doing what waitresses do. Apparently pyjamas were the new uniform for waitresses these days. Anja, her figure even more wonderful in the soft night-ware, caught sight of me and froze. I shrugged my shoulders helplessly and smiled. She took hold of herself and turned away to serve other guests. I hoped she would come over to speak to me later, but she didn't.

After we'd fed our fill and Berry had talked to everyone he wanted to, we crossed the river and were delivered into the maw of a true dance club called *Caesars*. It was in the underground level of an old warehouse and the beat made the oysters inside me get up and dance and I thought my ears would bleed. Berry and Maisie dove into the tumult with serenity and obvious pleasure. After a while, my being adjusted and I was lifted onto the beat and carried along on a continuously breaking wave of drum and base.

I washed ashore sometime that was more early than late, at the steps down to the docks. The tail-lights of the phantom, sweeping unstoppably up the empty road left a trail of phosphorescence on the back of my eyeballs.

I got as far as the security gate and discovered that although I knew that I knew the number, the knowledge of it wouldn't seem to get down to my fingers. I shook them a bit to see if that would help. It didn't so I rested my head against the cool metal of the gate.

It wasn't just the number, there was something else I was supposed to remember, something about Polly, or going back to Polly. Or not going back to Polly. Or…

Perhaps the chap coming would know. I felt the decking move a little under his weight. Or that could've been mine, it was hard to tell. I started turning round to ask him, and it went dark, very dark. And then someone hit me in the oysters. And gripped me hard by both arms and I was falling, falling, falling…

6

THE GUN ROOM

I woke up in the park; Hyde Park. I didn't know that at the time; I thought it was hell. A cold hell with scratchy twigs and appallingly loud birds. They'd dumped me under a bush near the bird sanctuary and taken my clothes, all of them. And everything else.

At least they hadn't done me any real harm or killed me. What an idiot. Me, I mean.

I got up, threw up, unpleasantly, and tried to give the poor woman staring at me a rueful smile. I don't think it helped. She ran off and was soon replaced by a pair of coppers. They tried not to look amused, but it didn't work, and that didn't help either.

They found me a blanket; it wasn't very clean, but then neither was I; and took me back to Polly with a mixture of kindness and suspicion. This was allayed when it turned out that I really did know the combination to the security gate. They gave me a half-hearted telling-off and left me to it. On some occasions, there are worse things to have about than a British policeman.

Aboard Polly, I went forward, leant over the bow and retrieved the spare key from its place, taped to the underside of the anchor hawsepipe. I went below and put some distance between me and the blanket. My God, it was good to get back into the shelter of my beautiful boat. I showered and cleaned my teeth and drank a lot of water. And then lay down on my bed and let myself off all things and all thoughts and let myself just be.

In order to live you have to eat; it's not optional. Some time later my stomach woke me up and reminded me of this. I dressed and went up to the cafe. There, I found a very beautiful and very angry woman waiting for me.

"There you are," Mel said. "You might answer your phone, you prick."

"Hello Mel," I said.

"Well?"

"Coffee and a full english please."

"Do I look like a waitress?"

"No pyjamas."

"What?"

"I don't know."

"What happened to you? You look like shit."

"I got drunk and forgot that someone I'd pissed off would be waiting for me. They were. They took my clothes and left me in Hyde Park. And my phone."

"All your clothes?"

"Yes. Some policemen brought me back."

"Serves you right." I could see this was cheering her up. "Why?"

"Isn't it the kind of thing they do?"

"Not the policemen, the person you pissed off. It was over a woman, wasn't it?"

"No." I thought about it. "Actually, yes."

"Typical. Who?"

"I don't know. They hang out over there," I nodded, gently, towards the *Sea Hare*. "Someone called Tony, probably."

"I meant, who was the woman."

"Oh. Her name's Anja. She's Russian. Never met her before. I mean, a couple of days ago. This chap was nasty to her, so I broke his nose."

"Oh. Fair enough, I suppose."

"Glad you approve, now…" I managed to attract the attention of a passing Henriques. He trotted over, clearly repressing a smile.

"Well, Henriques?" I said.

"Well, sir?"

"You were on earlier, weren't you?"

"When those two policemen brought you back from your night out, sir?"

"Do you see everything that happens around here?"

"Pretty much, sir."

"Well, stop smirking and get me a full english and a lot of coffee. Quickly."

"Yes, sir."

"Same for me, please," Mel said.

"Yes, ma'am."

When he'd gone, she said, "Now, let me look at you." And she looked at me for some time. I felt thoroughly looked at but I didn't mind; I've always liked and trusted Mel.

"Hi, Mel," I said.

"Yes, that's you alright. Where've you been, you bastard." It didn't seem to be a question. "I don't know whether I'm more pleased to see you, or more angry with you."

"You look amazing, Mel. You've grown into your looks. If that's not a wrong thing to say?"

"Thank you. It's not a wrong thing to say. Apart from being hung over, you look pretty good too."

"I'm not too bad."

"Fuck."

"Sorry."

"Oh, fuckit, give me a hug, you idiot." She reached out to me and I scooped her up into my arms and kissed her. She kissed me back and then she leant against me and beat my chest gently with a fist.

"I'm sorry I was a bit funny the other day, but if you ever just disappear again without saying anything, I'll…"

"I know. I'm sorry. Avus died, and…"

"I know. I know. Never mind. You've got over it now."

"Yes, I have. How did you know?"

"How long have I known you?"

"Since you had braces, as I remember."

"I never had braces," she said. "Since you tried to drown me in the apple-bobbing barrel at Aldermark village fete, actually."

"You remember that?"

"Yes. Since you were just a smart-arsed boy, instead of the shallow, selfish man you are now."

"Girls can be such a pain. You thought I was a smart-arse boy?"

"You were. Full of yourself to say the least. Nothing seems to have changed."

"It didn't stop you…" I raised an eyebrow, "in that hay barn…"

"Oh yes… Near your parents' house… I remember. We all make mistakes. I was young. What're you doing now?"

"Nothing in particular. What're you doing?"

"What I'm always doing. Which you clearly remember?"

"Er…"

"Fuckwit. I'm a journalist. I mainly work for Essence magazine, but I also do freelance work. I'll probably be editor of The Times in twenty years, if it still exists, but now I'm paying my dues; living on peanuts and doing whatever I have to."

"Okay. A journalist? Like what?"

"Yesterday I did something on sun-beds and cancer in Essex, tomorrow I'll probably be interviewing some self-promoting psych with a new theory on autism, or something."

"And today?" I said. It occurred to me that she was looking at me rather as I've seen a terrier look at a rat.

"Today I've come to see you."

"That's nice."

"Where've you been and what've you been doing?"

"I'm er, just back from the Caribbean."

"By yourself?"

"No, there was a girl with me."

"What's her name? What happened to her?"

"Soumaiya. She's living near St Maxime in the south of France."

"Did you split up with her or was she just a friend?"

"Er, neither and both. She was my house-girl in Morocco and she came with me when I left. She loves me but doesn't rate me as a husband. I think she wants to live a domestic sort of life and have children. She's good at that sort of thing."

"Did you love her?"

"How about you ask me a question I know how to answer?"

"You're a dangerous man, Simon Ellice."

"Hm."

"What were you doing in Morocco?"

"Messing about in boats, mainly."

"Not dealing hash, then?"

I looked at her.

"Heard of a search engine, have you?" she said, holding up her phone. "I looked you up while you were keeping me waiting."

"Ah."

"Who's Romeo Harak when he's at home?"

"A dead man, if I ever find him there."

"And Guy Wealden? I've heard of him, haven't I?"

"Probably. It's a long story."

"Which you're going to tell me."

"I didn't say that."

"You think I'd write about it, do you? Do a piece on you."

"I didn't say that either." This was all getting rather hard work for a chap in my condition.

"What kind of cow do you think I am? We're friends, aren't we? I wouldn't do a thing like that to anyone."

"Even me?"

"Even you."

"But you do want something, don't you? Apart from breakfast, I mean." It seemed to be taking rather a long time.

"What makes you think that?"

"How long have I known you?"

"Let's not start that again."

"So?"

"Okay, yes. I want something."

"Thought so. Mel…"

"What?"

"Stop talking and go and see if that mad fucking waiter is ever going to feed us, will you?"

"Oh… fucking hell. Okay, Si."

She did that and a disgruntled Henriques appeared carrying food and proclaiming that he'd just been bringing it. And coffee, thankfully.

"You got off very lightly, if you don't mind me saying so, sir," he said.

"Being left in the park?" I said.

"Others haven't been so fortunate."

"As it happened, I spent a small fortune on oysters at the *Sea Hare* last night in the company of a lord. Perhaps it helped," I said.

"What lord?" Mel said.

"Berry," I said.

"Oh, that would explain it," she said. "You getting really drunk, I mean."

"Sir?" Henriques said, looking plaintive.

"The earl of Beresford," I said. "Commonly known as Berry."

"I see, sir," he said, looking at me thoughtfully.

"You know what curiosity did to the cat, Henriques?" I said.

"I do, sir. You are a customer, and I am a waiter, sir."

"If you say so, Henriques. This, by the way, is Mel. Mel, this is Henriques. He will be pretending to be our waiter today."

"Your servant, ma'am," he said, bowing like he knew how to bow.

"Thank you, Henriques," Mel said, like she thought he meant it.

When he'd gone, Mel was about to speak but I shook my head and started eating. It was definitely the right decision.

"Typical," she said, and attended to her own plate. Or at least what was on it that she was fast enough to get before I did.

"Better?" she said.

"I need a nap now," I said.

"Don't you fucking dare."

"Mel, it's wonderful to see you, but do tell me what you want and let me go back to bed. You can come too, if you like."

"In your dreams. Do you know Hillary Stubbs?"

"I've no idea. Should I? Who's she?"

"She's a friend of mine. Or rather, she was. She's dead now."

"Oh. Sorry about that."

"She was found in a flat in Tower Hamlets two days ago. She died of an overdose."

"Oh dear."

"She went missing just before Christmas. I looked for her. Quite a few others did too. London's a big place."

"Yes."

"She was very lovely and very clever. I've known her since playgroup."

"Yes…?"

"Si…"

"Mel?"

"The thing is, I don't believe it."

"What don't you believe?"

"What happened. I simply don't believe she had a drug habit. Not like this anyway. It's just not possible. Not with Hillary."

"You said she died of an overdose."

"I know."

"People aren't always as okay as they look. It takes away the pain, makes them numb, and then…" I shrugged, attempting to look compassionate.

"But I knew her. I mean, I really knew her. That simply can't be what happened. If you'd known her, you'd think the same."

"Okay. If what appears to have happened didn't, then something else did. What do you think happened?"

"I don't know, but I want to know where she was for those six months. No one saw her. As far as I can tell, she was never in any of the shelters. What was she living on? She had no money."

"The streets. A beautiful girl can get money. Shit, even an ugly girl can get money, I think…"

"By selling herself, I know. And I still don't believe it. Not Hillary."

"What would you like me to do?"

"Do you know Susie Chesterfield?"

"Don't think so. Who's she?"

"Another friend of mine. Another friend I've known a long time. She got off her head at a party a few days ago. I had to sit with her for hours and hours afterwards."

"Yes...?

"But it wasn't anything she took herself."

"That happens too, doesn't it? One's supposed to keep an eye on one's drink, isn't one?"

"Yes, one fucking is. It was like what happened to Hillary. I don't know how exactly, but it was. This isn't right. Something's going on. I'm worried about Susie."

"Probably a stupid question, but have you mentioned this to the police?"

"I tried. You know what it feels like to be patronised?"

"Dimly. Okay, what would you like me to do?"

"Si, I want you to help me."

"Okay."

"I want to find out what happened to Hillary and I want to stop it happening to Susie. And I want you to help me."

"Oh. Okay."

"Okay?"

"Yes, of course."

"Oh. Good."

As it turned out, the idea of going back to bed, alone or in company, met considerable opposition. Action, immediate action, was the only acceptable thing. The food had helped, so I acquiesced, at least provisionally, refused to be specific or let her accompany me, ascended from the docks and fed myself into the tube.

I got out at Baker Street and wandered off in the direction of Marylebone. I'd assumed that Le Bonholmes would still be in Montague Row and they were. As before, there was just the name engraved on the glass door with nothing to indicate what they did. I stepped into the foyer and took the wide, carpeted stairs up to the first floor.

I heard the click as the doors unlocked themselves and refrained from looking for the camera. I pushed them open and stepped into the same Aladdin's cave that I'd first visited with Avus on my twelfth birthday.

Le Bonholmes was in Avus's opinion, and naturally also in mine, by far the best gunroom in London. There was plenty of glowing old mahogany and Persian rugs but the guns weren't behind glass and at one side of the room was a large table with a leather top and a scattering of disassembled parts, bore-snakes, rags and gun oil. It was a working room as well as a showroom. At Le Bonholmes they sell guns, not the idea of guns.

A well-groomed man in his mid-thirties got up from behind a computer screen and came over to meet me.

"Good afternoon, sir," he said.

"Good afternoon," I said.

"I don't believe I've had the pleasure…?" he said.

"Yes you have. You once made me a mug of tea. It was about ten years ago and I was here with my grandfather, Albert Ellice. He brought in a .375 Sako with a cracked stock."

"And he and Jimmy and my father spent almost all afternoon choosing the new blank. And just talking; telling stories. I remember. Mr Ellice…" he held out his hand.

"Simon. Call me Si."

"Charles Hibbert. My sincerest condolences on your loss."

"Thank you. Your father?"

"Fit and well, I'm glad to say. He's more or less retired but he still takes some of the older clients out to the range. He'll be sorry he missed you."

"As am I."

"Can I offer you some more tea? And is there anything I can do for you?"

"There may be. I'm hoping that Jimmy is still here?"

"He is, and will be delighted to see you. I can fetch him but I expect you'd rather go to him?"

"If I may. And tea would be very nice too."

"Excellent. I'll go and put the kettle on. I expect you remember the way?"

"I believe I do."

I went to the back of the shop, stepped behind the counter and opened the green baize door. There was the shabby, lino-floored corridor that I remembered and at the end the same steel door. I knocked, and the hard metal felt the same under my knuckles as it had when Avus had made me knock to save his.

"Come in," a voice said.

I swung the heavy door and stepped into Jimmy's lair; the workshop where countless firearms had been repaired, modified, re-stocked, and serviced over the decades. It was warm and brightly lit with florescent tubes. There was a long bench down one wall, a lot of racking on the opposite one full of guns, and all the equipment and tools that you would expect, including a lathe.

Jimmy was sitting at the bench on a high stool wearing a leather apron steadily working at the walnut blank held in the vice with a spoke-shave. He stopped working, the tool held in the air above the wood, and looked at me. Then he put his head on one side a little.

"Hello, Jimmy," I said, coming in.

"You've grown a bit," he said, his face breaking into a slow smile.

He put down the spoke-shave, got off his stool and took my hand. He had a good look at me with his clear hazel eyes. I didn't feel much older than I had when I'd last seen him. He didn't look much older either.

"Is Charlie making tea?" he said.

"Yes," I said.

"Good. I've got some biscuits too."

He fetched the other stool from its place against the wall and put it near his. I sat on it and he got back onto his and carried on gently stroking slithers of wood off the new stock emerging from the rough blank.

"I thought we wouldn't see his like again," he said, "but I could be wrong." His eyes twinkled at me with a cheerful amusement.

"You mean my grandfather?" I said.

"He used to turn up here looking like you look and it always meant trouble. At least for someone," he said.

"But not for you?"

"People who take liberties with their armourers don't generally live long enough to be a problem. What's the point in us providing it, if people like you don't use it. Are you going to tell me what you're after then?"

"I will, but in fairness I think I should tell you what I've been up to first. You might not want to know me."

"Go on, surprise me."

Charlie brought us mugs of tea and we dunked our biscuits and I told Jimmy all about my time in the Rifles and in Morocco, omitting nothing. As Avus told me, you tell the truth to the man who cares for your guns; if you can't, you shouldn't use him; if you don't, he shouldn't work for you.

And then I told him about Dad and Bill's proposition that I work for H.M. government, albeit unofficially, naming no names, of course.

"I think I see where this is going," he said.

"Thought you would. Do you think Jean would mind?"

"It'll cost you some stories," he said, smiling.

"You sure?" I said. "What about Charlie?"

"Do you think you're the first to think of it?"

"Obviously not."

"I'll give you a password for Jean. It may be wise if your friends buy a few dresses."

"In this case, it's more likely to be shirts I'm afraid. May I?" I got out my phone.

"Always the same you lot, charging through life like bull elephants. I'm supposed to pop out and get a round tuit anyway," he said, and I could see that he was amused.

"May I use the phone?"

"Of course."

I called Bill and he answered. Jimmy was about to go to give me privacy but I put a hand on his arm.

"Patience, Si. We're working on it," Bill said, when he realised it was me.

"Excellent, darling. Is the old man with you now by any chance?"

"As it happens…"

"Right. Let's meet for a quick chat, shall we?"

"Yes, but…"

"You're going shopping. Get a cab and go to Baker Street. There's an expensive country clothing shop called Hamptons. Dad will feel right at home and you can just lump it. A rather beautiful woman called Jean will meet you in ladieswear." That made Jimmy smile. "The password is…" I looked at Jimmy.

"Mauser," he said, patting the stock in the vice.

"Mauser," I said.

Jimmy resumed his work and we talked about guns we'd known; some old, some new. It seemed to me that to Jimmy, they were all the same, more or less. Plus ca change, plus le meme chose.

In a while, there was a tap at the door and a smiling Jean, Jimmy's charming and very lovely French wife, delivered a doubtful pair of men in the shape of Bill and Dad up the back stairs from Hamptons.

"Half an hour do you?" Jimmy said, going to the door and taking Jean's hand.

"Perfect," I said.

"Right. We'll go and entertain ourselves. Don't you worry about us."

They departed, looking happy and conspiratorial.

"Age before beauty," I said, hopping up to sit on the bench and indicating the stools to the others.

"Typical," Dad said, looking about.

"But very suitable," Bill said, taking a seat.

"You can both buy your wives something nice while you're here," I said.

"On my salary?" Bill said.

"It's only money," I said, giving him a grin.

"Having fun then, Si?" Dad said.

"Fun?" I said. "I've no idea what you're talking about. Now, I've got a few things I need from you both."

"You need from us?" Bill said.

"Go on, Si," Dad said.

"Thank you. Firstly, money. I want to spend some. Dad?"

"No problem. You're now on the board of something called Kunops Enterprises and have a legitimate income earned in various places including Nassau, the Bahamas and the Isle of Man. You'll have to send funds from Switzerland to where I tell you to, in due course, but no hurry for that. We had a certain amount left over from… well, you know what."

"Nice one, Dad. And Polly?"

"Papers will be ready for you to sign in two days and she's all yours."

"Thank fuck for that. Now, I want to know who owns two businesses. The *Sea Hare* down at the docks and the *Coma Club* in Soho. Dad, will you get onto that?"

"If you want me to. Any particular reason?"

"Partly because they put a bag over my head last night, took all my clothes knocked me out. I woke up in Hyde Park."

"You what!" Dad said. I explained.

"Nice of them not to hurt you," Bill said.

"That's one way to look at it," I said.

"Now you mention it, you don't look quite at your freshest," Dad said.

"But it's no reason for us to bother with them, surely?" Bill said. "I think you should be grateful and forget about it. We've more important things to do."

"No," I said.

"No?"

"No. You've persuaded me to start being useful, this is me doing that; it's a package deal. I want to know about these people."

"No problem. I'll start making enquiries," Dad said.

"Good. Now then, Bill, your turn. One of your colleagues has given a friend of mine the blow-off, and they shouldn't've done. You're going to make amends. I want to know about a girl called Hillary Stubbs who was found dead in a flat in Tower Hamlets two days ago."

"What do you want to know about her?" Bill said.

"Apparently, she disappeared for six months. I want to know where she was. My friend suspects foul play of some kind, and therefore, so do I."

"Oh, you do, do you? And that means we have to too, does it?"

"Yup. You're a policeman, go do your thing."

"Oh fuck. I've created a monster," Bill said.

"All this was your idea," I said. "Don't blame me."

"So, you've given us jobs to do, but what are you going to do now?" Bill said.

"Me? I'm going to go and get some more sleep, of course," I said.

7

SOME STRANDS OF HAIR

I woke to the pleasant sound of the halyards ticking against the mast and my first thoughts were of deep blue water and endless skies. Then the sounds of London in the background brought me back to present reality.

It'd been a good sleep and I felt well rested. I went topsides for a look at the world. The June sunshine had given way to a breeze scudding fluffy clouds over the tall buildings. The air, if not exactly fresh, was fresher. It was good to know that even in London, weather sometimes happens.

I'd barely sat down at what was becoming my accustomed seat in the cafe when Henriques appeared.

"Do you ever actually sleep, Henriques?" I said.

"Some of us have to work for a living, sir."

"Not currently getting much acting work then?"

"You wanted something, sir?"

"Double eggs-bené and plenty of coffee, if you think you could manage that."

"I will endeavour to serve you, sir."

"Don't put yourself out."

I'd brought the phone Bill had given me and a replacement for the one Tony and his mates had presumably taken from me before they dumped me in the park. I didn't think they would get into it, but the fact that they couldn't might intrigue them. Bill's phone binged a text, 'Guy's morgue one hour'. Fair enough.

I dealt with the offering Henriques brought me and headed up to Tower Bridge and started walking. When dodging the other pedestrians got tedious, I put my hand up for a cab and rode to the bottom of the Shard and went from there. After consulting a handy map on a signboard, I went down an alley and passed through the doors of a back entrance.

"There you are," Bill said, getting up from a bench. He was wearing those ugly glasses again and looking a bit grim.

"Here I am," I said.

"Good," he said. "Come and meet Hillary."

I followed him down corridors, through departments and down more corridors. We stopped at a discreet doorway where he held his warrant card up to a camera and we were buzzed through. Past the empty reception area with plastic flowers and waiting rooms we entered a world of stainless steel and the smell of disinfectant and lurking behind it, other things.

A young woman in a white coat looked up from a computer screen and said, "Ah, you'll be wanting Dr Krevis." She got up and went into another room.

"You seem very familiar with this place," I said.

"It's where some of my customers hang out. I come and visit now and then," he said.

"Bill." A cheerful middle aged scot with a thick moustache came out of the back room and shook Bill's hand.

"Mac. This is Simon. He'd like to meet the girl, and perhaps you could explain."

"Right oh. No problem." He shook my hand with a firm grasp and led the way through some plastic curtains into a large room with an operating table of the kind that deals with the dead, and many numbered steel drawers. He lifted a clip-board from a hook, consulted it and pulled out a drawer. "This is Hillary Stubbs," he said, respectfully lifting a sheet back to reveal the top half of a young woman.

I went and stood next to him, looking down at her. Bill began pacing on the other side of the room.

I wasn't unused to the dead but this was the first time I'd seen the official version. She seemed rather unreal at first; cold, pale and clean, and arranged so perfectly. The brutal Y incisions of the autopsy, so grievous to living flesh but administered after death to meat, dead matter, increased the effect. She should have been a waxwork, but she wasn't. She had thick, dark eyebrows and a mass of dark hair framing her face, a strong, slightly roman nose and dark blue eyes stared opaquely upwards. She would have been an attractive girl, not necessarily pretty but, in life, possibly beautiful.

"Cause of death, cerebral haemorrhage. Toxicology: metabolites of amphetamines, alcohol and a lot of cocaine. On the face of it, she had herself one hell of a party and died of it," Mac said.

"On the face of it?" I said.

"Well..." He stopped and looked at Bill.

"Go on, Mac," Bill said.

"Ahem, well, it has been suggested by some, that what I'm about to tell you is a load of bollocks."

"Not by me, Mac," Bill said.

"No. Okay then. The thing is, I handle a lot of corpses here, right?"

I nodded encouragingly.

"Right. And you sort of get to know the feel of them. The tissues; they're affected by everything we do. Work, stress, food, alcohol, tobacco and all the drugs. It's not that there's a specific test necessarily, but you generally know what kind of pressure each body has been under, and drug deaths, even accidental ones, don't generally come out of nowhere."

"She doesn't look like a drug user to me," I said.

"No, but that in itself isn't so unusual. I see plenty of healthy young people who you wouldn't know to look at them, weren't perfectly sound, apart from being dead. And in a way, they are. Their bodies are tolerating what they're doing to themselves. In a couple of decades it'll start so show on the outside. But for now, they look fine. Isn't that right, Bill?"

"Are you saying I drink too much, Mac?"

"I'm saying it's your round on Friday, and don't forget. No, if they quit everything, ate well and got some exercise, they'd soon be as fit, as… well as you look, Simon. In the meanwhile however, from the inside, they're telling me a story of G and Ts, uppers and downers and long hours of work and worry. But this girl, well if I didn't know she'd just died of a massive overdose of an illegal substance, I'd say… well, I'd say she hadn't even had a drink for six months."

"That's possible, I suppose," I said.

"Yes, possible but it seemed a bit funny so I tested her hair. No drug use, no alcohol, nothing for more than six months. As you see, she's got long hair so we go back more than a year. Before six months, modest alcohol but nothing else."

"So not just out of rehab then?" I said.

"No," Bill said, "I've dug out her case file. She started acting a bit weird last autumn, neurotic, paranoid, one minute hyper, the next dragging herself about. Then she disappeared. Everyone assumed a class A addiction. The family spent a fortune searching for her, but no luck."

"I was just about to sign her off last night when I get a call from Bill here asking me if I had any thoughts about her, and, well, I went out on a limb a bit and said I might have."

"That's interesting," I said.

"Yes, well, I suppose it is," Mac said.

"So I asked him to assume foul play and do everything possible to find out," Bill said.

"And now you think someone killed her?" I said.

"Er, yes…" Bill said.

"Very possibly," Mac said. "I put everyone else on hold and started digging and digging. And then finally I found it. God bless mass-spectrometry." He held up a sheaf of printed pages. "In her hair at about eight months. A very, very nasty combination of l-dopa, rohypnol and scopolamine. Any one of those are bastards and in combination they'll have you looking like you've been mainlining for years in a few days. And the scopolamine will prevent you from remembering who you are, never mind who gave it to you. Very sophisticated pharmacology indeed."

"Chemical gas-lighting, you might say," I said.

"Good way to put it. Exactly that, if you ask me," Mac said.

"Your friend was right, Si. Thanks, Mac, you can put her away now," Bill said.

"Anytime, Bill. You know you're always welcome here. And you, Simon."

"Thanks," I said.

He smiled at me knowingly and showed us out.

"You seem to spend a lot of time down there for someone who doesn't like dead bodies," I said, as I followed him back the way we'd come.

"I've a Calvinist streak in me that does it. I also make myself see the relatives when I could send a WPC."

"You seem a tad stressed, old thing," I said.

"My workload just doubled, or didn't you notice. I'm currently in two places at once. Can you remember the way from here?" He stopped at the junction of two corridors and stood where we could see down both.

"I think I can find my way out of a hospital, yes."

"Good. Take these." He pulled some folded sheets of paper from his inside jacket pocket. "I'm going out a different way."

I opened the pages. Various sheets of paper with information about Hillary and some photos.

"Why?" I said.

"You mean why did someone do this? I've no fucking idea."

"Quite cool in a way though, isn't it?"

"I knew you'd think that. What are we going to do about it?"

"We?"

"I'm helping you this time, remember."

"Quite right, so you are. Well, don't just stand there, go and get on with it."

"Oh, fuck off."

I wandered back thoughtfully through the teeming metropolis towards the river. Looking down at my home from the walkway down to the docks, it struck me again that, beautiful as she was, she really didn't belong where I'd put her. I would take her with me when I went to the Pyrenees. Perhaps I should set out soon and return her to Soumy's care. Things to do first though, apparently.

Breakfast seemed to have passed sufficiently to make elevenses advisable, so I returned to the cafe and spread the sheets of paper out.

"You've decided to become a talent scout for super-models, perhaps?" Henriques said, appearing with unabashed curiosity.

"Huh?" I said.

"The girl, sir."

I saw what he meant; she was strikingly beautiful.

"Not a super-model, Henriques, a rocket scientist, possibly."

"I see, sir. Will she be joining you sir?"

"I don't believe so, no."

"Shame."

"Not necessarily. Coffee and cake for two please, Henriques."

"If you say so, sir."

I tuned him and the rest of the world out and paid proper attention to the information on the sheets of paper. There were interview notes from parents, friends, employers, colleagues, tutors and the like, and screen shots from social media. Instagram, Facebook and others. There were photos of a happy, shiny girl receiving her degree and posing for family portraits. Photos of her bedroom too; a vibrant room full of books and clothes and pictures and sporting kit; the stuff of a rich and healthy life.

Then there were photos of an apparently drunken, but more probably, drugged, girl at parties and in clubs and restaurants and then there were photos of a nasty, filthy, squalid room and a dirty, tangled cadaver. Altogether, it was a sad and poignant collection of paperwork; the record of a beautiful, promising creature, broken, corrupted and trampled into dirty, decaying nastiness.

I looked at it all, stacking it into my brain as information to be held and sifted and sorted. Then I took photos of some of the photos with my phone. The happy alive girl, and then the dead one.

After that I stared into space and thought about it all, but not so vacantly that I didn't see Mel come through the archway into the dock and walk towards me through the wandering tourists and whatnot. She appeared to cleave the throng like a swan passing through lesser fowl.

"Are you ever not eating?" she said, putting her bag down on a chair and ruffling my hair with her hand.

"I got some for you."

"I see that. Thank you. It's true, then?"

"Looks like it."

She sat down and I told her what Mac had found and gave her the paperwork to read. She consumed the information and the cake.

"Bloody hell. I knew it."

"And you were clearly right."

"What a complete fucking waste," she said, turning to her coffee.

"Yes," I said.

"You're supposed to say that like you mean it."

"I do. Sort of."

"I know. Thank you."

"You're welcome."

"How did you do this?"

"Don't ask."

"How? Who? Why?"

"It's not important."

"Hm. Whatever, I suppose that you did, is the main thing."

She looked past me and I became conscious that we weren't alone. Henriques had joined us and was brandishing a pot of coffee.

"Hello, Henriques," Mel said.

"Good morning, ma'am. May I offer you some more coffee?"

"Er, thank you, yes please."

"And me," I said, putting my cup in the way of it.

"Sir."

"Thanks, Henriques," I said, looking at him.

"Anything else I can get you, ma'am, sir?" he said, holding his ground.

"Don't worry, we'll let you know," I said.

"Very good, sir."

"Be nice to him," Mel said, when he'd retreated.

"That was me being nice to him."

"Whatever. Anyway, this means…"

"That you're probably right about your other friend too. Susie, wasn't it?"

"Yes. What're we going to do?"

"I don't know."

"Oh, don't you?" She gave me the benefit of her full attention and it struck me how well her hazel eyes went with her raven tresses.

"What do you think we should do?" I said.

"You know why I used to like hanging out with you?" she said.

"My amazing good looks?"

"Huh?"

"Thanks."

"No, because a lot of the time you'd be up to something. Usually something stupid and dangerous."

"You ratted me out when I climbed the front of School House. Do you remember?"

"Only because they were about to catch you anyway."

"I got caught a few times, but you never did, did you?"

"It's a matter of brains."

"Fine. And your point is?"

"My point is, I know what you look like when you're up to something. So stop trying to wind me up and tell me how we're going to do this. You have a plan and I know you do, so stop fucking about."

"Yes, Mel. Okay, so this is a bit vague but…"

"Go on, surprise me."

"It's pattern recognition, if you like. You know how you find an animal's trail in the bush?"

"In Shepard's Bush?"

"Possibly. You don't start with the detail; you'd only get lost in that. You start with a diffuse focus; you let the whole of it come to you. You give the odd thing, the broken twig, the stem of grass that's pointing a different way, a chance to draw itself to your attention."

"If you say so."

"I do. And I've spent some time with the kind of people who do…"

"Bad things?"

"You could say so…"

"And don't care about other people?"

"Yes."

"Like you, you mean?"

"You want my help?"

"Sorry. Go on."

"I may possibly be qualified to notice the bent grass, the odd thing, the thing that doesn't fit the overall pattern. We'll let the police plod, and I'll do what I'm good at. Okay?"

"Yes, but you mean, us."

"Ah, yes. I've had a thought about that."

"What?"

"For all we know, could be you next, couldn't it?"

"Could it? Why would it?"

"You're a connection for a start. Did Hillary know Susie too?"

"Yes, we all know each other."

"I take it she's young, attractive and clever too?"

"Pretty much."

"So, there we are, three of a kind. I can't help feeling I should stick pretty close to you for a while," I said, smiling.

"Oh, do you? No chance, I'm not going there again, you bastard."

"It's nice to see you again, Mel."

"And you too. Now stop looking at me like that and help me catch these people."

"Me, help *you*?"

"You know what I mean."

"Whatever. You ready to do some work?"

"What work?"

"Let's you and me be a team and talk it through. I'll be the bastard doing it, and you can be Hillary. See what I mean? We'll each bring our own point of view and see what emerges."

"That's actually not a completely stupid idea," she said.

"Thank you."

"Well, come on then, do your thing."

"Okay. I've been thinking about how I would do this myself. Poisoning and kidnapping a girl. Or girls, I suppose. Supposing I'd decided to, for some reason, I'd want at least one person to do the actual poisoning. Someone above suspicion, and preferably, apparently harmless."

"Agreed."

"And further to that, I think they would have to be someone who doesn't just know her, but knows her in a context where people are drinking and probably taking drugs. By that I mean a peer; someone their own age. Probably thirty or less. Naturally mixes with them at private parties and nightclubs."

"You don't tend to get pissed in the company of great aunt Dorothy."

"I do, but I know what you mean."

"Agreed. And?"

"And, I'd also want a small team to do the actual work. Transport, storage, all that. You get me? There has to be some logistics going on here and that also is going to require a certain type of person. At least six of them, I would say."

"That many?"

"I think so. They've got to keep her alive and not let her get away. People need sleep. And they'd have to be not squeamish, certainly. And comfortable operating outside the law. I think she's a high-value item, whatever the value to them is. It's not like they've made off with some unknown street girl, is it? This was a girl that people would miss and spend considerable resources looking for."

"Agreed. So you mean, the mob?"

"Or ex-military or police, or similar. An organisation of some kind, definitely."

"That's all pretty obvious."

"Try and be nice. I think we know a few things about the boss, or bosses, of this thing too."

"We do?"

"Yes. He, or she, is persistent, plans ahead, is well-resourced, well-connected and securely established. This took planing and patience. It's not a crime of opportunity or impulse."

"Why the last two?"

"This isn't bread-and-butter crime; this is specialist. Whoever is doing this, must have a secure source of funds coming from somewhere else, and enough free time to indulge in this. And I would want to be a chemist or a pharmacist, or a doctor, or have one of those in my back pocket in order to do this. You don't just come by l-dopa, rohypnol and scopolamine at the local pharmacy."

"Okay, I'll go with all that."

"And we're talking about quite a specialised location too. It would appear that they kept Hillary alive and well for at least six months. For whatever reason. Somewhere abroad would be easier, but against that, you've got the risk of passport checks. Unless you're set up for fake documentation, which is getting harder, but is quite possible. Given the sophistication of the pharmacology involved, I think it would be easy enough to make the girls compliant and then just walk them onto a ferry or aeroplane."

"But…"

"But then why bring them back into the country to kill them? That makes a location here more likely. So, it's either a remote location or somehow very secure. We know they're not doped up for the six months and there're no signs of physical abuse. You would think they would shout or make a fuss if they could, wherever they are."

"Agreed. So, like where?"

"No idea, but I'll be working on it. Your turn; I've told you about the perpetrators, now you tell me about the victim. I particularly want to know what might make her valuable to someone."

"Valuable? Oh. Okay, I'll do my best. She's beautiful and clever. And young and well-educated. And well-connected and lives in London."

"No ransom?"

"No."

"You're sure."

"Quite sure."

"Okay. But she knows you and Susie."

"Yes, that's true and we have lots of other friends in common too. Including you, if you weren't always buggering off somewhere and if you bothered. She, she and Susie… well, they're the future. That's why it's such a bloody shame."

"Nubile."

"Nubile?"

"I mean in the Latin sense. Debutants. Breeding heifers."

"Marriageable, yes, very. But this is kidnap, not marriage. I mean, they don't breed from them. Do they?"

"Even I know that takes more than six months."

"Of course."

"But talk about marriage. I mean, forget the fluffy stuff and let's talk about the basics. I would see these as potential high-value brides for export to the Middle East, or whatever. Wouldn't you?"

"Trust you. Okay. Marriage, at its most basic is a trade of wealth against breeding potential. Wealth used to be land and to a degree, title. Title representing prosperity through access to patronage and opportunity. Breeding potential being youth and beauty. A plain girl with lots of acres could hope to get a vigorous second son with good prospects and pretty young girl with no money might get…"

"My Darcy."

"Exactly. Now it's holdings in BAE Systems and raw fame of course. The real debutants in today's world are the sons and daughters of Saudi princes, Russian oligarchs, movie stars, and internet giants; wealth and status in all its current forms. And, yes, there still is a 'season' in which they are shown off to prospective husbands. In that world, we don't even figure. Well, only very peripherally."

"That's very rational, but I'm not entirely sure. Put it this way, value is always perceived value, and that's seldom rational. There's a certain something about you, isn't there. I'm not sure what it is, but I'm sure there is. Did Hillary have a hereditary title, or something? Something like that?"

"No. Susie's a bit of an aristo, but Hillary's a prole."

"And you. Wasn't your great aunt, Duchess of Washingup, or something?"

"Walshrup. My grandmother, actually. But that's in abeyance now, and was never important."

"I've no idea if this matters or not, but, you're a certain class, you three, in a very British way. You can tell it from a thousand yards. Or at least as soon as you speak. And without being one of the actual land-owning aristocracy, what's left of them, you're pretty near the top of society, aren't you? And Hillary, I think."

"You shouldn't say that," she said, looking uncomfortable. "And stop including me; we don't know I'm anything to do with this.

"I know," I said, smiling. "Very bad form of me. But why would someone want to kidnap Hillary, keep her hidden for six months, and then kill her?"

"No idea. That didn't help much. What, the fuck, Si, are we actually going to do? Apart from look at twigs, or whatever you said."

"What I said. Until something better comes up, spend as much time as we can with our potential victim and potential suspects. Let's go hang out with this girl, Susie, wherever it is she does that."

"Your idea of helping is to just go out drinking and partying?"

"You got a better one?"

"You buying?"

"I don't suppose you are. Are you coming?"

"Of course I fucking am."

"Good. Where shall we start?"

"We'll start at the Meatball, of course. I already got tickets. It's tonight."

"You already got tickets?"

"You think I'm stupid?"

"Why did I bother saying all that then?"

"No idea. What're you going to wear?"

"I don't know. Does it matter?"

"It does if you think you're coming with me."

"Oh fuck. I'm going to have to go shopping, aren't I?"

"Yes, Si. You certainly are."

8

AN EXPENSIVE WOMAN

Mel gave me strict and explicit instructions, annexed Bill's bits of paper, and took herself off leaving me with the debris, the bill, and a recurrent Henriques.

"A very beautiful young woman, if you don't mind me saying so, sir," he said, collecting the debris with tolerable skill.

"Oh, do you think so?" I said. "I can't say I'd noticed."

"Really, sir?"

"Are you enjoying yourself, Henriques?"

"Just doing my job, sir."

"If you say so, Henriques, if you say so."

Back on Polly, I lay on a bunk and stared at the cabin ceiling. No good; Mel was right; time for doing, not thinking. And my body felt like it needed a good clearing out. I put on some trainers and loose clothes, went up and sat in the cockpit, just leaning back, my head barely clearing the teak-work and looking at everything and nothing. I've learned to trust that feeling of being watched and pay attention to it. Couldn't spot anyone though. I got up, went out through the gate, and started running.

Up past the Tower of London, the ancient fortress now looking friendly and almost toy-like in the company of skyscrapers, and on towards Westminster. The dirty, busy river was catching the light, as almost any water does, and was good company. There were plenty of other people on the paved pathway but there was space enough for us all and I wasn't the only one running.

St Pauls showed herself briefly between the other buildings and the Eye came into sight on the other side. I got into my wind and went over the grass of Temple Gardens almost at a sprint and then settled back down to a steady jog as I followed the river round the corner to Victoria Embankment, cut through Whitehall Place to Horseguards and then St James Park. Now I was running on grass. The waterfowl on the lake looked content enough, and so was I. It can't help being a city, but London is a place in itself; it's not like anywhere, it just is London. And I suppose it's beautiful in its own way. It was on that early summer's afternoon, anyway.

I carried on through Green Park, crossed Hyde Park Corner without getting run over, and entered the park itself. I kept off the paths and under the trees. I started to feel that I'd done enough running so I slowed down to a walk and a particularly lovely lime tree enticed me to sit down under it, so I did.

I leant back and looked up into the cathedral spaces of its branches. I'm not saying I could feel the sap rising in its trunk, but I'm not saying I couldn't either. A grey squirrel on a lower branch looked at me, flicked its tail once and went on about its own private business. I like lime trees. The scent of its flowers was falling in the air, sweet and refreshing.

When I was cooler, I pushed off its rough bark and went on my way, running again. Down past The Magazine, over the Serpentine, through the last of the park, past Kensington Palace, into Holland park, down a familiar street and up the steps to the door of my family's London residence.

Mum was out but Dad was in. He let me in and offered me tea. I sat by the window overlooking the park while he made it. He put the tray down and sat down opposite me.

"You look happy, Si," he said.

"Funnily enough, I am," I said.

"Being busy?" he said.

"I suppose it doesn't feel so bad having something to do," I said, grinning.

"That's good. I think I'm glad to be back at work too."

"Fine, but you aren't, are you? You're sitting here drinking tea with me."

"What are you two laughing about" Mum said, appearing with milk and the day's papers.

"Si's just been telling me to go to work," Dad said.

"Oh." She looked from one to the other of us and then understood. "Well, you'd better go and do that then."

"Well then, I will," he said. "What're you going to do, Si?"

"I'm going to do some shopping," I said. "And I'm hoping Mum will help me."

"Really, darling?"

"Yes. Will you?"

"Will I! Darling, I'd love to."

"Good, but may I have a little bite to eat first?"

"Of course you may, darling."

Dad went to change, reappeared in a suit, looking armoured and ready, and then left with a purposeful air. Mum made toast and fried things. I borrowed her iPad and looked up things.

We ate in comfortable silence for a while. Or rather I ate and she watched me.

"You sent him to work," she said when I got to the plate wiping stage.

"I did," I said.

"Thank you. That was very thoughtful. He needs to be back now, but he's not sure of his own strength."

"I know. Mum, d'you remember Melissa Franklin?"

"Oh, yes. Of course, you and she..."

"Hm. Dad told you about this dead girl?"

"Hillary Stubbs. I knew about her anyway, of course, poor thing. Your dad tells me everything now."

"That's good. Who knows, I may do the same."

"Go on then."

"Someone kidnapped her, but first they've subtly poisoned her so that everyone thought she had a habit."

"That's certainly what I thought. I'm glad in a way, if it's not the case."

"But why, Mum? Tell me about her, will you? And could you work me up a list of similar girls. Go through your address book. I'm wondering if Hillary was the only one. Suppose there were others?"

"You think there could be?"

"No harm in looking. Tell me about her, will you?"

"Okay. Well, she was the type of girl I would be hoping you would marry," she said. "Clever. Lots of character. Good education. Bound to want children. What else do you want to know?"

"Don't go there Mum. I'm not sure; go on."

"Okay, darling. Perhaps it'll come to you one day. Yes, I can do that; my address book, I mean. And there's Debretts."

"Really? I didn't know that still existed."

"Well maybe not Debretts exactly, but perhaps the guest list for the hunt ball. Some of the hunt balls, I mean. What are you thinking?"

"Thanks. For the moment, I'm assuming she was poisoned by a peer; a friend or acquaintance, an equal."

"I see that, but why?"

"No idea. The other way I can think of is in a social setting, I mean restaurants, clubs etc. As a waiter or something. See what I mean?"

"I do. London is a big place, but people are tribal and each tribe has its own places. It changes for the different generations but the principle holds. I remember the places we used to go…" She almost sighed.

"Talking of peers, I'm wondering if that's a factor too. What do you think? Heredity? Nobility? Breeding?"

"That's interesting. There's Mel, of course."

"She said not."

"She would, but she's real aristocracy all the same."

"She is?"

"Yes, but on the distaff side. Franklin isn't a patronymic."

"Oh, so what is it? A…"

"Matronymic, of course."

"Oh."

"It's a kind of distortion really; the line of descent, as it's usually seen, is all about the name, and the name comes from the man, but the whole business of having to have a son to pass it on is just so much nonsense; daughters do just as well, perhaps better."

"Oh. Er, I'd never thought about it."

"People don't. Someone explained it to me once. Grace, I think. It's like a mirror, in a way. If you flip the way you see it, it all looks different. There are some women who are directly descended on the distaff side since well before the conquest."

"The conquest?"

"When the Normans arrived, darling."

"Oh, the Normans. Of course."

"Yes. Very good record keepers, but socially conservative. There are some women about with the most amazing pedigree, if you want to put it that way, but they're called Smith or whatever, because they married someone, so you'd never know."

"Don't you mean men too? I mean if the man's mother was…?"

"Yes, but not really. It's generally seen that if you're looking on the female side, you don't count any male children. In some circles, anyway. Now I think of it, I'm not quite sure why. Perhaps it's because all the money goes down the male side, which is basically just unfair."

"Oh."

"Though I suspect that some of them have their own discreet banking arrangements. The women, I mean. It's noticeable that the ancient female lines seldom ever die out. That implies a continuity of funds, don't you think? It is easier in a way if you're a woman of course; we're less likely to be killed than you men are. Those lines of descent, like Mel's, have proved remarkably resilient; all you need is to have one female child, or for one of your female siblings to have one female child, and on it goes. Just like for men."

"Bloody hell."

"And of course, all these old matronymic families tended to marry into the old patronymic families that we all know of, like the Chesterfields for example, so it's all intertwined. Anyway, it's interesting, but it doesn't really matter, does it? We're all related if you go back far enough, and we're all just people, so who cares?"

"Some people might care. It's funny what people do sometimes care about."

"Hm…" She looked at me thoughtfully, but I couldn't tell what she was thinking.

"Mel was brought up by her mum and an aunt, wasn't she? I don't remember them," I said.

"In that lovely house on the outskirts of Effington, yes. And I'm sure they had a place in the South of France too, but I can't remember where. Why?"

"I've just realised I've never heard her mention her father."

"I think he died when she was very young, but I can't say for sure. It was always just the three of them as far as I can remember. Why, darling? What's this about?"

"I've no idea. But whatever, my job is clearly to get a social life," I said.

"You lucky thing."

"If I know Mel, she'll have lots of ideas. And I'm sure I can count on Berry too. It was nice to see him the other night. And he's practically the definition of the set we're talking about, isn't he."

"You be careful of him, darling."

"Berry's alright, Mum. Just a bit eccentric, that's all."

"Oh, how I wish I could come with you."

"I've got a feeling that wouldn't work too well," I said, smiling. "But tell me about the Meatball."

"My goodness, that's tonight. You're going, darling?"

"Apparently. Mel's got tickets."

"Well I never. Of course, how sensible."

"Yes, but what is it really? I've heard of it of course, but never been."

"I have. Many times. It's a charity fundraiser for women's shelters. Been going for years. Definitely one of the highlights of the season. There will be a lot of money about and a lot of drinking, and, if I know you, you'll love it."

"Oh, good. Why the name?"

"Meat, as in cattle market, I believe. The hottest young things in the city will be for sale. Just to be chosen is quite something. It's really the Congrieve Women's Foundation Ball, but everyone calls it the Meatball."

"When you say, for sale...?"

"Just for an evening. There'll be an auction and you can buy the right to spend an evening with a pretty young thing."

"But not the night?"

"That's up to the girl, I suppose, but no. So, you and Mel are going to be working on this together?"

"Looks like it. It's good to see her again. She's really grown up."

"You two always did look good together. I'm surprised you didn't..."

"Stop right there, Mum."

"Sorry, darling. I'm too young not to have anything to do." She sighed.

"Fine. So let's get out of here and do some shopping. Ready?"

"Oh, yes, Si. Never more ready."

It seems pretty stupid to own a car in London but I bought one anyway. I'm a bit sceptical about any vehicle that won't take a reasonable amount of gear and climb over reasonable sized rocks, but I didn't seem to need either of those particular attributes at the moment. Mel texted me an address and I turned up at it, with the help of the built in sat-nav, in an F-type Jag.

I'd rather associated Jags with old people but it had caught my eye in a window on Park Lane and it was growing on me. At some point, I would have to find out what all the multiple computerised settings did.

I rang the bell of a small Victorian terrace somewhere in the general direction of Crouch End. A plump young woman in a pink dressing gown and damp hair answered the door.

"Are you Stevie?" she said.

"Definitely not. I'm Simon," I said.

"Okay, you can come in."

"Thanks." I followed her into the cramped hallway.

"Whoop, whoop, man in the house," she called out, leading me down the passage. We had to get past a bicycle and there was washing hung on the radiator and the frame of the bike.

Mel was in the kitchen, standing up. She was wearing a ball-gown of lavender silk and lace and she looked like everything that was wonderful in the universe, right there in that untidy cramped room. I squeezed past the girl in the dressing gown to get to her.

"Thank you, Hazel," Mel said.

"You're welcome," Hazel said, standing there watching us.

"I meant, go away," Mel said.

"Oh."

"Now, let me look at you," Mel said to me, taking the lapels of my jacket gently between thumb and forefinger of each hand and inspecting me. "Yes, you will do."

"Hi, Mel," I said. "You look absolutely stunning."

"Thank you. I need a drink. Let's get out of this mad house. Have you got a taxi or something?" She picked up a handbag and a competent looking camera.

"I've got a car."

"Is it reasonably clean?" she said.

"Should be, I only got it this afternoon."

"Right, follow me and don't look left or right."

Another girl had joined the first at the bottom of the stairs. They watched us pass with great interest.

"Have a nice evening and be good," they called after us as we left.

"Have you any idea what it's like living with two other girls?" Mel said.

"Some idea," I said.

"Yes, knowing you, you probably have. You're joking!"

I held the door of the car for her.

"I stole it," I said.

"Fucking hell, Si."

"It's okay, we've got hours before they miss it. Get in."

"Just don't get me arrested, okay?" She gathered up her dress and got into the low car.

"I promise," I said, carefully shutting the door on her.

"Just how much money did you make in Morocco?" she said, when we'd pulled away.

"Enough not to have to work for a while."

"What's a while? A month? A year?"

"I don't know. Depends how fast I spend it. If I don't buy one of these everyday, it should last for a few years at least."

"Okay, you're buying the drinks tonight."

"I knew that."

"I'm just glad you're okay and you're back. Just try not to go away again without saying goodbye. Okay?"

"Okay." I pulled away and started driving under her instructions. We weaved about in the general direction of Soho and I parked next to a Landrover under a streetlight. We walked back to an unostentatious doorway in a plain brick wall. Above the door was the legend *Umbra Villus* and a stylish representation of a hare carrying a tray with a domed serving dish on it.

"Don't let anyone pick a fight with you, will you," Mel said

"I'm a lot harder to pick a fight with than I used to be," I said.

"Tell your knuckles that," she said.

I looked at my right hand. My knuckles were nearly back to normal but not quite.

An overweight gentleman in black and white stopped fingering one of his rings long enough to check Mel's name on a list and wave us through. We stepped into a cavern with gold pillars, ornate mirrors and no shortage of black velvet. There was a long bar, a stage and a dance floor, but most of the space, and it was a big space, was taken up with round tables covered in cloths the colour of clotted blood. A hundred or more people were there already and more coming in behind us. Dinner jackets, colourful cummerbunds and waistcoats, long gowns and short ones. Backless dresses, strapless dresses, dresses that were near a second skin. There was a lot to look at.

"And if you go off with another girl, I'll never ever speak to you again," Mel said.

"Mel!"

"I'm just saying."

"None of them are as beautiful as you, Mel," I said.

"You said that like you meant it."

"I did. I do. It's true."

"Thank you. You're not a complete disaster yourself."

"Thank you. You look like you know some of these people?"

"Half the fucking media world is here, you idiot. And the successful half at that. Of course, I fucking know them. The question is, do they know me."

"They look like an interesting lot. Which one's Susie?"

"Don't worry, you'll see her in a bit."

"Oh. Okay."

One group, including the girls, were in hunting pink, white britches and riding boots. It was a colourful crowd and a lively one. Everyone seemed to know everyone else. Men were standing in groups, men and women were standing in groups, men and women were moving between groups as they noticed a friend, or perhaps a lover.

"Let's get a drink, shall we?" Mel said, looking towards the bar.

We didn't make it. A man in a dinner jacket with a hint of makeup pounced on Mel to exchange air kisses, shake my hand curiously and begin gossiping with her. I grabbed a passing waiter and ordered martinis for us and a daiquiri for him and we were led off to join a group. These, at least, did know Mel, and clearly liked her.

I shook a lot of hands and practiced making comic or obscene associations with their names to help me remember them. Mel was drawn into conversation with an older man with a halo of silver hair around his crown and I found myself talking to an attractive young woman in long dress with an exquisitely laced corset. She had a magnificent figure and turned out to have the most extraordinary grasp of North African politics. We were having an argument about the persistence of cross racial slavery when Mel reclaimed me.

"Si, I'd like you to meet my boss, Harry," she said, introducing me to the man she'd been talking to.

"How d'you do, Harry," I said.

"Pleased to meet you, Si."

We shook hands. He was a tall chap with a slight stoop and a disarmingly gentle manner.

"Harry is the editor of Essence," Mel said. I must have looked blank as she added, "the magazine I work for, you clot."

"Of course. I'm afraid I've been away from civilisation for a while and I'm not very familiar with your world," I said.

"If you think there's anything civilised about the magazine business you're quite wrong," he said with a twinkle in his eye. "Just ask Mel."

"He may look like a big teddy bear, but don't be fooled," Mel said.

"It's all just a game, you know," Harry said, "but if you don't play games to win, they don't have any meaning, do they?"

"What do you call winning in your world?" I said.

"Blood on the carpet, mainly. Blood on the carpet. Preferably someone else's blood and someone else's carpet."

I liked the shrewd old buzzard. He really wasn't at all as meek as he looked. We talked about how empty life became without a challenge. I joined him in a whiskey sour. Mel had another martini, took some pictures of us and then held onto my arm, listening to us talk. By now the room was full and it was time to find our table for supper.

There were ten of us at the table. Luckily it was put together from Mel's kind of world and there were several people she knew, and a few plus-ones, like me, who weren't. We ranged in age from bright young things, fresh out of university, younger than Mel and me, to the eminence-grise, of Harry.

A serious, round-faced fellow on my left picked up on the fact that I was a moneyed layabout given to yachting, and asked me, in a voice loud enough to include the whole table, if I didn't get bored enjoying myself all the time. I answered him with a substantially true story of modern day piracy on the high seas, which left one of the girls staring at me with her mouth open. I made myself the victim not the pirate.

This led to more questions and to more stories, though I wouldn't let myself be the centre of attention for long and managed to elicit some scandalous stories of social, professional and sexual misadventure. I got the impression that their world was, in its own way, highly charged and more than a bit promiscuous.

Occasionally, Mel would break off what she was doing to take a picture of someone she found interesting. Sometimes it was me. No one seemed at all put out by this and plenty of other photos were being taken by cameras and phones.

Food came. Allegedly wild boar and ceps. It wasn't bad for food served to hundreds of people all at the same time, and the wine wasn't bad either. As everyone became more relaxed, or at least less sober, and the conversation became more specific and gossipy and work oriented, I was able to sit back and observe them. Mel, beside me, put her hand on my arm.

"Thanks for being here, Si. And it's nice to have you back," she said.

"Thanks for bringing me. And it's nice to be back," I said.

"Was that story about the fast boat true?"
"More or less."
"But not your part in it?"
"No."
"Thought so."
"I like your friends."
"Even Phil?"
"Can't blame the man for fancying you."
"You, you mean."
"Oh."
"Will you ask me to dance when this bit is over?"
"Of course."
"Not Stephanie?"
"Who?"
"The girl with the pneumatic bust."
"Huh?"
"The one you were so deeply engrossed with earlier."
"Oh, her. No."
"Good. She's a cow."
"I had no idea."
"You wouldn't, you're a man."
"By the way, where's the bait?"
"Susie?"
"Aren't we supposed to be keeping an eye on her?"
"Don't worry, you won't miss her."
"If you say so."

I let my eyes slide over the crowd, looking for anything interesting, looking for anything, as Bill might have said, that looked out of pattern; for the fox in the hen house. There were certainly plenty of chickens.

I made up little stories about some of the people I could see; this one a corrupt banker in debt to the gangs, that one a paedophile, that one a wife beater, her a dominatrix. None of the stories took root particularly.

"Did I mention how beautiful you are?" I said to Mel.

"Yes, but I don't mind you repeating yourself."

"So, this is your life then, living in London. Parties and going out ,and glamour and fine food, and all that?"

"I wish. Have you any idea how much it costs to go to this kind of thing?"

"Not a clue. But you keep up with the old crowd?"

"I see Helen now and again, and George and Stubbsie of course. Trouble is almost everyone's on a proper grown up salary apart from me. There's a limit to how often you can let someone else pick up the tab."

"I'll take your word for that."

My wandering eyes noticed a couple in mid-forties sitting at a table not far from us, not talking. His hand was on the table and hers beside it, little finger hooked into little finger. They looked a lot like each other, as sometimes happens with couples. His hair was jet black and hers was a soft strawberry blonde, but they both had the same lean intensity and effortless perfection of dress that only comes from innate style or unlimited funds. I struggle to care about how I look myself, but that doesn't mean I can't appreciate a good thing when I see it.

What caught my attention was that they were in their own bubble. They, like us, were on a table of ten but they weren't with the other eight and the other eight weren't with them. It was almost as if they were above all this, or perhaps doing a duty or a chore.

A waiter passed behind them and seeing that their glasses were nearly empty, leant down and spoke to the man. I saw his lips move so he must have replied but he didn't move his head one inch, and neither did his wife. The waiter went away leaving their glasses unfilled.

They were both looking in the same direction so I looked where they were looking, as far as I could tell.

"They're beautiful, aren't they," Mel said.

"Who?"

"The girls you're looking at; tonight's prizes."

"Huh?"

"Look at the card under your plate, you idiot."

"Ah." I did that. There was a printed sheet. It had photos, names and a brief biography of six attractive young people. Three young women and three young men. To my surprise, I'd recently met two of them.

A man left the table with the prizes and ascended the stage. His hair, what was left of it, had a good strong hint of ginger about it. He had on a bow tie, a very loud waistcoat and a considerable amount of ebullient charm. He tapped his glass with a spoon near the microphone and a sporadic silence fell. He tucked the spoon into the top pocket of his jacket and said, "Good evening, ladies and gentlemen."

A more solid silence descended.

"My name is Charles Dutton, though most people call me Charlie, and I have the honour of being your auctioneer tonight. Is that okay?"

"We're with you Charlie," a man shouted out from somewhere near the front.

"Thank you, thank you. Now, ladies and gentlemen, you all know why we're here, don't you?"

There was a certain amount of cheering and ribald comment.

"No, not for that. We're here because of Muriel Congrieve and the wonderful Congrieve foundation that she founded. Our world is often not very nice to half its population and it won't do. Ladies and gentlemen, it won't do. Will it?"

"No Charlie," the vocal comedian at the front shouted, backed up by others.

"No, it won't. Sadly, even now, there are people in the world who see women as commodities to be bought and sold. But we won't have it, will we?" He lent us a theatrical ear as more people shouted agreement.

"No it won't. So we need the walk-in centre and safe houses and resettlement programmes and all the wonderful people who spend their lives helping to make the world a better, safer place for women who are in deep trouble to continue, don't we?"

Various shouts of, "Yes, Charlie."

"But it all takes money. And so, if you are willing, I'd like to…" he paused… "sell you my children!"

We clapped and cheered.

"…and some of my friends' children!"

We clapped and cheered some more. There was a good feeling in the room. We had come together with the man and we felt that what we were doing was a good thing. Whatever it was we were doing.

"So there," Mel said, punching me on the arm.

"What?" I said, rubbing it. She was stronger than I expected, or at least, hit harder.

"Excellent. If you would, my dears," Charlie Dutton said, waving up the young people from his table.

The six handsome young people ascended the stage into the applause and stood in a line next to him. They looked out at us, self-conscious but confident. One of the girls gave a little wave to someone in the crowd.

"Now then, Ladies and Gentlemen," Charlie said, "we'll have no gender stereotyping here, if you please. You may bid for whoever you would like to spend an evening with, regardless of their gender, or yours. Am I clear?"

"Yes, Charlie," more than one person called out.

"These absolutely gorgeous young people have kindly offered to do their best to entertain you with their sparkling wits and stunning good looks for an evening. That doesn't mean that you can take them home afterwards, however. You'll find under your place mats a brief and mainly truthful resume for each of them."

"I fancy the filly in blue myself," one of the men at our table said. "Susana Chesterfield."

"Susana? Susie?" I said.

"Yes," Mel said.

"I think buying her for the evening is about as close as your ever likely to get to going out with her, Andy," one of the women said.

"You never know, she might take a fancy to me," he said.

"You'll have to buy her first and I don't believe you'll be able to afford it," Mel said.

"How do you know what I can afford and what I can't?" the man said.

"Go on, then. I dare you," she said.

"Which one of the men is going to go for the most then, girls?" I said. The women at the table had clearly been weighing up their merits.

"I say Jules," one of them said.

"Not Abe?" another said.

"He's cute but too boyish for me."

"I quite like boyish."

"You're old enough to be…"

"His big sister. I don't care."

On the stage, Charlie tapped his glass again to hush the chatter and said, "Ladies first, I think. If you wouldn't mind, Jess. Ladies and Gentlemen, my lovely daughter, Jessica Dutton."

There were sounds of appreciation and more than one whistle. The other young people retired, leaving the girl standing beside her father. The tall, elegant red-head with whom I'd had that enjoyable sparring match beside the Fyne brook. She held herself like a swan; beautiful and self-assured and walked about the stage, showing herself off to the right and left and then did a twirl and arrived back beside her father, looking out at the crowd, daring them to bid for her.

"I shall start the bidding at one thousand pounds," Charlie said. "One thousand pounds. It's not every father who sells his daughter, Ladies and Gentlemen, but in this case, let's make it worth it. Do I see a thousand? Anyone…?"

Several hands shot up and we were off.

"To you sir. And two… thank you… three…"

And on up. And then further up until the figures being called out began to seem quite high. The atmosphere in the room was changing; there was a frisson of sexual competition and excitement. I looked at my interesting couple. They were looking at the table where the other prizes sat, not at the stage.

The bidding warmed up nicely and after a good battle she fell to a handsome man in his early sixties at a table mostly full of men.

"Thank you, Sly. Sylvester Mountstevens, Ladies and Gentlemen," Charlie said.

We clapped the winner and watched Jess sashay down from the stage to join him. He stood up and received her with a low bow.

"Well, Andy, your girl might go for as little as that," Mel said. Andy was looking a little pale. "Do you think they'll take an IOU?"

Her brother, Jules, was next. He too had great presence on the stage. He encouraged the female bidders to save him from an old queen who was having fun putting up the price. In the end a dowager with diamonds at her throat bought him for a couple of thousand less than his sister. He ran down to her, knelt before her and kissed her hand. She looked delighted.

After that it was Susie's turn. I looked at her properly for the first time and saw what others had seen. She was coltish and slight, wild and raw, bones and angles and muscles and every bit as feminine as Mel, but the racing version. Her being, a statement of grace and potential. Fine golden hair, cut quite short, framing a passionate, classical face. The kind of woman everyone looks at in a room. Any room, anywhere, in any company.

"Ah, I see," I said.

"That took you a long time," Mel said.

"That's because I can only see you."

"Yeah, right."

True to his word, Andy raised his slightly trembling hand. It seemed like half the room did too. The bidding swiftly surpassed its previous high point and the bidders began to thin out. A man of middle-eastern, or possibly Italian, origin was going up in leaps and bounds against a very self-satisfied looking chap at a table of people who looked like bankers, possibly of the kind that starts with a w. They clearly both wanted her and hated to lose. The intense looking couple's eyes were now glued to the girl on the stage.

When the swarthy gent began to falter, I caught Charlie's eye and raised two fingers. There was a squeak from beside me.

"Si, what are you doing!" Mel said.

"I'm bidding for Susie," I said.

9

UNDONE

"With the gentleman to my right," Charlie said. "And you sir?" He turned back to the banker who also held up two fingers. "Ladies and Gentlemen, we seem to have a battle on our hands." He turned a questioning look at me. I nodded.

"Why?" Mel said.

"Just doing my bit," I said.

The entire room was engaged in the contest, turning their heads from him to me like in a tennis match. We went up tit for tat for a bit until he started to turn a bit pink about the jowls. When Charlie turned to me next, I held up five fingers.

"Fuck! Si, don't," Mel said, in a small voice.

"And five more, sir?" Charlie said, turning to the other man who nodded, as if in a daze.

"And you, sir?" He turned back to me.

"If I may," I said.

"You certainly may. Against you, sir?" he said, turning to the man.

"Er, yes," he said, in a slightly strangled voice.

"Maybe I'll have to go back to work sooner than I thought," I said quietly to Mel as I held up ten fingers.

"And ten, sir?" Charlie said.

"Yes please." I said.

"You stupid prick," Mel said. "Don't do it."

"I think I've done it," I said.

The other bidder was looking confused and started to raise his hand. I thought for a moment that he was going to match me but then he collapsed back into his chair, shook his head and pulled out a handkerchief to wipe his brow. The room broke into a storm of applause. I looked at the girl on the stage. She was looking at me and smiling. She really was extraordinarily beautiful.

I stood up to receive the applause and the girl, who came tripping down to me.

When it was quiet enough for him to be heard, Charlie said, "Thank you very much for that noble act, sir. I'm sorry to say I don't know your name?"

"Simon Ellice," I called out.

"Thank you, Mr Ellice. Your prize."

I bowed to the girl standing before me, bright eyed and looking at me with curiosity. The other men at the table got to their feet as well.

"Hello, Susana," I said.

"Hello, Mr Ellice," she said. "That was very nice of you."

"That was entirely selfish of me. Call me Si."

"Okay, Si, I will."

"Hi, Susie," Mel said.

"Oh. Hi, Mel," Susie said.

"This is my friend, Si," Mel said.

"Will you have a seat?" I said. A helpful waiter had brought a chair for her and the others shuffled round to make room.

"Thank you, I will," She said, and did.

"I'm going to insist on claiming my due. Do you mind very much?" I said.

"I suppose it could've been worse," she said, looking at me.

"That's the spirit," I said. "Let me get you a drink and then will you tell me how you came to be for sale tonight."

"Oh, that's Charlie, he's a sweetheart. No one can say no to Charlie when he wants something."

"I don't think any of the others are going to out-do you two," Harry said. The auction had got going again and a sandy haired chap with boyish good looks was up. The crowed were encouraging each other to join in. A male couple started bidding against each other for him, to the amusement of the crowd and the consternation of the victim.

There was no waiter handy and no clean glasses so I refilled my glass from a bottle and put it on the table halfway between me and the girl.

"Thank you," she said, taking it and drinking some and then putting it back in the same place. "So, Si. Who and what are you, with all this money to throw about on girls?"

"I'm me and I'm er... what's the phrase? A man of independent means. At least at the moment."

"At the moment?"

"Well, you know; money comes and goes."

"I see. Or rather, I don't. So, you don't do anything? Work, I mean?"

"Not as such. I may have to do some sometime, I suppose."

"Depending on how often you come to one of these auctions?"

"Pretty much. Or I may blow it all on... oh, I don't know, a chicken farm, tomorrow."

"You want a chicken farm?"

"I don't think so. But you never know."

"You get bored? Not doing anything."

"Sometimes I do. What about you?"

"Do I get bored?"

"I meant, are you a woman of independent means, but that's a better question. Do you get bored too?"

"You don't know who I am, do you?" she said.

"You're Susana…" I flipped over the card with the details on it, "…Chesterfield," I said. "Are you famous?"

"No, not particularly."

"Fabulously wealthy then?"

"Not at the moment."

"Ah well. I was going to ask you to marry me but now…"

"Oh fuck," she said and put her head back and laughed. "I needed someone like you tonight."

I put my head slightly on one side and grinned at her. "That sounds good. Have some more wine," I said.

"I think I will," she said, taking the glass and drinking.

This time when she put it down I picked it up and drank some too.

"So, what do you do?" I said. "Given that you seem to disapprove of me not doing anything."

"I didn't say that," she said. "I'm a lawyer, if you must know. Well, I'm going to be a lawyer. I'm on placement with Hutchenson and Grieves at the moment."

"Oh. That sounds good," I said.

"You haven't a clue who they are either, do you?" she said.

"No, but I'm sure they're excellent if you're with them."

"And I think I'm unlikely to marry anyone for a while."

"Very wise. Me neither. Do you like being a lawyer?"

"No, but I like using my brain and, unlike you, I'm not work-shy."

"Who said I was work-shy? Give me a minute and I'll remember some lawyer jokes," I said.

"Okay, Mr Ellice. If you currently do nothing, tell me what you've done before. You must've done something sometime."

"Ah well, as to that…"

She and I chatted on, in between watching the auction and clapping. I told her some lies but they were only lies of fact. She told me some things that were probably true but were also evasions. We got on very well and after a bit she topped up the wine glass and we shared it again. Mel talked to the man on her right and ignored us.

At their table, not far away, the couple were watching us. The woman's eyes were locked on Susie and the man was looking at me. For a tiny, fleeting instant, when our eyes connected, I felt the hairs on the back of my neck rise and then he looked away.

When the last lot was sold, Charlie thanked us all and told us again how wonderful we were and then suggested that we might like to dance. He led a slim, elegant woman who I took to be his wife, to the dance floor, the lights dimmed, the band, previously languishing in shadow, sprang into being and hit the beat. The couple stepped out and began to set an example with a will. People started to rise to their feet and join in.

"Susana," I said, putting my hand on hers.

"Call me Susie," she said, also looking ready to rise.

"Susie, if I give you my number, will you promise to phone me?"

"No, but you can have my number and call me," she said.

"Even better." I got out my phone and keyed in the number she gave me. "And now I must keep a promise, but I'll call you soon."

"Okay, Si. I'll count on it," she said.

I got to my feet, hung my jacket on the back of my chair, moved behind Mel and put a hand on her shoulder.

"Melissa Franklin, may I please have the honour of this dance?" I said.

"Oh. Okay, Si. If you want," she said.

We went off to the dance-floor and let the music have us.

Later it began to become late and a lot of what had been done up became undone. Some of the faces took on a sheen of sweat and others took on the glazed look of lots of alcohol.

We danced some and then we danced some more. It was good. I'd forgotten what it was to throw my body about to music. I'd forgotten what it was to dance with a girl who was like me in a room full of my own kind. If that's what they were. Anyway, it was good.

When we'd had enough of dancing, I went and leant against the polished wood of the bar to drink some water and watch the crowd. Mel picked up her camera and dived off to catch up with acquaintance and take photos.

Groups formed and unformed. Many of the older people had slipped away, though not Harry, who seemed to have endless stamina. Some people sat and watched those dancing. Photos were taken, perhaps deals done and alliances negotiated. My interesting couple were sitting not far from the dance floor watching Susie as she bounced and wiggled happily in a group of beautiful young things.

A well-dressed man in his early fifties came to the bar near me and, noticing me watching the crowd, said, "You Brits get me, you really do."

"How's that?" I said.

"Earlier on I mentioned to that lady there," he pointed to one of the women dancing; she was flinging it about in fine style and hadn't notice, or didn't care, that the straps of her dress had slipped rather and her décolletage was superabundant, "that I'd just done one of the best deals of my life while I'd been here and she said, 'that's nice for you,' and changed the subject like I'd said something dirty. And now look at her."

"I know. I'm sorry," I said.

"And that's another thing. People keep saying sorry and I never know what they mean."

"Sorry."

He looked at me sourly. I raised an eyebrow and smiled at him.

"Have a drink?" I said.

"Don't mind if I do. Thanks."

We got a glass of whiskey each and stood there watching the dancers.

"Will," he said, holding out his hand.

"Simon," I said, taking it.

"For all you sound so stuck up, you certainly know how to let your hair down," he said.

"We don't mean to sound stuck up," I said. "We just inherit it and have to live with it."

"Inherit it is right. You guys just have no idea how much history you have. It just kind of oozes out of you and you don't even see it."

"Oh, I don't know. I think about half of us are trying to get away from it and the other half are hiding behind it."

"No kidding?"

"Well, sort of. Here we are: class-bound Brits, defining ourselves by it. Our past, I mean. But it can be hard to reinvent yourself because of it. I think you guys have more freedom."

"Freedom maybe, but…" he appeared to take a deep breath, "Look, I know I'm not supposed to ask, but, you… are you… I mean, do you have a title or something?"

"What do you think, Will?" I said, giving him an understanding grin.

"I've no idea. For all I know you could be fifteenth in line to the goddamn throne. Or…"

"Just some commoner who went to a good school?"

"Yes, I suppose so."

"Will, it's like this. Class is like relativity: it all depends on where you're standing. He might think I'm upper class but she knows I'm middle class. If I gave a fuck I would definitely be middle class and as I'm talking about it at all I can't possibly have any real class."

"No shit?"

"Yes, but why do you care?"

"I don't know. It's just that it all goes back so far, you guys have... I don't know. Something we don't."

"A deeper, more secure, identity rooted in our history and traditions?"

"Are you joshing me?"

"Maybe a little. I think you have a bit of a crush on us."

"Come again?"

"An infatuation. A case of Anglophilia."

"Anglophilia. I like that. Yes, you've got it. My wife has it too. There she is, talking to Miss Dutton." He indicated a well-dressed woman in her forties who was talking to Jess.

"So, you don't think we're a bunch of over-educated, narrow minded, inbred, horse-faced idiots then?" I said.

"Well, maybe some of you but..."

His eyes were following Mel, who was coming over to us.

"Not her?" I said.

He looked at me like I'd said something incomprehensible.

"Now I know you're yanking my chain."

"Sorry." I gave him my grin. It all seemed very silly.

"Look, I don't just quite know what it is," he said, "but in my opinion, you've got some of the most beautiful, and the classiest, women in the world right here in this room. They look like angels; talk like the queen, ride like devils and party like, like... well like this."

"And some of them aren't entirely thick either," I said. "You have got it bad. Don't worry, they're perfectly human, just like you and me."

"If you can say that, you must be one of them."

Mel put an arm round me and said, "There you are, Si." She helped herself to my glass.

"How're you doing, Mel?" I said.

"Pretty good, Si."

"This is Will. Will, this is Mel."

He'd stopped leaning against the bar and had stood up straight.

"Hi, Will." She held out my glass and clinked it against his.

"Very pleased to meet you, Mel," he said.

"Will was just saying that there are some of the most beautiful women in the world in this room and he was looking at you when he said it," I said.

"That's true, I was," he said, looking self-conscious, "but I didn't expect you to rat on me."

"He's no gentleman, Will. But thank you anyway. Come on, Si. It's time to dance."

She put down the empty glass, took my hand and began leading me away.

"Nice to meet you, Will," I said, being led away.

"Likewise, Simon."

We danced and they did a slow number and Mel held onto me tight and said with a sigh, "I'm feeling young again tonight, Si."

"You are young, Mel."

"So I am."

"Mel?"

"Si?"

"Don't look, but you see that elegant couple sitting together holding hands and watching the dancers?"

"Yes."

"Do you think you could get a photo of them without making it obvious?"

"Yes. Why?"

"I'll tell you later."

"You better had."

"Thanks."

After a few slow numbers, we reluctantly disconnected ourselves and I went over to talk to Julius and Jess Dutton who were standing to one side of the dance-floor watching their parents dancing. They turned to me politely as I came up.

"Hello," I said.

"Well, hello. Mr Ellice, apparently," Jess said, looking at me thoughtfully. How interesting that we meet again so soon in such a different place."

"Simon might just as easily say the same about us, sis," her brother said.

"So he might. Did you find your Titania?"

"I did indeed. You may know her better as Grace Lievre. We had a cup of tea together. She's known me since I was born, more or less," I said.

"Simon Ellice. I thought that name seemed familiar," Jules said, grasping my hand. "Your parents live in…"

"Aldermark."

"Of course, we're almost neighbours. Well I never. That was amazing, by the way; it really helped to wake the evening up. Thank you very much."

"No problem. I don't feel the loser," I said.

"Different setting, different clothes, but equally at home, apparently," Jess said, looking at me through narrowed eyes.

"Don't start on him again, Jess. He's just done a nice thing for us," Jules said.

"Yes, but why? That's what I want to know," she said.

"Well..." I said, looking towards where Susie was dancing.

"Susie Chesterfield is something, isn't she?" Jules said.

"She certainly is. An American gentleman was just telling me that in his opinion you've assembled a good collection of the most beautiful women in the world in this room," I said, looking at Jess. As before, she returned my gaze with interest.

"Our Mr Wallace, I presume?" he said.

"Will?" I said.

"Willard, yes. He's quite the anglophile."

"Tonight, I am too," I said.

"You do look like you're having a good time," He said, with a sudden smile. "So am I, actually. It's been a successful evening, I would say. Don't you agree, Jess?"

"We do seem to have put the male urge to compete for the best breeding prospects to good use tonight, I'll give you that," she said.

"Don't say that, Jess. He'll think we're just cynically manipulating him for his money."

"But we are," she said.

"Yes, but we're not supposed to say so out loud," he said.

"Call me Si and feel free to manipulate me as you see fit," I said.

"See, my candour is disarming him," Jess said.

"Excuse her, Si. She's always been like this," Jules said.

"Anyway, I don't think the fiercest competition this evening has been between the men," I said.

"Well said that man," Jules said.

"You're right. I can feel myself wanting to scratch her eyes out now," Jess said, looking at Susie.

"You came second," I said.

"And that's supposed to be some consolation from the man who bid for her, not me?" she said.

"Next time I'll bid for you, I promise," I said.

"I'll hold you to that," she said.

"So will I," Jules said.

"I look forward to it," I said. "Tell me, where should I take Susie? I've been abroad for a while and this London isn't the one I used to know."

"Ah, the eternal and ever-changing city," Jules said.

"If I know Susie, you won't be taking her, she'll be taking you," Jess said.

"Sounds good to me," I said.

"What he means is, he'll follow her anywhere," Jules said. "One look from those magnificent eyes and he's her slave. What it must be to have that power over men, eh sis? Do you wish you had that, sister mine?"

"Enough, brother," Jess said. "I've admitted my weakness, now shut up or I'll punch you in the head."

"She would too," he said. "Well anyway, let's stop talking about sex and talk about money."

"If you like," I said.

"Boring," Jess said.

"No, it must be. Can I relieve you of a pile of cash, Si? By any chance?" he said.

"In case you disappear without trace," Jess said.

"I knew you were going to say that," Jules said. "Stop it."

"I'm only saying what we were all thinking," she said. "We still don't really know who or what this strange creature is."

"Yes we do. Anyway, the point of civilisation is that we don't say what we're thinking."

"I really wouldn't know you two were brother and sister," I said, grinning at them.

"See, he isn't in the least offended, are you," Jess said. "What would offend you, I wonder?"

"I don't know," I said. "But I appreciate the point. I could be tempted to skedaddle, now I've got her number."

"Yes, but now you're on your honour not to. Aren't you? Because it's been said," she said.

"Possibly," I said. "Or you could say the idea of doing a flit has been legitimised by us talking about it. And anyway, I'm not sure my honour is much to be counted on."

"Somehow that doesn't surprise me," she said.

"Don't encourage her," Jules said. "She'll be analysing you in a sec."

"He might like it," she said.

"I might at that," I said.

"Ahem," he said, giving a little cough. "On the matter in hand...?"

"Ah, yes. I can't say I have exactly that much on me in notes and as I didn't know I would be bidding, I didn't bring a cheque book," I said.

"And now we know your honour is doubtful..." Jess said.

"Well I for one am sure you're good for it, Si," Jules said, taking a notebook out of his pocket and unclipping a pen. "What's your address by the way? Do you have somewhere in town, or should I put down Aldermark?"

"Wise Policy. St Katherine Docks. London."

"How enchanting. What is Wise Policy?"

"She's a yacht," I said.

"What do you mean by a yacht?" Jess said.

"I mean a twenty-five metre ketch-rigged Andre Hoek. I call her Polly," I said.

"Bloody hell, you really do mean a yacht," he said. "And you sail her?"

"That's what she's for. I'm just back from the Caribbean via the South of France."

"You bastard," Jess said.

"I'm deeply and truly envious," Jules said. "Do you have a more land-based address at all?"

"Nope. Give me some bank details and I'll send you the money tomorrow. I promise not to leave on the next tide."

"Okay. Will do." He started writing on his pad.

"Thanks. And add your phone number and I'll invite you to come and have a proper look at her and maybe drink a cocktail or something," I said.

"Phone numbers, you mean," Jess said. "Give him mine too." She took the pad and pen and added her number.

"I may even send you a text in the morning to let you know that I've remembered the money," I said.

"Good. You do that," Jess said, folding the paper into the palm of my hand and giving me the full wattage of her attention. "What is it you do, Si? When you're not visiting Titania or purchasing heiresses, I mean."

"No chance," I said, smiling. "You'll have to beat me first. On horseback, I mean. I'm assuming you haven't forgotten your promise?"

"Beating you will give me great pleasure," she said, taking her hand back. "Whenever you like, Mr Ellice."

"Excellent. Give me a couple of days and I'll give you a call. By the way, do I take it that you're part of all this…" I waved a vague hand to indicate the higher purpose, "… the foundation and all that. Or are you just here as cock-bait?" I smiled into her eyes.

"Hah!" Jules said.

"I may be. What's it to you?" she said.

"Do you help any kind of woman? Not just the well off and respectable?"

"Oh, yes. Bring me your dribs, drabs, sluts, slatterns, whores and wantons," Jess said. "If she's a spilt-tail, we'll help her. If we can."

"Sister! Don't be so crude," Jules said. "Sorry about that, Si. Truly we are the more sensitive half of the species."

"Aren't you just," Jess said.

Something in the room behind her caught my eye and I looked to see what it was. A girl in a black dress was walking back from the direction of the toilets. There was something disjointed about her movement.

"Oh dear," Jules said, following my gaze.

"Natasha," Jess said. "Poor thing."

We watched the girl walk to the dance floor. It was a jittery walk which turned into a jittery, jigging dance. She wasn't part of any group, but dancing by herself, apparently unaware of other people. A girl had to move out of her way and then she crashed into a man who was too drunk or oblivious to notice her. She lashed out at him with a fist. It was a girl's punch that did no harm but it upset him and he tried to talk to her.

People were moving towards her. She turned away and started dancing to herself again. An older woman approached her and tried to talk to her but she just put her head down and ignored her. The woman stood near her, not knowing what to do.

"Come on, sister. We're needed," Jules said.

"Okay, brother. Follow me," Jess said.

The two of them walked onto the dance-floor and sort of surrounded the girl and managed to ride her back towards the anxious face of her friends at a table. The older woman came behind them looking ashamed and embarrassed. The girl took a swing at Jess but she just seemed to take it as a dance move and went with it, talking to the girl all the while.

They kept her moving towards the door, letting her jiggle away to the tune of whatever demons had hold of her, while coats and jackets were fetched and then they ushered her out into the night.

I drifted into Harry, or he drifted into me.

"Having fun?" he said.

"It's been an interesting evening," I said.

"You two know each other quite well; you and Mel."

"I suppose we do."

"Try not to get her into too much trouble, won't you."

"What me?"

"Yes, you."

"Hm."

I shook his hand and wandered towards the door. Mel appeared as if by magic and put her arm through mine.

"There you are, Si."

"Here I am, Mel."

We walked out into the street, taking with us the glamour and the shabbiness and all the conversations of the night. My ears still rang from the loudness of the music. We found that it was morning. I mean really morning. The sun was up and everything.

"Do we have breakfast or go to bed?" she said.

"Both. Breakfast first."

"Are you still drunk?"

"I feel a bit light-headed. Now, where's the car?"

"Don't be stupid. Follow me and sing out if you see a taxi."

I followed her and we walked through the quiet streets and neither of us minded that we didn't see a cab. The sunlight was catching the tops of the buildings and the paved courts of Lincolns Inn were serene. When we got onto the grass of the fields I wanted to run, so I did. And did a couple of cartwheels too.

"You're mad," Mel said, catching up with me.

"I'm alive," I said.

"So I see," she said, and she was smiling in spite of herself, and the brief run had made her look pink and fresh, and the way her hair was starting to come down at the back without her knowing, was charming.

"I'm amazed you can run in heels," I said.

"I can do anything in heels," she said.

We found a café that was open next to Smithfield market and sat drinking coffee and eating black pudding and bacon and eggs and baked beans and fried tomatoes and mushrooms and toast. There was a lot of rough and friendly greeting and talk between the white-coated men and women of the market and a lot of coming and going. We sat with them looking very different in our evening clothes and some of them smiled when they saw us.

When I had some food inside me, the light-headedness went and I began to feel sleepy. Mel had gone quiet too.

We paid and easily found a cab back to her house. She leant against me in the taxi, her head on my shoulder, almost asleep. The driver smiled at us in his mirror. Being leant against by Mel was very nice and I sat there watching the early morning streets passing by and feeling how much we felt like a team; just like we had before, many years ago. I also thought about Soumy and wondered how she was.

Outside her door, I put my arms around Mel and kissed her.

"Bloody hell, Si," she said.

"Yes, Mel," I said.

"Are you coming in, then?"

"Yes, Mel," I said.

10

A CAN OF WORMS

I woke up in a bed that was too soft and too small. I didn't mind in the least. The room wasn't a lot bigger than the bed but it nevertheless had a lot in it. Mainly clothes. A certain amount of makeup, a desktop mac balanced on a shelf with lots of post-it notes stuck to it and piles of magazines.

I needed a pee so I slid out of bed, opened the door and discovered a small bathroom on the other side of the landing. It wasn't that clean but that didn't matter much because you couldn't see much of it for products of kinds beyond my comprehension, and a number of bras and knickers hung up to dry.

I got back to Mel's room unobserved, shut the door and got back into bed. She stirred a little so I slid an arm under her and pulled her against me. She was deliciously warm and soft and sleepy. She raised an eyelid to look at me and then shut it again. She snuggled in against me, pushing her face into my chest and taking a bit of my skin gently between her teeth.

We didn't surface for another hour, enjoying the perfect sufficiency of our tiny world in the bed and each other's bodies and the languor of the morning after the night before. When we did, Mel went downstairs to make tea and return with it while I sat up and flicked through some of her magazines in a half-attentive way.

"Well, Si," she said handing me both mugs and climbing over me to get back into the bed.

"Well, Mel," I said.

"I wasn't going to do this."

"Do what?" I said, smiling.

"You know perfectly well."

"Sorry."

"No you aren't. Stop looking like the cat that got the cream and give me my mug."

"Okay, Mel."

"Fucking hell, Si. You just spent more than I earn in a year on an evening with an airhead deb. You bastard. Why?"

"Is she an airhead deb?"

"No, she's very clever and quite wild. You're going to get on with each other."

"I thought we were. I would've bid twice as much if you'd been in the auction."

"That's nice."

"It's true, too."

"I want to believe that. But why? I was going to introduce you to her anyway, for fuck's sake."

"You're right, I did get a bit carried away. You believe Susie's in danger?"

"Yes, I do."

"You've told her about this?"

"Er... no. Not yet."

"Okay, we'll get to that. I think it's highly likely that whoever we're looking for was in that room last night, don't you? I like to think I've got their attention and now I intend to get in their way. We'll see who takes notice."

"Oh. I see."

"Give me your camera."

"Why?"

"Just give me your camera."

"Fine."

She did that and showed me how to scroll through the photos. I found one that would do. It was of some other people, but in the background was the girl with long dark hair who'd got into a state at the end of the night.

"Who's that?"

"Natasha Wilkinson. Why?"

"You know her?"

"A little. Why?"

"She was off her face at the *Coma Club* the other night, and again last night."

"So?"

"What's she like?"

"Nice. Clever, generally good fun. But sensible. Or, it used to be; we've never been in the same circle that much."

"Rich?"

"In a quiet way. Old money. Nothing that serious, but comfortable."

"So posh. Like Hillary and Susie. Are you sure she was drunk?"

"I don't know. What're you saying?"

"How do we know there aren't others?"

"What do you mean? You think…?"

"No idea. Could be, couldn't it?"

"You think… Fuck. What're we going to do?"

"Have breakfast."

"Yes, but... I don't think I have anything in the fri..."

"Let's go back to Polly and have a shower and get some food."

"Your boat has a shower?"

"Of course she does."

"A proper shower?"

"With hot water and everything. I might even have some soap somewhere."

"Okay. I suppose anything beats staying here."

We got into some clothes and Mel threw a few things into a bag, including her camera, and then we made a swift and stealthy exit to a minicab, which took us back to *Umbra Villus*. By some miracle the car didn't even have a parking ticket. I drove us to the docks with Mel navigating. I was glad of the help.

I punched the numbers into the security gate, noticing Mel memorising them as I did so, and led her along the walkway.

"Which one's yours, anyway?" Mel said.

"You're looking at her," I said.

"I am? What, this one?"

"Yes, this one. Come aboard."

"No!"

"Yes. Come below and take your clothes off."

"My God, she's lovely. What did you do to deserve this?"

"That's a long story."

While Mel was in the shower, I sat at the chart-table and connected her camera to my laptop. She'd done an excellent job of capturing the atmosphere of the evening and there were lots of good pictures of lots of people. Including the couple who'd been so interested in Susie and the girl who'd been taken away in a state.

And me. I looked like I'd was enjoying myself.

I let the camera delete the photos as they were uploaded; it would piss Mel off but that couldn't be helped. Then I dug out the piece of paper with the Dutton foundation bank details and Jules's and Jess's phone numbers on it, transferred the money with a small sigh and sent them both a text. Then I phoned Bill.

"Morning, Bill, I need you to do some more work for me."

"What do you mean, morning? What now? I'm starting to worry about hearing you say that."

"There's a girl called Natasha Wilkinson. About twenty-two, dark shoulder-length hair, five foot seven or thereabouts. I want to know if she's alright."

"Why?"

"I watched her getting into trouble at the *Umbra Villus* last night, and I have a feeling."

"I know your feelings. I'll send a woodentop now. That it?"

"No, there's a couple I want to know about. He's dark, she's blondish, early to mid-forties, both slim and very well dressed. No idea who or what they are, but they didn't look like they belonged. You can crosscheck against the guest list if that helps, but be careful how you ask for it."

"You'll have to give me more than that."

"I've got photos."

"That should do it."

"Good, I'll text them to you in a sec. Can I put in for expenses?"

"No. What kind of expenses?"

"I bought a girl last night. She was quite expensive."

"What do you mean, bought a girl? How expensive?"

I told him.

"Fucking hell. Where do you expect me to find that from?"

"I don't know. I'm sure you or Dad can siphon some off from somewhere for me."

"That's the road to hell. You do realise that?"

"Go and do some work and stop worrying," I said, and hung up on him.

"I bet you don't have a hairdryer," Mel said, coming in wrapped in a towel.

"Second drawer down, beside the bed," I said.

"I don't believe it," she said.

I had a quick wash while she got into a proper state to deal with the world and then we went up to the café for some breakfast. Unusually, we were served by someone who wasn't Henriques.

"I could get used to this," Mel said, taking a good sniff of her coffee and looking at the scene.

"I'm not completely sure I could," I said. "My girl seems hemmed in and contained here, surrounded by all this. We're too far from the sea."

"It's pretty cool though, isn't it? She looks amazing amongst all this concrete and stone. Very beautiful. You call her she, but isn't Wise Policy a more masculine name?"

"All boats are female."

"You really sailed her all the way to the Caribbean and back? Just you and the girl."

"Yes."

"I'm envious."

"Hm."

"Hm."

My phone rang. I answered it, "Hi Angel, how're you?"

"What the... Oh, you're in company," Bill said.

"Well done," I said.

"Yeah. Anyway, you were right. She's gone," he said. "Middle of the night. Seems to have just walked out of the house and disappeared."

"Are you..."

"I shouldn't be, it's too soon for her to officially be a misper, but of course I am. Or will be shortly. CCTV, phone records, interviews, all the actual police work. Do you want my job?"

"Well done, darling."

"Oh fuck off."

I disconnected and looked at Mel, who was looking at me.

"Who?" she said.

"Natasha walked out of the house in the middle of the night," I said.

"Oh fuck. How do you know that?"

"I just do. Look on the bright side. If she's another one, then our poisoner was definitely in the room with us last night."

"That gives me the creeps."

"I wonder how many more there have been. The phrase, can of worms, comes to mind."

"The person you were just talking to; your policeman friend...?"

"She's on it now."

"She?"

"Leave it."

"Whatever. Poor girl. What're we going to do?"

"I'm going to phone Susie. What're you going to do?"

"Why?"

"To arrange a date, of course. What was the period of preparation with Hillary?"

"If you sleep with her, I'll kill you."

"Mel..."

"Shut up. What do you mean?"

"I mean, how long did they go on poisoning Hillary before the made off with her? Perhaps we could use Susie as live-bait. How many times has this happened to her so far?"

"You bastard. I don't know."

"I mean, with her consent, of course. How many times did it happen to Hillary?"

"Knowing her, she might. You mean actually catch them poisoning her?"

"Or trying to kidnap her."

"That's a hell of a risk. Quite a few. Hillary, I mean. I haven't counted."

"If I can, I'll try to spend the evening with Susie and not let her come to harm. Is that okay with you?"

"I'll come too."

"No, you won't. If she isn't going to be with me and I don't find out that she'll be somewhere safe, then you should go and talk to her. Don't you think?"

"I suppose so."

"I'll let you know. Now, isn't it time you went to work?"

"They can manage without me. This is more important."

"I mean, isn't it time you went to talk to Natasha's parents and friends? And Hillary's. I want to know more about the pattern. And I want to know who was repeating the story about them having drug habits. Is someone spreading it about? They'll tell you things they won't tell the police. And you'll notice things the police won't notice because you're one of them. How does our poisoner know when it's safe to kidnap the girl and people will assume she's dropped into bad company and waste time looking for her? All this has been done to prevent people making connections between the disappearances. I'm starting to think there have probably been more girls taken. If you're going to go to the effort of setting this up, for whatever reason, you might as well do several, don't you think? Have you looked?"

"Oh, fuck. You're right' it's the kind of thing people don't talk about."

"No, it's the kind of thing people try to hide when it's them, and are happy to talk about when it's other people. Go and talk to them."

"Imogen something... I remember now... hang on..." She had her phone out and the look of a terrier about her again.

I remembered that I was going to phone Susie, so I did, and she answered.

"Hey Susie," I said.

"Who's that?" she said.

"Si Ellice."

"Oh, great. I was just thinking about you."

"That's good. What were you thinking about me?"

"What're you doing tonight?"

"I don't know. Going out with you perhaps?"

"You're not squeamish, are you?"

"Not in the least."

"Good. Pick me up at nine."

"Okay. Where will you be?"

"I'll text you."

"Great. Should I wear anything in particular?"

"Only if you want to." She disconnected.

Well, that was easy. And intriguing.

I was ahead of Bill at the gunroom, so I sat on a stool and carefully stripped, cleaned and oiled a pair of Hollands while Jimmy delicately removed the foresight from a Blaser straight-pull and cut a thread on the end of the barrel to take a suppressor. It was an honour to be entrusted even with this menial task, but we both knew that if the arrangement was going to work, I had to fit in with him and not interrupt his work too much.

In the spirit of reciprocity, I told him the story of my recent doings.

"You've taken up rescuing damsels now, then?" he said, smiling.

"Don't you think that's a reasonable occupation for someone like me?"

"Up to a point, I suppose."

"Oh. Up to what point, exactly?"

"Up to the point where they need more from you than fighting for them probably."

"I might develop emotional maturity and the capacity for commitment one day," I said.

"And I might develop a taste for lycra and ballroom dancing," he said.

"So you might," I said.

The door opened and Bill and Dad stepped in. Bill looked knackered, as usual. Dad looked better.

"Afternoon, officer," Jimmy said. "Afternoon, Mr Ellice."

"Hello, Mr Jameson," Bill said.

"Hi Jimmy, hello, Si," Dad said.

"Would you like some tea?" Jimmy said. "And a biscuit. You look like you could do with one."

Bill looked at us; Jimmy calmly removing the tiny burs from the thread he'd just cut with a needle file, and me working gun-oil into the details of an action with a cotton bud. He put his bag on the bench, leant on it, and said, "Do you know what. I think, I will. Thank you."

"I'll send Charlie along with some," Jimmy said, rising to go. "Be easy, I'm ahead of myself today and I know Jean won't mind sharing a pot with me. Take your time."

"I've turned all my phones off," Bill said, when he'd gone.

"And so have I," Dad said.

"So I should think," I said.

"I like it here; it's like the world stops and I get to breathe again," Bill said.

"No one makes you do it."

"And you would take up growing cabbages?"

"I'm not the one complaining."

"True enough. Bill, sit down for fuck's sake and tell me what's eating you."

"You and whatever you've gone and stirred up, that's what's eating me."

"That's interesting. What've I stirred up?"

"MI6," Dad said. "Bill's inadvertently woken up the spooks and they want to know what he's up to and why."

"That'll be that couple I asked you to find out about then, won't it," I said.

"Yes. He's a Russian. Name of Pogodin," Bill said. "When I started looking into them, the result was a chap from MI6 turning up at my office looking serious. According to him, they're dangerous, or at least he is, and they aren't short of a few quid."

"I thought I recognised that look."

"Guess what his line of business is," Dad said.

"Prostitution?" I said.

"No, pharmaceuticals. Drugs of all kinds."

"Ah ha."

"Ah ha, indeed."

"Rodion and Lada Pogodin," Bill said. "He is CEO of Russo Pharm. Care to guess what they specialise in?"

"Psychoactive substances?" I said.

"Have a gold star. Maybe four or five on the list, but big business nonetheless. Leading the way with outsourcing to South America, Africa and the East. Very well networked sort of chap. My spook isn't actually saying he's regarded as a threat to national security, but the mere fact he turned up like he did, says it for him. And the fact that MI6 are bothering to track his whereabouts and who's interested in him."

"Threat, as in how?" I said.

"Substances as agents of disruption, would be my guess," Dad said. "If you wanted to come up with new addictive compounds and get them manufactured and brought into the country under the guise of something harmless, Mr Pogodin would be your man.

Or easily could be."

"I see. Does he have an organisation in this country? Of the kind that could make girls vanish and keep them vanished, I mean?"

"Can't say. Easily could have. With these Russians, if there's a distinction between business and organised crime, it's a faint one. I'm going to lean on the spook a bit and see what I can get, and Bill's going to see if he find out about their movements and associates and all that, independently. I don't trust the spook not to filter whatever he tells me."

"What made you notice him?" Bill said.

"It was the way they were looking at one of the girls."

"Looking at her, like how, exactly?" Bill said.

"I can't say it was hostile exactly, more hungry," I said.

"Hungry?"

"He'll be talking about foxes next," Dad said.

"Wolves in this case, I think," I said. "Yes, hungry. And I got the impression that they resented other people being near her. Me, at least."

"That's the kind of thing your average policeman just doesn't say," Bill said.

"Anyway," I said. "Talking of girls, what about Natasha? Have you made any progress yet? Anything interesting in her phone?"

"You're starting to sound like a copper," Dad said, smiling.

"Don't worry, it's only pretend," I said.

"Well, the real policeman here can tell you that there's nothing unaccountable in her phone history; she left it on her bedside table, so we can't use it to locate her," Bill said, consulting his notes. "Didn't take a handbag or purse, or anything. We've checked all the obvious places, like friends and family and hospitals and night shelters. Nothing at all. Nothing on social media either and no sightings on CCTV, in the vicinity of her house. She must have left the house between o-three hundred and o-six-thirty, by which time her mother was awake."

"Why?" I said.

"Why did she leave the house?"

"Yes."

"Mac has a theory."

"Go on. I like Mac's theories."

"He reckons that as the body starts to metabolise the l-dopa and its effects become less severe, the subject is likely to become restless, but because of the rohypnol, which disables memory and will, they probably won't get up and do something self-directed. He thinks they might just get up and do routine tasks or wander about."

"Chemically induced sleepwalking?" I said.

"That's a good way to put it. Mrs Wilkinson found Natasha about to take their lurcher to the park in her nightie one morning three weeks ago. She seemed confused but just went back to bed when her mother suggested it."

"Still compliant because of the Scopolamine."

"If Mac's right, yes. I'm having enquiries made along similar lines with the families, friends and colleagues. Or I will be. Have you any idea how much work that is?"

"So, she just walked out into the street and was picked up?" I said.

"Presumably, yes," Bill said. "The camera over the wine shop on the next street shows the vehicles that enter her road from that direction. Someone could have come in from the other direction, turned around and left the same way, and we wouldn't know about it. I'm working on that."

"And the vehicles that you do know about?" I said.

"We're doing what we can to trace them now. Luckily several of them were taxis, which helps. The only interesting thing so far is a silver-grey transit which went down her street at four this morning. We've got ANPR hits for its plates from Solihull and down the 303 not far from Andover. The timing's too close, unless it got a lift from a passing Chinook. I've got local boys hunting in both directions but nothing so far."

"That will be it," I said.

"Yes, it probably will, but we'll check the others anyway," Bill said, with a sigh.

"The fake plates are a sign of something well planned and organised," Dad said.

"Speaking of organisations," I said, "what can you tell me about the *Coma Club* and the *Sea Hare* and whoever owns them?"

"You've still got your Russian girl on your mind?" Dad said.

"What's that?" Bill said.

"He means the girl from my first night back," I said. "The evening I hit that chap and you took me home for supper."

"What's that got to do with this?" he said. "Isn't she's just a hooker?"

"I'm not saying it has anything," I said. "But Natasha was drugged in a venue belonging to the same people who own the Russian girl, wasn't she, Dad?"

"This place, *Umbra Villus*, belongs to the Greens?" Bill said.

"Yes, it does," Dad said. "Actually, there may be a tie up, of a sort. I managed to have lunch with Tony Beech. He's the head of Organised Crime at the Met," he added, for my benefit, "and he got one of his lads to put something together for me." He took a folder out of his briefcase. "Shall I give you a quick synopsis?"

"Please," I said.

"Okay, the *Coma Club* belongs to a family called Green. Grant and Leila, brother and sister, ages unknown, address unknown. Apart from the *Coma* and the *Sea Hare* they appear to own a dance club south of the river called *Caesar's* and, indeed, the *Umbra Villus*."

"I take it all back," Bill said.

"Don't get carried away," Dad said. "It's actually almost inevitable that there would be a connection. Let me tell you what Tony said about them."

"Go on," I said.

"Basically, he said, don't bother."

"Why?" I said.

"They're fake. Everyone knows it. It's all just pretend."

"What do you mean?"

"They first appeared about ten years ago in a pub in the Eastend, and since then they've built a chain of the coolest places in town. That's what they're really about, not crime. They probably do a bit of prostitution, which would explain your Russian girl, and some coke. Almost more as a service to their customers than seriously. The organised crime façade is just marketing. Some people even say that they don't exist."

"How come?" I said.

"All you ever get is someone in a hat and dark glasses passing regally by, or standing up to receive applause in a crowded venue and then being whisked out of sight. They're there, but no one actually knows them. It's just theatrics. It's a thing to make the venues seem cooler; give them an edge. Like a harmless reference to the Krays, and all that."

"Hm," I said.

"You don't seem convinced," he said. "Anyway, they undoubtedly have the knack of being 'in' with the in-crowd. They're the hottest venues in town, and have been for a few years. If you go about with the cool crowd, then you will inevitably be going to their places."

"I have been," I said. "Am I right in thinking that each of them has an image of a hare, or some variation of it, on their branding?"

"Er, yes, you seem to be right about that," Dad said, flicking through his notes and showing me some familiar logos. "It comes from the unofficial boxing club over their first pub," Bill said. "It had a logo of two hares boxing and they carried on with the theme."

"Interesting," I said. "And pyjamas, I believe."

"Pyjamas?" Bill said.

"Anyway, Natasha being drugged at the *Umbra Villus* could easily be pure coincidence," Dad said, "Assuming she was, and really is a victim, not just another girl with a drug problem of her own making. There's a holding company which owns everything and at this point I've no idea who owns that. Probably just some astute businessman. Do you want me to try to find out?"

"Yes please," I said.

"I knew you'd say that," he said. "Working for you has turned out to be unexpectedly hard work."

"Funny how he always ends up in charge, isn't it," Bill said.

"Yes, I've noticed that too," Dad said, smiling.

"So, apart from a bit of hired muscle minding the girls, I don't suppose they're much to worry about," Bill said.

"You could be right," I said.

"But you don't sound like you believe it?" Dad said. "Why's that?"

"I've actually no idea. Maybe it's just because they left me in the park without my clothes. I'll get over it. Now then, before we go, have you two considered the obvious question?"

"What question?" Dad said, smiling.

"Hillary, for definite. Possibly Natasha and possibly Susie. Who else?"

"Who else?"

"Now you've gone and done it," Bill said. "I've been trying really really hard not to think that thought all day. I suppose I'll just have to go and find out now, won't I."

"You were quite right, Bill," I said, grinning at him. "It's good to have something to do."

"Next time I have an idea, I'm going to go and throw myself in the river, it'll be easier," he said.

"We've got a lot to do," Dad said. "I'll let you know about the Russians as soon as we have something. What're you going to do?"

"I'm going to go and look after the next victim, if that's what she is. I've got a date with her tonight, as it happens. It's a chore but I'll man-up," I said, grinning.

"I'm sure you will," Dad said.

"What's her name?" Bill said, with pen over notebook.

"Susana Chesterfield," I said.

"What? You mean, *the* Susie Chesterfield?" Dad said.

"Presumably," I said. "What do you mean?"

"About twenty-five, quite tall, fair hair, stunningly beautiful?" he said.

"Sounds like the girl in question," I said.

"Susana Chesterfield, only daughter of Sally and Steven Chesterfield, Duke and Duchess of Bicester, heiress to about half of the Cotswolds?" Dad said.

"If you say so," I said.

11

LET IT SNOW

I assumed nine meant nine, so I drove to an address in Belgravia in time to ring Susie's bell at nine. It was the kind of address where you expect the butler to answer the door, but she answered it herself, and I was glad that I'd made an effort with my clothes; she looked like a special occasion all by herself.

"You'll do," she said.

"I suppose you will too," I said.

"Got transport?"

"A car." I pointed to the car.

"Good. Come on then."

"Where to?" I said.

"Thrawl Street. Back of Spitalfields."

"How about you navigate."

"You don't know London?"

"Does anyone really know London?" I held the door for her and managed not to shut it on her dress.

"So, who and what are you exactly, Mr Simon Ellice?" she said, when we were sitting side by side in the small car.

"I'm your proud owner tonight, and I've some idea that you're supposed to be nice to me."

"No, this doesn't count. You'll have to do that another night. And I haven't made any promises to be nice to anyone. Ever. Dad looked a bit funny when I said who I was going out with. You're one of the Hampshire Ellices." It was a statement, not a question.

"I did grow up in Hampshire, but I'm not aware of it being a crime."

"So, what is it about you that's raised his hackles? Are you disreputable in some way? I'm pretty sure you are."

"Me? No, I'm the very epitome of respectability. My father's a pretty straight stick too. He may have been thinking of my grandfather."

"Ah ha. Tell me more."

"Albert Ellice was a gambler and a soldier. Sometimes a shit and sometimes a hero, invariably a philanderer. He generated a certain reputation that clings to the name."

"I see. You knew him well?"

"Yes. He taught me to shoot and fish and hold my drink. And a few other things."

"I envy you."

"You have no grandparents?"

"Yes, but yours sound more interesting. And you're a straight stick, are you?"

"Me? Straight as a die."

"What is it you do, again?"

"Actually, I'm a wandering knight. I rescue damsels and slay dragons."

"I'm starting to think Dad may have been right; you're clearly mad and possibly dangerous."

"Does that mean you'd rather I took you home?"

"Fuck no."

"Thought so. Where are you taking me, by the way?"

"Ever heard of the *Subvello Club*?"

"I may have. What is it?"

"Wait and see. I think you're going to like it."

We left the car on a single yellow line and walked towards a pub called The King of Malta. It was a big Victorian corner building with lights blazing from large uncurtained windows. In these relatively quiet streets, it was like a beacon in the night. We dived into the big room and I followed Susie through a throng of people, men, and women with hard, but friendly faces, sometimes battered faces, short, fat, tall, thin, everything. T-shirts, jeans, chinos, trainers, tattoos, piercings, rolling and lilting East End accents. It was loud and I liked it.

Apart from some of the men politely moving a little to let Susie pass, they paid us no attention. She led the way through and up rough, uncarpeted stairs to the floor above. A man in a dinner jacket with scarred knuckles grinned at us knowingly, received Susie's name, looked at me carefully and then let us into the big room above the one below.

The door had the name '*The Subvello Club*' on it and under that was a drawing of two hares with gloves on, boxing. I can't say I was that surprised.

There was a lot less light up here and the windows were covered in heavy curtains. Most of the space was filled with tables and a lamp on each one made pools of illumination; showing faces and throwing shadows; a deceiving light. There was a bar at the back, lit like a stage, with three barmen hard at work serving a knot of people in front of it. In the corner of the building, the prow thrusting out into the night, a man was playing boogie-woogie piano on an old upright, stroking out the beat in a meditative, self-absorbed way.

Around him were the accoutrements of a band; a set of drums, guitars leaning on stands, microphones etcetera. In front of that, there was a clear space. The tables bordering the space were arranged in a curve so that it seemed like a small arena or possibly, dance floor.

It was hard to tell how many people there were in the room but there was the subdued buzz of at least a hundred, and more were coming in all the time. A girl in silk pyjamas passed us bearing a tray with bottles and glasses.

I followed Susie as she navigated between the tables looking for someone she recognised.

"Susie! Over here." A girl jumped up, came over to us and threw her arms around her. "I'm so glad, so glad." It was Maisie.

"Hi Maisie. This is Simon."

"Hi Simon. Nice to meet you." She took my hand and held it and looked up into my face with her big, liquid eyes and then reached up, put her hands round my neck, pulled my head down and kissed me firmly on the lips. Again. "I'm Maisie, by the way."

"I'm glad to meet you, Maisie," I said.

"Come with me, Simon." She took hold of my hand and started leading me away. I looked at Susie. She shrugged, and motioned me to go with the girl, so I did.

There were four people already at the table, chairs close together, talking and laughing. Two men and two women. The men got up to welcome Susie and she exchanged kisses and hugs here and there.

"Everyone, this is…." Maisie said.

"Simon," I said.

"Simon," Maisie said, presenting me as if I were a precious object.

"Hello, Simon," voices said, faces smiled, hands were raised to give a wave.

"Have some champagne, my dears," one of the men said.

"Thanks Melvin," Susie said. "Si, let me introduce you. This is Melvin and Harriet, Harry to you, Graham and Felicity, or Flick if you don't want to offend her."

I shook hands or exchanged nods and waves with them all. Someone put a glass of champagne in my hand and Maisie pulled me down onto a chair beside her.

"Don't mind Maisie," Susie said, taking a chair on the other side of me.

"I don't," I said.

The room was rapidly filling up and it was hard to hear the others over the general sound of talking. Susie leaned close to me and said, "Well?"

"Interesting," I said.

"It's almost time," she said, taking my arm.

Everyone at the table was watching the man at the piano so I did too. He finished the piece with a fine glissando and stood up. As he came into the circle of light I saw that it was Berry. Once again, there was a feeling of inevitability about his presence.

He came to the table and received our applause with a bow. People at the other tables clapped him too.

"Thank you, my friends. I am but the handmaiden to greatness, but thank you. What have I been missing? Si! Bloody hell. You bastard. Fancy finding you here." He pulled me into a bear hug.

"Susie brought me," I said, when he put me down.

"Susie! My darling, how wonderful. I didn't know you knew Si."

"I don't, he bought me," Susie said.

"Don't you mean, you brought him?"

"No, Berry, he bought me. It was a purchase. I am now his property, my lord," she said, and I could hear the different levels of meaning in the phrase.

"Are you, by God. Si, you're a very lucky man."

"I know it, Berry. I know it well. And they tell me she comes with quite a few good acres," I said, grinning at her to show that I understood. She cheerfully gave me the finger.

"So they say," Berry said. "Are you planning to breed from her?"

"Stop it, Berry," Susie said, punching him hard on the upper arm. "Enough now. I am not a horse."

"No, of course you're not, darling. But if you were, you would be a thoroughbred."

"That's very vulgar of you," she said.

"I can't help it, it's the atmosphere," he said. "Are we alright for everything? Anyone? I think I could use a small libation myself."

"I would Berry, but it's a dead un," Melvin said, turning the bottle upside down into the ice-bucket.

"Tragedy! Let me see if I can catch that girl's eye," Berry said.

He'd barely said it before one of the pyjama clad girls who were working the room came over and said, "Your pleasure, milord?" in a slight Polish accent and whilst looking charmingly available.

"Ah, good question," he said. "What do we want?"

"Champagne please, Berry," Susie said.

"What about you, Si?"

"Suits me. It's actually not too bad," I said.

"No, it's actually not. Let it be champagne all round then."

"Can we have a dish of the day please, darling?" Maisie said.

"Count us in, Berry," the man called Melvin said.

"If you wish, my darlings, of course we can. And a dish of the day please."

"Very good, milord. Two champs, one dish. I will fetch that for you now."

"Better make it three I think," Berry said.

"Very good, milord."

179

"They take a bit of getting used to, don't they?" Berry said when she'd gone.

"It's the pyjamas," I said.

"Isn't it just," he said. "Now, Maisie, darling, put the man down a minute and let me talk to him. How're you finding the fleshpots so far, Si?"

"So far, rather fine. London is actually entertaining me rather well. I expect I'll get bored and wander off in a bit, but for now I can report that I'm having a good time."

"Well done. Proud of you, my boy," he said. "And you actually appear to be wearing something that isn't a hessian sack." He fingered the cloth of my shirt with appreciation.

"Wander off, where?" Susie said.

"I don't know. Where would you like to go?" I said, smiling.

"Be careful with this one, darling," Berry said. "He's apt to do what he says he's going to. It can be unnerving until you get used to it."

"Does he?" Susie said.

"Yes, and come to think if it, you can be a bit the same, can't you?" He raised an eyebrow in her direction.

"I don't know what you mean," she said. "How do you come to know Berry then, Si?"

"He used to beat me up when I was a kid," I said.

"When I could catch him," Berry said. "Wild as a berry, brown as a ferret. Guard your pheasants and lock up your daughters, schools out and Si's back. Happy days, happy days."

"You hated the country," I said.

"That's true," he said. "And now I own a sizeable chunk of the great muddy pointlessness. Can't stand the place, wish I could sell it, but the lawyers won't let me."

"I'm planning to just pretend mine doesn't exist," Susie said. "See what happens. I expect someone will step in. Nature abhors a vacuum and all that."

"Nobless oblige," I said, with a straight face. "I feel for you both."

"Be quiet, commoner," Susie said. "What do you know about anything?"

"I'm going to turn mine into a golf course," Berry said.

"You wouldn't?" Susie said.

"Or perhaps a theme park. Druids-r-us. Build some tumuli and discover a previously unknown ring of stones in the White Wood. Stonehenge, Avebury and Wentworth Hall, that's the thing."

"You'd never get away with it," Susie said.

"You're probably right. Okay, I'll just turn it into an agri-business. Plough up the meadows and fell the woods. At least that would make some money."

"They'd never let you," Susie said.

"I wouldn't ask them. Have you ever tried putting a tree back up after you've felled it? Doesn't work, trust me."

"What are you actually doing with the hall and the estate, Berry?" I asked.

"Pretty much what Susie said. I'm ignoring it and hoping it'll go away. It does make a fine party venue though, doesn't it, darling?"

"That is about all they're good for," Susie said.

The champagne arrived. With it came a silver serving dish with a domed lid. I assumed it was food, but it wasn't. There was also a glass of short straws and when the lid was lifted it revealed a neatly domed mound of white powder and a razor blade.

No one seemed to mind when I declined. It went round and they each cut out a line and bent their heads to it in turn, expertly chasing it up with the straw, Susie and Berry not the least.

"That's not bad," Berry said.

"That is quite good if you ask me," Maisie said. "I feel… I feel… So glad." She twirled her fingers about in the air and then delicately wiped her nose, lost for words.

"Are you… in training?" Berry said to me.

"My abstinence? No, it nearly killed me once and I've been a bit wary of it since."

"I see. You look as strong as an ox now. If you don't mind my saying so."

"That's the effect of sailing," I said. "I expect city life will soon begin to take its toll."

"Sailing where? What in?" Susie said.

I told her about Polly and about my recent travels. Around us the pitch of conversation brightened.

"She's here? In London?" she said.

"St Katherine Docks, yes."

"I'd love to see her."

"You'd be very welcome. You all would," I said. "Perhaps we should have a party on her, what do you think?"

"Oh, yes please," Maisie said.

"I think that sounds like a charming idea. I'll come," Berry said.

The room was packed now and there was an air of expectation in the crowd. Some smartly dressed young men walked through the crowd and took up position with their instruments. An attractive woman in a long, flowing gown picked up a microphone and tapped it.

"One two, one two," she said. Her voice was husky and delicious and commanded our attention. "Good evening, lords and ladies, it is time… yes, it is time."

Enthusiastic clapping, whistles and calls broke out.

"Here we go then. Everyone ready?" Berry said.

"Bring on the first sacrifice," Maisie said.

I raised an interrogative eyebrow to Susie.

"You'll soon find out," she said.

"Our first contender is, I believe, Mr Eli Brown. Will you step forward please, Mr Brown?" the woman said.

An athletic looking young man with shoulders like any two other people, his head carried forward on a muscular neck, strode through the crowd to cheers from one section of the room. He skipped from side to side, loosened his neck and then turned to face us. He had a slightly scarred face, but not in an unattractive way. He started undoing his shirt cuffs.

"There you are, my sporting lovelies. Mr Eli Brown. We will now play you a little song while you place your bets and then we will begin. Five minutes. Five minutes, ladies and gentlemen."

The room was full of money. People were calling out odds and notes were being made. Touts were visiting each table but much of the betting was happening within the tables, or between one table and another. Everyone seemed to be speaking at once and everyone seemed to be placing a bet with someone. The band struck up and the woman started singing. She was very good; it was a bit of a waste really.

"Yes, but who's his opponent?" I said, to Susie.

"Who indeed. That is the question," she said.

"The Visitor, that's all we know," Berry said. "It won't be a fair fight but it may be an interesting one. Do you fancy a little of my money at four to one?"

"For him?"

"No, dear heart, against him."

"If you're backing the house, let's call it six?"

"That's a bit steep, a hundred at fives?"

"Done," I said.

"You have been. My hand on it. What about you, Graham? You're usually good for a punt."

More bets were placed around the table.

The woman came to the end of her piece and held the long, last note alone and then finished to a crash of cymbals. The young man with the shoulders had peeled off his shirt and wound some tape around his knuckles. He was dancing and shadow boxing this way and that. He had a nice fluid movement and a reach like an orangutang. The lights, such as they were, dimmed. A pair of spotlights came on, in the ceiling above him. He looked out expectantly into the crowd.

"Vi-si-tor. Vi-si-tor. Vi-si-tor." Someone began banging a table and calling out the word. Others joined in.

The woman tapped the mike again and said, "Ladies and gentlemen, all betting to cease forthwith. Pray silence for tonight's Visitor."

The banging stopped abruptly and an expectant silence gripped us. Heads turned this way and that, scanning the crowd.

"Will the gentleman please show himself," she said.

The silence continued for a few more heartbeats and then a man at a table not far from us got to his feet and walked forward. He wasn't as tall as his opponent and when he took his jacket off and passed it to a girl it was obvious that he was more slightly built. There were murmurs from the crowd.

"He's giving away at least a couple of stone," I said quietly.

"Sssh. You just wait," Susie said, in my ear. She was hanging onto my arm and leaning forward to get a better view.

The man flexed his fingers and then took hold of his shirt collar. He gave it a sudden pull and it came completely off, coming apart at the back. He pulled his hands out of the cuffs and tossed it to the girl holding his jacket. There was a sigh in the room. He was as lean as an east wind and had muscles like a racehorse. The phrase, 'well put together' didn't cover it. He brushed his long black hair back from his eyes and flexed his shoulders. He didn't look at his opponent once.

"Well, there we are then," the woman said in her husky voice, looking appreciatively at the man. "The Visitor, my lords and ladies. D'you think he'll do?"

There was a burst of applause and more whistling and shouting. The man ignored us and slowly and carefully taped his knuckles.

When it died down sufficiently she resumed, "You all know this, I'm sure, but I will state The Rules. The Rules are: no objects to be used; bodies only. There are no rounds; we begin, continue and end. No interfering with combatants. Victory by surrender, knockout or death. Are we all clear?" She looked at the men.

They faced each other, looked at each other and then turning their heads only slightly, nodded to the woman.

"You may begin." She stepped smartly backwards out of their way.

And without any fuss, they did. The big chap, Eli, went straight at the smaller man, trying to crowd him against the people surrounding the space, his fists working at impressive speed. It was a good strategy; one solid blow might end it right there. The other man was being forced back. He had his guard up but it wasn't keeping out those fists and he was ducking and dancing to keep them from connecting. A long straight right just clipped his head and he was running out of room. Any second he would be forced off balance and the big man would get a good target.

Then, as he was almost completely out of room, the Visitor seemed to lean back and his guard opened, exposing his head. The bigger man's rhythm changed as he lined one up to take him out. Faster than thought, the Visitor's shoulder un-corked and his right went through. He hadn't been off balance, he'd drawn his man in and got him to open up. There was blood on the big man's face and the rhythm of his attack was, just for a second, disturbed.

The smaller man didn't follow up, but stepped out and round, forcing his opponent to turn and instead of punching, kicked for his knee. His foot connected as the other's weight came forward onto it so it didn't break, but it must have hurt. A sigh, like wind in the corn, rippled through the room.

The fight settled a bit; both men in the centre of the space and taking care. The big man was more than just a slugger; he was keeping the other at a distance with his reach and trying to read him. He kept the leg that had been kicked behind him. He didn't try to force the other man back this time, but reserved his strength; letting the Visitor come to him.

He, in his turn, wasn't rushing now; he moved with the other, testing his reach and his timing. Twice he kicked out and missed but it didn't put him off balance and it made the other man more careful.

They danced like that for a bit; neither man scoring a real hit. Then the Visitor stopped, stepped back and put his arms down. He waggled his head, loosening his neck and looked at the crowd. The big man stood and watched him warily.

"Vi-si-tor, Vi-si-tor, Vi-si-tor," they shouted.

He shook himself once more, put his hands up and went back to it.

When the attack came, and it came very soon, it was half over before we'd realised it had started. The Visitor seemed to float forward into the other's space and punch hard into his kidney with his left. This time he didn't back off. He stepped in right and put his right hard into the man's solar-plexus. His head was wide open but the big man couldn't get there in time. The Visitor swept his left up and out, deflecting Eli's right arm, his knee rising into the other's crotch. The three blows stopped the man dead.

He finished him with a perfect headbut to the centre of his face. We all heard the wet, bone-breaking sound of it. The man didn't fall but he was no longer there. The blood started to flow down his face and drip off his chin onto the floor.

The Visitor stepped back and held out his hand towards the girl who was holding his clothes. She threw him a towel and he used it to wipe the other man's blood off his face.

He stood in front of his opponent, hands down, waiting. The big man tried to lift his hands and step forward but his feet weren't with him. He went down, hitting the floor hard. His shoulders heaved and then slumped down; he was out and it was over. The room went wild. I dug my money clip out of my pocket and passed Berry a couple of fifties.

"You're a gentleman, whatever they say," he said. "I shall spend it wisely."

"Don't do that, Berry," Maisie said.

"Oh, all right." He looked up and caught the eye of a waitress.

"Well, Si?" Susie said

"That was a classy piece of fighting," I said.

"What a body that man has. Who is he, do you think?" she said.

"I've no idea, but if you told me he was Romany I wouldn't be surprised. That's a man bred to it, I'd say," I said.

Two stocky men in DJs gently rolled the casualty onto a stretcher and took him away. Someone else mopped up the blood. The woman started singing again and everyone started talking and drinking and having a snort of coke here and there and settling up with each other.

"So, tell me about this now," I said to Susie, when she raised her head from the dish of coke.

"Gladly. This happens once a month. They never say who they are. All the Visitors are special. Sometimes they fight in masks. They say that even international pro fighters come to fight here, but I don't know if it's true," she said. "The local toughs put themselves up and usually get beaten, but not always."

"Sounds like a quick way to lose your career to me. It seems like all the world comes to watch, whatever." I'd been looking at the crowd. "I'll bet you there's judges, police chiefs and politicians in this room."

"I'll point some of them out for you, if you like," she said.

"Go on then," I said.

We put our heads close together and turned away from the ring and towards the crowd. She directed my eye, describing this person or that and giving me a brief biography of each of them. It was very interesting and I learnt quite a bit, including that she had a very good memory and that we were being carefully watched by two familiar lean, intense faces further back in the room.

"Interesting," I said. "Now I think I'd rather look at you." And did so.

"Oh, would you," she said, but she was smiling and looking at me too. The pupils of her eyes were very wide.

"Thanks for bringing me, by the way. I'm having an interesting evening."

"I'm glad. So, Si, are you going to put yourself up?" she said.

"I'm glad too. So glad," Maisie chipped in, looking at me wistfully.

"What do you mean?" I said.

"Are you going to put yourself up?" Susie said.

"Oh, do," Maisie said.

"To fight, you mean?" I said.

"Yes, of course," Susie said.

"No," I said. "Not in a million years."

"Go on," she said.

"You must be joking. That guy would kill me."

"Don't say that. Go on. Be my hero. Take your shirt off and show us what you've got," she said

"No, Susie," I said.

"Go on. It would be fun," Maisie said, squeezing my arm. "Do it for us."

"Hey, Berry. Back me up here," Susie said.

"What's that, Susie?" he said, leaning over.

"Tell Si to fight," Susie said.

"Are you really going to fight?" the girl called Flick said, leaning over.

"Don't do it, young man," the man called Melvin said. "You're surely too young and too good looking to die tonight."

"He can if he wants to," Maisie said.

"If the man doesn't want to fight, I don't see why he should," Berry said. "I don't think you should fight, Si. Besides, don't you have to put your name down or something?"

"That's just a technicality," Maisie said. "You could fix it, darling."

"I want you to fight for me," Susie said, looking at me intently.

"I don't want to fight, and I'm not going to," I said, meeting her eye.

"Well said that man. Now who's for some more champers?" Berry said.

"Berry, you're a diplomatist," Maisie said.

"Pass me your glass, darling and we'll drink to it," he said. "What about you, Si? Would you care for some more?"

"Love some." I stopped looking at Susie and held out my glass. Berry upended a bottle over it.

"That's another one gone the way of all bottles," he said, shaking the bottle disconsolately.

"Don't worry, here's reinforcements," Maisie said, as a waitress arrived with yet more champagne and coke. Under cover of the delivery and collection of the numerous empties I managed to swap Susie's glass for mine, tip the contents of that onto the floor and get it refilled from the bottle.

"Hooray for the *Subvello club*," Susie said.

"Hooray for the Visitor," Maisie said, her eyes fixed on that gentleman.

The silver tray of coke started going round the table. When it arrived at Susie, Berry said, "Should you, darling?"

"Yes, I bloody should," she said, and bent down to snort another line. "And who made you my keeper, anyway?"

"No one, dear heart. Forget I spoke," Berry said.

"Simon's my keeper tonight, aren't you, Si?"

"Am I? Do you need keeping?" I said.

"Keeping? Who could keep me? I'm sunlight glinting on wet cobblestones after summer rain, that's what I am," she said.

"You look a lot less ephemeral than that to me," I said, putting a gentle hand on her arm. It was hot.

"Don't you lay hands on me, you coward," she said, pulling it away.

"Okay. Sorry." I took my hand back.

"Hey, Susie. Are you going to bet on the next one?" Flick said to her.

"I might. What kind of man is he?" Susie said, turning her back to me. "A real man, I expect."

"Sorry about that, old thing," Berry said. "The old Bolivian marching powder seems to be giving her trouble tonight."

If that's all it is, I thought to myself. If that's all it is.

12

KNOCK OUT

"Perhaps it's a dodgy batch?" I said, to Berry.

"No, trust me, it's the real thing," he said. "Have a look at it, it shimmers like angels' wings."

It was certainly pearlescent but I wouldn't have made any connection with angels myself.

"Can we keep her off it?" I said, quietly.

"Not easy, old sport. Besides she's safe enough here and there's no great harm."

"It's not that. I sort of had a feeling that later on she and I might get it on, but I can feel my chances slipping away."

"I see what you mean. Sorry, old man."

"When you've been at sea as long as I have…"

"Stop, you're breaking my heart. Have you met Maisie, by the way?"

"I have, but…."

"I don't suppose I'll be much use to her at this rate."

"Darlings, are you talking about me?" Maisie said.

"No, darling."

"I don't believe you."

"Cross my heart."

"I don't believe you have one, Berry. Oh, look what's just stood up over there."

"What?"

"If I'm not mistaken, that's the next contender."

She was right. A man with a shaved head had stood up at a table over to our right and was slowly unbuttoning his shirt. He was, maybe, an inch taller than the Visitor and compactly built. He carefully took his shirt off and hung it on the back of his chair. He had a hard, oak-like look about him. He gave the impression that if you hit him, he wouldn't mind much. Having said that, his face was apparently unmarked. There was a composure about him that I really liked.

"Well, Berry?" I said.

"What, old thing?"

"Where's your money, sport?"

"I don't know. Where's yours?"

"Same again?"

"No way."

"All right. Fours?"

"Could do evens, I suppose."

"Is that it? Against the Visitor?"

"Look at the man. I call that a sporting bet."

"You do?"

"I do."

"Okay, evens. One large."

"One bag of sand?"

"More if you want."

"No, that'll be fine. A grand it is."

We touched hands on the bet. Over at his table, the Visitor put down his mug of tea, got up and started doing a few stretches. This time he looked at his opponent.

The singer finished her number and the two men stepped forward into the silence.

"Mr Edward James, ladies and gentlemen. Mr James," she said.

We clapped the man and he turned to us and gave us a brief nod of his head. We didn't matter to him more than that. The Visitor kept his eye on him all the while.

The singer was about to speak her piece but it wasn't needed; they just began. There was no mad rushing, but they took their part of the space and started to feel each other out.

The leaner man appeared to have a slightly longer reach and the other had more muscle mass and looked like he would take more to put down. For a few seconds, it was more a dance than a fight; the Visitor trying an occasional jab and Mr James keeping his head moving, his feet moving and his hands flying in shorter jabs, uppercuts and hooks. He didn't extend himself, but if the Visitor got too close and any of them landed, it could easily be serious. The crowd were silent; they knew that this was only the beginning.

Mr James started to move forward in a loose, fluid sort of way. He kept driving with his fists but he was ducking and sending in long straight lefts which were coming near the mark. He didn't stick to one track but would move left and left and then right; I could see he was a hard man to know where he would be.

Then the Visitor got one in. It was a counterpunch. He seemed to be moving back with the other's one, two, three but he drove in and connected to the man's jaw. It was a familiar move and a good one but bought him no more than the chance to move round into more space. James was right back at him, tucked in and swinging.

I began to think that I might be taking some money off Berry; I didn't think the Visitor would get away with that again.

He must have thought so too as he changed tack. He stepped back and dropped his hands. James calmly walked into him and took one in the body as the Visitor feigned a sudden uppercut right and instead put his head right down and drove a straight left through the other's guard. It didn't do him as much good as it should though; in that stance, he couldn't snap his fist back and it was more of a push than a punch. It moved the man back but it cost him a glancing blow to his head. A little blood from above his eye ran down his cheek.

If anything, the other man seemed to like the last exchange. Far from weakening his legs, that blow to the body seemed to have encouraged him. I wondered if he was one of those fighters who take heart from a little pain.

They circled a bit and then both seemed to decide to stop messing about and go in hard. It was scrappy and both of them were wide open with big punches flying and mainly missing. Mr James went head down and took a blow to the side of his head but got in one or two solid blows to the Visitor's torso. They clinched for a second and then broke; both looking the worse for it but neither more staggered than the other.

It was the Visitor who moved first. He closed in, needling the other man with long-range jabs and when he began to counter with his welter of weaving, ducking blows, he anticipated one of his long lefts and got in a one-two. His right going through the other's guard to his nose and then his left going over to his ear. Now it was Mr James's turn to begin to bleed.

The heavier man soaked up the pain like it was nothing and it probably was nothing, but I knew that that wasn't the problem. He'd been read and for the moment, he didn't have an answer.

The Visitor resumed his jabbing and the crowd were encouraging him. I thought that this might go down as a classic fight at the *Subvello*. I had a quick look at the faces of the others at the table; they were all enthralled.

Mr James tucked himself up and worked away. He'd given up the long, low left and stuck to the steady onslaught of ducking and weaving and punching that had driven the Visitor back before. It was driving him back now. The man was impressively fit. The Visitor was jabbing and dancing, light on his feet as ever, but I could see that he was saving himself. He was giving no more ground than he had to and all the time there was the chance of his counterpunch going through, but that wasn't it. I began to think I knew what was about to happen.

The Visitor was running out of room again and I knew he could have pivoted out of it but he didn't. The other man was driving him and he'd been punching like a machine gun for several seconds. The Visitor counterpunched and missed, his hands falling away. The other saw his chance and drove in, looking for his knockout. What he got was thin air as the Visitor went right down, and he no longer had the speed or balance to react quickly enough. The Visitor put his fully loaded left into the man's body and then drove an uppercut into his jaw.

Even then the man wasn't completely done. He rocked back and stepped back but he wasn't going down. If it had been a boxing match he would have lost and that would have been that. This wasn't a boxing match.

The Visitor stepped sideways round the man and as his leg came straight, kicked it sideways. We all heard it break.

He went down, holding his knee, and started moaning quietly. One of the men at the next table over vomited onto it. The Visitor shook himself, swept his hair back from his face and went back to his table.

I looked at the others. Berry was looking at the man on the floor with interest. Maisie looked vacantly on as if she hadn't understood what had happened. Melvin looked like he might be next to throw up. Graham put a hand on his shoulder and said, "Are you all right old thing?" Their girls didn't seem to be much affected.

I turned further round to see how Susie was doing and I didn't like what I saw; she was pale and shaking and the pupils of her eyes were so big that she hardly seemed to have any iris left.

I got my money clip out and took off a sheaf of notes. I was going to speak to Berry but he was talking to someone at a nearby table so I spoke to Graham instead.

"If I give you this, will you settle up for me?" There was talking and shouting breaking out from the crowd now.

"Don't worry, there's no…"

"Thanks," I said, putting the money on the table and ignoring him. People were beginning to get to their feet.

I got to my feet, bent down and lifted Susie onto my shoulder.

"Hang on, Si. Don't do that," Berry said.

I ignored him and headed for the door. People got out of my way and then closed behind me.

The man at the doorway looked at me and seemed inclined to bar my way.

"I think she's OD'd I said. Berry will settle up for me."

"You're with his lordship, sir." he said, making way for me. "Okay, turn left at the bottom. No need to go through the bar."

I took his advice and carried the girl straight through the kitchens and out of the back door onto the street. I dumped her into the passenger seat of the Jag and got in the other side.

"Hey, Susie. Look at me," I said.

She looked at me.

"How're you feeling?" I said.

"How…?"

"Can you put your seatbelt on?" I said.

"I'll tr…" she reached up and tried to pull it down but she didn't seem to have enough strength.

I put my hand on her forehead. It was very hot and she was sweating. I took her pulse. It was going up around two hundred.

I took her belt and plugged it in, started the engine and began running red lights. I didn't have far to go.

I managed to find Whitechapel road and there was the Royal London Hospital. I drove straight into the ambulance bay, scooped her out and carried her in through the self-opening doors. Luckily it was a quiet night.

A staff nurse took one look at us and guided me into a bay. I put her gently down on the bed and stepped aside so that he could get to her.

"Alcohol, cocaine and something else," I said. "Her name is Susana Chesterfield and I can't give you any medical history."

He took her pulse and her blood pressure and examined her eyes. She wasn't unconscious and she cooperated with him willingly but he didn't like what he saw any more than I had. He put an oxygen mask over her face and said, "Stay with her, I'll be right back." He pulled the curtain to, and left.

I got my phone out and called Bill.

"Hello…" He didn't sound very awake.

"Hi, Bill. It's Si. I've got a live one for you."

"Oh, er… A live one what?"

"Susana Chesterfied's been poisoned. She's in the Royal London. I need you to get samples of her blood to Mac."

"Bloody hell."

"Thanks. I'll catch up with you tomorrow. I'm off to bed now. Make sure no one takes her from here, won't you."

"Oh, sure. I'll just clear up for you, as usual."

"Thanks, Bill." I disconnected.

A young registrar appeared, conferred with the nurse and examined Susie.

"You were with this girl when she took whatever she's taken?" she said.

"I've seen her drink champagne and snort some coke. She's unusually compliant and I think she's hallucinating. You're the doctor, but in my opinion she's taken something else, but I don't know what."

"That could be whatever the coke was cut with," she said.

"Possibly, but I'm pretty sure it was pure," I said.

"In your opinion. I take it you're an experienced user?"

"No, but other people who appeared to know what they were talking about, said so."

"She is unusually compliant," the nurse said.

"Okay, you can leave her with us," the doctor said and turned to start finding a vein. "But stay in the waiting area, please. We'll need to talk to you in a bit."

I wanted to stay with Susie but it wasn't wise, so slid off. As I pulled out of the space, a marked police car pulled in. I drove the quiet streets and left the car in the docks' car park and walked through to the basin. It was really late now and there wasn't anyone about.

I intended to go straight to bed, but for a moment I stood by the railing, looking across the water at Polly and listening to the silence. It wasn't the silence of silence, but the silence of everything happening elsewhere and nothing particular happening there.

I let myself through the security gate and listened to my footsteps on the boards as I walked to Polly. I swung myself up onto her, feeling her move ever so slightly under my weight, and stepped aft to the cockpit. I wasn't alone.

"Hello, Si."

"Hello, Mel."

She had her feet up along the seat and was leaning back, looking at me. She got up and came towards me and I stepped down to her. She looked at me carefully in the diffuse light.

"You look tired," she said.

"Now you mention it, I am a little."

She put her arms around my waist, so I put mine around her.

"Come on then, Si. Let's go to bed."

"I like it when you say that, Mel."

"I seem to like it when I say it too."

"Come on then."

13

LIVE BAIT

In the morning, languorous and satisfied, we'd got to the point of having tea in bed again and my head was full of the night before. I gave Mel the full story, which helped me and was, in any case, necessary.

"Poor Susie. So you completely failed to look after her then," Mel said.

"It was a lot harder than I thought. There were so many people and so much distraction, but I'm still surprised I didn't see anything. I was right next to her and her drink was right beside me except when she was drinking from it," I said.

"Good thing you were there in a way."

"Nice of you to say so. And nice of you to be here too." I looked at her thoughtfully so that she would see that I was thoughtful.

"I came to tell you something," she said.

"What?"

"And you're right; I came to see if you would bring Susie back here."

"I didn't."

"Only because she was off her head and in A and E."

"Not necessarily."

"Look, Si. While we're working on this together you can lay off fucking other girls, okay. After that, you can do whatever you want. As you always do."

"I wasn't particularly planning…"

"Don't bother, I know you. We're doing this together, aren't we?"

"Yes, you're right, we are."

"So?"

"Okay."

"Okay, you won't fuck anyone else?"

"Yes."

"Okay. Good."

"What did you come to tell me?"

"I did what you said." She pulled some sheets of paper with printed pictures and words out of her bag and passed them to me. "Cecilia Brinkworth, Fiona Asher, Jane Hamilton and Imogen Westhall."

"Four more? Seven all together."

"So far. There may be others. Jane is missing, the others are dead."

I leafed through the sheets and looked at the girls' photos, and was struck once again by how beautiful they all were. Clever, beautiful, and well-connected?

"Any more aristos?" I said.

"Yes. Cecilia and Jane."

"And the others are old money?"

"Actually, yes."

"Interesting. We need to talk to Susie."

"Why?"

"What do you mean, why?"

"I just think…"

We were interrupted by someone banging on the hull. It was an impatient sort of banging. I ignored it and read the bits of paper a bit more thoroughly. The banging stopped.

"Are you going to go and see who that is?" Mel said.

The banging resumed.

"I hope they can swim, whoever they are," I said, taking my dressing gown from the back of the door.

When I put my head out, I found that there was a tall gentleman in a suit putting his foot on the gunwale in preparation to coming aboard.

"Don't do that," I said.

"Oh, there you are," he said, and stopped. "I need to talk to you."

There was a young man in a maroon blazer and paisley tie, who I recognised from the harbour master's office, standing behind him.

"Go to that café," I pointed, "and order me coffee. I'll meet you there shortly," I said.

"No. I need to talk to you now," he said.

"Mr Chesterfield, if you come aboard my boat without an invitation I will toss you over the side."

He looked at me. He was clearly a man used to others doing what he told them. Come to that, so am I.

"Oh. Right then. Don't be long." He turned away and strode off with the young man following him. I went back down to Mel.

"It's okay," I said. "Just an angry father."

"Whose?" Mel said.

"Susie's. I'll go and talk to him."

"Poor Susie," Mel said.

I had a shower and put some clothes on and went up to the café. The man was there, but no coffee. He glowered at me.

"Good morning, Mr Chesterfield. Did you order me some coffee?"

"It is not *Mr* Chesterfield, and you can get your own damn coffee. Sit down. I've something to say to you."

"Hang on…" I caught Henriques' eye, he was looking at me anyway, and he came over.

"Good morning, sir. Sir," he said.

"Morning Henriques. Coffee please; you know how I take it. And for this gentleman…?"

"No thank you," the man said.

Henriques gave me a face that was so studiedly blank it almost made me laugh, and slid off.

I sat down and said, "Right, what can I do for you, my lord?"

"How do you know who I am? We've never met."

"I can see the resemblance to your daughter," I said. "And the list of men of your age and class who are likely to turn up and be angry with me this morning isn't such a long one. I assume you think that what happened to Susie last night was somehow my fault?"

"You took her somewhere and got her off her head, on drugs," he said. "To the point where she nearly died."

"No I didn't," I said. "She took me, and I had nothing to do with the drugs she took and she didn't come that close to dying. Also, I was the one who took her to hospital, just in case. As you well know."

"Yes, I know that. My daughter didn't have anything to do with that kind of thing until you showed up, Mr Ellice." The way he said Ellice wasn't nice.

"We both know that's not true."

"What I'm telling you, Mr Ellice, is that you are not welcome here. You will stay away from my daughter. Do you understand?"

"Or else, what?" I said.

"Or I'll see to it that your past catches up with you."

"So, you came to see me today, believing me to be, what?"

"I know you to be a drug dealer and a murderer but in this country, we still have the rule of law."

"Well, I appreciate your candour, and I really like Susie, so I'll be nice to you. Ah, thanks." Henriques brought the coffee.

"Oh, will you." He looked at me with anger and some confusion. I felt for him. Not that much, but a bit.

"When was the first time this happened?" I said.

"The first time what happened?"

"The first time you became aware that Susie was taking cocaine."

"My daughter doesn't, didn't, have anything to do with drugs until last night."

"You'll be telling me next that you've never taken any yourself," I said.

"I have never taken cocaine," he said. I believed him.

"Last night," I said, "I sat in a room watching two men beat each other senseless for my entertainment. As it happens, I enjoyed it, but I'm certain that it was laid on and hosted by a local crime family. There was enough snow going around to send a herd of elephants into orbit. Susie was kind enough to point out a few of the judges and policemen and politicians in the crowd for my entertainment, so unless you're a complete idiot, you know very well what goes on."

I looked at him. He looked defiant but he didn't deny it.

"And you must also know that Susie and her set all indulge pretty freely in coke and probably have done since they were teenagers. Now, when did you first become aware of her getting into trouble with drugs?" I said.

"She doesn't," he said. "Why do you want to know?"

"I just do. Are you going to tell me?"

"There is nothing to tell. If you stay here, I will see to it that you regret it. One way or another."

"Fair enough. Now if you'll excuse me, I've got things to do," I said, slurping down the last of the coffee.

"I haven't…"

"Goodbye, Mr Chesterfield. Thanks for coffee."

As I walked back to Polly, it occurred to me that I might be confused by all this, but I definitely wasn't bored. The phone that Bill had given me rang. I sat down in the cockpit and answered it.

"Hey, Si. You were right," he said.

"It happens. What about?"

"About that girl. Susana Chesterfield. She is definitely another one; scopolamine, rohypnol and l-dopa. Mac's just finished running the tests. She's doing fine, by the way and he says hello. There was something that looks like a nicotine patch stuck to her skin under her dress. Who put it there? Tell me and I'll go and arrest someone. Or something. I take it you can at least give me a short-list of suspects this time?"

"Can I? I don't know that I can do that exactly, but the Pogodin's were there."

"Were they, by fuck. Why couldn't it be someone else. We'll need real evidence before we can go anywhere near them. Even then, it'll be a shit-storm."

"Where can I find him? What're his movements?"

"Pogodin? What're you going to do?"

"I don't know. Have a closer look at him, probably. Possibly, have a chat."

"Why don't we let the spooks do that?"

"Are you worrying about me?"

"No. It's just that… okay, maybe a bit. It's the way the chap from MI6 looks when he talks about him. Why don't I at least see if I can get hold of a bit of backup?"

"Yes. Good idea. Get Freddy. I want to do a thing with him and a few of his mates anyway."

"What kind of a thing?"

"It's just a vague idea at the moment, but it'll be in the cause of making the world a better place," I said.

"Not for someone, I'll bet. I'm not sure he's forgiven you for last time yet."

"Exactly. I've pissed him off so much that it would be beneath his dignity to fail me."

"Fair enough. I'll sound him out on the matter."

"Good. Now tell me where I can find the Pogodins. What's his mode of being? I think it's quite likely he'll come to me sooner or later, I might as well go to him first."

"Does the phrase 'international incident' mean anything to you?"

"Nope. Anyway, who am I? I'm just some low-life drug smuggler. You don't even know me. Don't worry so much."

"Okay. Well actually, he has been behaving a little differently recently, according to the spook. His main base is Moscow and it's unusual for him to be in London so long. And he's travelling with his wife, which he doesn't usually. It's almost like he's on holiday, if people like him have holidays. I mean apart from on their yachts or whatever. I can also tell you that they've been staying at a country hotel. Twice so far; a place called…" he consulted a notebook, "Melton House in…"

"Hampshire," I said. "Near the village of Acton."

"You know it? Of course, that's where you're from."

I was silent for a moment, thinking.

"I can hear you thinking," he said.

"I feel thoughtful."

"Why?"

"I'm from Hampshire."

"Yes, I know. And?"

"So's Mel and Jane, I think and… and… I need to think about this."

"You think this hotel might be something to do with it?"

"Seems unlikely, but who knows. I've been to many a ball there. Nice place. Just out of curiosity, how do you know that? You're tapping his phone?"

"How the other half live. No. Fat chance of that. PNR hits put his Merc on the 303 at Micheldever but not at Andover, and then back at Micheldever. I knew you'd want to know, so we made a list of places where they might stay and the hotel's booking system was easy enough to get into. They pretty much all are. I didn't just tell you that, by the way."

"Nice work, Bill."

"Thanks. And I'll probably regret it, but since you're being nice, I'll tell you that they have a reservation for tonight and tomorrow night, too."

"Excellent. I'll see if I can join them for breakfast. Have you identified any more victims?"

"We're working on it. I've got a couple of constables making lists now. Should have something to say about that this afternoon. There's a misper just turned up dead in Tower Hamlets, but she's a librarian or something; not our demographic. Was, I mean. I'll check anyway though."

"Good. Got a pen?"

"I'm a policeman, of course I've got a pen."

"Then write down, Cecilia Brinkworth, Fiona Asher, Jane Hamilton and Imogen Westhall. Four more posh girls for you."

"You're joking? Are you sure?"

I thought about that. If Mel said they were, they would be.

"Yes, actually, I think I am."

"Oh fuck. Say them again."

I said the names again slowly so that he could write them down.

"Shit. This just became a major investigation. I'm going to need more people. It's going to get out, you know that, don't you?"

"Whatever."

"Fine. Anything else, or can I go back to work now?"

"Yes. You know you were going on about tracking phones and all that the other day?"

"What about it?"

"You know where I am, don't you?"

"I might do."

"Thought so. In which case I need the number of a phone which co-locates with me at some specific times and places. Can you do that?"

"I can get it done. Why?"

"Because it will be the number of the phone belonging to a Russian prostitute called Anja. I think she must have one so that they can tell her where to go and what to do. I want to talk to her somewhere in private, and if you give me her number I can use it to go and find her, can't I?"

"So, you're not a complete luddite after all."

"Apparently not. You don't have anyone down here keeping an eye on me, do you?"

"Why the fuck would I? I'm short-staffed as it is. Why?"

"I have a feeling I'm being watched, so you can look at all phones colocating with me. And I'm going to text another number to you too. I want to know about any phones that colocate with that as well."

"Fucking hell. Anything else?"

"Not for now, but I'll let you know."

"What are you going to do now?"

"Have breakfast, of course."

I made my way back down to the saloon, where I found that Mel had got dressed and was skilfully piling her raven tresses into their accustomed order. I fetched the sheets of paper that she'd made up on the other girls and started looking through them again. And then I took photos of the photos with my phone.

"Well?" she said.

"Huh?" I said.

"Susie's dad…?"

"Oh, no problem. About that; us doing this together, I mean. I have something to say."

"Oh, do you? What?"

"You know I was in the Rifles for a while?"

"Yes, but I'm not entirely clear why you left. There were some contradictory rumours."

"Maybe another day. Anyway, people shot at me and I shot back. There was a certain amount of violent death and quite a bit of danger."

"Which, I'm sure, rather suited you."

"Er, I suppose so. And Morocco wasn't an entirely peaceful experience."

"Another story you haven't told me yet. And your point is?"

"If we carry on digging about with this, I'm pretty certain that some one'll try to kill me pretty soon. They might kill you too and that would make me feel bad. I'd rather it didn't happen."

"I'm glad to hear it, but that's just tough. This genie won't go back in the bottle. Stop being a prick and start treating me like an equal."

"I am. I'm just saying, I'm just not sure I'm going to be able to protect you, that's all."

"You don't have to. I'll be fine."

"You can't possibly know that. Is there anything on this wide earth would make you leave it to me for a bit? Just for a few days, perhaps."

"Death might do it. Mine, I mean, not yours."

"Oh fuck."

"It's me, Si," she said. "Remember? Mel Franklin? Not some helpless, witless bint you just fucked. When did you ever know me get into trouble?"

She was right of course.

"Okay," I said. "But if it gets dangerous, will you promise to run away and hide?"

"No. What aren't you telling me?"

"Nothing."

"Yes, you are." She looked at me, and there was no escaping how well she knew me.

"Oh shit."

"Just stop prevaricating and tell me why you're suddenly worrying about it. You can start with why you deleted the photos on my camera, you bastard."

You just can't get anything past Mel.

"You know what I mean by a thousand-yard stare?"

"As in, PTSD?"

"In this case more as in, I've seen a lot of shit and I've done a lot of shit and if you bother me in any way, I'll squash you like a fly."

"A bad dude?"

"In this case, probably a very bad dude. You remember the couple who were watching Susie at *Umbra Villus*?"

"Who I no longer have photos of?"

"Their name's Pogodin, they're Russian and he's CEO of a high-level Russian pharmaceuticals company. And I'd rather you didn't come to his notice. And if you've got a problem with that, you're not in my gang." I stuck my tongue out at her.

"That's quite sweet, but don't worry about it, I'll be fine. How do you know this? Your friend again?"

"My point is, you don't look them up, or anything like that. I'm serious. And I'm worried about you hanging about with me because of them. It wouldn't mean being left in the park with no clothes this time. They were there last night; at the boxing club; watching Susie; watching me with Susie."

"Oh, were they. Pharmaceuticals; so they could get the l-dopa and so on?"

"Easily."

"We still need to know why."

"I know. And this boxing club; it has two boxing hares as its logo. The same hare, the same people; I'm sure of it. They're called Green apparently; brother and sister."

"Yes, the Greens. Everyone knows about them. You think there's a link?"

"It's a hell of a coincidence if there isn't. Three incidences of poisoning in three different premises."

"Okay. So?"

"So, I want to find out more about them and I may piss them off again doing it. I really must move Polly."

"Where to?"

"Oh, er..." My other phone interrupted me. It was a message from the number I'd saved as 'Susie C' and it said, 'let me in, will you?'. I went to the window and looked out. There was a woman in a big hat, scarf, sunglasses and a long coat at the security gate.

"Who's that?" Mel said.

"Could be anyone," I said, and went up to let her in.

"Hey, Susie," I said, holding the gate for her.

"Hey, Si," she said, taking off her sunglasses so that she could look at me and I could see her. She looked pale and shaken and self-conscious and proud and troubled. And very, very beautiful.

"You just missed your dad," I said, smiling.

"He just missed me," she said, pulling her hat brim down a little. "I was in the other café waiting for him to bugger off."

"He wanted someone to blame," I said.

"Yes. About that, I came to say sorry. And thank you," she said.

"And he's worried about you."

"I know. I'm not usually like that. I don't know what happened. I can't seem to remember, but they say you picked me up and took me to hospital. I told him not to..." I could see her clear, sharp mind hunting about for what had happened, and not finding it.

"Not your fault," I said.

"Yes, it was. I don't usually… I don't know what happened, but…"

"No. I mean, it really wasn't your fault. You were poisoned."

"You mean it was bad snow? I don't…"

"They didn't tell you? Obviously not."

"What? I don't understand."

"And me, as it happens. Will you come aboard for a bit and I'll explain."

She looked at me, undecided. "Who would do that? Why? How do you know?"

"It wasn't me. We can go to the café instead, if you'd rather?"

"This is your boat?"

"I call her Polly. Yes."

"She's very beautiful."

"Yes, and she has hot running coffee and toast."

"Okay."

She followed me onto Polly and down the companion way to the saloon. My bulk hid Mel until I stepped aside.

"Oh," she said, when she saw her.

"Hello Susie," Mel said.

Again, there was that thing between them. I couldn't tell if they were friends or enemies but there was something.

"Hi Mel, I didn't know…" Susie said, looking from Mel to me. "Are you…?"

"It's complicated," Mel said, cutting her off.

"I suppose it might be," Susie said, looking at me again.

"We're old friends," I said. "And Mel's got me helping her to find out what's happened or happening to six girls who are now missing or dead. We think you're about to be next. Have a seat and Mel's going to tell you all about it while I make coffee and toast. Okay?"

"Oh. Okay." She sank onto a seat and looked at Mel. I went to the galley and set about doing the things that are necessary for life.

When I came back with a tray full of the good stuff, Susie was looking very thoughtful, not to say, dazed.

"You really think this is real?" she said.

"Yup," I said.

"How? I mean... was it in my drink?"

"No. It was in an adapted nicotine patch stuck to your skin under your dress. The chemicals involved are all easily absorbed that way. I assume you didn't notice anything?"

"Nothing. There was such a crush and I... How do you know that?"

"He's got a source," Mel said. "Someone in the police or something like that. He's not saying."

"This couple who were watching me at the auction. And they were there last night. Mel says you bought me because of them?" Susie said.

"Yes, basically. It seemed like a good idea," I said, smiling.

"Just who the fuck are you, Si? And why are you doing this?"

"Don't get excited," Mel said, "He's just a selfish bastard who gets bored and does exactly whatever he feels like all the time."

"If you say so," she said, looking at me doubtfully.

"But he's not the actual poisoner," I said. "The Russian, I mean. He didn't come anywhere near us. And neither did his wife."

"It's someone I know, isn't it?" Susie said. "We've been talking about it. Trying to make a list. It has to be, doesn't it. Someone who knows all of us."

"It doesn't have to be," I said, "but I agree it's likely. Assuming it's only one person."

"Fuck," she said, with feeling. "What're we going to do?"

"You could take a holiday," I said. "Possibly somewhere like New Zealand. And don't tell anyone where you've gone. And take Mel with you."

"How would that help?"

"It would keep you safe."

"I see. But why take Mel with me?"

"To keep her safe as well."

"Oh. No. I'm staying right here and I'm going to help you catch this bitch and find out what happened to the others. You can use me as bait, if you like."

"The fish does seem to already be on the hook," I said, looking into her troubled and beautiful eyes.

"You are a cold-hearted bastard," Mel said.

"It makes sense though," Susie said. "Besides, I want to. And we have to find Jane and Natasha before they get killed too."

"Good for you," I said.

"I'm not saying being poisoned was fun," she said, "but I was a bit bored and all this is rather exciting."

"Me too," I said.

"Oh, for fuck's sake," Mel said. "I am the only slightly sane person round here."

"If you were sane, you'd take me seriously about keeping away from me while this is going on," I said.

"What do you mean?" Susie said.

"I mean, I'm quite certain I'm going to be attracting unwelcome attention pretty soon and I don't want Mel getting caught up in it. Tell her, will you."

"Oh. I see. I expect Mel will do whatever she wants to."

"Apparently so," I said, and then a thought struck me. "Tower Hamlets."

"What about Tower Hamlets?" Mel said.

"Hang on." I said, and got a phone out.

I hit the entry for Bill and he answered immediately.

"Hi darling," I said. "That dead misper, what was her name?"

"Hang on, I've got it here… Wendy Russell. Why?"

"Wendy Russell," I said out loud, watching Mel and Susie. They didn't react. "Where's she from? Where're her family from, I mean?"

"Er... somewhere called... Claydon. In Suffolk, I think."

"Thanks. You said she was found in Tower Hamlets?"

"That's right. Why?"

"I want to have a look at her."

"No chance. There'll be a woodentop on the door, and forensics all over it shortly."

"Okay. Just text me the address anyway, will you."

"Why?"

"You don't want know. Just do it because I'm asking you to, you control-freak."

"Oh, fuck. Okay, mein führer," he said, and disconnected.

Mel and Susie were both looking at me.

"You aren't going to like what I'm going to ask you do to now though," I said, to Susie.

"What?" she said.

"Wait," I said. "Wait and keep yourself unavailable to be poisoned for a bit. Can you do that?"

"Why?" she said.

"Because there are a few other things I have to do first. Things we have to do first." I looked at Mel.

"What?" Mel said.

"We'll start by going to visit someone called Wendy," I said.

"Oh. Why?"

"Good," I said. "That's settled. Susie, would you please go home and hide? Do some study or something. Just don't leave the house or have any visitors. Just for a couple of days."

"That may possibly kill me," she said.

"I said you wouldn't like it," I said, grinning.

"You're going to have to make it up to me afterwards," she said, grinning back.

"Oh, fuck," Mel said. "That's all we need."

14

RESIDUE

The gods of traffic were reasonably kind to us and we made it to Whitechapel in less than a week. I was assuming that however bad it was for us, it would be equally bad for everyone else, and the amount of traffic made it easy for me to keep an eye out for anyone following us. Further down the Mile End Road, I made Mel take the wheel and wait on a double yellow while I ran into a DIY shop and returned with two disposable white coveralls, a box of latex gloves, disposable face masks and disposable over-shoes.

"Ah, I see," she said, deftly pulling out into the traffic. "What happens if we get arrested for impersonating soco?"

"Get you, with the police jargon. We run," I said.

"That'll be a sight. Well, don't just sit there; put yours on," she said, grinning.

That turned out to be rather tricky in the small car. And amusing. And then we swapped places so that she could change too.

"Why didn't you tell me not to wear a skirt?" she said.

"Never occurred to me," I said, grinning.

"Just keep your eyes on the road," she said.

"Not a chance," I said, pinching a bit of exposed flesh.

Mel's impressive knowledge of London got us close, and a patrol car and a few listless onlookers told us exactly where. I estimated from the angle they were looking up to, that it was on about the fifth floor. We drove round the corner out of sight and parked by a row of small lockup garages. I got out, put up the hood of my overall and pulled the cords so that the opening in it tightened round my face. With the face-masks on as well, we looked like scary, androgynous zombie creatures from some evil science lab. Mel got her camera bag and we walked into the stinking stairwell at the back of the block of flats.

"Do you think the car'll be okay?" I said.

"I doubt it," she said.

"Thanks."

We went on up the unpleasant concrete stairs, our footsteps echoing back at us. There were a bunch of kids on the fifth-floor landing.

"What to fuck do you think you look like?" one of them said to me. The others laughed.

"Someone who's already lived longer than you're likely to," I said, pushing him out of the way.

"Filth," he said, and spat at me.

I thought about dangling him over the edge, but there were more important things to do. We went out onto the balcony that ran along the front of the building and gave access to the flats. There was a uniformed officer standing outside one of the doors about halfway along.

"So, Harry doesn't mind you skiving off then?" I said.

"He doesn't know. Why're we talking about that now?"

"Because I don't know anything about football," I said.

"So, you don't know how Spurs did last night then?"

"No, do you? Afternoon," I said to the officer, raising a hand.

"Two-one to West Ham," Mel said.

"Haven't you forgotten your box of tricks?" the man said.

"Just a quick look-see and a few photos for the boss," Mel said, holding up her camera bag.

"But they've got an ID," he said. "Her purse is on the floor, just by where it was. I called it in an hour ago."

"Don't ask me. Ours is not to reason why," she said, moving for the door.

"Are the others going to be long? One of those bloody kids is going to throw something at me any minute."

"There's something on, up Hackney," I said shrugging.

We were just going in when he said, "Oi! Put your bloody paper boots on then."

"Fuck. Thanks," Mel said.

We put our paper boots on, and latex gloves, and entered the room, stepping over a pile of postal junk on the floor. At first sight it wasn't too bad. Apart from the smell. There was a big poster of a Manga character on one wall and a few cactuses on the windowsill. There was a pile of books by the sofa and next to them, a glass bong with the head of Yoda. In one corner, there was an acoustic guitar on a stand. Someone had given it a necktie and put a hat on it. There were a pair of shoes where its feet might be. Mel took photos of it.

I picked up the purse that was lying on the floor and pulled out the contents. There was a library card, a bank card, a card with her name and national insurance number on it, a photo of a dog, a few receipts and some small change. I laid them out on the floor and Mel took pictures of them. Then I put them carefully back.

"Ready?" I said. "We probably don't have long."

"Of course," she said.

We went into the bedroom and joined the corpse. She'd started to swell and her lips had drawn back over her teeth, revealing her livid, purple gums. Her open eyes were sinking back into her skull and I suspected that it wouldn't be long before the putrefaction in her intestines broke through the skin and she collapsed. Her tongue had swollen and protruded between her clean, white teeth, mocking us.

The smell had layers of rotten eggs and sweetness and a deep staleness that was more than just the long un-changed air in the room.

"Just concentrate of capturing all the information. Take it like a jigsaw; piece by piece," I said.

"Shut up, you idiot," Mel said, working away with the camera.

I examined the tourniquet on her left arm that was biting into the swelling flesh and the hypodermic that lay on the duvet. They didn't tell me anything. Her nails were neatly square-cut and unvarnished. Her glasses, on the table beside the bed, were clean. Her clothes were not expensive but not worn either, and apart from their current circumstances, not dirty. When I tried to imagine her as a living girl, I saw her in a library or maybe a council office.

To my surprise, Mel put down her camera and pulled back the duvet exposing the whole of the rotting body. She took photos of every part of it, pulling back the clothes as much as possible.

I stood back and looked at her and the room in general.

This room was more untidy than the living room. It had piles of clothes; a man and a woman's, on the floor and over a chair. There were more books, another Manga and an art poster of a stylised girl with her back to us. Someone had doodled on this one, which was a shame. I bent down and read some of the backs of the books.

"Help me turn her," Mel said.

"What?" I said.

"Help me turn her, you idiot."

"Bloody hell. Okay, if you want," I said.

"I want."

We did. It wasn't fun but nothing actually came apart, and Mel completed her set of photos. She even gently ruffled the girl's hair, looking for who knows what, and then we turned her back.

"Poor cow," Mel said, respectfully replacing the duvet.

"Let's just quickly look in the other rooms and then I think we should go." I said.

"Agreed," she said, snapping away.

The kitchen wasn't clean but I got the impression that it had been tidied and then left. There was some dust on the surfaces. The milk in the fridge had long turned to cheese and the lone banana was a mummy of its former self.

While I was investigating the cupboard under the sink, my brain made a small connection. When I was done, I went back into the room with the girl in it and took a photo of the poster with a doodle on it with my phone.

The tiny bathroom was similar; not pleasant but not appalling. Several cap-less tubes of toothpaste were curled up dead on the sink and the small bin was overflowing. I wouldn't have used the bath unless I was pretty desperate, but it didn't actually have anything growing in it.

I met Mel in the front room. The figure of the officer moved over the doorway, blocking the light.

"She's a fruity one, isn't she," he said. I didn't believe his nonchalance for a minute.

"I've seen worse," I said.

"The rest of your lot have just pulled up," he said.

"Great. Come on, let's go and give them a heads up and help with the kit," I said to Mel.

"Can't you stay here a moment? I'm busting," the constable said.

"Let's just keep those kids back where they are, shall we. We won't be two minutes," I said and walked towards him. He backed up to let me past.

"Don't forget to bring up a scene sheet," he called after us. "You haven't signed in yet."

"Don't worry," Mel called back, "we won't."

"What does she look like?" the mouthy kid said, as we turned into the landing.

"She hasn't exploded yet, but she's about to," I said.

"Cool!"

We pushed past them and went down two flights of stairs as fast as we could. I stopped, and started stripping off the protective clothing. Mel did the same. We bundled it up tight and I put it under my arm.

There were the sounds of many footsteps coming up to us. I took Mel's hand and pulled her as quickly and quietly as we could manage down the last few steps and onto the balcony at that level. There were more police cars in the space below and a big transit labelled 'incident unit'. A longwheel base Landrover drove slowly past and went out of sight.

I turned Mel to face me, put my arms around her waist and gently rested my forehead on hers.

"How're you doing?" I said.

"Fine," she said. "How're you doing?"

"Oh. Fine," I said.

The footsteps passed by and no one came out onto our level.

"I think they'll work down and up from her floor," I said.

"Can we go now?"

"Yes, let's."

We met one tired looking man in a suit and tie coming up but he didn't bother to pay attention to us and hurried past. The car was still there and undamaged, though a couple of kids with skateboards had appeared and were looking at it. They looked at us with equal curiosity. We got in and drove off, but not too quickly.

"I think they must have thought we were dealers," I said, when we'd got back onto the Mile End Road heading west.

"What?" Mel said.

"Why they didn't touch the car. Who else would have a car like this round here?"

"Fuck, Si."

"What?"

"Poor girl, dying alone like that. Some people do just die of drugs."

"Maybe. I'm pretty sure that that was one of our girls."

"Why?"

"I'm not sure."

"She wasn't."

"Why not?"

"Because…"

"Yes?"

"Because she's not like us, I suppose. What you said before…"

"Wrong class?"

"If you want to put it that way, yes."

"Imogen, Hillary, Cecilia, Fiona, Jane, Natasha, Susie and Wendy?" I said.

"She seemed sort of mousy," Mel said. "Harmless, I mean."

"She's a girl," I said, looking at Mel. "And from her photo ID, a very pretty one."

"Which also could be pure coincidence," she said.

"I don't believe that," I said.

"Hm."

"Mel…"

"Yes, Si?" she said.

"You're less squeamish than I thought you'd be."

"Si, I'm not squeamish at all."

"Mel…"

"Si?"

"Do I really know you?"

"No, Si. Not really. But don't worry about it. What's next?"

"I don't…" I got out Bill's phone and read my texts, "… actually, I do." I pulled over and found a place to stop.

"Your deep throat?" Mel said.

"Something like that. You take the car. I'll meet you at Polly in a bit."

"Me take this car?"

"Yes, why not." I got out.

I watched her drive away, silver bangles and red nail-varnish catching my eye as she put her arm out to wave goodbye. I liked the little car but she looked like she belonged in it. Then I stepped into the Oxfam shop just there and stood at a display of second hand books, looking out through the window. Sure enough, a couple of minutes later, the same Landrover passed by. Well, I was sure it was the same Landrover, even though it had a different number plate today.

I went and sat on a bench and phoned Bill.

"What now?" he said.

"Hi, Bill, how's your day going?" I said.

"I don't even begin to believe you care. Now, stop winding me up and… Oh fuck…"

He disappeared for a bit so I entered one of the phone numbers he'd texted to me in the tracking app on the phone. The result seemed almost inevitable: Tower Hamlets.

"Right, sorry about that… you there?" he said, reappearing.

"That girl, Wendy Russell, I want to know about her family."

"What about her family? Why?"

"What her background really is. Just trust me. I'll tell you why later."

"Oh, fuck."

"Thanks, Bill."

I hung up on him and started walking back the way we'd come; back towards Tower Hamlets. On the way, I bought a big bunch of flowers in a flower shop. I like buying flowers.

The flashing dot on the phone led me to a urine soaked lift of a tower block not far from the one we'd been in earlier. After a couple of false casts, I navigated along the balcony of the seventh floor to number 724 and tapped politely on the door.

After a while a female voice called out, "What?"

"Flowers," I said.

"Who for?" the voice said.

"Number 724 is who. Do you want them or not?" I said.

"Okay, hold on."

The door opened a crack and stopped against the chain. An eyeball examined me suspiciously from under a fringe of blonde hair. I gave it a winning smile and displayed the flowers.

"Okay. Leave them by the door," the owner of the eyeball said.

"Sorry," I said, and jammed my toe into the gap so that the door couldn't be shut.

"Fuck off, whoever you are," she said, and tried to push the door shut. It bent a certain amount but didn't catch. It wasn't much of a door.

"I want to talk to Anja," I said. "Let me in or I'll blow your house down."

"Anja, some arsehole wants you," the voice called out. "Come and deal with it."

As she stepped back from the door, I took the opportunity to put my shoulder to it. The staple holding the chain to the doorframe came away with no great resistance, and the door flew open. I stepped in, closed it and went through into the main room. Anja was standing in the doorway to what I assumed was a bedroom. She looked groggy and not properly awake and was wearing a dressing gown that she hadn't managed to do up properly. She was holding a mobile phone and was clearly torn between trying to find a number on it and looking at me.

"Don't phone them," I said. "It will only cause trouble. I brought you some flowers." I held out the flowers.

"It's you again. Who the fuck are you?" she said, looking at me and then at the flowers. "How did you come here? Why were you at the club? Are you following me? I thought you weren't one of them, but I was wrong."

"Not exactly. I'm sorry about the door. Would you like me to mend it?"

"Good idea, mister," the first girl said, coming out of a different door, now with some clothes on and looking at me. Another frightened female face appeared looking over her shoulder.

"What do you want?" Anja said.

"Help, actually. Will you help me please? And in return, if I can, I'd like to try to do what you asked. Help me, and I'll help you."

"No. I cannot help you, and you cannot help me. Now go away or I will call the men."

"Okay, call the men. That would be a good idea. It will show them that none of this is any of your doing and I can ask them a few questions."

"They will just kill you and dump your body in the river," the blonde girl said.

"Sure. Tell them I'm unarmed will you." I lifted my shirt and did a little twirl to demonstrate that I was unarmed.

"They will kill you. Do you understand?" she said.

"Sure. It's okay. I don't want to cause you any trouble, I just want to find some girls. Girls who are in trouble. I seem to have taken it up as a job. Go ahead, call them."

"Okay, just go away, will you. We don't want any of this," the blonde one said.

"Just tell me what I want to know and I'll go away," I said, getting out my phone.

"What girls?" Anja said.

"These girls," I said, holding it out and showing her the photos of Hillary, Cecilia, Fiona, Imogen and Jane. In each case, photos of them alive.

I made them all look. They didn't want to but I put the phone in their faces and made them. I watched their faces for any signs of recognition, but I didn't see any.

"Any thoughts?" I said.

"We don't know them," the blonde said.

"Shame. You're all here against your will in one way or another, aren't you?" I said.

"No, we're not," the blonde said.

"Some girls get to go home," the quiet one said.

"Shut up, Kazia," Anja said.

"We don't know these girls, so you should go now," the blonde said.

"Okay. You're owned by the Greens, aren't you?" I said.

There was a flicker of fear in Anja's eyes. The others looked away from me with closed faces.

"They're people who do slavery and they might have these girls locked up somewhere. Or maybe have connections who could get them for me. There are people who would be happy to pay a lot of money for them. You can have that money if you help me find them. Can you?"

"I have told you, we cannot help you. You cannot help us. Go away," Anja said.

"Even if you haven't seen them, tell me where I could look for them and then I will go." I looked gently at the quiet one and gave her my nicest smile.

"We don't know," the blonde said.

"He could mean the garden," the quiet one said. "With the wall; where the screaming was."

"Shut up Kazia, you know nothing." The blonde turned on her and the poor girl put her head down.

"We can't help you, Mr. So now you fuck off, Okay," Anja said.

"Unless you're going to beat us up. Are you?" the blond one said, turning back to me and standing in front of Kazia.

"Or rape us, if that's what you want?" Anja said, stepping forward beside the blonde. She undid her dressing gown and held it open. "Is that what you want?" She stood in front of me, showing herself to me naked. "Mr English gentleman. Is this what you want?"

I looked at the quiet one and saw that there was no way I was going to get to talk to her then.

"My mistake," I said. "Can I borrow a pen? Just in case any of you change your mind."

I wrote the number of the phone Bill had given me on the inside cover of a magazine, did my best to knock the screws that had held the staple for the chain back into to the door frame and let myself out. Two and a half angry stares followed me out.

As I got out of the lift at the bottom, a heavy-set man was stepping into the other one. He had black eyes and tape over his nose. Just before the doors closed our eyes met and I recognised him as the man I'd hit at the docks. Tony. He recognised me too. I could hear him trying to get the doors open. I thought about following him up but it was too late. He would be calling his friends right now, and me getting cornered in this horrible tower-block wouldn't help anyone.

I carried on out onto the streets round a couple of corners, trotted along to the nearest tube station and disappeared into the anonymous sea that is London.

15

NUTTERS

Back on Polly, I found Mel at the saloon table working at a laptop. I passed her and went down to the engine room where I got out the Sig Sauer P226 automatic pistol that I keep in what looks like one of the engines air-filters, but isn't. Mel followed me and watched me do that.

"What's that for?"

"I don't know. It's time to go." I replaced the cover, being careful not to leave scratch marks on the screw-heads.

"Where?"

"The country. Via your place, I suppose. I've booked a hotel room for us for tonight. We should possibly take a toothbrush and a change of underwear."

"A hotel, where? Why?"

"I'll tell you on the way. I don't want to hang around here just now."

"What've you done?"

"Mel, just get your things, will you. I've got a few other things to find and then we're out of here."

"Oh fuck. Here we go again."

At the docks' car park. I opened the car from a distance with the key and then swept the underside as well as I could with a mirror on a stick.

"Really?" Mel said.

"Yes," I said.

"Whatever."

I put my bag in the boot, slid the Sig out of my trouser waistband and put it under the seat and we set off into the city.

"Right then, Si. What the fuck?"

"Equals?"

"Of course."

"We're off to interrogate the Russian. Okay with you?"

"Definitely."

"Good. Fuck this."

"What?"

"All these bloody cars. You're driving. I need some more sleep."

I pulled over and she willingly swapped with me.

Before I let myself settle down, I reached into the back for a phone-charging lead and saw that the Landrover had taken up station four cars behind us.

I woke to her saying my name and the crunch of gravel under our tyres. We'd just turned into the fine avenue of limes and the hotel was revealing itself between the passing tree trunks. It stood out in its lawns, square and uncompromising; a fine piece of Georgian exuberance with a Palladian portico.

Mel was driving slowly and looking at it too. In front of it, a girl in a pink dress was chasing a West Highland Terrier about on the grass and a boy, younger, in a perfect miniature tweed suit was swinging his legs on a bench next to his nanny.

"I haven't been here since that ball when you went off with Tabitha," she said.

"I don't remember that," I said. The sleep had done me good, and I was feeling like food. What with one thing and another, I hadn't given lunch the attention it deserved.

"You wouldn't. What're we here for? I mean, do we have a plan? Are the Russians here?"

"We're just a pair of young lovers, of course. Let's check in and order something to eat."

We followed the drive round to the back of the house, left the car in the wide gravel car park and walked back. The path led through box hedging to the old stable yard which now contained the outside pool and spa facilities. The sun was low enough to throw shadows from the buildings across the flagstones and a dragonfly was cruising in and out of the light and shade, hunting for his supper. A girl in a nurse's uniform was sitting in one of the chairs that was still in the sun, reading a book with an air of patience. Not far from her, an elderly man in a wheelchair with a rug over his knees was dozing.

We followed the path to the back entrance, and then a corridor past the kitchens to reception. The place still had the confident informality that I remembered. A charmingly efficient young woman signed us in and led us up the wide staircase to a light, high-ceilinged room that looked out over the gardens. Mel sat on the four-poster and bounced up and down experimentally.

"Will it do?" I said.

"I'm in heaven."

"Come on, let's eat while we're still alive."

"You think we're in danger?"

"I mean, I think I'm about to die of starvation."

I wanted to eat on the terrace but Mel vetoed the idea so we sat at a nice round table at the back of the dining room. A thoroughly acceptable Haut-Medoc went down nicely with some wood-pigeon followed by a slow-roast rib of beef. At the far side of the room, Rodion and Lada Pogodin were also having supper. I refrained from looking at them and so did Mel.

"What?" Mel said, noticing that I was looking at her.

"I was just appreciating how beautiful you are."

"Thank you."

"In a way, I'm flattered that you asked me for help."

"I..." She stopped herself.

"Was it Grace?" I said.

She looked at me, not answering.

"You could always fool me, couldn't you?" I said.

"Of course. If I wanted to."

"That day at the marina... You weren't surprised to see me. You knew I would be there. You were just pissed off with me.

"You went away without saying anything."

"I'm sorry."

"I know. We did that."

"Well, Mel. I don't know what the fuck you're really up to, but if you want my help, you're welcome to it. Is your friend in the Landrover going to join us for desert?"

"Sometimes I hate you."

"That's your problem. Who is he?"

"Who's your friend? The one you keep phoning?"

"Can't tell you. Not my secret to share."

"Same here."

"Fine."

There was one of those silences for a bit.

"Si," she said.

"What?"

"Nothing. Shut up. Finish your pudding already and take me to bed."

"Oh. Okay, Mel."

In the morning, I was feeling good. That's what Mel said anyway, and she was right. I got out of bed and opened the window wide to let it in the beautiful early-summer morning. The only clouds were fluffy and high up and the air had the sweet crispness that promises well for the day. Outside, the blackbirds were busy on the lawn and a pair of wood pigeons were calling out their domestic bliss from one of the lime trees in the avenue.

I had a big stretch and yawned enough to nearly split my head and then shook out my limbs. It was good to be alive.

"You look like a self-satisfied cat that just woke up and is considering how many mice to slaughter," Mel said. "Or possibly whether to go back to sleep."

"You look like a great reason to come back to bed," I said, doing that.

"No. No more. Now tell me, what the plan is, if you have one."

"Sure." I made a gentle grab for her but she slapped my hand away and got out of the other side of the bed.

"I said, no. It's time for work now."

"Oh."

"Don't look at me like that."

"Aw."

"The plan, you prick."

"If I must, but I think better after…"

"No, you don't. After, you get sleepy like every other man."

"That's actually true."

"So?"

"This Russian; I'm sure he's not a man to mess about with."

"And your point is?"

"I don't know. This London gang…"

"Them again. What about them?"

"It all feels effective, impersonal. You know what I mean?"

"Yes… sort of. So?"

"These two; they seem human somehow. It doesn't fit. I just think we shouldn't assume anything."

"What do you mean?"

"Let's try to do this without making an enemy, if we can."

"Yes, but how?"

"I don't know, but I thought you could subtly keep an eye on them and see if you can figure out how to get them alone for a bit. Just for a chat."

"Oh, *I* can, can I. And what're you going to do, while I'm doing that, you complete shit?"

"And I expect your friend in the Landrover will give you a hand. I'm going to take a gentle stroll in the English countryside."

"Why?"

"Because I want to, and because I've promised to go and see Grace," I said.

"Oh."

"That's okay with you then?"

"I suppose it'll have to be. Just don't be long."

We had an excellent full English on the terrace. Three tables down, it appeared that Rodion and Lada Pogodin did too. Mine came with lots of excellent coffee and a considerable amount of unexpressed hostility from the direction of Mel.

"There's a spa," I said.

"I know there's a bloody spa," she said.

"And perhaps you could make friends with some of the staff."

"Do you think I'm stupid?"

"I think you're beautiful," I said, smiling. Her anger had made her look very fine. "You can text me if you learn anything."

After some more coffee, I left a conflicted but purposeful Mel heading towards the outside pool with sunglasses, her laptop and a notebook, and walked through the more formal gardens and then through some of the shrubberies beyond to the car park. There was a familiar looking longwheel base Landrover sitting at the back of it under a tree, but no sign of any occupant.

The powerful little Jag wanted to leap down the avenue of limes but I made it restrain itself, and then we followed a tractor towing a muck-spreader to the end of the lane. I hadn't driven it on a proper road yet. I went right, away from the village, passed the turnings for the old Abbey grounds and Home Farm, and shortly afterwards pulled up on the gravel drive of the Dower House.

Rather than making Giles answer the front door, I walked through the gateway into the garden. Grace was at a table under a Mulberry tree and Hermes and Apollo were lying on the grass not far away. As usual they raised their heads briefly to see who I was and then went back to sleeping. Grace looked up from her tablet and saw me. She didn't let her face show it, but I was certain she was annoyed.

"Simon," Grace said. "I didn't know you were coming."

"Sorry," I said.

"You don't look it," she said.

I'm pretty immune to these things, but a sensitive flower might have withered somewhat at this point.

"Well, Grace," I said, "considering you hired me to do a job for you, without telling me, I've come to ask you to explain yourself."

Hermes and Apollo sat up and looked at me. Giles appeared and stopped dead-still and looked at me too. I had the impression that time stood still and held its breath.

"Ah, yes. I'd forgotten what it's like to be spoken to like that," Grace said. "And I am glad you've come. I want to talk to you."

The dogs lay back down and Giles said, "I'll fetch some more tea, my lady."

"I mean no disrespect," I said, "but you got me, not someone else. And I don't like it when people get me involved in something without being straight with me about it."

"Explain what you mean."

"Mel came to find me and asked me to help her. Are you going to tell me it wasn't you who got her to do that?"

"No. I did that."

"Good. So, now tell me why, and what you know about it all."

She looked me dead in the eye, coiled and alive and as friendly as a north wind.

"Why is easy; because you're a hunter and I want something caught and killed."

"Caught and killed, not prosecuted and questioned?"

"You'll want to kill it when you find it."

"Will I?"

"I believe so. What I know, is very little. The daughters of my friends are being preyed upon like so many sheep. Precious, beautiful girls are being taken and used for something and then killed. I want it stopped, but I do not want it talked about. You are a suitable person to do that for me."

"I see. Or at least, I think I see."

"You have the instincts and the training of a hunter and you're one of life's natural killers. Through your father, and this policeman, you now have the resources of the state to assist you. I want you to find whoever is doing this, and when you do, I expect you to either deal with them as you see fit, or inform me and I will."

"You will?"

"I am not without resources."

"I see. My relationship with Bill, and Dad for that matter, isn't a one-way street. They may have their own opinions about what should be done, when and if, I find these people."

"Mr Smith has a reputation for good sense and discretion. More importantly, he has his own sense of what is right and wrong and is willing to put that ahead of what people call the law."

"You seem to know him. And Dad?"

"I've never managed to discern any strong moral sense in your father, but his loyalty to his friends is beyond question. And to you."

"Fair enough. What's the connection with this area?"

"I didn't know there was one."

"Two of the girls come from families that have connections to the Hampshire/Wiltshire area. So do I, so does Mel and so do you. That's obvious, isn't it?"

"I don't know."

"And one of the people who has my attention at the moment, a Russian pharmaceuticals oligarch, is staying at Melton House, just down the road from here. Don't you find that strange?"

"Yes, I do."

"And?"

"And, I will think about that and tell you what I can."

"What you can?"

"Yes. What I can. Tell me about this Russian."

I told her what I knew about him. She didn't comment but looked thoughtful.

"Also, do you know anything about some London people called Green?" I said.

"They own eating and drinking places in London, I believe."

"But you don't know anything about them beyond that?"

"No. I imagine my son would, but I've never set foot in any of them, nor do I intend to."

"Does the name Wendy Russell mean anything to you?"

"I don't think so, no."

"Is there anything else that you should tell me? Anything else you know or suspect that you haven't told me?"

"That I should tell you, no."

"I see."

We looked at each other in silence for a bit. Whatever we had been to each other before, we were something different now.

"Next time you want me to do something for you, ask me directly," I said.

"We will see," she said. "I may do, or I may not."

"I see," I said, and I didn't refrain from letting her see how I felt about that.

"You were a good choice for this," she said. "What are you going to do now?"

"Right now, I'm going to go for a walk on the estate with my lovely gun. If you have no objection?"

"Not in the slightest."

I sat with her and we drank the tea that Giles brought. By mutual consent, we left the main subject of conversation be, and talked about her garden and the rising year instead. There was still a deal of tension between us, but it was a more honest thing now.

"Here you are, Master Ellice," Giles said, returning with the gun and a bag of cartridges.

"Thanks, Giles," I said, giving him a wink.

I hung the open gun over my arm, the bag over my shoulder, gave them both a cheery smile and headed for the garden gate.

The long meadow had been cut and baled for haylage. The big round bales stood about where they had been dropped, like a mysterious agricultural henge. I paused to smell one, it smelt wonderful, rich and warm and friendly with a hint of fermentation already. Then I wandered through them in the direction of the path that led down to the hedge towards the White Wood.

I followed it with no great expectation of game; if I was serious about that, I would've been up and about much earlier. My best chance would lie in the margins of the wood where there was more cover. I glanced down the barrels, to be certain, slipped a pair of cartridges in and shut her; an unloaded gun is just a complicated stick.

I stretched my legs happily, the short stubble brushing against my trainers and the ground under-foot hard and cracked in places. It was good to be off the tarmac and out of the city.

Having the heavy, smooth, familiar feel of the gun in my hands gave me that old frisson of excitement. I moved her about gently in my hands getting to know the balance of her.

When a bunny scuttled for cover, she was up and the hammers back without any conscious thought on my part. I put her at him with deliberation and plenty of time and tumbled him over, welcoming the gun's kick into my shoulder.

The rabbit, when I picked him up, was sweet and rabbity and soft and quite dead. This year's buck; good eating. I squeezed out his bladder with my thumb and then paunched him with my pocket knife, shucking his intestines into the long grass. I threaded one hind leg through the achilles tendon of the other and hung him on a branch of the hedge in the shade. I would pick him up on the way back.

Where the field turned the corner, it gave onto a bridleway into the wood. I followed it in. It was deliciously dappled in there and had the feeling of privacy that you get when you're within the trees. It drew me on, and before I'd expected it, I came up against the walls of the old Abbey that intruded into the corner of the wood.

It was a serious piece of wall; old but sturdy. On top of it were strong metal uprights holding wire. A thick roll of razor wire, as it happened. As far as I could remember that hadn't been there when I was a kid. I walked along beside it, idly looking for wrens' nests in the moss and wondering how I might get a look over it.

One of the magical things about a wood is that moving through it constantly reveals and hides what is not far from you. This means that if you are quiet and alert, you may find yourself coming as a surprise to a deer, badger, or fox going about their business. Alternatively, you may be subject to surprises yourself.

I was standing looking up at the wall when a voice disturbingly close to me said, "So, who're you to be carrying a gun on this land, then? Eh?"

I turned round and saw a shortish, stocky chap of indeterminate age looking at me with shrewd, dark eyes from only a few feet away. He had on an old corduroy cap, his clothes were dull browns and greens but they were neat and clean and his trouser legs were tucked into his socks. He had an old, but rather nice looking, double barrelled twenty-bore over his arm and was accompanied by what looked like a cross between a long-legged jack russell and an ill-tempered yard brush.

"Morning." I said. "I'm Simon and I'm a friend of Lady Grace. Who're you?"

"Are you? You don't look like someone who would be friends with her ladyship. Though you never know." I presumed he was referring to my clothes, which were my normal worn and scruffy outfit.

"I am, honestly," I said.

"Don't I know you? Didn't I once chase you out of the east spiny? And caught you too, as I remember."

"And cuffed me good and hard, but didn't tell on me," I said.

"So I did. That makes you one of them, I suppose."

"I'm Albert Ellice's grandson."

"Of course you are. I'm Herbert Morningstar, but I won't be called Bert so people call me Morny."

"As I well remember. These days, people generally call me Si," I said. We shook hands.

"Well, Si. I don't suppose I have to chase you off this time, which is good as I'm not sure I could any longer."

"I'm glad we don't have to find out."

"Was it the east spinney? I'm not sure now," he said, looking at me questioningly.

"I can't remember," I said.

"Ah, well. Never mind. You'll be staying with her ladyship?"

"I'm at the hotel, actually. Just a spur of the moment thing."

"I see. Well, I'll probably see you about. I must get on now so I'll wish you a good morning. You'll be leaving this piece quiet; there's does with fawns hereabouts I'd rather not see moved. There's a mort of rabbits in the old conygres and down by the orchard yonder, if you've a mind. And plenty as'll take them off you, if you've spare."

"Thanks for the tip, I'll not trespass on your preserves this time."

"Not mine; I'm only steward, and a passing through, like. But I appreciate it." He moved to go.

"Morny," I said.

"Hm?" he said, pausing.

"There's wire on the wall?"

"Yes."

"Why?"

"To keep the nutters in, of course."

"What nutters?"

"Psychiatric patients. You've been away a long time. That's a loony bin now."

"I didn't know that."

"Yup. There's some really mad and bad nutters in there. Apparently."

16

A SCREAMING PEACOCK

I walked back out of the wood and found my rabbit with no trouble. There'd been no communication from Mel and I didn't feel like going back to the hotel yet, so I turned in to the yard of Home Farm to say hello to the girls who ran it. There was an old Landrover, a short-wheel base one this time, in the inner yard but no sign of Lizzy or Cal or Julie. I hammered on the kitchen door of the house and waited. Nothing happened except a bumble bee passed by.

For the want of any other plan, I took the path round the side of the house. It went through an arch in a high wall. Beyond was a walled kitchen garden of about two acres. It was fantastic. Laid out in beds of vegetables and soft fruit, salad and flowers for cutting. There were tomatoes, pumpkins, brassicas of all kinds and colours, the flowery tops of carrots, a bed of sunflowers reaching up and in between them all, companion plantings of herbs, nasturtiums and marigolds. I took the nearest path and started walking through it, enjoying the scents and luxuriance. Honey bees were working the dwarf lavenders.

"What do you know, it's the wandering hay chucker," a woman said, stepping out from behind a trellis of sweet peas. It was Julie. She was still wearing the same dungarees.

"Hi, Julie," I said.

"You seem to be armed," she said, looking at the old gun with interest.

"And potentially dangerous," I said, opening the bag to reveal the rabbit. "At least to the rabbits."

"You can have a go at the ones in the orchard, if you like. They've a habit of trying to get in here and they're not welcome."

"I can imagine. Thanks, I just might do that," I said.

"But don't shoot Champion."

"Champion?"

"The wonder horse."

"Ah. Does he look like a rabbit?"

"No. He doesn't look much like a horse, but he doesn't look like a rabbit either."

"Then I promise not to shoot him. This is amazing, by the way. I'm very impressed."

"We're not having a bad year so far," she said noncommittally, and then stood there looking at me.

"And it's a lot of work and you have to get on with it?" I said.

"It keeps growing," she said, smiling. "And the weeds with it."

"If you're willing to pay me in a drop of cider and possibly a crust of bread, I could lend you a hand for a bit," I said.

"Lend me a hand?" she said. "What are you, some kind of itinerant agricultural knight errant?"

"If you like," I said. "What would you like me to do?"

"The potatoes need earthing-up. But it's pretty hard work," she said.

"Do you have me down as a work-shy weakling?" I said.

"Not as I recall."

"Well then."

"You'll find a spade and a big hoe leaning on the wall over there," she pointed, "if you go and fetch them and meet me over there," she nodded to a wide area of spuds at the far end of the next section, "we'll find out, won't we."

"Yes, boss."

I'm not one of nature's natural gardeners, but I can handle a spade and the exercise in the fresh air and sunshine was just what I wanted. Julie was right, it was hard work and by the time I'd been doing it for an hour the rows started to look longer.

It took me another half to finish and I was glad to stand up and have a good stretch. I took my tools with me and went to find Julie. She was tying up a row of tomatoes and pinching out unwanted shoots.

"Okay, what's next?" I said.

"You've done it?" she said.

"I have," I said.

"Oh?"

"Don't you believe me?"

"Let's have a look, shall we."

We went over to the potatoes and she walked up the ends of the rows, looking down them with a critical eye.

"Hm," she said.

"Any good?" I said.

"It'll do," she said. "Have you ever…" she was interrupted by the deafeningly loud screech of a peacock which had taken up position on top of the wall near us, "… have you ever shot a peafowl?" she said.

"Yes, as it happens," I said.

"Well, feel free to do it again. Noisy, bloody things. Made me jump."

"So, why do you keep them?"

"We don't. The bastard things wander over from the Hall. I don't think anyone feeds them over there."

"I quite like it. Reminds me of home," I said. "Not that we ever actually had any. I probably mean the Hall."

"Bloody strange kind of thing you are. I was going to say, have you ever planted out a bed of courgettes, but you probably had people to do that kind of thing for you."

"No I didn't. And I haven't. But if you show me how, I'm willing to have a go," I said.

"I expect you will too. Right, follow me, my lord," she said.

By the time she relented and called it lunch, I'd done quite a bit of gardening. There was soil right under the nails of every finger, my trousers had taken another step in the direction of dissolution and my back was telling me I was being unkind to it. She seemed to take some satisfaction from all of this.

She'd passed a big plastic bucket full of weeds to me and bade me follow her towards the compost bins and I was asking myself where I'd put my gun and rabbit, when we were interrupted. A slim, elegant woman of middle years appeared from behind the runner beans. She was wearing light summer clothes, which seemed slightly too formal for some reason, and a large floppy hat and was carrying a long wooden trug. She seemed vaguely familiar, but I couldn't immediately place her.

"Ah, there you are, Julie," she said. "I was passing so I thought I'd pick up the flowers for tonight. Are they ready?"

"Yes, Mrs Dutton," Julie said. "I put them in the shade by the rhubarb."

"Ah, well done. Who's this then?" she said, looking down at me from a considerable social hight.

"My name's Simon, Mrs," I said, letting a little of the speech of the village slip into my voice. "From over Aldermark way. Just helping out a bit."

"Very good. I'm glad you've found someone, Julie. He looks a bit stronger than Cal." She assessed my physique dispassionately.

"I can drive a tracre alright too, Mrs," I said.

"Glad to hear it. Now, Julie, you'll have the boxes ready for the house this afternoon?"

"I will, Mrs Dutton," Julie said.

"Good. Can you deliver them, do you think? Charlie's given Chris the day off." I got the impression that staff having time off wasn't a concept she readily accepted.

"I'm not sure…" Julie said.

"I'll drop them round, Mrs," I said.

"Very good. Right, I'll leave you to it," the woman said. She turned and went and I could see that we'd ceased to exist for her in the instant.

"I always fucking do," Julie said, when she was sure that the woman was out of earshot.

"Your best customer?" I said.

"Francesca Dutton. Our biggest customer. And she likes me to know it," she said. "Snobby cow. Why did you do that?"

"What? Offer to deliver her stuff?"

"No, pretend to be local."

"I am local. Couldn't be bothered to try and explain myself, that's all."

"I don't think you're explicable. Actually, yes, why did you offer?"

"To help you, of course."

"Thanks. I think."

"And there's a girl I met the other day who I'm supposed to be having a race with. A red-head. She lives there, doesn't she?"

"You know Jess?"

"That's the one. Met her by the ford on a horse the other day. She's promised to lend me a mount."

"You're going to ride with Jess Dutton?"

"That's the plan."

"Fucking hell, that sort of makes sense in a weird way."

"Seems like it to me. Is it lunchtime yet?"

"Suppose it might be. Bread, cheese and a drop of cider?"

"With all my heart."

I followed Julie back to the farmhouse. The door led into a hallway with stairs straight up ahead of us. To the right was a sitting room. We went left into the kitchen. The walls were thick and the windows small, so it was cave-like and cool. There were plain wooden cupboards along the wall and a range where the chimney must be. In the centre of the room was an old pine table with wooden chairs round it. Lizzy was sitting in one of them working on a laptop. She had on a loose pink top and shorts. She looked more tanned and healthy and vital than last time, if that were possible.

"Oh, it's you again," she said, looking at me and then the gun I was carrying.

"He's been gardening this time," Susie said.

"Hi Lizzy," I said, smiling.

"Was he any good?" she said.

"I've known worse," Julie said. "I'm letting him have a bit of lunch."

"Is it that time already?" Lizzy said.

"Yes. Put that away and let's eat," Julie said.

"Outside," Lizzy said.

"If you like," Julie said.

Lizzy shut her laptop, got up and went and opened the door and went out into the back garden. Light flooded into the dark room. I stood Thomas up against the wall beside a long-case clock and followed her out. She had nice legs. Not that clean, but very nice.

There was a paved area with a table and chairs, beds of herbs and roses. A heavy scented honeysuckle climbed trellis on the wall. The lawn needed mowing and the flower beds were a riot of granny's bonnets and lupins and foxgloves and hollyhocks.

"This is where we usually eat in the summer," Lizzy said, carefully lifting a tray of drying seed-heads from the table.

"I can see why," I said.

"Well, don't just stand there; go and fetch stuff," she said.

We ate bread with lettuce, tomatoes, cold sausage and cheese and washed it down with a little rough cider. Butterflies flickered about on the buddleia and hoverflies hovered, and then zoomed and then hovered, over the flowers. The sunshine was warm and the only sound from beyond the garden was a lawnmower in the distance, occasional punctuated by the call of a peafowl. I may have eaten a better meal, but this one was definitely up there.

"That's an old gun you have there," Lizzy said.

"My grandfather's," I said. "Would you like the rabbit?"

"You don't want it?" Julie said.

"I'm eating at the hotel I think," I said.

"You're staying at Melton House?" Lizzy said.

"And he's just spent most of the morning gardening," Julie said.

"Yup," I said.

"You are an odd sort of being," she said.

"We should probably be nice to him. He might do some more," Lizzy said.

"You are being nice to me," I said. "But you do seem a bit short handed. No offence to Cal, of course."

"None taken. Yes, we had a chap called Ray, but he disappeared," Lizzy said.

"Disappeared?"

"Ran off with one of the girls from the Rectory over by Effington," she said. "Pretty thing called Ivanka."

"The Dutton's place?" I said.

"That's them," Julie said. "How did you know that?"

"Native as the coney, me," I said.

"Yeah, right," Lizzy said.

"I am," I said.

"If that's what happened," Julie said.

"What do you mean?" I said.

"Julie thinks they're buried in the White Wood," Lizzy said.

"No I don't," Julie said. "It just doesn't make sense, that's all. Ray loved those cows and there's no reason I can see why they'd have to run off. Maybe one of the other Poles at the Hall didn't like it; well, tough. It wasn't like she wouldn't have been able to do her job or anything. Or him either."

"Perhaps she was married to someone else," Lizzy said.

"So? In which case, she could've got un-married," Julie said. "Or just got on with it anyway. People do, you know."

"I know," Lizzy said. "What's your explanation then?"

"I don't have one. I'm just saying it's odd, that's all."

"And bloody inconvenient," Lizzy said.

"Perhaps they got eaten by the nutters?" I said.

"Could be," Julie said.

"Morny was telling me they keep some real psychos in there?" I said.

"You know Morny?" Julie said.

"Since I was a kid."

"Well bloody hell, perhaps you are a local."

"You wouldn't know it," Lizzy said. "They keep themselves to themselves, the inmates, but I think it's more a case of lost souls than man-eating monsters. We supply them with quite a lot of produce. Meat and veg."

"Lost souls like this odd fish here, perhaps," Julie said, indicating me with a smile. "That's where you're really from, isn't it? Explains everything."

"Who runs it?" I said. "Perhaps I should go and find out. At least I'll bet the grub is good."

"Chap called Dr Simm. Don't see much of him, but he seems nice enough. They sponsor the village fete," Julie said.

"And are good neighbours," Lizzy said.

"Why in the White Wood?" I said.

"Why what in the White Wood?" Julie said.

"Why did you say thingy and whatshername were buried in it?"

"Oh, that's just what they say about it. Have you been in it?" Lizzy said.

"Not really. A bit when I was a kid, but not much. I met Morny in the outskirts of it near the Abbey wall this morning," I said.

"That doesn't surprise me," Lizzy said. "He haunts the place. There's a track right into the middle, if you can find it. I've been there, but only once. There's a clearing with a big stone and the Fyne brook rises there. If ever there was a spot where Druids sacrificed maidens, that's it."

"It's just a big wood, is all," Julie said. "But it's thick and tangly and people don't go in it much. I don't believe they ever did sacrifice people. That's just Romans making up stories. You know; history is written by the victors."

"Speaking of which," Lizzy said, starting to collect up our plates. "We should get back to the fight."

"That we should," Julie said. "What about you, Mr wandering whateveryouare?"

"Hang on, I'll find out," I said, and checked my phone. No communication from Mel.

"Girlfriend?" Lizzy said.

"Wife, probably," Julie said.

"My boss," I said. "No, I'm free. You can have me a bit longer, if you want me."

"Oh, we want you," Lizzy said.

"What is it you do again?" Julie said.

"Whatever you tell me to, Julie," I said.

"Well then, now I'm telling you to go and find the barrow. Cal's probably left it somewhere near the pigs. And we'll go cut some stuff and then load you up and send you off to make your delivery. Okay?"

"Fine with me." I said, and ambled off with the swallows passing over my head.

Cal was in the outer yard leaning on a muck-fork. "It's you again," he said. "I'll be thinking you're after my job soon."

"Don't worry," I said. "I think you're irreplaceable."

"I expect I am," he said, complacently.

Over the hedge, I watched the top of a van appear from the direction of the Dower House and approach us. It was a silver-grey transit. A silver-grey transit…

"There's a van coming," I said.

"So there is," he said. "They do that."

"Where's it going, do you think?"

"That van?" he said, looking at it more closely.

"Yes," I said.

"Oh, tha's going to the nut-house," he said.

"How do you know that?" I said.

"Cos tha's the kind of van they have there," he said.

"You know a lot, Cal," I said.

"I does, doesn't I," he said.

17

FACES OF DESIRE

Landrovers are a funny business. They get to be like the old dog that hangs around the yard; smelly and a bit difficult, but you're never going to shoot it until you absolutely have to. I got the one belonging to the farm up into second gear at the third try and discovered that it would respond to the steering if you gave it enough notice. Luckily there was nothing coming when I got to the road; why I thought it would have effective brakes, I've no idea. I trundled past the Dower House and on into the village and the stupid thing made me smile in spite of myself.

I rattled and bounced my way up to Edgar's Cross and took the bridleway that cuts the corner off the road proper and, having effectively circled back around the other side of the White Wood, pulled into the forecourt of the Rectory on the outskirts of Effington.

It was bigger than I expected; clearly the God business had been lucrative in this diocese at some point. The Victorians had added a section that filled in the space between the main building and the old stable block. It was slightly lower than the original Georgian bit, so it didn't spoil the look of the place too much, but there was quite a lot of it.

I passed through a gateway and found myself in a yard with industrial sized wheelie bins along one wall, a couple of small vans and, in a covered space, a Bentley and a new Mercedes Sprinter with blacked out windows. There were four entrances into the various bits of the Victorian section and associated buildings, and beyond that, a wide archway leading to the stables. I could see the open doors of a couple of loose boxes, but no horses in residence.

I parked next to one of the vans and opened the back door of the landy. It was stacked high with veg, fruit and salad in boxes and old paper sacks. I lifted a big bunch of sweet peas off the top and headed through a small gate in the wall near the entrance to the stables, which my instinct said would lead to the gardens. It did.

I let myself be lured away from the house, through rose beds and then into a long section of raised lawn with a deep bed of perennials running along between it and the bordering wall. The bed was a mass of colour and scent and sound. Full of butterflies, hoverflies and honey bees. I paused to smell a pink phlox that was bursting out of a patch of queen anne's lace. I wouldn't have minded lying down on the soft grass for a bit.

The lawn terminated in a sizeable bronze of Artemis. I passed her and took the path back towards the house. Between the trees, I had occasional views of the house. Seen from here it was serene and lovely in its setting of lawns and flowerbeds and trees. Some of the upstairs windows of the main house were open and I could see a woman in a uniform making up a bed through one.

The Victorian section looked more closed up, but not entirely as, at that moment, there was movement at one window. The net curtain prevented me from seeing any detail and it wasn't repeated.

There was a path through some arching roses that led to the side of the house furthest from where I'd parked. I took it and it led me to an orangery. The door was shut and the plants had been arranged so that they obscured the interior. I walked slowly and did my best to catch glimpses of the inside. I could see the back of someone's head between some palm fronds and at one point I think I saw a slippered foot. That was all. No sign of Jess.

Further along, the French doors of a lovely big drawing room were open onto the terrace. Francesca Dutton was sitting at a table studying a piece of paper through reading glasses. She had a pen poised over it and beside the paper on the polished mahogany was a black short-wave radio receiver. I entered.

She looked up, frowning.

"'Scuse me, Mrs Dutton. D'you want the flowers here?" I said, holding them out.

"Oh. Who… Oh, yes," she said.

"Simon, Mrs Dutton. From the farm," I said, dipping my head. "Delivering the veg and that, like I said."

"Of course. Thank you. You give them to the kitchen. And the flowers. They will know what to do with them."

"Yes, Mrs Dutton."

"Oh, and, Simon," she said.

"Yes, Mrs Dutton," I said.

"The outside staff don't come into the house," she said.

"I'm sorry," I said.

"You weren't to know," she said.

I was just leaving when Charlie came into the room. He was walking quickly and had the air of a busy man organising things.

"Ah, there you are," he said. "Mrs P doesn't eat…"

He stopped when he saw me.

"I know, she told me," Francesca Dutton said. "This is Simon. He's just started at the farm."

"Er, you mustn't …" he started to say.

"I've told him," she said.

"… Okay, good. Have you got the…" he stopped paying me any attention and I made a suitably bucolic departure.

When I got back to the yard, I grabbed a box of veg from the Landy and went exploring. One of the doors leading off the yard had a stack of boxes and trugs outside it, so I ignored it and tried one of the others. It opened onto a bare lobby with the blank doors of a lift and simple wooden stairs.

Through the next one, I found myself looking into what appeared to be a staff room. There was a TV in one corner, tables chairs, two armchairs by the fireplace, a kettle, a fridge, half-filled ashtrays, a row of hooks by the door with a number of coats hung up on it. A man looked up from a paper and grunted at me.

"Co z tego?" he said.

"The kitchen?" I said.

"Does this look like it?" he said.

"No," I said and backed out.

The next door, a wide one, revealed a massive wood-fired boiler. There were heavy bins on wheels, some of them full of chipped wood, and a neat conveyor belt system for filling the hopper above the beast itself. I had a quick look through the glass peephole and saw an almost white-hot light within its belly. In hindsight, the tall stainless steel chimney sticking out of the roof above it would have been a clue to what was in there.

The kitchen, when I pushed the swing door open, was big and well equipped. There was a lot of very clean stainless steel and three people hard at work. The biggest and oldest looked up from peering into a massive oven and narrowed his eyes at me.

"Who are you and what do you want?" he said. His English was good but he had a Polish accent.

"I was sent from the farm with your vegetables," I said, raising the box.

"About time. Greg, take them in." He went off to do something else without giving me any more of his valuable time. One of the others, Greg presumably, took the box from me and said, "You bring."

"I'll bring and you can help," I said, giving him a grin.

"Ugh," he said, but came out with me, and, together we carried in the supplies. I gave him the piece of paper that Julie had given me, and he made a mark on it, and that was it. I filled the Landy with the empties from by the door and persuaded the poor old thing to point its nose homeward and off I went again.

An acerbic text from Mel finally summoned me back to the hotel, so when I got back to the farm, I left the Landy to sleep in its corner, hung Thomas over my arm and accepted a sack of carrots for the hotel and a warm smile from Julie.

"Say goodbye to Lizzy for me, wherever she is," I said.

"I will. She's out fetching in the coos for the evening milking," she said. "Feel free to come again any time."

"I would like that," I said, and let myself enjoy the swallows again as I walked through the yard. Actually, I thought, I really would like that.

Grace wasn't in evidence when I walked in through the garden and into the orangery, but I found Giles in the kitchen. He accepted Thomas and promised to clean her. I put the bag of carrots in the boot of the little car, where they took up most of the space, and drove back to the hotel. There were people enjoying the sunshine on the terrace as usual. I followed the drive round to the back, parked, retrieved the carrots and started wandering back towards the hotel.

"Ah, my man," a voice said, from not far away.

I turned round to give it some attention. There was a chap who might have been a decayed Guards officer standing by a slightly rusty XJ6 Jaguar. He was looking at me from a moral and social height and with some impatience.

It would have been unsporting to hit him, so I said, "Afternoon, sir," instead.

"Good. Come here will you, and give me a hand with this lot," he said, opening the back door of the car and ignoring the fact that I already had a sack over one shoulder.

I attended at my best bucolic amble. I hadn't bothered to expect anything, but if I had, it wouldn't have been a pile of large books. I obligingly held out my spare arm and onto it he piled two volumes of the Almanach de Gotha, a battered Burke's Peerage, a volume of Debretts, and something else that had a title in a language I couldn't read. They were none of them small, and altogether it was a lot of book. He himself carried a briefcase and a large scroll done up with a purple ribbon.

"Handsomely does it then. Doesn't do to be late. Follow me," he said and led off through a gap in the box hedging. A path between magnolias took us past outbuildings and a massive LPG tank, half frozen. I paused to look through a doorway into the courtyard containing the beautiful outside swimming pool. A couple were swimming steady lengths but otherwise it was deserted.

The man swimming looked up and watched the chap I was following. With his hair plastered down over his forehead, I didn't recognise him immediately and then the quality of his gaze reminded me. It was Mr Pogodin.

"Don't dawdle there," the idiot said, holding the door for me.

I gently deposited the books on a nice round mahogany table in a little sitting room, as directed. He could have thanked me but it didn't occur to him. I followed him out into the hallway where he rang the bell on the reception desk.

"Will you let Mr and Mrs Wallace know that I'm here. I'm in the Peacock room," he said to the young woman who appeared from the cubbyhole office behind it.

"Good afternoon, sir. I take it, they're expecting you?"

"Of course, girl. I wouldn't be here otherwise, would I."

"Very good, sir. May I take them your name?"

"Don't you know me? I'm here often enough. Major Smythe. And we'll have some coffee, if you can manage that?"

I lowered an eyelid to the receptionist as I passed behind the major and wandered off in the direction of the kitchens. She gave me an answering flicker of a smile.

I passed my burden to a junior kind of chef person and retreated upstairs to our room. Mel was lying on the bed with her laptop on her lap, chewing a pencil and looking cross.

"There you are. Where've you been?" she said.

"I've been gardening," I said.

"Why? You're filthy. Get off!"

"Ah, well. To what green altar, O mysterious priest, lead'st thou that heifer lowing at the skies, and all her silken flanks with garlands drest?" I said.

"What did you say?" She sat up, drew back and looked at me like I'd just said something terrible.

"Easy," I said. "It's only a line of Keats that was running in my head. Just musing on why someone might've wanted our girls. I've been reconnoitring the landscape, that's all. Listening to the local gossip, that kind of thing."

"Oh." She seemed to relax a bit. "Why?"

"Rodion and Lada must be here for a reason. You've got the hotel covered so I was checking out the environs. Grace says hello. How's that going by the way?"

"You are a shit. What did you find out?"

"I found out that the peacocks from hall still wander about and annoy the locals."

"Is that all?"

"Pretty much, but I had a very nice afternoon."

She tried hitting me and I let her, a bit.

"Feeling better yet?" I said, reaching for her.

"You're filthy. Get off."

"Okay, I'll go have a shower."

A shower was all I got. We had supper on the terrace, and so did Rodion and Lada.

"I'd forgotten how great it was growing up round here," I said.

"It soon gets old," she said. "There's actually nothing to do here."

"I shot a rabbit," I said.

"Why?" she said.

"Just felt like it," I said.

"Correction; there's nothing to do here apart from killing things and farming things. I'll bet you there's hardly a decent place to eat, apart from here, for miles."

I thought about the lunch I'd had at the farm and didn't comment. My phone received a message from Berry, 'Just thinking of popping out, care to join us?'. I showed it to Mel.

"The party seems to be carrying on in town," I said.

"Does that man actually do anything at all like work?" she said.

"Not that I know of," I said.

"It's hard to take him seriously."

"He used to have a pretty serious right cross."

"Sometimes there's not much more to you men than having sex and hitting people," she said.

"Sometimes, there isn't," I said, and sent back, 'gone to rehab, but planning to relapse on my return'.

"And drinking too much and not taking anything seriously," Mel said.

"It's what I'm good at," I said.

"If you go out partying with Susie instead of me, I'll kill you," Mel said. "Or have you killed."

"I'll take that as a no then, shall I?" I said, smiling. "What does he mean, by that?" I showed her the return text from Berry, which said, 'planning a visit to the monastic brethren tomorrow if you're back?'.

"Fucking hell," she said. "I'll bet he means the Friars. Trust Berry to be a member of that."

"The what?"

"It's a kind of… club, I suppose. The Pied Friars."

"You don't sound very sure."

"It's… well, it's definitely the coolest place in town, and…"

"You've never been there?"

"You have to be invited."

"And you never have been?"

"No. For some reason, I never have."

"You just were," I said, waving my phone at her. "Should I say yes?"

"But it's not work, is it?"

"Is it the kind of place we might find beautiful posh birds hanging out?"

"Probably the poshest. Or, at least the coolest."

"I should say yes, then? I promise to go with you, not Susie."

"Oh, alright."

"Don't force yourself." I texted Berry back in the affirmative.

"Talking of work, don't say their names, but tell me what you observed today and what the plan is," I said.

"I told you," she said. "Nothing. He swam. She swam. She read a magazine. He read a book. They took a walk in the garden together. He had the occasional cigar. She doesn't smoke. He made three phone calls. She sent a few texts. I think."

"So, they're waiting for something?"
"Oh. When you put it like that, yes."
"I wonder what."
"Yes."
"And why here?"
"Good point."
"Then we'd better ask them. You have plan for that?"
"Yes, of course. Stop looking at me like that and listen carefully…"

As the sun touched the beech trees in the west, I left Mel sipping a glass of old brandy, passed into the hotel, fetched a carrier bag which had appeared in our room, and slid out of the side door and into the lovely gardens beyond.

Not far from the gateway into the orchard, I found a bench. It was a secluded spot; hidden by the curving path and the tall flowers in the borders. I put my phone on silent and started listening to the sounds of the encroaching evening.

Almost an hour later the light was softening and the songs of the blackbirds were loud in the thickening evening air. My phone vibrated and received a text, 'coming'.

I took a blue boiler-suit out of the bag and put it on. There was a plastic gorilla mask as well. I put that on too. And then I carefully fitted the moderator to the Sig. Then I called myself an idiot and took my shoes off and put them, with the bag, behind a fuchsia.

The Russians appeared, holding hands and walking along like a couple in love. He had a small cigar glowing in his right hand. He saw me, or rather he saw a largish man in a blue boiler-suit wearing a gorilla mask holding a gun, and, warned by the subtle communication between them, she looked up and saw me too. They didn't break step but I saw that they came alert together, as people do who live with the constant possibility of danger. I could feel the weight of his attention.

"Good evening Mr and Mrs Pogodin," I said.

"You know who I am," he said.

"Yes."

"You want money?"

"No, just a few questions."

"My wife will go." He said it as a command, not a suggestion.

"No," I said, and that was a command too, but it had the gun to back it up.

"You will start to die soon," he said. "But it will take a long time."

"Well, if we're being dramatic," I said, "you look like lovers, so I will lay you down together. I have a place prepared for you. It's in a nice place in the woods and I will put some flowers over you."

"What do you want?"

"I'm going to ask you some questions. If you don't answer, I will kill you and be content not to know. If I believe that your answers aren't the truth, I will kill you and be content not to know. If you answer, and I believe you, I may kill you anyway. Or I may not." I raised the gun and centred it on his chest. "Do you believe me?"

"What questions?"

"You were watching a girl called Susana Chesterfield at a place called *Umbra Villus* in a particular way. Why?"

"That is your question?"

"Yes."

"The answer is, that it is not your business."

"Ah well, it's been nice meeting you. Shame it was so brief."

"Wait," Lada said.

"Are you going to answer the question?" I said.

She put a hand on her husband's arm and spoke rapidly in Russian to him. He looked stony-faced but didn't speak. She turned to me, held herself up and stared hard into my eyes.

"Look at me," the woman said.

I looked at her. She was a beautiful, slim, elegant woman. "Yes?" I said.

"I lost my daughter. Our daughter. Twenty years ago. She died."

"Yes?" I said.

"That girl."

"Yes?"

"Do you not see?"

"What?"

"That girl. She looks as she would've looked. If she had lived. We have tried, but…"

"The girl, your daughter?" I began to see it now, there was a distinct similarity. "What of it?"

"Yes. That girl. The girl you won at the auction. Suzana Chesterfield. Do you not see how much she looks like me? As I was at her age. She could be my daughter." She put both hands over her belly and looked at me. Looked at me nakedly, letting me see her hunger. "We will have one last try and that will be it. This is our last chance. That is why we looked at that girl that way. Do you not understand? I think you are a young man; perhaps you cannot understand."

"Perhaps," I said.

"One day perhaps you will want a baby in the way I do," she said. "In the way we do." She took her man's arm and held it protectively.

"You're telling me that's the only reason you were looking at her?" I said.

"I just wanted to be near her while we waited. That is all. I felt that it would make it more possible. I know it's not, you would say, rational, but…"

"So, you mean the girl no harm?" I said.

"Harm! No. Absolutely not! What I wish is that she is my daughter, but she isn't, so we will try once more to have our own," she said. "Maybe this time…"

"And that's the reason you were looking at the girl? The only reason?" I said.

"Yes. I swear it. We did not disturb her. I don't think you can understand what it is like," she said. "We are just waiting and hoping, that is all. I saw her picture in a paper and I wanted to be near her, because... I do not really know why... my husband..." she glanced up at him and I saw his face soften for an instant as he returned her look, "now, I have told you, so do what you wish."

"Thank you," I said.

We stood there looking at each other for a moment while I thought about it.

"You are protecting her?" Lada said. "You are protecting the girl? You are a friend of hers?"

I didn't deny it.

"Good. That is good. She is very precious and very beautiful."

"In which case," I said. "Please accept my apologies. I thought that you might be a threat to her, but I see that I was mistaken. I would like to forget this, but that may be difficult?"

"There will be no problem with that," she said. "My husband will not have you killed for wishing to protect the girl." Looking at his face, I wasn't entirely sure whether to believe her or not, but it wasn't worth worrying about then.

"Okay. If you would care to return to the hotel, that would be good," I said.

"Thank you," she said.

They turned round and started walking away. Before they passed out of sight the man turned his head briefly to look at me once more. I was glad of the mask.

When they had gone, a familiar voice, from behind a clump of hollyhocks, said, "Fucking hell."

"Mel?" I said.

"Poor cow," she said, standing up and delicately stepping out from between the flowers to join me on the path. "It's not them. She really, really wants a baby and I believe she really cares about Susie."

"You're supposed to be safely in the hotel," I said. "Supposing he comes back. Or they check to see who's not accounted for?"

"He won't," she said, with complete certainty. "Don't worry so much. Now take that stupid stuff off and let's go and have a walk in these beautiful gardens before it's time for bed."

"Me, not worry so much?" I looked at the way they'd gone.

"Yes."

"Oh. Okay."

I underwent the necessary transformation, tucking the sig into my trouser waistband under my shirt, just in case. I put the boiler suit and mask back in the bag and tossed it behind the hollyhocks, and then put my arm around Mel's shoulders and she leant against me, and we walked circuitously back towards the hotel.

"How did you get to be so stealthy?" I said. "I was sitting right there and I didn't see or hear you getting behind those hollyhocks."

"You think you're the only one who knows the countryside? This is my landscape too and I have soft shoes on. Besides, you were miles away."

"Was I?"

"Yes."

"I must have been."

There were swallows here too, chattering and fliting to and from their nests under the eaves of the building. We watched them for a bit and then went to bed.

18

THE WHITE WOOD

My internal alarm woke me at 2 am, as I'd asked it to. Mel was snoring sweetly; a gentle sound almost like a purr. She stopped when I slid out of the bed. I sat on the windowsill enjoying the cool night air and listening to the silence of the countryside until she resumed. A fox barked briefly in the distance.

I dressed silently, slipped out of the room and tiptoed down the stairs carrying my trainers. There was no one at reception so I went into the library and stole the binoculars from their place on the sill of the window that overlooked the bird-table. Then I passed through the kitchens, let myself out of the back door, put my trainers on, buttoned the glasses into my shirt, and trotted silently off to the car park. The Landrover was no longer in its place, well that one anyway, there were a few others. I got as quietly as I could into the little Jag and started driving. It wasn't easy interpreting the patches of shadow and starlight but I managed to get the car onto the drive, and then down it without lights.

It was too dark between the high hedges of the lane so I turned them on and regretted the loss of my night vision, but it couldn't be helped. It seemed like only a few seconds before the turning for Home farm came up, but it must've been longer. I put my lights out and drove into the outer yard at barely walking speed and stopped the engine. The door shut when I held the catch and pushed hard. I didn't touch the remote lock on the key because that would've flashed the indicators as it locked the car. I stood leaning on it for a bit listening and letting my eyes adjust to the darkness again.

No lights came on from the direction of the house. No dog barked. Nothing happened except the pale shape of a barn owl passed silently over my head. I smiled at him in the darkness, wishing him good hunting, and then went to look for the ladder that I'd seen leaning against the wall of the barn. I found it; it wasn't a great ladder as ladders go, but it was in two parts and adjustable and it would have to do. I put it over my shoulder, went out into the long meadow and started following the hedge towards the borders of the White Wood.

Part way down I stopped to listen and sniff the air. The night sounded like it should, and smelt like it should. It smelt like home and I realised that I felt deeply happy.

The beginning of the wood wasn't too bad, being mostly beech and quite open, but there was no way to move silently. The wood got thicker and the darkness darker and it got harder to move quietly carrying a ladder.

I put it carefully against the trunk of a big beech tree and sat down with my back against its smooth bark. I focused on my breath, cleared my mind and let the sounds and scents of the wood seep into me. Letting the wood forget about me. It was quite cool now but the tree felt warm against my back. There were noises off but they weren't threatening. Mice, a hedgehog perhaps. I smiled into the darkness, appreciating the delicious feeling of being alone in a wood in the dead of night on my own native soil.

I stayed like that until the quality of the light changed and the first fingers of moonlight found their way down through the canopy. It was a waxing moon, more than half-full, and its arrival was a ghostly, silver sunrise.

The extra light made it easier to navigate so I got up, shouldered my burden and pushed on into the wood. In due course, more or less where I expected to, I found myself confronted by the wall.

Someone had cut the undergrowth back beside it, which was interesting, and that made it much easier to move. I laid the ladder down and started following the wall. Not much further on, it turned a corner and just beyond that a vertical line of moon-shadow revealed the presence of the doorway that I dimly remembered from my childhood maraudings. I explored it, partly with my eyes, and partly by touch. It had been filled in very neatly and very thoroughly with what felt like modern engineering brick. So much for that idea.

I went back to my ladder, and with infinite care, extended it to what I guessed to be the correct length. I picked a spot where there was deep shade from an overhanging tree and some ivy had grown up into the razor wire, carefully settled the ladder in place and went up. The feet of the ladder sank a bit into the soft ground.

When my head passed the masonry, I could see the grounds of the Abbey quite clearly. The old monastic buildings were gone, presumably robbed of their stones during the reformation, but the structure of the terraces and gardens had survived. It was serene and lovely in the silver light. I carefully unbuttoned the binoculars from my shirt, putting the strap over my head, and began to study the scene.

In place of the cloisters there were now modern buildings. They wouldn't have been bad buildings if you found them in Milton

Keynes, but here they were wrong. There was only one structure that matched the loveliness of the place and that was a pretty, hexagonal wooden summerhouse with roses growing over it that was the focal point of three paths, bordered by tall, neatly clipped box hedging. I got the glasses out of my shirt and started having a good look at the buildings and their environs.

The only light was coming from a low building furthest from me, nearest to where the entrance must be. It flickered; a guard perhaps; watching a TV with one eye and the monitors of the security system with the other.

A quick shaft of light against the far wall indicated that someone had come out of the building with a light on. Presently a figure appeared from behind it. He was wearing dark trousers and a pale tunic; I couldn't tell what colour they were in the moonlight. He had short hair and looked youngish and in reasonable shape. He tucked a chunky, black radio into the pocket of his trousers, and began walking round the perimeter of the grounds. He moved steadily, unhurriedly, and I could tell that he was listening and looking carefully. I trusted to the deep shade and sheltering ivy to keep me from his gaze and stayed dead still.

He went all the way round, often disappearing from sight behind buildings and shrubs. When he got back to the beginning he didn't stop but carried on part of the way round again and then cut back through the middle of the grounds. I would be willing to bet that he didn't do his patrol the same way twice running, and that the intervals between patrols weren't regular either.

He returned to his lair and I resumed my observations.

There was a movement at one of the open windows of the largest building. I steadied and focused my glasses on the darkness inside. There was a girl sitting on a chair, just back from the window, looking out. She had no doubt watched the guard as I had. She was young, had dark, shoulder-length hair and was dressed in pyjamas.

The White Wood

She stared out into the garden, her chin resting on her hands, her elbows on the windowsill.

As I watched, a form appeared behind her. It was another girl, slim and fair and also in pyjamas. She put her arms around the seated girl and held her, resting her head against hers. They were still, for a few minutes and then the one standing straightened up and gently led the other away. They went from view and didn't reappear.

A male tawny owl made his 'hoo-hoo-hoo' not far from me and was answered by a 'kwee-kwick' from a different direction. I decided it was time to go home to bed, so I eased my muscles, a little stiff from being still, clasped the binoculars against my chest so that they wouldn't bang against the ladder, and shifted my weight onto my right foot in preparation for taking the first step down.

The right-hand leg of the ladder sank further into the soft ground, causing the top to pull against the wire. The wire sagged and rippled a bit, with a small but unpleasant shiver of metallic sound. I shifted my weight onto the left side, stepped down one and put my hand against the ivy to steady it. To me, the sound had seemed appallingly loud, but I didn't think it could've carried far. I very carefully wiggled the ladder a bit to see if it wanted to slip again. It seemed to be reasonably okay so I went back up and peered over the ivy to see if anything was stirring.

The serene moonlight gardens and buildings were silent and without movement. A roe deer barked further into the wood. I stopped looking at the view and let my eyes rest on the razor wire beside me. Something about it had caught my attention. There was a cable running along inside the loops just in front of me. It was clipped to the wire and reminded me of co-axial TV cable. It was slightly bent where the top of the ladder had caught against it.

Then a jay screamed its warning a couple of hundred yards away.

Was the moonlight bright enough for a sparrowhawk to be hunting? Or was it just complaining about a fox passing beneath its roost? The harsh call had an uncertain note as if it was unsure about the threat. You can often tell what they're on about by the way they call.

I looked at the cable again and decided I didn't like it. I got as quickly and silently as I could down to the ground, buttoned the binoculars back into my shirt and looked at the ladder.

The jay screamed again, at bit nearer now; it must be following something.

I left the ladder where it was, and went back into the trees and squatted behind a small holly bush to see what would happen.

What happened was that two men in dark trousers and white tunics ran fast but quietly from the right and stopped underneath the ladder. One squatted, looking at the ground for tracks, the other studied the woodland. Neither of them said a word. I kept dead still and said a silent word of thanks to that little bird.

Two more, appeared from the other direction. They all squatted down together, eyes on different quarters of the wood, and had a brief conference. None of them looked out of breath. They each pulled up their trouser legs and unsheathed a long knife strapped to their calf. I watched them and regretted the Sig, currently nestling at the bottom of my bag at the hotel. Then, at a nod from one of them, they set out on diverging courses into the wood. They were going to sweep the area.

The longer I waited, the nearer to me they would be when they saw me, and see me they would, so I turned my back on the holly bush and started running.

I heard the hiss of a command behind me and running footsteps. I knew what they would be doing; two directly behind me and one out on each side, flanking me so that I couldn't turn. They had an advantage over me; there were four of them, if any one of them tripped on the uneven forest floor it didn't matter, they could afford to take more chances than I could. They could run me down.

The White Wood

I love the woods. They were always a playground and a refuge when I was a boy. The spaces that the trees make, the moving light and the endless possibility of seeing without being seen. I'd had the odd skirmish with keepers as a boy and that had been quite exciting at the time. Now it looked as if I was about to die in this quiet, friendly, English wood; quickly and painfully and soak my blood into the decaying leaves.

The canopy kept out most of the moonlight but there was still enough of it filtering through for me to be able to make out the shapes of the trees and to head for the gaps between them. This was mainly beech wood here, quite open and uncluttered. I ran into the silent spaces, desperately seeking the best way in the deceiving light. My feet made soft scuffing noises and I could hear theirs coming up behind me too. I'd started with a hundred yards lead, but I'm built too heavy to be an endurance runner, and without looking round, I knew that they were gaining on me. If I were to alter course I must do it soon or their flankers would be close enough to intercept me. Any change, right or left, would bring them closer.

If I tripped or got held up they would close on me and it would soon be over. I would fight, but there were four of them and I had no doubt about the outcome. Not if, but *when*, I tripped or got held up. I attempted to settle myself to the task, not moderating the pace of my initial flight but being in my mind as if I would run right through the wood and out the other side. Let me be a nimble footed boy again tonight.

The beech trees began to give way to oak and ash and yew. This meant that more light got through to the understory and more hazel and bramble and briar were able to grow. The way ahead was becoming confused, a wall of cover rising up in front of me. I skirted a clump of hazel, was forced right by brambles creeping in from a clearing made by a fallen beech on the left, I could not tell which way to go but lunged on, wisps of nettles and ground elder catching at my feet, bracing myself against a fall.

And then I hit the ride. I nearly missed it and blundered on but a wall of brambles on the far side of it gave me pause and I realised what it was. It cut straight into the wood and must have been maintained, as it was clear. The surface was beaten earth with faint wheel ruts and even some grass growing on it. The undergrowth along its sides was correspondingly dense because of the extra light it let in.

I would have gone left, the way out, but that would take me back towards them, so I took the way on, the way in to the heart of the wood. I heard a cry of frustration as the right-hand flanker danced about trying to find a way clear to get to me. I saw his white coat through the undergrowth as I ran on the path, and heard the others break through and accelerate towards me, their footsteps louder on the beaten earth.

I was in a tunnel now, sometimes open to the sky and sometimes branched over by the trees. This must be the path that led to the clearing in the centre that Lizzy had spoken of. The problem with it was that it was good underfoot. They were beginning to close on me again and my lungs were on fire and my legs in danger of cramping. I must get off the path again and quickly.

The deer and wild boar have their paths, and I must find one leading off the track, or if I made it that far, the clearing, would be a killing ground. It couldn't be far now. I could see a lightening ahead that must be it.

I was wrong, it wasn't the clearing, but a huge dead-fall. An old and massive ash had lost its battle with gravity and crashed to the ground, shattering itself and taking several smaller trees with it, opening up a patch of the night sky, the bright moon looking down into it.

Perhaps it was the clear air, the relief from the increasing claustrophobia of the trees, perhaps a flash of inspiration from the boy coming to aid the man. I leapt for it, as for salvation, and scrambled up onto the trunk. I ran, careless of my footing, along it, swinging round the impeding limbs and into the tangle of upper branches, ducked my head under, pushed down and through, sliding past the smooth bark, going with the, once vertical, now horizontal direction of their growth, my weight bringing down the tapering branches. Falling to my hands and knees as they released me I was through and into the cover of the darkness beyond.

I was still for a moment, tried to calm my breathing, and knew that they had lost me. Only for a moment, but it was something. In the darkness, they had missed my leap and had run on. They were coming back and spreading out and I heard one of them calling to the others in words I didn't know. I heard boots on the bark of the tree trunk.

Now that they had lost contact with me, my dark brown trousers and shirt gave me an advantage. Their white tunics made them far more visible to me than I was to them. If I could move without sound I might have a chance.

I couldn't. In the stillness of the night wood, every rustle and swish of cloth or skin against foliage carried. The ground was a minefield of small twigs and trailing bramble fronds. I moved away as quickly and quietly as I could while they got through the branches of the fallen tree, but when they stood and listened they soon picked me up again. I carried on away from them as quietly as I could in a rapture of concentration, trying to slow and quiet my breathing. My whole being tuned to my fingertips and my ears, my sight almost useless in the darkness. They called to one another as they caught the sounds of my movement, no need for silence on their part. I didn't know the words but the sense, 'to the right a bit, there he is, there,' came through with complete clarity. Even so I hugged to myself the knowledge that, for the moment at least, they couldn't actually see me.

The darkness gave way a bit and I decided that I was coming on the clearing itself. I could run there, perhaps regain the ride, but my legs were shaky and the thought of giving up the darkness wasn't welcome. I backed into the shelter of an old oak and put my hand on its rough bark. They had gone silent and were waiting for me to move again and betray my whereabouts.

Another thought. I felt carefully at my feet until I found a small dead branch and shied it into the darkness in front and to my left. It landed with a suitably subtle rustle of the bushes and one of them called out, directing the hunt towards it.

Covered by the sounds of their movement I clung to my tree and felt about for a way up. It was an ancient thing, split and hollow and leaning in towards the clearing, away from the competition of its fellows. I put my hands into the crack and my feet against the trunk and started to pull myself up. Dangling there felt horrible and I expected a stabbing pain in my back or hands gripping my feet to pull me back down every second, but every foot gained was a foot towards sanctuary. If I could get up it, even if they found me, which they might not, they could only come at me from below.

They had gone silent again, listening intently for me in the darkness. I stopped and stayed put, my sinews cracking and my muscles on the edge of cramping, and listened with them.

Someone moved away to my right. The sounds of his feet treading the leaves was very distinct in the deep silence.

"Czy to ty, Jerzy?" a voice called out from twenty feet behind me.

"Tak," came the reply.

"Gdzie jest ten drań?" the voice behind me said.

"Gdzieś w pobliżu Ciebie, szef," a voice back and to the left said.

"Cisza, będziemy czekać," the voice of command said.

Silence settled on us again. And we waited together, them not knowing that they were so close to me. Waited for the first person to lose concentration or patience and move.

But it was no longer complete silence. In the distance, there was the sound of an engine. Just a murmur of sound, but there.

I thought about this and asked myself if it could be carrying from the road, or from the environs of the Abbey grounds, or from the Hall. Or perhaps the Rectory which also bordered the wood. There was little or no air movement and no indication of the branches moving above me, so the sound wasn't coming down the wind. It was growing stronger. I believed that someone had driven across the long meadow, into the wood, and was coming up the ride. In a Landrover, by the sound of it, or possibly two. In the dead of night without lights on.

"Pieprzyć to, pójdziemy," the voice of their leader said.

"Tak, szefie," one of the others said and they began to move carefully away from the clearing.

I took the opportunity to get further up my tree and settle myself in the fork of a high limb, holding close to the main trunk. I hoped that I wouldn't be silhouetted against the sky and that if I were, I would look like part of the tree, which was a misshapen, irregular thing. The noise the Landrovers were making, it was definitely at least two, easily covered any sounds I made. Holding on, both arms round the trunk, my cheek against the rough but friendly bark, I began to feel a little of the nightmare of being hunted pass away.

I dimly saw a pale form pass beneath me, moving back towards the fallen ash. From my vantage point he was an insubstantial being, dangerous, perhaps, in his domain, down of the flat earth, but irrelevant to me, up in my aerial retreat.

My tree, leaning in as it was, gave me a partial view of the clearing. A more vigorous tree would have obscured my view with its branches but this old thing had few enough. Many of the trees round the clearing were ancients like this one. They must have been spared the axe of the Georgian ship builders for whatever reason, and had grown too hollow and irregular to be worth harvesting since.

In the moonlight, I saw one Landy pull up to one side of the clearing. It had a large trailer behind it, and this was stacked high with old railway sleepers. Two large dogs, appeared and started quartering the space. From the sounds, I could tell that two more Landrovers with trailers pulled up, also heavily laden. Doors opened and men got out and started doing things.

The dogs picked up a scent, gave low growls and started following it. I could hear them circle the bottom of my tree and then go on in the direction my pursuers had taken.

I briefly considered going down to say hello, but it didn't seem sensible, so I just concentrated on being part of the tree and hoped they'd go away soon, whoever they were.

Which they did. There was about half an hour of swift and purposeful activity without the sound of a single human voice, and then the vehicles started up and trundled off again.

I sat and waited until the sounds of the night wood returned; the rustling of mice in the leaf-litter, the tawny owls speaking to each other. I let myself very carefully down into the relative darkness below. No one, human or canine, appeared and tried to kill me.

The easiest and quietest way to leave would be to go into the clearing and pick up the path from there, so that is what I did.

There was a low bluff of rock to one side of the clearing and from its base a small stream ran. The birth of the Fyne brook. It curved a circle round part of the space and disappeared into the wood. I walked out into the moonlight to see what the visitors had been up to. The grass was surprisingly short and even. Presumably rabbits and deer kept it down.

There was a large slab of rock not far from the centre of the space. On three equal sides of it hay bales were laid out to make rows of seats facing it. Further back, between each was a hefty pyramid of sleepers set ready to burn. Someone was clearly planning a party, or a celebration, or something. Three groups of seats. Three bonfires.

The White Wood

I followed the tracks of the vehicles and easily found the lane that led back towards the long meadow. I followed that for what I guessed to be half way and then cut away into the wood and eventually made my way out into the meadow.

There was more than the first hint of the coming day in the sky when I parked the car back in the same space in the hotel car park. I thought about phoning Bill, but sent him a longish text instead, and retreated to bed, not forgetting to return the binoculars. Mel snuggled up to me without waking. I was tired now, but it seemed like a long time before sleep would come.

19

HARE'S EARS

Mel woke me unreasonably early with demands for breakfast. When I was sufficiently with it, I responded by trying to get hold of her, but she got out of bed, put her dressing gown on and ordered room service.

"Ughhh," I said.

"Come on, sleepy head. I'm going for a shower."

And by the time she had, breakfast arrived.

"So, what did all that really achieve?" she said, dunking a soldier in her soft-boiled egg.

"I felt it achieved something," I said.

"I don't see how. It doesn't help us find Natasha, does it?"

"It might do, and we've got a lovely room with a lovely bed..."

"...you can forget that."

"I'm sure it would help the thinking process..."

"Never mind the thinking process. In so far as you're capable, which I'm not too sure about. Where did you go in the night?"

"Ah, the sleep that ravels up the sleeve of care, balm of hurt minds, chief nourisher in life's quest... I mean feast. Where do we go. Who can say."

"Your trousers are damp and they have green stuff on them that they didn't yesterday. Where did you go, and why didn't you take me with you?"

"I didn't want you to get hurt."

"That's patronising. You should see me as an equal, or..."

"As a superior, I know. It was something someone said. Something about a walled garden and screaming."

"Who said what?"

"One of Anja's flatmates."

"Anja... oh, your prostitute. What do you mean, flatmates? You know where she lives? What walled garden? What screaming? Is that why we left London in such a hurry?"

"Possibly." I gave her an account of my visit to the flat in Tower Hamlets without being at all specific about how I found it.

"I see. You should've told me, prick."

"I just did. Anyway, I thought I'd check out any walled gardens we came across."

"Well, it's obviously not the one here. So, where've you been?"

"The nuthouse. It's a big walled garden, isn't it? I went off to have a look over the wall."

"You went into the White Wood last night?" She looked at me as if I'd done something unimaginable.

"Yes. Why not?"

"What did you see?"

"Nothing."

"Oh."

"I thought it was worth a go, but I was wrong. Hey ho."

"You don't get screaming in the White Wood."

"Yes, you do."

"No, you don't."

"Yes, you do." I stopped looking at the sausage that I was dealing with, and looked at her instead. She looked very serious and a little pale. "You get vixens screaming in the White Wood," I said.

"Oh. Foxes. Yes, of course."

"What did you think I meant? And possibly peafowl from the Hall. The sound could easily carry that far."

"Okay. Sorry, you're right."

I made Mel play her half of a love-struck young couple while we checked out, in case there were any suspicious Russians about, which there weren't, and then we got on the road. As I passed the turning towards Acton, and the Dower House and the asylum in the wood, and pushed on towards the A303 and London, I wasn't sure if I was heading away from the problem or towards it. We drove for a while, not talking, just thinking about it all.

I enjoyed the drive. At least until the M3 delivered us into the outskirts of the teaming metropolis, but it didn't make anything any clearer. Rather the opposite. No Landrovers trundled along behind us this time, but then that may have been because they couldn't keep up.

"There's something I don't know," I said.

"Like, who's doing it?" Mel said, waking out of her own reverie. "And why."

"No, something else. There's something there in front of me and I can't see it," I said.

"Like what?"

"Strangely enough, I don't know. Doesn't it seem to you like there's a family feeling about it all?"

"No. What do you mean?"

"Imogen Westhall, Hillary Stubbs, Cecilia Brinkworth, Fiona Asher, Jane Hamilton, Natasha Wilkinson and Susie Chesterfield.

And possibly Wendy. There's something about that group of girls that I can't put my finger on. Any thoughts?"

"No."

"Is it money or school or university or location or employment?"

"I.Q.?"

"Possibly. Is this some kind of girls' club, or something? Do you all belong to some secret society?"

"Like what? The 'we've all slept with Si Ellice' club?"

"I never met Natasha before or Susie and Cecilia, er Fiona, possibly, I can't remember."

"Typical."

"Or looks. It could be that; you're all stunning. You could all have been on stage at that do the other night."

"Would you have bid for Susie or me?"

"I'd have bid for whichever of you the Pogodins were looking at."

"For all the good that did."

"I'm trying, okay?"

"Very."

"Anyway, we've ruled out the Russians, so let's concentrate on the Greens. Is it really not possible to pin-point one person who was at the locus of each poisoning? If we find the poisoner, the chances are we'll be able to find out the rest of it."

"Obviously. You'd think it might be, wouldn't you."

"But it's not? You've been trying to narrow the field haven't you? That's what you've been concentrating on with your laptop."

"Obviously, again. I've been through every facebook page, insta account, everything I can think of to figure out who was where when. No fucking use."

"But you've got a list? A list of possibles?"

"A long list, yes. I've been over it fifteen thousand times and I can't identify any one person I know about who was definitely there when each of all seven of them were poisoned. As far as I can tell. But if you assume more than one poisoner, the permutations are fucking endless."

"Oh well." I pulled over into a handy bus lane and stopped.

"What now?" she said.

"Bloody traffic. You can drive; I need some more sleep."

"Oh, okay."

I dozed a bit and eventually, a few thousand of the planet's other inhabitants got out of our way sufficiently for us to make it to the docks where Polly welcomed us back with her usual imperturbable loveliness. Although it was a bit early, we dumped our bags and went up to the café for lunch.

We sat down and I let my eyes wander over the walkways and the people and the cafes and restaurants. And past the *Sea Hare*. It all looked utterly normal and harmless and I was quite certain it wasn't.

A passing Henriques suffered a slight disruption to his stride as he noticed us. Not long afterwards he came over, looking self-conscious.

"Good afternoon, madam, sir," he said.

"We're here again, Henriques," I said.

"So I see, sir."

"How're you, Henriques?" Mel said.

"Very well, thank you for asking. How're you?"

"Very well, thank you," Mel said.

"And so am I, by the way," I said. "Hungry though."

We ordered various things to keep ourselves going and he wrote them down and then failed to go away.

"What's occurring, Henriques?" I said.

"I am standing here taking your order, sir," he said.

"I can see that, Henriques," I said.

"I am not standing here telling you that when I go back inside I'm going to make a phone call and tell someone that the man they're looking for has come back."

"You're a gentleman, Henriques."

"I am not, and neither are you. But I would rather they didn't catch you."

"I'm grateful. Any particular reason? If you don't mind me asking?"

"You were nice to the girl. She is very beautiful and it would be a shame if… well, you know."

"You're a romantic, Henriques."

"I am an actor, sir."

"I hadn't forgotten."

"And a very good one, I'm sure," Mel said,

"Go and make the call, Henriques. It's fine."

"Oh. Now I don't want to."

"Yes, but why…?" Mel said.

"I'll explain in a sec. Henriques…" I said, catching him as he was about to leave.

"Sir?" He turned back to me.

"You're a brave and fearless man, aren't you?" I said.

"I'm nothing of the kind, sir."

"No, you're an actor. Are you afraid of the Greens, Henriques?"

"Mortally, sir."

"Thought so. Why?"

"Because it's all a set, sir. It's all make-believe."

"And you should know."

"I do know, sir."

"I agree. And we can't see what's really behind the flats, but it's probably not very nice, is it?"

"You put it correctly, sir. In my opinion. Now, may I…?"

My phone binged with a text from Berry, 'have you returned to civilisation? Are you coming out to play?'

"Hang on, Henriques, bearing in mind that you're an actor…"

"Yes, sir…?"

"Have you heard of the Pied Feathers?"

"The Pied Friars, sir?"

"That's the one."

"Of course, sir."

"Have you ever been there?"

"Yes, sir. Many times."

"What sort of place is it?"

"In my opinion, it is the beating heart of the city, sir. The epicentre of civilisation as we know it."

"Is it, indeed. So, it doesn't belong to the Greens, then?"

"Definitely not."

"How do you get in?"

"You have to be invited, sir."

"Why do you think they called themselves Green?" I said.

"Perhaps their name is Green," he said.

"I doubt it; everything else about them is made up, isn't it?"

"I believe you're right, sir. Yes, there will be a reason."

"Thank you, Henriques. Yes, do go and…"

"I will, sir."

"What the fuck?" Mel said, when he'd gone.

"Did I not mention that that chap, Tony, who's nose I broke, saw me in the vicinity of Anja's place the other day? I'm quite certain that Henriques has gone off to let them know I'm back, on pain of pain, if he doesn't."

"Wherever you go, there is trouble."

"I thought that's what you liked about me."

"No, that's only your money, nowadays."

We ate in silence for a bit. I could see Mel was thinking. Come to that, so was I.

"Tower Hamlets again," she said.

"You've had a thought," I said. "Care to share?"

"No."

"Oh. Well what about the Friar's tonight? Fancy it?"

"The Friars? Tonight? Why?"

"For one thing, I want to talk to Berry."

"Why?"

"I know he can look like a bit of an idiot, but he isn't really. I'll bet he knows something about the Greens."

"I doubt it; why would he?"

"He spends enough time in their places. He's practically their best customer. He's probably met them, if they exist. I want to pick his brains. Why not?"

"Good luck with that."

"I'll go by myself, if you want to wash your hair."

"You fucking well will not."

"Okay, Mel," I said, smiling. "Whatever you say."

"I just want to find out who's doing this, and I'm not certain this will help."

"You have a better idea?"

"No. Well there's something I want to follow up, but not this evening."

"In Tower Hamlets, no doubt. Good. I've had an idea about our poisoner too."

"Oh yes?"

"We have the bait; I've thought of the trap."

"Susie?"

"Yes. We've got to narrow the field somehow. Why don't we offer her up in circumstances where we have more control."

"How?"

"Let's throw a party on Polly tomorrow."

"How will that help?"

"You and Susie can put out a general invite and make sure you include everyone on your list of possible suspects. It's very short notice, so most people won't be able to come, but someone who really wants to get at Susie, will. The best way to catch our poisoner is surely to, well, catch our poisoner. In the act, I mean."

"She might get poisoned again."

"She's up for the risk. It should be much easier to spot them on Polly than in some dark, crowded club. And there'll be two of us. Three of us, even. We'll all stay sober, but pretend not to. We'll be very careful and watch her like hawks."

"You think the poisoner would come?"

"Why wouldn't they? How can they know that we're trying to catch them? How would they even know we know they exist?"

"True. So, your idea to help Natasha and Susie, is to go to a club tonight, and then have a party tomorrow night?"

"Yes."

"Just fucking typical."

Lunch arrived and we ate it. Mel looked thoughtful, and occasionally looked at me, and otherwise said unusually little. The place got busier as it became nearer to lunchtime. I took advantage of Mel's relative preoccupation to gaze absentmindedly about, but it all looked perfectly innocent. A tramp with a small dog shuffled onto the scene and took up a position in the sun against a wall. I considered bribing him to keep his eyes open for me, but given his apparent consumption of whiskey, this would probably be futile.

"What're you doing this afternoon?" Mel said.

"I don't know," I said. "I could go and talk to Susie about this party."

"No. I'll do that. Like I said, you can keep your hands off other women for the time being."

"I was only... That's a bit hard..."

"Don't bother. Can I have the car?"

"Why?"

"I want to use it. And give me a key to Polly."

"Oh. Okay."

"I'm moving in."

"Oh. Er. Are you? You're not worried about Tony and his mates then?"

"No."

"Is that because whoever's driving that Landy will be watching over you?"

"None of your damn business. The Greens, I agree, let's at least rule them out. I assume you have a plan for that?"

"So, you're agreeing with me about them now?"

"Provisionally. Well?"

"Er, not yet, but I expect I will sometime."

"So, what are you going to do this afternoon?"

"I might just have a brief nap."

"Typical."

"I was up half the night," I said, and raised a hand to fetch Henriques and the bill.

"Are you content, my lady?" he said, when he arrived, handing me the bill.

"Far from it, Henriques," she said. "But lunch was excellent. Thank you."

I walked Mel to the car, just in case, and watched her drive away with the utter assurance that she seemed to bring to everything.

When I got back, I stood in the shelter of the covered walkway and surveyed the scene. There were the usual dinners and drinkers, people passing. Office people and a few tourists. They all looked perfectly normal and like they belonged, and yet I felt uneasy. It's a feeling I've learned to trust.

The only two people who looked at all out of place, were the beggar with the small dog, and in my usual scruffy out-door clothes, me.

Out of fellow feeling, as I passed them, I squatted down to stroke the dog. He seemed to appreciate that and had nice silky ears, even though his main coat was rough. The man stared vacantly ahead and gave off whiskey fumes. I put some change in his hat and he grunted something that may have been thanks.

Back on Polly, I put my feet up and settled down to think. It occurred to me again that it was nice having something to do; I'd missed the feeling. Even if I didn't necessarily know what I was doing.

Or did I mean something or someone to hunt? I sat there and took myself back to those evenings alone with Avus in his gun-room and listened to his voice in my head. Food, shelter, belonging… think about the quarry's hierarchy of needs, what its nature is. What's its natural habitat? What're the habits and location of what it eats?

I phoned Bill.

"Hey, Bill. How's your day going?" I said.

"You sound cheerful," he said.

"I'm alive; it's a good start."

"I suppose it is. Cup of tea?"

"Yes, and a biscuit."

I got to the gunroom before Bill, so Jimmy put me to work again and I told him about being chased through an English wood and up an English oak tree.

"Well, like I said, what's the point of people like me supplying it, if people like you don't use it," he said.

"But I didn't have anything except my pocket-knife on me," I said.

"My point exactly," he said, grinning.

"How was I supposed to know I would find someone who wanted to kill me in an English wood?"

"Maybe because you went looking for them?"

"That's a very good point."

"I know."

Bill knocked and entered at Jimmy's summons, rubbing his knuckles. Jimmy smiled his slow smile and said, "That's me then. I'll just pop along to the factors for a new glass hammer."

"Couldn't get some chocolate biscuits while you're there could you?" Bill said.

"There's a plate of them just there, officer. And a mug of tea, still hot. Sit down, man."

"Thank you, Jimmy. Thank you very much indeed." Bill put his bag on the bench and pulled himself up onto a stool. I slid the mug and biscuits towards him. Jimmy softly closed the door with himself on the other side of it.

"Well, Bill," I said.

"Well enough, Si. What are you doing to that? And what is it, by the way?"

"I'm cleaning it. It's a Greener side-lock and if it was yours, you could probably swap it for a two-bed flat in Hackney."

"What do you know about two bed flats in Hackney?"

"Very little. What do you know about Noor Abbey?"

"How sure are you?"

"Pretty sure. They use the same vans as the one that spirited Natasha away. I think I saw her and that girl, Jane, but I can't be certain. Whoever it was who tried to catch me in that wood, they weren't any kind of normal security guards. There's more to that place than nutters, I'm certain of it."

"Okay..." He flipped open his notebook. "Noor Abbey medium secure mental health hospital is run by one Dr Nathan Simm. It has 32 beds and specialises in treatment resistant conditions. And rich clients. Last Care Quality Commission inspection was eighteen months ago; no concerns whatsoever. Excellent record-keeping, patient safety, statutory compliance, all that bollocks. Families are happy. Clients seem to do well. As well as can be expected anyway.

Basically, when you've accepted that mad uncle Wilfred isn't going to get any better, and can't be let loose amongst the population, this is where you send him. If you're loaded, that is."

"Can you think of a better place to hide a few girls?"

"Not off the top of my head, no."

"Any connection with the Greens?"

"Not that I can find so far. Nor to our Russian friend either. But, yes, it really is full of nutters. And not harmless ones either. Question is, what're we going to do about it?"

"Go search it, for fuck's sake."

"How?"

"With enthusiasm and lots of men, of course. Preferably about now. What the fuck are you waiting for?"

"Small matter of a search warrant."

"Really?"

"Yup. This is this country. Don't have a choice."

"So, go get one."

"Based on what?"

"I don't know. Lie. Information received, or whatever."

"Won't work. I need something that at least looks like evidence."

"Fuck. Okay, I'll think of something. Is Freddy coming out to play?"

"You were right; he's keen. He'll be here in a few days."

"Good. Talking of the Russian, I had a chat with them and I don't think it's him."

"Did you, by God. And you're apparently still alive. How? Why?"

"Why am I still alive?"

"No. Why don't you…"

"Babies. I think it's about babies…"

I gave him the gist of my encounter with Rodion and Lada.

"I'm not sure if that's a disappointment or a relief," he said.

"Is there a fertility clinic, or something like that around there?"

"Not that I know about."

"Well, find out. And there is something," I said. "I realised afterwards. She didn't ask what we were protecting Susie from. Lada didn't ask."

"Oh…?"

"That doesn't seem right to me."

"Does she care? She's probably as cold and ruthless as her husband."

"Quite possibly. But perhaps she didn't ask because she already knew."

"Yes, but they live in a world where they need constant protection, she probably assumes it's the same for Susie."

"Oh. I suppose it could be that."

"You want to go and ask her?" he said.

"Are you trying to get rid of me?"

"Not until I've finished with you."

"Okay. So, I'm assuming you've not been completely idle. Tell me who's doing the actual poisoning then," I said.

"Well, we've done a fuck load of work in a very short time. We still have quite a few people to interview, and bear in mind we're often asking about things that happened over a year ago, or even two now, so the information isn't good, but no one person looks like they had opportunity to do all the poisonings. Rather the opposite, in fact, what with people taking holidays and so on. I have quite a long list of people who know or knew one or more of our victims. Do you want it?"

"Yes, please."

"By the way, do you know, I'm supposed to be arresting you this morning? Or rather, organised crime are."

"I thought we'd got over that in Nador?"

"Not me, old son. The eleventh Earl of Bicester has got it into his head that you're a very bad fellow. He's right of course, but we've explained that there's the small matter of evidence. He's not happy about it."

"I feel for him. What about Wendy?"

"Ah, yes you were right about that. How did you know?"

"She's an aristocrat then?"

"Was. Yes. Poor as a church mouse, but the genuine thing. Her uncle was the Duke of… Chumley-something… I can't remember but I've got it written down. How did you know?"

"Have a look at this." I got my phone out and showed him a photo:

"What's that?" Bill said.

"Looks like a pair of hare's ears to me," I said. "Think about it."

"So? Think about what?"

"Hare's ears. It was doodled on the poster in Wendy's bedroom."

"Hare's ears… Oh. Fucking hell. Hang on…" He opened his briefcase and pulled out a bunch of files and started going through the contents. "Hang on, it's… got it." He passed it to me. It was the room with the dead Hillary in it. On the shelf behind the sofa was a mannequin's head, and on that someone had put a pair of those bunny ears you sometimes see girls wearing at parties. The tips of the ears had been bent down. "Bloody hell." He carried on looking until he found the same pictures for Imogen, and there it was; a greetings card with an artistic drawing of a hare pinned to the wall not far from the body. The ears on the drawing were bent down.

"Well?" I said.

"Fuck. He's marking his kills. The cocky bastard."

"What's the Green's logo?"

"Oh fuck. A hare."

"A hare with bent down ears. Still think the Greens have nothing to do with this?"

"Okay, I'm going to take them seriously now."

"About time."

20

BACCHUS EST DEUS

I returned to Polly and contemplated her environs. There were plenty of flats overlooking the basin; a single shot from a window... but I was sure that wouldn't be the way; Tony would want something much more personal. Well, nearly sure. I watched one of the girls from the cafe go over to the tramp and his dog and give the dog some scraps. The man looked at her as if to say, 'what about me?', but didn't appear to speak.

Henriques was flitting about the tables of the cafe, as usual. Did the man never sleep?

Sleep. It would all bear thinking about and perhaps a lie down would help. I went down into the cosy sanctuary of Polly and failed to remember to make the cup of tea that I intended to make before I lay down on the comfortable bench seat in the saloon.

My phone woke me, as phones have a habit of doing. I responded to the summons and found a taxi driver piling suitcases into a heap beside Mel and the Jag in the carpark. It was a quantity of bags, which in my world, equates to moving house.

"There you are. Have you got any money on you?" Mel said.

"Do you think you've got enough stuff?" I said, walking gingerly around the pile.

"Don't give me that crap," she said. "Pay the man and get carrying, it's almost all you're good for."

"It may cost you," I said, making a grab for her.

"Don't even think about it," she said, stepping behind the pile and levelling me the kind of look that usually comes with a calibre.

"Glad to have you, Mel," I said.

"Glad to be with you, you bastard," she said, smiling. It was a very good smile.

I did my Sherpa duty and dumped a handful of Mel's bags on the big bed in my cabin.

"I'm having this one," she called, from the next cabin.

"Why?"

"Because I say so."

"Oh."

"Don't worry, I'll know where to find you, if I want you."

And, as she didn't seem to want me at that point, I lay on the bed and watched her unpack, which actually was rather nice. And we talked about this and that and time sort of slid by without anything in particular happening, as it does sometimes.

"What're you wearing?" she said, looking at her watch.

"This. Would you like me to take it off?"

"If you're coming out with me, you're not wearing that."

"Oh."

"Now, go away."

"Oh."

"I want to get dressed."

"I don't mind."

"Si, get the fuck out of my room. Now."

"Yes Mel."

I went off to wash and change and appeared in the saloon wearing bits of what Mum had helped me buy. Mel was investigating some of the storage lockers.

"Something you wanted?" I said.

"Just seeing what you've got," she said.

"Almost anything you could want, I expect."

"I doubt it. You ready?

"I'm ready. You look ready," I said. "In fact, you look amazing." And she did too.

"Thank you. I've seen you look worse yourself."

"Well, come on then."

We stepped out into the evening to go and see what it would bring.

"My spine's tingling a bit," I said.

"So's mine," she said.

"If we aren't being watched right now, then I know fuck all about anything," I said.

"You and me both," she said.

The beggar with the small dog was still sitting under his plane tree, so to propitiate the gods, I dropped a note into his hat in passing. He grunted something again.

"He could OD on that; you've probably just killed him," she said.

"Perhaps," I said, not really caring one way or the other. "Anyway, I think he's just a drinker. I mean him no harm."

"That's what men always say," she said, holding my arm tightly.

We made our way up to Tower Bridge Road through the perfectly normal London evening and picked up a black cab to a street in Soho, as directed by Berry by text.

I think I'd expected another discreet doorway off a quiet street but we found ourselves at the ornate Palladian doorway of what appeared to be an old-fashioned gentlemen's club on a relatively busy street. It said, 'Pilgrim's Club' in gothic lettering in the fanlight.

We rang the bell and a bright-eyed young man in a maroon and navy uniform and cap attended the intercom. West African via the Eastend, by his accent.

"Yes, lady and sir?" he said.

"We're here to visit Father Berry," I said.

"Ah, do come in," he said, pushing the button, opening the door for us and then locking it behind us.

We entered the foyer of what undoubtedly was, or had been, a genuine Victorian club for a certain type of ecclesiastical gentleman. There were framed photos of men in cassocks and frock coats from the very dawn of photography, no shortage of mahogany and leather, ancient books behind glass. The subdued electric lighting seemed to be the only thing at all modern. I couldn't decide if the cheerful young black man was a neat touch or an incongruous intrusion of modernity. Was he a free man earning good money on the night-shift, or a slave of empire still serving a tyrannical master. It seemed inappropriate to ask him.

He led us past his cubicle, through the boot room, down some lino-covered stairs, through a heavy door into a cellar lined with wine racks. The racks were full of bottles. Some dusty, some not.

"Is this your first time at The Pied Friars, my lady, sir?" he said, noticing us looking at our surroundings.

"Yes," Mel said.

"Then you're in for a treat. If you'd care to just wait there for a few moments, someone will fetch you. Enjoy your evening."

He made a polite exit, shutting the door behind him. I went over to have a look at it. There was no handle on this side.

"This is a steel-lined door," I said.

"I suppose it's good to keep all this wine safe," Mel said.

"Presumably we're being watched," I said, noticing a camera lens in one corner of the room.

There was a hydraulic sigh and a section of wine-rack moved out six inches and then swung away from the wall to reveal Maisie. She was resplendent in a shimmering, floor dragging, pale peach gown and with a tiara in her hair.

"Hello, darlings," she said, skipping over the threshold to greet us, kissing me on the lips. She smelt of Jasmine. "I'm so glad." She took my arm. "You must come with me."

"You can take me anywhere, Maisie," I said, looking deep into her fathomless eyes and seeing no one there.

"Can I, darling?" she said. "I'm so glad." She pulled me into what seemed to be a tunnel. Mel followed.

"Do you like it?" she said.

"It's wonderful," I said.

"Bloody wonderful," Mel said.

"Well, come on then," she said, skipping a bit and leading me on. So, on we went.

We were in a concrete passageway with heavy steel beams lining the roof. After a slight descent and a shallow corner this broke into a wide staircase of cut stone which had been capped off above us but spiralled away below. There was sound and light and warmth coming up to us. Maisie let go of my hand and tripped lightly down. We followed.

"Ta-da," she said, waving her arms and twirling her fingers exquisitely.

We were in the arched vaults of some medieval cellar or dungeon. The yellowish stone had been cleaned and the place was warm and dry. It seemed to have been not so much deliberately converted into something, as to have just happened. My main impression was of rugs and sofas and people, none of them matching. And art on the walls, and music and the smell of marijuana and possibly bread. It was hard to tell how big a space it was, as many of the archways between the supporting pillars had been blocked off with hanging tapestries and cloths, or piled up furniture, or all kinds of things. The result was many rooms, some only partial, leading off each other. Each one was different and each one had its different occupants.

"I expect you'd like a drink," Maisie said.

"What an amazing place," I said. "Yes, I think we would."

"There are rules," Maisie said, as if repeating a lesson.

"Tell us the rules, Maisie," I said.

"The only rules are, that everything is free and that you must contribute. More or less. If all you have to give is money, then give that. If not, give art, or music, or dance your heart out, or bring food, or collect glasses. It doesn't really matter. You may be passionate but not angry and if you bring anyone who turns out to be a nuisance, then you lose your membership."

"How do you become a member?" Mel said.

"By magic," Maisie said. "If you want to use anything or change anything, you may, but leave the place richer for your passing. Ready?"

"Yes," we said.

"I'm so glad. So glad. Follow me, my darlings."

We followed her, stepping aside to let a couple of young men carrying a beautifully made wooden canoe pass.

"I think they're doing the Lady of Shalott tonight," Maisie said.

"I don't know what I was expecting," Mel said, "but Tennyson wasn't it."

"I wonder how they got the canoe in here," I said.

The place seemed to go on and on; different spaces opening up as we moved through it. The bar, when we came to it, was crowded, and made me think of Jack Vetriano. There were people sitting at round tables on bentwood chairs talking all around us. Some of them were playing chess or draughts.

At the bar, a young American girl asked me what we would like to drink, but when I turned to ask Maisie and Mel what they wanted, Maisie, had disappeared and Mel was looking around her with complete absorption.

"Hey, Mel," I said.

"Huh?" she said, turning to me.

"Drink?" I said.

"Yes," she said.

"Maisie?"

"Huh? Oh. I don't know."

I got us a pair of massive Zombies and I dropped some notes into one of the bowls on the bar. I looked again at the surface of the bar. It was a dark resin but things had been set into it before it had been polished. They were pale and familiar.

"Do you think?" I said, tapping it. The American girl smiled and nodded.

"What?" Mel said.

"The Pied Friars," I said.

"Oh," she said.

"Maisie said, everyone makes a contribution," I said.

"So she did."

"Cheers." I raised my glass.

"Cheers, Si." She raised hers.

We gently touched glassed and drank. They were bloody good Zombies.

"Shall we have a look around?" Mel said.

"Damn right," I said. "You wander where you will and I'll come with you. After we've had a look, we'll maybe come back here and sit over there." I indicated a sumptuously appointed alcove. "I think most people will come to the bar at some point and I'd like to watch."

"What an interesting crowd," Mel said.

We started moving through the people, from one space to

another. I can't remember all the things there were to see, and a part of what was there, was under construction, so it would have been different later anyway. In general, there was a kind of division in the people; there were lots of art students, or artists anyway, drama and music, not just visual stuff; and there were older people with money who liked being around the bright young things. It wasn't clear cut though; there were all kinds of people. I think if you were genuinely into something that was there, or had a talent of some kind, then there was a place for you in the Pied Friars. Or if you had money and appreciation, and weren't an arsehole.

Some things looked fairly permanent. The bar, the dancefloor, which had more of the original inhabitants, this time set in Perspex, and a million stars shining down from the black velvet that lined the arch above. There was a kitchen, which was the source of the smell of bread and many areas which were basically just for chilling out in; sitting and talking, or getting wasted in, or both. I got the impression that if any area stopped being used much then it was okay for anyone to take it over and change it.

We found the canoe in an area with seating round the walls and a clear space in the middle. A picture of a river flowing down a gorge was projected onto a sheet and framed by a small forest of willow branches. To one side, a girl in a small amount of muslin was reading earnestly to one of the young men who had been carrying the canoe. Presumably the performance would be later.

When we'd seen most of it, we stopped and Mel leant against me and took a pull at her Zombie and said, "How have I not been here before, and how am I going to manage not to write about it?"

"Well, you're in good company on that one," I said.

"What do you mean?" she said.

"Come back here a moment, and I'll show you."

I led the way to a dimly lit area with deep leather sofas that we'd just passed. There were a dozen or so people and a strong smell of dope. We went in and I sat down next to Harry, the owner of Essence magazine and Mel's boss. He looked at me benevolently and passed a joint on to the girl in cropped jeans and a cropped t-shirt who was next to him.

"Hello, Harry," Mel said, taking a place opposite him.

He had the grace to look embarrassed.

"Hi, Mel. Hi, er... I'm sure we've met," he said, looking at me.

"Simon," I said.

"You old bastard," Mel said.

"Sorry," he said. "Couldn't trust you not to write about it. Welcome to the Friars."

"Thanks a lot. Is that Frankie from layout?"

The girl with the spliff and, now I noticed it, a belly-button piercing, waved it in confirmation and hello.

"Men!" Mel said.

I sat back and made myself comfortable and decided that I'd better not take a drag. Mel got over herself and decided she would, and did, and then it was funny, not serious and we were all talking and Harry was smiling at us benevolently.

After a while I got an urge to be moving about again so we gave them our love and went back to wandering.

My eyes had got used to the place, and its shifting light and patterns now, and I was seeing more, or at least I thought I was. It could have just been the Zombie and the passive smoke. We navigated back to the bar without getting lost and got another drink each.

"Will you light my Zombie please?" I said, to the elderly man in tails who'd made it.

"With pleasure, sir," he said, turning up the flame on his lighter and skilfully dipping it down into the drink without burning himself. "And you, madam?"

"Yes please," Mel said.

We took our glasses of soft blue flame to the alcove and a couple of people moved a little to make space for us. We sat, close, and leant back. The flames flickered down and went out.

"My cherry is hot," Mel said, trying to catch it with her long, red-nailed fingers.

"I'm sure it is," I said.

"Isn't it nice doing things together again, Si," she said, rubbing one of her ankles against mine.

"Me too," I said.

We were silent for a bit, watching the people and sipping our drinks and being alone with each other in a crowd of others.

"Why are you cross with me a lot of the time?" I said. "I am doing my best to help, honestly."

"I know. I'm trying not to fall in love with you again."

"Ah, sorry…"

"…don't say anything."

"…sorry…"

We sat in silence together for a bit and then I said, "London is… I don't know…"

"Yes, isn't it," she said.

"Bigger and more full of different things than most other places," I said.

"Yes, it is, but I thought you didn't like it?" she said.

"Ah, but which it? There are many Londons. I like this one."

"There are indeed many Londons and I like this one too."

Maisie reappeared, and with her was Berry. This time he was in immaculate black and white, his thick mane of hair shining in the soft light They came in and went to the bar; a king and queen. They didn't see us.

"If this place is anyone's, it's theirs," I said.

"People in their element," she said.

"London, or just here?" I said.

"Both."

"We should go say hello," I said.

"Do we have to?" she said.

"I want to," I said.

"Well, go on then. I'm going to wander about."

"Oh, okay. Don't get lost."

"Don't be silly."

"Meet back here later."

"Okay."

Mel gave me a fairly friendly punch in the chest and slipped off through the crowds. I got up to go and join Berry and Maisie at the bar. A man with a pint in his hand got in my way. I stepped politely sideways to go around him and there was another one there too. They both had the glassy look of those who are a bit drunk and not in a great place with it.

"Hey, fella. How're you doing, my friend?" one of them said, swaying slightly.

"Fine thanks."

"It's a good place, no?" he said.

"Is this your first time at the Friars?" the other one said. "It's ours."

"Have a drink with us," the first one said, raising his nearly empty glass.

"Thanks, but I'm just…"

"Si! There you are," Berry said, seeing me.

"Berry, Maisie, hello," I said, grinning at them.

"Si. How wonderful. I'm so glad," Maisie said taking immediate possession of me again, and kissing me full on the mouth.

"As Maisie says, how wonderful," Berry said, giving me the usual bear-hug.

"These chaps…" I started to say, but the men were no longer there. "Never mind. What an amazing place."

"I pride myself on being in the most interesting place in town on any given night of the week," Berry said, modestly.

"Berry, you're the master," I said.

"He is, truly," Maisie said.

"By the way, I meant to say," Berry said. "That was the right thing to do the other night, Si. With Susie, I mean. I'm sorry it wasn't me, and I owe you for it. Thank you."

"Anytime. Damsels in distress…" I said.

"Quite," he said. "Now let's get you a fresh drink and then you must come with me; I'm going to show you my favourite place."

"I'm in your hands, Berry. As always."

With a refreshed glass in one hand and Maisie clinging to my other arm, I followed him this way and that through the rich and crowded place. At one of the back corners, we entered a space that I'd not really noticed before. On a small scale, it was a kind of pastiche of a baronial hall. Heavy carved furniture arranged around a stuffed deerhound in front of a fake fireplace; logs in the grate, surrounded by flames of coloured tissue paper. A range of dead animals looked down at us from above but most of the wall space was covered in armorial bearings. It was strange and it reminded me of many other places.

"I come here every time," Berry said, taking a seat.

Maisie took the seat next to a small side table and began to cut a line. I sat next to Berry and looked at the walls. Something was wrong.

"Isn't that the Royal Family's…?" I said, looking at the achievement over the fireplace.

"Look again, dear heart," Berry said.

I did that while he got up and went over to the table for a snort.

There was something funny about the layout of the images, and the lion had a strange expression on his face. After a bit, I realised that the unicorn's erection was almost fully inserted into him, which presumably explained it. And there were swastikas where no swastikas should be, and the motto wasn't right either.

"Ego sum Deus," I read out.

"No, 'Bacchus est Deus'," Maisie said, grinning at me and twiddling her fingers.

"I don't think it'll be here much longer," Berry said. "Not enough people appreciate it."

"I think it would take a certain kind of person to get the point," I said.

"Like me, you mean?" he said.

"I get it," Maisie said.

"Me too. Sort of," I said, looking round at other achievements. Some of them were familiar, and all of them were corrupt and obscene and funny. "And I'll bet Susie would too. Is this all the major families of England?"

"She does, and it is," Berry said. "Most of them anyway."

"So, where's yours?" I said.

He pointed to one beside the fireplace.

"'Contumeliam ante prandium', dishonour before..." I said, attempting to read his motto.

"Breakfast," he said.

"Of course. Is that a rabbit eating a baby?"

"Could be. Vert, a cony salient, preyant, sable upon a child waddled gules, to be precise. The fourth earl is supposed to have provided one to Richard the Second in time of need. For what need, isn't known. I suspect it simply records some particularly egregious piece of fawning; arse-licking being the family's forté."

"Is this your room, Berry?" I said.

"Man's got to have a hobby," he said.

"Noblesse oblige," I said, raising my glass.

"Fuck you," he said, raising his.

"And me," Maisie said.

"And you, Maisie," we said.

That seemed rather funny at the time. I nearly choked on my zombie and Maisie came over and patted me on the back. Afterwards she sat on the arm of the chair and draped herself against me.

"Tell me, Berry," I said. "Tell me all."

"Tell you what, Si?" he said.

"How come?" I waved a hand at the obscene armorial artwork surrounding us.

"Oh. I just snapped, old thing. One day I just snapped. Uncle Fitz-fucking-whatthefuckdoyouknowaboutit-william was going on at me about custodianship and passing it all on intact to my heir, when I suddenly thought, 'Is this me? Is this me he's talking to?' and I decided it wasn't. That's all. This is my response to the situation."

"You mean you decided to be an actual person, not just a link in the family chain; guarding and handing on The Heritage?" I said.

"Got it in one, dear heart. I did that. Well I tried to. Turns out to be harder than you would think. Bloody lawyers. I'd have to go broke and have it all taken away from me. I did this to make myself feel better."

"I'm impressed. In my head, a host of elderly forebears are putting you up against a wall without benefit of a blindfold," I said.

"And you, old son? Does your soul cry out, 'Blasphemy! Blasphemy!'"

"Take a wild guess," I said.

"I don't know," he said. "People can be, surprisingly bothered by all this nonsense," he waved a hand at it. "Nobility and ancestry and all that crap."

"Does it, fuck," I said. "I'm with you Berry. I'm with you all the way."

"Iconoclasts we stand," he said, raising his glass to me.

"Iconoclasts we fall," I said.

"Bravo," he said.

We drank to that.

"You are funny, you two," Maisie said. She stopped draping and went to cut some more coke.

"Save me a smidge, sweet pea," Berry said.

"Here you are, darling. Come and get it," she said.

They bent their heads together in a friendly contest for the white powder.

"Right," he said, standing up, wiping his nose and putting a thoughtful finger against his coat of arms, "now I've had my fix, tell me, Si…"

"Yes, Berry…?"

"Tell me, Si… tell me about you."

"What about me, Berry?"

"Nature abhors a vacuum, isn't that what they say?"

"They do. I believe, say that."

"My point…" He stared into space for a minute.

"You have a point?"

"Yes, I do have a point," he said, coming back. "And it is this. You, Si, are a vacuum. Are you not?"

"I am?"

"You are."

"If you say so…"

"Quite a solid one," Maisie said, squeezing one of my biceps.

"I have known you some time…"

"And I you…" I said.

"… exactly, and in that time, I've never known you to not be planning trouble, causing trouble, or, occasionally running away from the trouble you've just caused. Where you are, dear heart, there too is trouble. Sooner or later, and usually sooner, trouble will be. Spill a little, old thing. Tell a fellow what's in the wind, will you?"

"Berry…"

"Here you are in my neck of the woods, and if you aren't up to something, I'm bloody sure you soon will be. What is it?"

"I don't know what to say."

"That's unlike you."

"Isn't it. Okay…" I thought about it, and said, "what do you think of the Greens?"

"Grant and Leila?"

"You know them?"

"Of course, I'm one of their best customers. Or haven't you noticed?"

"I have. They exist then?"

"Oh, yes. That's all nonsense, but clever nonsense, don't you think?"

"I suppose so. You've met them?"

"Well, yes and no. Why do you want to know?"

"I'll tell you. Are you on commission with them, or something?"

"Don't be so crude. I enjoy a certain status and, how shall I put it, latitude. This is the life that suits me and, if my presence lends a certain aura…."

"I see."

"It may have been a while since I actually paid a bill as such, if you understand me."

"Ah, I see. Death duties and all that?"

"Crippling, dear heart. I live on credit and other people's snobbery. There it is."

"Ah. Sorry about that."

"Forget it; this is the life I choose, but tell me, old friend. What the fuck are you doing here, and are you going to wreck my life?"

"Me? No. Why?"

"You and I are known to be friends and you have… How shall I put this… I've been deputed to have a word."

"By the Greens?"

"Indeed."

"That word being, 'fuck off, or else'?"

"Pretty much. They're by no means the worst of their kind, but if you will poke a hornet's nest…"

"You may end up at the bottom of the river?"

"I couldn't comment on that, but, Si, what the fuck...?"

"Berry, you know I occasionally get a bit bored?"

"I do indeed."

"Well, as it happens, the first night I was in London I met this girl and..." I gave him a pretty close version of my encounter with Anja and her minder and then the evening I bought two hours of her time and had supper with her.

"So, you want the girl?" Berry said, smiling.

"I suppose I do," I said. "I went to see her, where she lives, but she told me to get lost. I could see she's frightened though. I don't know what I'm intending exactly. I could see she wanted to be free and..."

"As the moth to the flame... you want some excitement, and probably a fight, and rescue the girl and fuck her?" The idea seemed to amuse him a great deal.

"Possibly something like that," I said.

"And then what?"

"I don't know. Sail off into the sunset with her, perhaps."

"Like that ever happens," he said.

"It does," I said. "Well, it might."

"So you're not here for any other reason, then?"

"No. Not at all. Like what?"

"I'm glad. I happened to tap your name into a computer the other day. Just out of curiosity. You've been busy, old thing. I assume they've done the same. I think they may have been wondering if you're the advance guard of a hostile takeover, or something of that nature. You see what I mean?"

"I suppose I do. But no, not by me. Whatever you think I did, I'm not planning to do it again."

"If you're sure?"

"I'm sure."

"Well then, if it's only a girl you're chasing, I'll sleep easy in my bed. When I eventually get there. I hope you get her, and may she bring you everything you deserve. Are you willing to buy her, by the way?"

"I could be. How much?"

"No idea, but I suppose I could ask. Am I participating in the sale of a woman?"

"Seems like you might be."

"Well, anything to help a friend. Don't suppose it's the first time a Lievre has done that."

"Berry, you're a brick."

"To Si and his insatiable appetite for interesting women," he said, raising his glass.

"Fuck you too," I said.

"And me," Maisie said, watching herself twiddle her fingers in the air.

"By the way, are you two coming to our party?" I said.

"What party?" Maisie said, coming back.

"Are you having a party, old thing? How civilised."

"It's really Mel and Susie's idea. Tomorrow. On Polly, if you would care to...? And do invite anyone... I'm new in town and could do with expanding my network."

"Of course. So, Susie's part of this, is she? I thought you two would get on. She's quite something, that girl."

"You're not wrong, Berry. There's something about her, isn't there?"

"Grace, my boy. Grace is the word. She has more of it than the rest of us put together. Yes, of course we'll come. With all my heart."

"And mine," Maisie said. "So glad, so glad."

I left them to the enjoyment of the strange place and their haze of coke and alcohol and went in search of Mel. I didn't find her, but I did find a pint of water, which seemed like a good idea. A tall, dark-eyed girl in a bandana and boiler suit, and carrying a shovel, stopped in front of me, casually tore off a piece of the flat-bread she was carrying and held it up to my face. I took it into my mouth and bowed to her. She smiled and curtseyed and swept off on whatever errand she was on. I wondered what the shovel was for and part of me wished that I was more than just a passing visitor there and tried to decide what kind of space I would belong to, or make.

The flat bread, which had been excellent, left an impression and gave my body a message, so I went in search of its origins. The warm scent of baking led me on to an area that was mainly tables and chairs for eating, filled with people and a haze of marijuana smoke, and beyond that the kitchen, or at least, a selection of the appurtenances of a kitchen variously piled up and scattered about, and in it, three young people kneading and rolling and mixing and whatever. A girl in dungarees, this time a relatively short and wide one, was delivering breads and pizzas to and from an oven with a shovel. I got my bread and started eating it as I went off to look for Mel. I found her in the bar.

"Hey, Si. There you are. How's Berry?" she said, tearing a lump of bread off the whole.

"Mad as ever," I said. "Get up to anything interesting?"

"Yes, everything and everything and everything. This is the best place in the whole of London. Probably the whole world."

"It's not so bad, I suppose," I said, grinning.

"What do you want to do now?"

"I don't know. What do you want to do?"

"I want to dance."

"Okay, let's go dance."

We finished the wonderful bread and drank some water, and then we went to the dancing place and danced. It was full of other people losing themselves to the music and the feeling was very good.

We came away warm and sweaty and quite a bit more sober and all the things that had brought me there seemed a million miles away.

"Well, Si," Mel said, leaning against me.

"Worth coming then?" I said.

"Fuck me, yes."

"What would you like to do now? We could go and look for the Lady of Shallot, or we could go and do what you said."

"What?"

"Go home to bed."

"Oh, not yet."

"Okay, let's go and be cultural then."

"Not without a drink in my hand, we can't."

"I suppose another one wouldn't do much harm. Could you manage a snack, do you think?"

"I expect I've just expended a few calories. Go on, why not. Give me some money and go fetch."

"Yes, Mel."

If anything the place became more crowded as the night went on. Mel went to the bar and I headed for the kitchen. This time, there was a queue. I joined it and watched the people around me; as contented as I'd been for a long time.

At the back of the space, behind a bank of three massive fridges or freezers was a scullery; tables piled with dirty dishes and against the wall two big Belfast sinks. A sound system on the wall above them was blaring out Abba and two fat men in sweat and grease-stained whites, alternately washing and drying and dancing, and occasionally pausing to kiss. What a variety of people there are in the world, and what a variety of ways of being busy and happy.

One of the drunks who'd tried to button-hole me earlier walked past me; I recognised the dragon on his orange shirt. He'd clearly sobered up, as he was now walking upright and purposefully. He passed me and I saw that he had a tattoo on the back of his neck. It seemed familiar so I tried to make out what it was, but he kept moving and was gone.

I found Mel in the alcove near the bar and squeezed in next to her. She handed me a Zombie and said, "You took your time, I was about to go and get another one."

"Here, have some bread, or I'll have to carry you home."

"You can carry me home, if you like, Si."

"Mel, I fully intend to."

I put my arm around her shoulder and offered her the bread, held between my teeth. She took hold of her side with hers and we had a tug-of-war with it until it was gone. It was fun and my stomach was grateful.

"We've just been dancing on the bones of dead monks," she said, chasing the bread down with the last of her zombie.

"I don't suppose they mind," I said. My mind had wandered back to that tattoo.

"But I mind," she said.

"Do you? Why?"

"They keep whispering to me."

"Do they? What do they say?" It was a diving eagle. A diving eagle with a lightning bolt in its talons.

"You don't believe me." She pulled away and looked at me.

"Yes, I do." Her pupils were as wide as they could easily go.

"How're you feeling, Mel?" I put a hand on her arm. It was hot.

"They say the stones are cold," she said. "They want me to move them up into the sun. You have to help, come on." She waved her arms about a bit.

"Oh fuck," I said.

"No. No fucking yet," she said, swaying a bit. "Nine days abstinence, you know that. Got to be…"

"Mel, I think…" I said, taking the remains of her zombie off her and putting it on the floor.

"…no. I said, no. You'll have to wait…" she pulled away from me some more. Her movements weren't her own.

"Mel, sit still. Don't move, hang on…"

She did as she was told and let me put a hand under the fabric of her dress. I couldn't find anything.

"Shut up, Si. Just…"

"Mel, we're going to go home now. Hang onto me, and don't let go."

I walked her out of there and I took her glass with me. Ascending the stairs was going up into a cool silence. I pressed the knob by the door and it sighed open. Mel was a hot diffuse presence that, compared to her normal self, felt like an absence. At least she was willing to do what she was told now.

The doorman greeted us with a restrained disapproval, but accepted a fifty pound note in exchange for fetching a minicab. I loaded her into the back of it and made her scoot over so that at no point could the car leave without me.

I needn't have worried; our Lebanese driver was clearly just a man driving a minicab. I talked to him a bit in Arabic and watched a long-wheelbase landrover pull out into the traffic a few cars back and follow us. I phoned Bill and he answered, more or less.

"Ugh? Oh, Si."

"Morning Bill."

"Is it? I suppose it is. What's up?"

"Could you get a couple of uniformed officers to hang about the docks in fifteen minutes?"

"St Katherine docks?"

"No, San Francisco docks."

"Why?"

"Does it matter?"

"Yes, I can."

"Thanks. Do that and go back to sleep, I'll phone you in the morning."

"Ughhugh."

We parked on Thomas More Street, by the archway into the basin, and I led a dopey and increasingly sleepy Mel out across the space under the cynical eyes of a couple of policemen who clearly thought they were looking for something much more interesting than us. Other than them, we seemed to be completely alone.

In my cabin on Polly, I bossed her about enough to get her undressed and into bed and told her to go to sleep. She lay down like a lamb and closed her eyes. Her skin was cooler now. I wrapped the dirty glass in a clean plastic bag and then made a mug of tea and sat on the bed next to her. She didn't stir. She wasn't nearly as bad as Susie had been, but I didn't intend to go to sleep myself until I was certain that she was sleeping naturally and couldn't choke on her own vomit, or anything like that.

In any case, I had a great deal to think about. I drank the tea and then hunted out some chocolate and a banana. I could tell that as soon as I put my head down, I would go out like a light.

Bill's phone, which was on silent, vibrated, indicating a text. Bill had questions? No, it was from an unknown number, 'Mr can you help me pls'. Odd.

I sent, 'who?'.

'Anja'. Of course I had given her this number.

'Where are you?'

'Docks'

'Wait'

I checked on Mel and decided that she was sleeping normally. A trap? Probably. Fuck it. I fetched my Sig, screwed on the suppressor, put a round into the chamber and topped up the magazine. Would the docks have CCTV? Probably. Had the officers wandered off. Probably.

I went up and sat in the cockpit and looked and listened. It really was the witching hour; the whole place was unusually quiet. I couldn't see a single person anywhere, not even the drunk and his dog.

I sent, 'Where are you?'.

'I can see you'

The walkways and spaces were lit by the streetlights, but some of the doorways were in shadow.

'Come out. I'll meet you'

I closed and locked Polly, just in case, stepped off her very gently and walked to the security gate. It lets you out just by pushing, so I did that and then let it back against its catch as softly as I could. There was a metallic clang as the lock engaged.

A shadow detached itself from the darkness under the awning by one of the restaurant doors and came towards me, hesitantly, as if walking was painful. It was Anja and she was alone. When she came into the light I could see that she had the thick, puffy look of someone who has been carefully beaten about the face. When she was a good way out from the shadow of the archway I went to meet her. The gun was in my hand and I was looking past her into all the dark spaces.

"Hi," I said.

"Hello," she said, and the word didn't come out properly.

"Fancy seeing you here," I said.

"I..." she said. She seemed to stagger and not have proper use of her legs. I stepped close and put an arm around her, holding her up. She hesitated and then let herself lean against me. I felt something in my upper arm, nothing much, like a scratch or something. I stopped looking into the shadows and looked at her.

In the orange light from the lamps I could see that her lovely deep blue eyes were troubled.

"I'm sorry," she said softly, holding onto me.

"That's okay," I said.

The eyes were getting bigger and they were becoming fuzzy. And then I was becoming fuzzy too and my edges were blurring and then I was falling and I couldn't stop myself and I was falling and falling but not ever landing.

21

THE GODDESS OF THE SANCTUARY

After some time, which I knew was some time but could've been a few minutes, or perhaps a few years, I was present enough to hear the banging and to know that the banging was coming from outside me.

Shortly after that, I started moving my hands a little; just one finger at a time. That seemed to be okay so I opened my eyes. The light hurt, so I shut them again but it was too late; my body was coming back and it was very, very unhappy. I clenched my fists and my teeth and my mind and concentrated on trying not to exist, but it didn't work. After what seemed like a long time, the churning nausea subsided a bit. I opened my eyes again and managed to keep them open. There was a badly painted ceiling above me so I looked at it until it became familiar.

When there seemed to be nothing else to do I sat up. And then I wished I hadn't. I managed not to throw up by swallowing hard and staring at the opposite wall. I made myself breathe as slowly as

I could through my nose and that helped. Though it also brought me the smell.

When I'd come back a bit more, I admitted to myself that I did know what the smell was and started looking about me to see where it was coming from and whether it was from me.

I was on a raised bed of the type osteopaths and the like use, in a brightly lit room with no windows. The walls were just painted brickwork and the floor was lino.

One man was slumped against the opposite wall. His head was hanging down and there was blood dripping from it onto his lap. Another one was curled up on the floor in a still spreading pool of his own blood. He was clearly the source of the smell. There was absolutely no question about whether they were dead or not.

Apart from feeling like shit, I seemed to be unhurt. I even had my phone and wallet and keys still in my pockets.

The banging stopped. I looked at where it had been coming from. There was a heavy steel door, painted the same colour as the walls, and it was bolted shut with heavy bolts, top and bottom. There was a similar door on the opposite side of the room and it was shut but not bolted. Apart from a few old wooden chairs, a stainless steel sink with a calendar with naked girls on it hung on a nail above it, a fridge and a kettle, and me, that was about all there was. Oh, and a car battery, some wire and a pair of pliers.

I got down carefully onto a bit of the lino that didn't have blood on it and gave my legs a chance to stop trembling.

It was very quiet. I couldn't hear any sound apart from my own breathing. I looked at the dead man nearest me, the one with the pool of blood round him. There was a bulge under his t-shirt where it overlapped his trousers. I leant over, so that I could lift the shirt, and extracted my Sig. I eased the slide back and saw that there was a round in the chamber and then thumbed off the safety. This made me feel better.

I went to the unbolted door on shaky, but strengthening legs, and gave it an experimental pull. It swung smoothly on oiled hinges. Through the gap I could see a corridor and the entrance to another room. I still couldn't hear anything.

There didn't seem to be any purpose in waiting, so I swung the door enough to get through, stepped out, and then swung it back against my fingers so that it couldn't bang, and then slipped them out. Now I could see the entrances to two more rooms and that the corridor ran into nothing one way, and turned a corner out of sight the other. There were no windows and no CCTV cameras. I went forward as quietly as I could and looked into the rooms and then round the corner.

Wherever I was had no windows and felt like it was underground; it reminded me of the subterranean parts of one of the schools I'd been to. They hadn't bothered to plaster the walls and pipe-work and wiring ran along the ceiling. There was intermittent lighting by fluorescent tube and the paint job was reasonably fresh but not inspired; just a universal yellowish cream.

There was no need for caution; I was alone apart from one more dead man. He was face down at the end of the corridor where it met what I took to be the front door of the place. This was another heavy steel door but it had a monitor mounted on the wall near it. There were some wires dangling and a shelf which I suspected had been the resting place for a CCTV recording system. Whoever had killed the three men had taken the evidence of their identity with them.

It would've been nice to see whatever the camera outside was seeing but the screen was blank.

I stepped over the dead man and was about to try this door when something about him made me stop and look at him more closely. He appeared to have been skilfully killed by a knife-thrust from behind through the ribs and into the heart. What had caught my eye was a tattoo of a diving eagle clutching a lightning bolt done rather crudely in blue ink on the back of his neck. Different shirt, same man. That made me think a bit and the thinking made me come back to myself a bit more. Which was about time.

I had a proper look at the door. It wasn't a bad door as doors go, but someone appeared to have given it a very bad time. The frame of it was so badly buckled that the deadlock had been forced out of its housing. I tenderly pulled it inwards and had a look. Apparently whoever had done this, had used only one blow. I opened it enough to have a peep outside. All I could see was an utterly ordinary looking and completely deserted bit of ex-industrial London. So not underground after all. Full daylight, but still very early morning, as far as I could tell.

I was going to leave then, but I didn't. Instead, I put the safety back on the Sig and tucked it into the waistband of my trousers. Then I shook my limbs out and rubbed my hair with both hands.

"Fuck!" The word was hard against the hard walls and the hard light.

"Fuck!" Now I felt angry as well as sick. I went back to have a proper look at the place and its inhabitants.

One of the rooms had metal framed bunk beds, another had two tired sofas and a TV, another had a pool and table-tennis tables. Neither of these had any occupants, alive or dead, or anything that to my slowly clearing brain might represent a clue. That left the one I'd woken up in.

I took out my phone, re-entered it and started taking photos of the bodies, especially their faces and injuries. The man against the wall had been stabbed over the heart and hadn't bled much at all; externally, anyway. The other had had his throat cut to the extent that when I pushed his head to get a better shot, it moved quite independently to his body. The sweet, sour, disturbing smell of that much fresh blood had got stronger in my brief absence.

Both men had similar tattoos of the eagle and lightning bolt. One on his upper arm, the other on his left calf. Both were heavily built men in their late thirties or early forties. They had short haircuts, hard hands and hard faces. On the whole I was glad that they were dead, whoever they were.

The hammering on the inner door resumed. I debated whether to see who it was or not. It might be a fellow victim or it might be another member of this unsavoury crew. On balance, I felt that it was probably a victim. And anyway, feeling like I was, if it turned out to be another tattooed thug I didn't have any objection to making my contribution to the body count. I drew the bolts and swung the door, stepping back.

I was half right and half wrong: it was Anja. She looked at me, and at the gun in my hand, with fear and confusion and then saw the dead men on the floor.

"You killed them?" she said.

"Not me," I said. "You drugged me." I looked past her and saw a toilet and shower. She seemed to be the only occupant.

"I had to," she said.

"Who are these?" I said, pointing to a dead man.

"The men," she said.

"Oh, the men," I said.

"Yes. Who killed them?"

"Don't ask me. I know fuck all, frankly," I said.

"Who are you?" she said.

"Do you know where we are?" I said.

"No. Yes. It is one of their places. I haven't been here before but I've heard of it."

"The Greens?"

"Of course, the Greens."

"Where are we?"

"London," she said, shrugging her shoulders, it looked like it hurt. "South of the river."

"Hm. I'm thinking of leaving. Would you care to come with me?" I said.

She looked at the dead men and I could see that she was feeling pretty bleak.

"I have to," she said.

"No you don't," I said. "I can lock you back in."

"They will still kill me," she said. "Now they will kill me for sure."

"Okay. In which case, er… follow me." She followed me cautiously.

I took a couple of photos of the dead man by the door and said, "Ready?"

"I suppose so," she said.

We stepped out into the street. There were concrete buildings and a road and pavements, and further down, a few parked cars, but no people moving. It was very good to be outside the building and in the fresh air. I wanted to run away somewhere, but I didn't.

To our right, at the junction I saw the brief light and movement of a car passing. The other way seemed to lead to an even quieter street or maybe a dead end. The building we'd stepped out of seemed to be the back of some Victorian warehouse. Low by the standards of the buildings around it but massively constructed in London red brick.

We turned to the right and started walking. The girl took my arm again and held onto it tightly. It was a good idea for both of us. It was fresh, almost chilly, and I welcomed that.

It was only a couple of hundred yards to the end but it felt like a long way. We found ourselves at a bigger road with occasional cars and lorries passing.

"What chance of a taxi, do you think?" I said.

"How would I know?" she said.

"I don't know what to think about you," I said.

While I was holding my phone and asking my brain what to do with it, a taxi appeared. The driver answered my raised hand, pulled up and put his window down a bit to have a look at us. We must have looked like we'd been having a fairly serious night out, but he accepted that we weren't a problem, and unlocked his doors.

While the girl was getting in I looked down the street to fix it in my mind. The back lights of one of the parked cars not far from where we'd been, came on and it pulled out of its space and trundled off down the road away from us. I recognised the distinctive square shape of a Landrover.

When we got to the docks, I tucked the Sig under Anja's coat as we walked to Polly. I was almost holding her up now. The steadily strengthening daylight helped though I was feeling very tired now as well as sick.

There were one or two people moving about, but I didn't see anyone follow us or take any interest in us at all. I punched in the numbers, held the gate for her and made sure it was shut. She found getting aboard difficult so she must have been beaten in other places too. I put her in the saloon and then went to check on Mel. She was sleeping soundly and looked fine, so I went into the galley to put the kettle on.

"You aren't going to do anything like that again, are you?" I said, going back to Anja. "Like drugging me, I mean. Or letting anyone in, if I get some sleep? I need some sleep."

She looked at me helplessly.

"Okay, I'm too tired to worry about it now," I said.

She started to shrug her shoulders but it hurt so she stopped.

"Would you like some tea?"

She nodded. I made us some tea and put sugar in it and gave her a shot of brandy and some painkillers too. She tossed the pills down with the brandy and then sat cradling the mug and looking at me.

I took her hand bag from her and up ended it on the table. There was the usual heap of bits and pieces and a phone. I took the battery out of it and put it in my pocket and then put the bits back down on the table. I should've done that before. She watched me without speaking or showing any emotion.

"We should get some sleep," I said.

"Okay," she said.

She was trying to look at me but she wasn't really there anymore, so I put her to bed in the spare cabin. She just rolled over onto the bunk and held herself and started to cry.

I went back to the main hatch and locked it, took my shoes off and then went to the aft cabin where I sleep. Where Mel was sleeping. I sat on the bed with my mug of tea and caught sight of myself in the mirror. I didn't look great but I was alive.

I went back to the girl, undid her laces and very gently pulled her boots off. Then I took the blankets off the top bunk and put them over her. She must have been awake but she didn't move while I did this. Then I lay down next to Mel, slid the Sig under my pillow and let go.

When I woke up, there was a warm, heavy presence lying comfortably against my back.

"Anja?" I said, softly.

"Ugh…?" a voice said near my ear.

"Mel?" I said.

"Ughhuh," the voice said.

That was okay then.

When I woke up again it was because we were having an earthquake.

"Are you awake?" Mel said.

"Mel?" I said.

"That's me," she said.

"Where am I?"

"In your own bed on Polly." She stopped shaking me.

"Oh. How? What…?"

"Anja drugged you."

"Anja?"

"The Russian girl you've been harassing. It'll come back to you."

"Oh yes. Is she...?"

"She's okay.. She's badly bruised but otherwise okay."

"Mel, are you...? Didn't you...?"

"I feel like crap, actually. What happened last night. We were dancing and then..."

"Oh, fuck. I'll tell you in a minute. God, I feel..."

"I can see. Don't move, I'll be back in a minute."

I wasn't going to.

She went away and came back a bit later with a glass of milk and a slice of toast with some honey on it. I sat up and tried eating and drinking. The food didn't taste right and I didn't manage much of it. My body felt slack and dirty, like I'd been sweating badly, and my mouth was horrible, and my head felt like someone had filled it with cement. I was alive though. And apparently in good hands.

"Fucking hell, Mel. Thanks," I said, when my brain had cleared a bit more.

"You're welcome."

"I feel like shit."

"Welcome to the club."

"Mel, we're not winning this one..."

"What do you mean?"

"I was right; you are one of them. One of the victims, I mean..."

I caught her up with events a bit.

"Oh fuck."

"Indeed."

"I thought I was just hung-over."

"How're you feeling you look..."

"Like shit. I know. I'm okay. Where did they take you?"

"It's the back of *Caesars*, I think."

"And someone killed them and let you out? You were lucky."

The Goddess of the Sanctuary

"It seems I have a guardian angel." I looked at her and thought about Landrovers and decided all that had better wait until my brain was functioning a bit better. Then I had a thought. "Go to the cupboard over there, will you. Second drawer down at the back. Should be medical stuff. Get a syringe and a needle."

"Please."

"Please. And then take a bit of my blood. If you can do that. Please."

It turned out she could. She pulled the belt out of my trousers and used that as a tourniquet and expertly found a vein.

"Good. Now give me my phone, please."

"Which one?"

"Both of them. And go and make some coffee, will you?"

"I see you're feeling better. They're beside you and I put them on charge."

"Ah."

She went and pointedly shut the cabin door. I managed to focus sufficiently and phone Bill.

"Are you hung-over? You don't sound quite yourself?" he said.

"No, I'm not hungover. I'm going to leave a couple of things for you at the gunroom. Pick them up and get Mac to look at them for me, will you?"

"Can do. What things?"

"A glass and some of my blood."

"Oh…?"

"Thanks. Can I tell you later? I need to drink some coffee and think."

"You do that, old son. Wouldn't want you to tire yourself out."

"Is Freddy here yet?"

"No. Doing some tidying up in… You don't need to know. Sorry, two more days. He'll be touched to know you're missing him."

"Go find out what a diving eagle holding a lightning bolt means."

"What?"

"As a tattoo. Just go do it. I'll text you in a bit."

I disconnected and got myself out of bed and into a pair of trousers and went to see what was what. Anja and Mel were in the saloon and Anja was in my dressing gown and had damp hair. She still looking battered, and vulnerable but more human nonetheless. Mel was applying makeup to hide the bruises.

"Good morning, Anja," I said.

"Good morning," she said, not looking at me.

"Don't mind him," Mel said.

"No, don't mind me," I said.

"He didn't mean to get you into trouble," she said. "He never does. It's just selfish thoughtlessness, not malice. He won't hurt you intentionally."

"You do remember that I just got poisoned, do you?" I said.

"And you think that makes you special?" she said.

"Fair point," I said.

"You haven't seen her bruises," Mel said.

"I'm okay," Anja said. Her voice contradicted her.

"No, you're not," I said. "You're in deep trouble, and it's at least partly my fault. I'm sorry."

"So, you should be," Mel said. "We need to get her somewhere safe."

"Yes, I've got…" I started to say when my phone interrupted me. It was a message from Susie, 'Are you in?'. I went to the window and looked out. There was the woman in the big hat, scarf, sunglasses and a long coat at the security gate again. I texted her the gate code and watched her make her graceful way towards us.

"What're you looking at?" Mel said.

"Sunlight glinting on cobbles," I said, and went to unlock the door.

"Hey, Si," Susie said, swinging down the companion way. "Is Mel here? I've come to make this party happen. Oh."

"This is Anja," I said. "Anja, this is Susie."

They greeted each other and took the few nanoseconds it takes one woman to assess another.

"Hi Susie," Mel said.

"Oh, yes. Hi Mel."

"Anja's Russian," I said. "She was forced into prostitution by some unpleasant people called Green, who've taken her young daughter from her and now I've got her into serious trouble by using her to try to find out about them. They beat her up quite badly last night and they'll probably do a lot worse if they get their hands on her again."

"Oh," Susie said. "That puts my problems into perspective. What can I do to help?"

"Good. You can lend me your hat and scarf and coat and... No, better idea, just swap clothes, will you? I mean..."

"You mean, someone's watching us?" Susie said. "You're going to take her away as me?"

"Yes. Well, probably. Do you mind?"

"Of course not." She began taking things off.

"What's happening?" Anja said.

"I'm taking you somewhere safe," I said.

"Where?" Mel said.

"Good question," I said. "Anja, will you put on Susie's clothes please? I want to disguise you."

"I could..." she said, holding my dressing gown tighter. They were all three looking at me.

"Leave the room, you idiot," Mel said.

"Ah," I said, and left them to sort themselves out.

While they were doing that, I went up to the foredeck and leant on the rail and phoned the number I had for Jess Dutton.

"Jess Dutton," the voice said.

"Hi Jess. This is Si Ellice," I said.

"Si. Well, hello. Are you phoning to arrange your humiliation? I'm in town at the moment but I'll be home for the weekend."

"That's a very good thought…"

"But not the reason you phoned?"

"Not exactly. You work for that women's foundation, don't you?"

"I do a bit. Why?"

"Good. Can I bring you one? She needs to be got somewhere where she can't be found."

"No problem, it's what we do. When do you want to bring her?"

"Nowish? Say about an hour."

"Okay. Hang up and I'll text you the address."

"Thanks."

"No problem." We disconnected and sure enough a few seconds later an address came through.

I went back down to see how the girls were getting on. Susie was wearing my dressing gown now and looking much more at ease than when she'd arrived. Anja was wearing Susie's clothes and although they fitted pretty well they didn't make her look much like Susie. She was looking better too though. If I wasn't mistaken, Mel was pissed off, but trying to hide it.

The three of them were having a discussion about which shoes Anja should wear.

"They don't fit," Anja said, holding one of Susie's up.

"Don't worry, it's the walk, not the shoes," I said.

"What do you mean?" Anja said.

"I need you to walk like Susie," I said.

"How do I walk?" Susie said.

"Like a yearling colt," I said. "Slightly gangly but with immense grace and latent inner spring."

"There he goes," Mel said. "How's that supposed to help, you clot?"

"Don't worry, we'll wing it," I said. "Come on Anja. Let's you and me go and take a walk."

"What are we supposed to do?" Mel said.

"I don't think I should go home in your dressing gown," Susie said, smiling.

"Could you use some of Anja's or Mel's clothes?" I said.

They both looked at me as if I was an idiot. Apparently not, then.

"Okay. I'll buy you some. You two can stay here and… Are we having this party?" I looked at Mel.

"I don't know," she said, hesitating.

"Why not? What's up?" Susie said.

"Right. I'll leave you two to sort that out. Come on, Anja," I said, and led the way.

To my surprise, they each gave Anja a hug. She followed me up into the June sunshine. Well it was more or less sunshine; there were a few clouds about and a bit of a breeze. Not a bad day.

"Now then, Anja, think of me as your bodyguard, not your minder. You're a wealthy, powerful woman with complete freedom in this world. My job is to carry your bags, keep you safe and do whatever you tell me. Ready?"

"I will try."

"Head up, shoulders back, don't walk behind me."

"Okay."

Maybe no one was watching us. Maybe they were. If they were, I didn't see them. We walked past the drunk and his dog, through the busy walkways of the docks, and out into the workaday streets beyond. I let the first passing taxi go, and the next, and stopped the third. It dropped us in Oxford Street where we dived into Marks and Spencer through one entrance, emerged from another and went round the block to Oxford Circus tube station.

Anja and I sat side by side in the relative intimacy of a half empty Bakerloo train and swayed together as it took the curves.

"Well?" I said.

"Where are you taking me?" she said.

"I'm taking you to someone who will look after you and keep you safe," I said.

"It doesn't matter," she said.

"Are you being Russian now?"

"What do you mean?"

"Hopeless, looking on the dark side, doing tragedy. You know what I mean."

"No."

"Unless you know where your daughter is and that she's safe, what happens to you doesn't really matter?"

"You have any children?"

"No. Don't suppose I ever will. Not my kind of thing. Well, I don't think so, anyway."

"Then you know nothing."

"Fair enough. If you know where your daughter is, or where she might be, I'll go and have a look for her."

"It is no good. I think she's in Poland."

"Then I will go to Poland."

"You will go to Poland?"

"Yes. Why not?"

"They will kill you."

"You keep saying that. Do you mind if they kill me?"

"No. Not much."

"Thought so. You haven't got anything to lose now, have you?"

She thought about that in silence. Or, possibly she didn't.

"Anja, would you please consider trusting me? Just a little," I said. "I would like to make amends, if I can."

"I do not believe you."

The Goddess of the Sanctuary

"I don't blame you. Mel trusts me. I think Susie does too. You could trust me a bit."

"They are your kind of girls. I am not."

"Anja, you are my kind of girl."

"No."

We rode along in silence again. She stared at the opposite side of the carriage and as far as I could tell, I didn't exist.

We changed at Embankment, got out at Southwark station and started walking. I could tell that she was still in some pain but I didn't want to take a cab and she didn't complain. We passed into quieter residential streets and navigated to our destination, which turned out to be a rather pretty brick house on Lynton Street. A discreet sign indicated that this was the Congrieve Womens' Walk-in Centre. There was an entry system complete with camera above our heads. When I pressed the buzzer a voice over the intercom enquired our business. I gave my name and was told to wait.

There was a brief delay and then the door opened to reveal Jess Dutton. In the strong daylight, I could see that she had a scattering of freckles across her nose. Her flaming red hair was loose about her shoulders, she looked healthy and vigorous and like she came from a very different world to the one that Anja and I had been inhabiting recently; a cleaner, lighter, brighter place.

"Hello, Si," she said.

"Hi, Jess. This is Anja," I said.

"Hi Anja." She held out her hand.

Anja took it carefully and said, "Hello," quietly.

"Whatever's been happening to you, it's about to get better. I promise," Jess said. And she said it with such simplicity and confidence that I could see it did Anja good. I believed her myself. "Now, come with me and we'll make a start." She held the door open for her.

"You will help me?" Anja said.

"I will," Jess said.

"Okay," Anja said, taking a breath and stepping through into the lobby.

"Sorry, not you. No men in here," Jess said, stepping in front of me so that I couldn't follow her.

"Okay, er…" I said.

"That's okay." She smiled at me comfortably. "Go away. I'll phone you in a bit."

As she shut the door I noticed that it swung smoothly with the weight of a serious piece of glass and metal and I'd be willing to bet that the inner one wouldn't open until it was shut and locked. No one was going to get through that door unless they were invited.

Instead of retracing my steps, I went on towards Bermondsey, where I caught a Jubilee train to Baker Street. I turned my phone off and trotted along to Le Bonholmes, where I left a package with my blood and the dirty glass with the ever-helpful Charlie Hibbert.

I was crossing Marylebone Road, and had only just turned my phone back on, when it rang. It was Jess.

"Hi Jess."

"Well, that's a story," she said.

"Anja's told you all about it?"

"She has, poor thing. I thought you looked a bit hung over, but it seems I did you an injustice. It also seems I got to find out what you do without having to humiliate you."

"You did?"

"She said that you're trying to find some girls?"

"That's true, I am. One girl mainly. Her name is Jane Hamilton. I was at school with her brother."

"So, you're a private investigator, or something? PI Si?"

"Very good. No, not at all. I'm not currently doing anything else and I said I'd help, so I am. Or at least, I'm trying to. Not sure I'm doing any good."

"Ah, I see. So, maybe we still need to have our race after all."

"We should definitely have our race."

"I agree. Anyway, there's someone here who wants to talk to you. Here she is…"

"Hello," Anja's voice said.

"Hi Anja, how's it going?" I said.

"It is okay," she said. "But…"

"Go on," I said.

"It's near Sanok. I heard one of the men say that. And there was a wind pump with no things in the yard."

"Where the missing girls might be?" I said.

"No. Not her," she said, and I heard the bitterness in her voice and realised my mistake.

"You mean where your daughter might be?" I said.

"Yes. She might be there."

"Okay. And Sanok is where?"

"Sanok in Poland," she said it like I should've known. Perhaps I should.

"Okay. The yard; was it a farm yard?" I said.

"Yes. It was a farm. Yes. Near Sanok. We were there for a week and then, when there were more of us, we came here. There were trees and I think it was high up. That is all."

"A wind pump with no sails? One of those old metal ones?"

"Yes, that is right. No wings. Just the tower."

"Good. That may be enough. I'll look for it. Thank you for telling me. How will I know her?"

"Her name is Irena. She is five years old and she has fair hair, like me."

"Do you have a photo?"

She hesitated and then said, "Yes. I have one."

"Good. Keep it for now. I will get Jess to make a copy and give it to me."

"Yes, okay. Jess said I should trust you. She is very nice."

"She is, isn't she. I'm sure she'll see that you're safe now."

"I think so too. And…"

"Yes?"

"Okay. There is a place in this country. Where they kept us. A lot of us. Before they brought us to London."

"Great. Tell me about it, please? Where is it?"

"I don't know. They took us there in the back of a van. They always do that. There was a wall. A high wall round a garden and buildings. It was in a forest. There was no sound of cars and no lights at night. And there was the sound of screaming sometimes in the wood. I think it was…"

"Foxes?"

"Yes, foxes…" she seemed to disappear.

"Okay," I said. "Do you have any idea where in the country it might…"

"Sorry, Si, we've got to go now…" It was Jess's voice, "…transport is here. I want to get her home now, but you can talk to her soon. Okay?"

"Er…

"Call me."

"Okay, I…" The call went dead.

I sent Bill a longish text about high walls in woods and then set off again. As I walked along through the metropolis, it occurred to me that perhaps there were some benefits to civilisation after all. Particularly if it came in the shape of an immensely competent, forceful, and rather attractive, red-headed girl.

22

LET IT RAIN

When I got back to the docks, Susie was still with Mel on board Polly. She was also, as I'd hoped, still in my dressing gown.

They had a tablet, Mel's laptop and a notebook, and they were looking absorbed and serious.

"What've you got there?" Mel said, taking her pen out of her mouth and eyeing the bags I was carrying.

"Some clothes for Susie."

"You bought me some clothes?" Susie said.

"I'm not saying I don't like you as you are, but I thought they might be useful," I said.

"Let me see." She got up, grabbed the bags and started pulling what was in them out.

"What about me?" Mel said.

"You already have clothes," I said. "Quite a lot of them, in fact."

"How did you do that?" Susie said, holding up a dress.

"What?"

"Buy this dress? It's perfect."

"Oh, that was easy. I went into a shop and told a girl what I wanted, she fetched it and I paid for it."

"But it's the right size, the right style, the right length, the right colour and even the right neck line. How did you know?"

"I'm not entirely unobservant," I said.

"About some things," Mel said.

"Speaking of which," I said, picking up the notepad, "What're you two up to?"

"Planning a party, of course," Susie said.

"We have double bait now," Susie said, giving me a mischievous smile.

"So, we do," I said.

"You seem doubtful?" Mel said.

"Have you noticed that some fucker seems to be able to poison us at will?" I said.

"Are you still feeling poorly?" Mel said.

"Yes, but…"

"No one will pass that security gate unless we let them in. I want to know who's doing this," she said.

"So do I," Susie said.

"We know it's the Greens now, don't we?" I said.

"Yes, we do," Mel said.

"The authorities know it too now. We can leave it to them to go through everything they are and everything they have. I'm sure they'll find Jane and Natasha."

"Fine, but I still want to lay my hands, or your hands, on whoever did that to me last night," Mel said. "I don't know who it was, but I want to, and I mean now; not at sometime in the future when someone else does something. Understand?"

"And me," Susie said.

"I suppose so," I said

"Good. So, c'mon, Si. Let's have a party," Mel said. "When did you ever say no to one of those?"

"Oh fuck." I looked at them. Mel was right, I was a little tired and I hadn't eaten anything for weeks.

"Why don't you go and have a sleep, Si?" Susie said, reaching over and taking my hand.

"Good idea," Mel said, getting up and stepping between us. "Come on you. Come with me." She shepherded me into the big bed and undid the buttons of my shirt and pushed me down and took my socks off my feet. The softness of the bed holding me up was too much, I lay back and she stroked my hair. "It's okay, Si. Leave it to us now. Okay?"

"Okay, Mel."

Someone took hold of my head by the hair and started shaking it. I didn't seem to mind much.

"Whaa…?"

"It's seven o'clock, Si. Wakey, wakey." The shaking stopped and something sat on me. I was pretty sure it was Mel.

"Huh?"

"It's seven o'clock."

"Oh, good."

"I said, it's seven o'fucking clock."

I pushed her off and sat up.

"Okay, it's seven o'clock."

She looked beautiful and soft, and delicious so I reached out and tried to pull her down to me.

"No you don't." It didn't work and I found out again how strong she was. "Get up. Get up now. We have things to do."

"Mel, have you gone off me, or something?"

"I told you, not now. It's party time."

"Oh." I sat up and put my fingers in her hair and caressed the back of her neck. She pushed me away.

"Now, stop that and get the fuck up."

"I am up."

"Don't be crude."

I stood under the shower for a bit and then appeared in the saloon in my dressing gown, which no one else was using at the time.

"Hey, Si." Susie quite unselfconsciously greeted me with a kiss.

"Hi, Susie," I said.

"Right, we've still got a lot to do, so let's focus," Mel said.

"Yes, Mel," we both said.

There was that interesting tension between them again, but also, as it turned out, a natural team spirit. Somehow they had purchased and got delivered a lot of things to drink and hired things to drink them out of, and hampers of food and plates and all that. And then, for some reason that escaped me, managed to buy more clothes.

"We're doing Caribbean," Mel said. "This is yours." She held up a loud shirt. A very loud shirt.

"You want me to wear that?"

"You're bloody well going to wear it," she said. "Go and put it on and get busy. I need you to do the lights and get some speakers outside and what happens if it rains?"

"You probably should, Si," Susie said. "I know her when she gets like this."

"So do I," I said.

I put on some shorts and sandals and the shirt in question. It was a very cheerful shirt and it did alter my mood. I didn't say that though, but got on with rearranging my home to suit their commands.

A man with a big hold-all appeared at the gate and called out to be let in, in broad cockney. He turned out to be Henriques in a boiler-suit and cloth cap.

"You ordered a barman, Ma'm?" he said, bowing to Mel.

"Henriques, there you are," Mel said. "I knew you wouldn't let me down. Follow me."

When I next descended the companion way, I found him in bowtie and tails, having clearly taken charge of the bar while appearing to relish taking orders from Mel and Susie.

It wasn't long before what could be done had been done, or was being done by someone else, so I went and sat at the back of the cockpit and surveyed the scene. It looked pretty good to me. I'm not saying I hadn't had a party or two on Polly before, but surprisingly, I had a good feeling about this one. And that had a lot to do with Mel and Susie; two utterly beautiful women, each in their own very different way.

Perhaps feeling me watching her, Susie slipped away from the others to join me. She sat down beside me and slapped my thigh a few times in a rather delightful way.

"We're having a party then, Susie," I said.

"So we are, Si," she said.

"Do you think anyone will come?"

"I believe they will, yes."

"Because you're here?"

"Yes..." she hesitated, weighing that up, "and because Berry will be. And because of you too, I think."

"Me?"

"You caused a few ripples the other day."

"When I made a certain purchase?"

"Yes. And you and Mel..."

"Me and Mel...?"

"You make an interesting couple."

"Ah. We've known each other a long time... but we're not... I mean, we're definitely friends but..."

"I see. Good, yes. And there's a story, isn't there? Dad's an idiot in some ways, but he's not entirely wrong, is he? About you, I mean?"

"Ah."

"I looked you up a bit." She looked at me, searching my face.

"I see," I said, returning her gaze and wondering what she thought of me.

"All that about drugs…?"

"I never said I was a saint."

"Actually, you did. Are you really trying to find Jane and Natasha?"

"Yes. And whoever poisoned you."

"Why?"

"Because Mel asked me to, and because I have nothing else to do," I said.

"Yes," she said, giving one definite, very charming, nod of her head.

"Yes?" I said.

"Yes, I believe that."

"Good. So, are you ready to be bait?"

"I am the bait, that is what I am. I will appear to drink, but barely do so. I will appear to let my hair down, but I will be watching. And I will assume that one of my friends is going to try to poison me." She sighed.

"It makes you sad," I said.

"Yes. Will you keep me safe tonight, Si?"

"I will do my best."

"Of which, no man may be asked more. And Mel, of course."

"Of course."

"Okay then. Unless I'm mistaken, here we go. Look."

I followed her gaze and saw that there were people approaching the gate, and if they were going to a party, it was a party I wanted to be at. And then behind them, more people.

Mel ran to the gate and there was shrieking and kissing and exclamations and shortly after that, I was wondering how only four more girls managed to make Polly suddenly seem small. I'd barely got their names before there were more, and more, and Polly was full of people and it was a party.

Even as I greeted people and tried to remember their names, I noticed that the lighting that we'd done was very good and the music was wonderful and I was having a good time.

At one point, Berry and Maisie stepped onto the deck and I thought of that song by Carly Simon, but it was an unkind thought. He gave me the usual hug, which I returned with interest and Maisie did a twirl of sublime happiness and then greeted me with her usual lack of reserve. And it's true that in that mysterious way of theirs, they brought a certain extra magic to proceedings.

I was still taking it very seriously, and I defy anyone to have noticed that Mel and I spent the evening playing a kind of tag. Wherever Susie was, one of us would also be sure to be. That way neither of them was ever on their own. The only trouble was, it quickly became so crowded that it was hard to see past the bodies. We kept moving; doing our hostly duty, helping to make it all go with a swing, not that it needed much help, and checked in with each other regularly and swapped observation posts. On one of those occasions, Mel punched me quite hard on the arm and said, "We're going to do this again when it's just a party."

"If you say so, Mel."

"I do."

There was a lot for us to do. Apart from keeping an eye out, I made a determined effort to have a proper conversation with as many people as possible; hoping that something about one of them would suggest something to me. It's not that I wanted Mel or Susie to be poisoned as such, but in this increasingly nebulous and frustrating business, it would be rather good to get my hands on someone slipping something into a glass of champagne or casually pressing a doctored nicotine patch against skin.

The girls played their parts fabulously. They shone like stars; laughing and joking and very clearly having a very fine time with no hint of restraint or self-consciousness. Susie's grace and naturalness had an effect like gravity on us all. For me, or any one of us, to be looking in her direction, was nothing out of place. Mel too, with her warmth and directness and the power of her personality commanded us. They were two equal and opposed celestial bodies and they bathed us in their light.

They both knew everyone, and with perfect naturalness, made sure that they spent time with everyone. And though they both appeared to drink deeply and often, they also often contrived to put their glasses down and to lose track of them, and then find them again. I had plenty to do to keep up with them.

In all this, I found myself making easy connections with lots of people too. Either through mutual friends, or school, or university, or the army, or often Hampshire, and they with me. I am a sociable chap when I choose to be, and it was a pleasure. I can't say I've ever felt that I belonged to any particular group, but if I did, this could have been it. I don't know why I hadn't realised it before, but the name, Ellice, had meaning in this world. In that company, I was someone because of who I was; my family and our history and connections, not because of what I did, or because I was the one telling everyone what to do. It was a novel feeling.

Henriques did an outstanding job; his punch was the real thing, and though he contrived to make sure that everyone had whatever they were drinking in abundance, he did it with such natural charm and confidence that there was no question of him being there as any kind of servant. At one point, I gave him a wink over the shoulder of the beautiful young woman he was deep in conversation with, which he returned with a perfectly dead-pan face, which I took to mean exactly what I thought it meant.

Though I say it myself, we did a fine job of making everyone feel welcome and special. I turned a blind eye to Maisie and several of the others snorting coke off the saloon table, though it cost me a pang.

After a time, the last of the light went out of the air, intensifying the feeling and the intimacy of the party. There was laughter and excitement bubbling out of the fore-hatch, groups of people were here and there, everywhere on the deck and in the saloon and in the cockpit. At a moment of pause, and having Susie in my eye-line talking to, or rather being talked at, by one Henry Fitzroyce, I moved to the back of the cockpit to check in with Mel, who was there. And to pause and survey the scene. It was a fine scene, for all that it was in the city. Even perhaps for that very reason. Life in London. If I was honest, there was something rather good about all this.

There was a feeling of weather in the air and I was glad that I'd rigged the tarpaulin over the cockpit. As I pushed through the throng to the back of the boat, a man and woman rose from the seats beside Mel, and I was aware that they were looking a little uncomfortable.

"Hello, er... Simon," the man said, extending a hand. "I hope you don't mind. His lordship said you wouldn't and..." It was the love-struck American from the evening at the *Umbra Villus*.

"I don't at all, Wi..." I said, racking my brains.

"Willard Wallace," Mel said, coming up behind me. "And of course he doesn't mind."

"Call me Will. And this is my wife, Caitlyn," he said.

"It's very good of you, if you're sure," she said, taking my hand, and offering a charming smile in return.

"I am delighted to have you here," I said, and as far as I could tell, I may well have been, though that name rang a bell somewhere else too.

"We're having such a wonderful time in your city and, by the way, tell me why you've got those extra two shrouds so far aft?" Will said.

"You sail?" I said.

"I do a bit," he said, grinning.

"Ah well," I said. "That's a good question. That's to help me set up a code-zero."

"A code what?"

"Oh, there he goes," Caitlyn said.

"Do you think they realise it's only a few bits of rope?" Mel said.

"It's like an asymmetrical spinnaker," I said, ignoring her. "The thing is, if you…"

I got so caught up in talking about sail-plans; Will was a serious sailor, and by the way he was talking, a well-funded one; that I forgot all about Susie for a moment, but then there she was being dragged towards us by Maisie. We all stopped talking to see what was up.

"Darling," Maisie said, looking up at me from close to.

"Yes, Maisie?" I said.

"You tell him, Susie," Maisie said.

"No, you tell him, Maisie. He won't mind," Susie said, lowering an eyelid in my direction.

"What would you like, Maisie?" I said.

"I want Berry to sing his song," she said. "Is that alright?"

"My love, you and Berry may do any damn thing you please with my good will," I said.

"Oh, thank you." She reached up and pulled my head down to kiss me, in the way she did. "Will you go and tell him please?" She looked up at me, pleading with her big eyes. "He won't believe me."

"Okay." I was going to argue, but it just didn't seem worth it. I went to Berry, who was sitting on the roof of the cabin, swinging his legs and talking to one of the Thompson twins. He looked down at me in a friendly, but rather absent minded way and raised his glass to me in salute.

"Berry," I said, returning the gesture.

"Si," he said.

"Maisie wants me to ask you to do your song."

"Does she?"

"Yes."

"Shall I?"

"Yes. I think you should."

"Very well, I will. Er... in which case, would you?" he indicated the nearest speaker from which the current selection of music was emanating.

"One second," I said, and nipped below to hit the relevant switch.

Into the sudden silence, the sound of voices was loud, and then self-conscious as people reacted to the change, Berry started tapping the beginnings of a rhythm with his thumb against his now empty glass and it began to catch at us. And then he gave a kind of grunt and started to sing. At first it was just one note, but it was a strong and growing note and it over-rode all the conversations and everyone stopped to listen, and then it broke and dipped and rose and took over the rhythm from his tapping on the glass, and then it became words and we followed them, and went with them. I'd forgotten what a master he was; strong and utterly confident and entirely with what he was doing.

I didn't actually see Mel arrive in the centre of the cockpit, but there she was and there was a space around her and she held herself quite still, but full of tension and our attention shifted from him to her, and then she began to move and the way she moved fitted the song and it was all one perfect thing. Everyone on board was on deck now, lining the rails and taking up the cabin top and every inch of the cockpit apart from the bit Mel was dancing in.

And in the centre of the crowd, the song, and Mel's dancing, began to build together and she faced Berry and he smiled at her and bowed a little as he sang and she curtseyed as she danced and then turned back to us and they worked up to the refrain together and eased into a more contemplative verse, and we all went with them.

They took us with them twice more and then to my complete surprise Henriques stepped into the cockpit with a guitar that I had no idea was on the boat, and stood before Berry. Berry smiled and gently nodded and Henriques hit a chord and it was the perfect cord that supported and surrounded Berry's soaring voice, and they swung into the beginning again, and again, we all went with them, but this time we were starting to hum, or even sing, with them and the whole thing was growing and deepening and we were all in it together and it felt like it was all that there was of us and all that there was, or needed to be.

And then, before we could have enough of it, they took it to the end together, facing each other and arriving at one note that gathered everything up, and us with it, and came together into a perfect stop that reverberated into the silence. And then came the applause that none of us started or consciously thought of, but which was sprung out of us like water gushing from a fountain.

And, as that eased, we were left better and cleaner and emptier and moved in some way, and satisfied and wanting more. Mel stamped her foot on the deck and said, "Girls!" and pointed at the foredeck.

I don't know who started the sound system again, or how they found the music that they chose, but someone did, and as they did, the first fat drops of rain hit the deck. Most of us moved under the tarpaulin or into the cabin, but there were six women on the foredeck; Mel and Susie and Julie Whitsmith and Tamara Asty and Becky Rice and Sophie Mole. They made a circle and they didn't seem to care about the rain.

Let it Rain

Mel pulled the pin out of her hair, so that it all fell down around her and they all looked up into the rain, accepting it and letting it soak them. They moved in together and took each other's hands and ducked their heads and then flung them up and shook them, scattering water like dogs, and separated and turned and began to stomp.

I've no idea what made them dance like that. Whatever it was, it came out of some place that I'd never been to. Their skin was slick and shining from the sodium lights on the quay and their clothes clung to them and became much more part of them than they had been before. They were not naked but they were revealed and were elemental and beautiful, each one. I wanted to join them but I couldn't. There was no place for a man among them at that moment. Or any other woman, come to that.

"Wow. Will you look at that," Will said.

"Is there anywhere on earth you'd rather be?" I said.

"I'll say not," he said.

I'm not saying I wasn't moved by it all, but I was still mindful enough of the evening's task to wonder if there was something going on that I couldn't see.

Most people stood and watched the girls dancing and one or two slipped back to their conversations. I noticed that Berry was sitting by himself at the back of the cockpit, so I went to join him.

"Well, Si, you seem to have thrown a party," he said, bowing his head slightly.

"I think it sort of threw itself," I said. "I didn't know you could get this many people on Polly without sinking her."

"I may have to change my mind; perhaps you do belong in the city after all."

"Don't say that, I'm in denial about the whole subject."

"Well, whatever you've done, you've got those girls dancing like some maniacal devotees of an orgiastic Dionysus. Did you put something in that rather excellent punch?"

"Apollo in this case, I think. It was your song that did that, and you know it."

"It may be. It may be. I didn't know Mel could do that, though. Have you liberated something within that very fine bosom?"

"Not me. She seems to have, I don't know, come into her power, but not through anything I've done."

"Women are powerful as women, not as men, aren't they? Not everyone knows that."

"That's profound, Berry."

"It's true though."

"I'm not arguing with you."

"Not that we're entirely redundant yet, are we. The masculine principle."

"Don't think I ever had any principles."

"Well said. So, you and she…?'

"Friends. Good friends, but I think that's all. She's changed…"

"Interesting. You look like a team, and that's a fact."

"I suppose we are."

"But a team doing, what?"

"Oh, just having fun," I said, concentrating on the dancers. Something had tugged at my attention again. Something wasn't right.

"Fair enough, Si. No one's going to say that you're not good at it."

"Huh?"

"Throwing a party."

"Oh yes."

Part of my brain was listening to him, but it was only Berry; the dancers had my real attention. In particular, Susie; that was what it was; she had started to move without her usual grace and now she was staggering back out of the group. Her foot caught on the harness line, she fought to catch herself and failed, arms flailing. She hit the rail with her thighs and tumbled over into the black water below.

23

IN WHICH CASE, APHRODITE

I passed my phone to Berry and went in after her. When I got to her, she was trying to swim but it wasn't going well. I put an arm round her and she hung onto me and pushed against me, pushing herself up in the water and me down.

I took a breath and let that happen, my head going under, and then kicked out with my legs, pushing us both up so that I could get a breath. She relaxed a little and I got myself behind her and held her up so that she felt a bit safer. When I got my head out next, I said, "Susie, lean back on me. I'm going to swim us over to the ladder." She did that, laying back against me. She almost stopped trying to swim or do anything at all. At least this made it easier and it was no trouble to kick us backwards to the rusty metal rungs of the ladder that came down to the water not far from the Polly's bows.

I put her onto it and walked her up it, my body behind hers making a cage around her so that she couldn't fall. Mel received her into a big towel and others were there too. Henriques held an umbrella over them, getting a soaking himself from the still heavy rain. Mel held her while she vomited until she was empty and it was only a slimy mucus coming out of her.

When I'd spat out a bit of the dock water and wiped the worst of it out of my hair and off my face I swept her up and carried her back aboard Polly.

The party had come to a halt, and people were standing about looking cold and wondering what to do with themselves. I took Susie down to the saloon, being careful not to bang her head on the sides of the companionway, and put her down on a bunk. Mel came with me.

"Hot shower and then bed," I said.

Susie looked disorientated and was very compliant, in that now familiar way. Mel sat beside her and took her wrist so that she could feel her pulse and then looked into her eyes and then moved a finger in front of them.

"I think she'll be okay," I said.

"I agree," she said. "No call for A and E tonight. I'll take her into the shower. Come on, darling, you come with me now." She took Susie's arm and guided the poor, sodden, confused girl into the shower. I put the kettle on and surveyed the disarray of my home, which was strewn with dirty glasses and wet clothes and other things.

"That was interesting," Henriques said, coming in. "Fluids is what she needs now..."

"There are some electrolytes in the third drawer," I said, pointing. "I'll just..."

"Go and see to your guests. Do that. I've got this."

"Thanks."

The crowd had already thinned somewhat but I found a largish group sitting about under the tarpaulin, talking quietly and not wanting to leave without saying something. They looked like they weren't quite sure what had happened. Apart from at least one of them, of course. I smiled at them remembering their faces and names and made light of it all and told them that Susie was just having a shower and was fine.

"Trust Susie," Berry said. "Well that was a memorable end to a memorable evening, Si."

And the end, it clearly was. Will shook my hand and Caitlyn kissed me and they went. The younger ones went off in a group, huddling together for warmth, unconcerned by the rain in their complete wetness, shepherded by their men, and me with a big umbrella, into a fleet of taxis that someone had made appear.

Soon, only me and Henriques and Berry and Maisie were left sitting in the cockpit. The rain was loud on the tarpaulin. Maisie was on Berry's lap, apparently mostly asleep.

"Well, there you are, you see," Berry said, smiling at me over Maisie's drooping head.

"I see what?" I said, sitting down and sweeping some more of the water out of my hair.

"Where you are, there trouble and drama are. How is the poor girl?"

"Susie? She'll be fine."

"What was it this time? I didn't even see her do a line," he said. "Did she just trip? Is she unwell, or something? The other night…?"

"She didn't," Maisie said, raising her head. "I offered, but she said she would stick to the champagne. Poor thing."

It wasn't clear whether Susie was a poor thing because she'd fallen in the dock, or because she was off the nose powder.

"Hm," Berry said. "There's another dimension to this you may not have noticed."

"Oh?"

"Unless I'm mistaken, we've been papped," he said, looking

towards the other side of the basin.

"Huh?" I said.

"Oh, fuck," Henriques said, and practically dived down the companionway.

"We've been entertaining more than just ourselves, and, unless I'm losing my eyesight, that pale thing sticking through the railings is a long lens," Berry said.

"Oh."

Now that he mentioned it, that persistent feeling of being watched was pretty strong. I looked out across the dirty water, a way to walk, but not so far in distance. The railing was lined with people, most of them under umbrellas. Some of them had phones held out in front of them, and, yes, that definitely was a long lens with a man crouching down behind it. I looked along the line of faces. One of them caught my attention because he was clearly looking directly and personally at me. Tony.

"A friend of yours?" Berry said.

"Fetch Aled will you, darling. I think I need to go to bed," Maisie said.

"On the way, my sweet. Come on, we'll meet him over there." He eased her off his knee and stood up. "Well, Si. I don't mind knowing you, whatever they say. Anytime you're having a party..." He gave me what seemed like a heartfelt hug and half led, half carried Maisie away, through the gate and across the walkway and into the darkness beyond.

I went below. The saloon was empty but some kind soul, Henriques presumably, had stacked a lot of the debris of the party back into the containers in which it had come. I fetched a damp cloth from the galley and wiped away the pair of hare's ears that someone had drawn in the fine dusting of coke on the surface of the table. Then I used a little isopropyl alcohol and tissues from one of the lockers to finish the job.

In Which Case, Aphrodite

"You've done that before," Henriques said, coming in from the galley in a boiler suit and cloth cap with a large hold-all.

"Not necessarily for cocaine," I said.

"Blood, I expect," he said.

"Possibly."

"It's been an interesting evening."

"Finally, you've stopped calling me, sir."

"Sorry, sir."

"Thank you, Henriques." I offered him my hand, wondering about him again.

"You're welcome..." he let the 'sir' hang and took it.

We went up and found that quite a lot of the watching crowd had dispersed, presumably sensing that the fun was over. It was getting late again, or in fact, early, and finally the dock was becoming quiet. He did a little dance step and said, "Oh fuckety, fuck, fuck fuck."

"Indeed, Henriques," I said, softly. "Indeed. Good night."

"Good night, sir." And then he went quickly and was gone.

I had one last look around the now almost empty dock, and went down and locked the door behind me. In my cabin, Mel and Susie were sound asleep side by side. I looked at them for a minute and then went and fetched my Sig from its hiding place, sat on the bench seat in the saloon, put my feet up, put the gun on my lap and wondered how long I'd manage to stay awake.

We didn't make an early start. Not early at all. Eventually, I was woken by the sound of Mel filling the kettle. I opened an eye and decided that we seemed to have made it through the night okay, even if my back was broken.

"That's very sweet," Mel said, coming in and ruffling my hair.

"Oh, er... morning," I said, picking up the Sig from the cabin floor and laying it on the table.

I had a shower and discovered that my dressing gown was unavailable, Susie had it, so I sat in a towel with them in the saloon and we sipped coffee together and tried to wake up. Or at least Susie and I did; Mel seemed fine. It took me a minute to realise that Susie was in a bit of a state.

"I'm sorry. I did it again. I must've... I don't know what happened to me," she said. "I'm not usually like this." She looked helpless and unhappy and twisted her fingers together and looked at the table.

"Ah," I said. "What exactly do you remember?"

"I don't... I think we were dancing and..."

"You were drugged," I said.

"I... oh... what...?"

"Oh, sweetheart," Mel said, sitting down beside her. "You've been poisoned again. Don't worry, I'll tell you all about it."

"Poisoned? Again?"

"That's interesting," I said.

"Shut up and go and do something useful," Mel said.

"Like what?" I said, giving my head a few gentle thumps to see if that would help.

"I don't know."

"Oh. Okay."

I took my coffee topsides and sat down in the cockpit and phoned Bill. He seemed annoyingly cheerful.

"I take it, that was another poisoning?" he said. "Susana Chesterfield, I mean."

"You know about that then?"

"I could hardly help it. Unless I'm mistaken, you've just taken your credentials as a dubious character to another level. Well done."

"That wasn't my intention."

"So, you know who it is?"

"No."

"Oh. But you've surely narrowed the suspect pool for our poisoner. I take it you're going to be sending me a list of everyone who attended your little party?"

"Any second now. Start with a chap called Henriques, he's a waiter at the cafe here."

"Henriques who?"

"I don't know. How many Henriques can there be in the world?"

"Fair point. Good. Judging by the photos that are all over the internet, that was some party."

"It feels like it this morning," I said.

"Bloody typical of you, but well done."

"Maybe. I'm not sure yet."

"Oh, relax; we think we know where the girls are, and what happened last night is bound to help us catch the poisoner. It has to be one of those who were there. It'll be old-fashioned police work now. How many; about thirty, forty?"

"About that, but I don't feel happy."

"You poor thing. Why?"

"I think it's because whoever did that last night was too clever."

"Cleverer than you, you mean?"

"Very possibly, yes."

"Bloody hell. You must be feeling crap."

"No, I'm feeling beaten. The bastard signed it. In the cocaine dust on the saloon table."

"That's very cocky."

"What was in my blood?"

"Etorphine."

"What?"

"It's what they use on elephants and other pachyderms. Appropriate really. Veterinary use only. Usually lethal to humans so it must've been a very moderate dose."

"It didn't feel like it."

"Mac says it would make you feel pretty rough but should wear off quite quickly and leave no lasting damage, assuming you survive in the first instance. He's very curious about how it got into you."

"So am I."

"The Russian girl…"

"Anja."

"Yes, Anja. Didn't buy it in Boots, did she?"

"Probably not. How did the Greens get it?"

"Exactly."

"But they clearly did," I said. "What about the glass I gave you?"

"Yup. The usual combination: rohypnol, l-dopa and scopolomine."

"And I have no fucking idea who did that either."

"Don't worry, Si. We'll get him. Or her."

"You're telling *me* not to worry. Now I'm worried. You looked up the tattoo?"

"The diving eagle. Yes, I did." That sobered him up a bit. "And I've told Freddy. You think you can get us what we need to get into the Abbey? He'll be ready."

"One way or another, I will. It's time to kill a few people."

"Yes, but let's make sure they're the right ones."

"That's better; now you sound worried."

"Oh, fuck off."

Back in the saloon, I found a more present Susie waiting for me.

"You went in after me," she said, getting up and taking hold of my arm.

"After I let you get poisoned," I said.

"Here," Mel said, offering me her phone. "Have a look."

I watched a video of a lot of very wet and barely clad women dancing madly on Polly's foredeck. Even on the small screen, I could see that Susie wasn't right. Then she stumbled and went in, falling like a rag doll, not fully aware of what was happening to her.

In Which Case, Aphrodite

Then there I was going in after her. It was a good dive, clearing the rail by inches and arcing down cleanly into the water.

"Thank you. Again," Susie said, giving me a kiss on the cheek.

"No problem," I said.

"Mel told me and I remembered. I'm me again now."

"You definitely are. Do either of you have any idea who did this?" I said. "Of the people here last night, I mean."

"We've been talking about that. Not me," Mel said.

"Nor me," Susie said. "I was being very careful and then suddenly…"

"Nor me," I said. "Will you write a list of everyone who was there for me."

"We have." She gave me her notebook.

"Oh. Good." I took a photo of it with my phone. "In hindsight, it wasn't the best idea I've ever had. What about the Wallaces?"

"They talked to me a lot," Mel said.

"Didn't talk to me at all," Susie said.

"Fucking hell," I said.

"What's up, Si?" Susie said.

"I feel out-classed, out of my natural environment and out of my depth," I said.

"Bloody hell, Si. Is this really you?" Mel said.

"Yup. All I've managed to do so far is get Anja beaten up and you and Susie poisoned."

"Oh, you poor thing," Mel said.

"Be nice, Mel. He's doing his best," Susie said.

"Even I am human," I said. "Susie?"

"Si?"

"Will you go home now please? I have to go somewhere and do something, and it would help a lot if I knew you were safe. And you, Mel."

"Okay," Susie said.

"What things?" Mel said.

"I'm not going to say, so don't ask." She looked at me, and for once, didn't make anything of it.

"Fine. In which case, I'm going to take Susie home," Mel said. "We're going to take a taxi from Thomas More Street. I'm going to talk to the Duke."

"Oh. Good."

And when I get back I want us to do something together before you go off and do whatever you have to do, okay? Have you got time for that?"

"As long as it doesn't take too long. What?"

"You remember I had an idea about Tower Hamlets?"

"Yes."

"Good. We're going to go and check it out. Okay? You and me."

"Yes. And after that, you'll go somewhere safe for a few days?"

"Yes. If that's what you want, I will."

"It is."

"Good." She got her phone out and sent a text. There was an instant reply. "Okay, let's go," she said. "Si, you need to be decoy for us."

"Huh?"

"Go on up and you'll find out. Go and buy a newspaper, or something."

"Oh. Why?"

"Just go and do it."

"Oh. Okay."

I put trainers on, got money and keys and went out into the day that was already more or less afternoon. It was drizzling, which seemed about right. As I passed through the gate a woman leapt up from a café table and came to intercept me. There was young man with a camera with her and he was taking photos of me.

"Hello, Mr Ellice. It is Mr Ellice, isn't it?" she said.

"Not me," I said, walking on.

In Which Case, Aphrodite

"It is Mr Ellice, isn't it. Mr Simon Ellice. I'd like to talk to you about last night, Mr Ellice. You're quite a hero, you know. Diving in like that to save the beautiful heiress. People want to know…"

I walked through them without making eye contact but they followed me like a remora follows a shark.

"People are saying that you're a drug dealer, Mr Ellice. Is that true Mr Ellice? Was it cocaine that you supplied that caused Susana Chesterfield to fall into the water, Mr Ellice? Why don't you want to talk to me, Mr Ellice? What have you got to hide, Mr Ellice?" She was almost skipping to keep up and holding out a digital recorder. The temptation to toss her into the dock was almost overwhelming.

"Where are you going, Mr Ellice? Is it to meet one of your suppliers, Mr Ellice?"

I ploughed on, wondering if I could get them to follow me to somewhere with no CCTV cameras. The homeless man's dog barked sharply at her as we passed, so he obviously felt the same way I did. I looked back very breifly, as I led them into the tunnel, and saw two figures slipping quickly through, the now unguarded, security gate and away.

They came with me to buy bacon and eggs at the supermarket two streets away and back again, and the woman barely seemed to pause for breath. What use to anyone, photos of me doing some shopping would be, I couldn't imagine. I slammed the security gate in her face and returned to Polly angry as well as fed up. Perhaps it was as well that I now had her completely to myself.

I put the kettle on and went into the cabin that Mel had appropriated and started going through her things. I didn't know what I was looking for, but the only interesting things I found were some pills and a wooden box. The pills were of two kinds; Cilest and Clomid. I didn't know what that meant, but I would look it up. The box was beautiful; it was round, made of oak, looked old, and had three running hares exquisitely carved on the lid. Their ears interlocked, so that actually, although there were three hares, and each hare had two ears, there were only three ears in total.

I tried to open it, but I couldn't see how and was afraid to try too hard. I carefully put it back where I'd found it, in the bottom of a draw under a stack of clothes.

More bloody hares. I drowned a teabag and put some bacon on to fry and attended to my other phone which had beeped.

It was a text from Jess Dutton, 'are you in?'

I thought about her lovely green eyes and pale skin and decided I was.

'I am, but there are journalists hanging about,' I sent.

'No problem. Send the gate code and put the kettle on,' I got back.

Oh well, whatever. I did that and constructed and demolished a couple of serious bacon sandwiches and not long afterwards there was a tap-tapping on the hull. I went up and found a woman in a baseball cap and dark glasses looking at me.

"Hi Jess," I said. "Come aboard."

"Thanks. Now this *is* a boat," she said.

"Come and have the tour," I said.

She stepped up onto deck and down into the cockpit with easy grace.

"I wasn't far away and I had a whim to have a look at your boat," she said. "And at you."

"Well, here we both are," I said. "Tea?"

"Thank you."

We went down to the saloon and she shrugged off her leather jacket and pulled off the hat, letting her thick red hair cascade around her shoulders.

"Have a look about," I said, waving an expansive hand to indicate that she should wander at will.

Exploring even a twenty-five metre yacht doesn't take long, and by the time I'd drowned a couple of tea-bags, she was back. She sat

In Which Case, Aphrodite

at the table, crossed her legs and looked at me.

"Simon Ellice," she said, accepting the mug.

"Yes?" I said.

"Just saying your name," she said.

"Okay," I said, and sat down opposite her.

"I'm still trying to work out what I think about you," she said.

"Are you?" I said.

"Yes. You seem to be quite notorious."

"You mean the party last night?"

"You didn't invite me."

"I will next time, if you like."

"Good."

"But you came to see me anyway. In spite of the paps."

"Oh, I don't care about them." Her eyes flicked in the direction of the dock where the journalist was. "You may or may not be a drug-dealer, but that was fairly decent of you to bring Anja to me."

"I'm not, and thank you."

"I didn't think you were. Though you do seem like a man with a purpose, but I'm not entirely sure what it is." She was frowning beautifully.

"Ah," I said.

"Well?" she said.

"Right now, I'm not sure," I said.

"Are you not?" she said, raising an eyebrow. "Apart from finding this missing girl. Jane Hamilton, you said?"

"Yes," I said. "Sort of. I can't say I'm getting anywhere with that."

"And you're used to knowing what you want and getting it, aren't you?"

"I suppose I am." I looked at her and she was looking straight back at me. "You're rather used to getting what you want too," I said. "Aren't you?"

"Maybe I am," she said, not taking her eyes from mine.

"So, what do you want now?"

"You know what I want now."

"Yes. Do you know what I want?"

"Yes."

"Well then," I said, and leant forward and kissed her. She didn't so much kiss me back, as bite me, pushing me back and climbing on top of me. Her body was hard and her hands strong and her nails long.

After we'd done that for a bit, we cooperated briefly in getting her top off and my shirt lost some buttons. I picked her up, one arm behind her back, my hand in her long, thick hair, the other beneath her. She wrapped her legs around me and I carried her into the main cabin and threw her on the bed.

We got enough of our clothes off and fucked until she cried out and bit the pillow.

Later, I pulled the rest of them off, and mine, and lay on her as she softened and we began again.

Later again, I lay back and ran my fingers over her fine pale skin. She had a few freckles on her back too, and fine, long limbs and small feet. She looked at me and her eyes were green and still predatory.

"We didn't drink our tea," she said.

"No," I said.

"I want some now."

"You know where it is."

"Men. You're always useless afterwards," she said, and got up and went out.

She brought me a mug of tea too. I sat up enough to drink some. She gathered up her clothes, sat on the bed and started putting them on, still watching me.

"That's better, I needed that," she said.

"Me too," I said, raising my mug.

"I didn't mean the tea," she said, laughing.

"Oh, I did," I said, grinning. "What else?" There was no doubt, I was feeling much better.

"Thank you, Mr Ellice. I must go now." It occurred to me too that that would probably be a good idea. Mel couldn't be far away.

"Can I talk to Anja again, please?" I said.

"Why?"

"She was telling me things I need to know."

"No."

"Why not?"

"It's the rules, that's why not. What do you want to know?"

"She has a photo of her daughter. I've promised I'll find her and get her back, if I can. A copy would be useful."

"You're serious about this then? You're going to help her?"

"I think I am," I said. "If I can."

"Maybe you're alright, after all. I'll... Oh, fuckit; not all men are shits, I suppose." She fetched a pen from the chart-table and wrote on the back of an envelope and gave it to me.

"Thanks," I said. It was an address in Balham.

"You be fucking careful with that. Okay?"

"I promise."

"They don't allow phones, well only the landline, so just go knock on the door when you're ready. I'll let them know you'll be coming. You can buy her lunch or something and bring her back. Just for an hour. Okay? Be nice to her."

"I will."

"Hm. I must go," she said. "Don't move, I can find my way." She expertly bunched her hair up and settled the baseball cap over it and then she put a hand on my chest and pushed me back against the pillows and leant over and kissed me hard one more time. "And you still owe me a race, Mr Simon Ellice."

24

UNDER THE INFLUENCE

Perhaps I hadn't realised how much I'd needed the release of sex, or perhaps it was some lingering effects of the Etorphine, or perhaps just yet another late night; either way I must have slept very deeply, as the next thing I knew was Mel shaking me.

She went to her cabin to pack, and I showered and put on fresh clothes. I gathered the sheets from the bed and threw them into the laundry bin.

"Ready?" she said, when I emerged dressed and sensible.

"Tower Hamlets?" I said.

"Yes, come on."

We put our heads down and walked through the steady light rain to the security gate. The woman and her cameraman were still there. We pushed through them, keeping our heads down and ignoring them. The bloody little shit with the camera danced about in front of us, almost tripping us up, taking photos. On balance, it was a good thing I'd decided to leave the Sig on Polly.

"Don't do it," Mel said, under her breath, sensing my intention.

"Later," I said, meaning it.

We passed the homeless man and his dog; they'd acquired a rather nice umbrella and seemed to be a permanent fixture now; and pushed on into the covered walkway.

"There's no CCTV here,' I said.

"Stop it," Mel said.

It was a relief to shut the car doors on them, and even the chap with the camera had the sense not to get in the way as we drove out.

"So, you're a journalist, are you?" I said.

"Of a kind," she said. "But not that kind." She got her notepad out of her bag, flipped it to the right page and started telling me where to go.

"Well, Mel," I said, when we'd gone far enough to have got away from where we'd been.

"What?" she said.

"You tell me what you're not telling me and I'll tell you what I'm not telling you."

"I can't."

"Won't."

"No, can't. I really, really can't. Sorry."

We drove in silence for a bit and when we got onto the Mile End road, I said, "Well, at least tell me what the fuck we're doing now."

"Yes, okay. I've been thinking about flats," she said. "And asking about. If you don't have much money and you need somewhere to stay, I have it on good authority that there's a man who will find you somewhere for a consideration. In Tower Hamlets. Do you see what I mean?"

"Not immediately."

"We might want to house a few working girls. Or we might want to leave the body of a faked OD we wanted to dump."

"Ah. Good. Yes, I'm with you."

"Now, who owns most of the low-class accommodation in Tower Hamlets?"

"Is there any other kind? No idea."

"The council, of course. We are going to go and see one William Herbert who works in the estates department of the borough council and who will give you a key and the address of a currently unoccupied shithole in return for sex or money."

"Are you going to offer him sex or money?"

"Neither. I thought you might just be nasty to him a bit."

"That sounds like a much better idea. I feel exactly like doing that."

"Yes, I can see that."

"Won't he be at work?"

"Not today, apparently. He phoned in sick this morning. I checked while you were having your nap."

The rain eased back into a light drizzle as we passed Mile End and turned into a maze of small roads with mainly two or three story blocks of flats. 1960s architecture at its most anodyne. There were a few 1930s semis which seemed cute and old-fashioned in comparison. Mr Herbert's house was a bungalow that had been squeezed into a gap between two of these. There was a newish Vauxhall in the drive and its bonnet was quite cold. I leant idly against the corner of the wall, just out of sight, and Mel went to the door.

"Ready?" she said.

"Completely," I said.

"Here goes then." She rang the bell.

Nothing happened. She tried again.

"Perhaps he's on the job," I said quietly.

"Shush. I can hear someone coming."

There was some fumbling and the door was slowly opened.

"Yes...?" a low-pitched voice said.

"Mr Herbert?" Mel said.

"Yes."

"I'm in a bit of trouble, Mr Herbert. One of the girls said you might be able to advise me. About my housing situation."

"I see. I think you'd better come in," the voice said.

I stepped smartly round and followed Mel close as she went in. I needn't have worried; there was the shape of a big man moving away down the hallway with his back to us. He had on old corduroy trousers and a cardigan that hung from his rounded shoulders. He was moving with a slow, lumbering gait like a bear just woken from hibernation. I shut the door behind us.

He turned round and looked at me.

"Ah, I see," he said. "We'd better go in there. I'll be with you in a minute." He pointed to a doorway into a sitting room. "Would either of you like a cup of tea?"

"We're alright, thanks," Mel said.

"Make yourselves comfortable. I'll get my mug," he said.

We went into the room. There were china ornaments on the mantelpiece and the armchair matched the sofa. Some prints of scenes from formula-one racing hung on one wall.

Mel perched on the front edge of the sofa and I went over to the window.

"This doesn't seem quite right," I said, under my breath.

"He seems a bit weird. I almost felt like he was expecting us," she said, under hers.

He came back down the hall and into the room. He was carrying a shotgun and he pointed it at me.

"Oh, fuck," Mel said.

His eyes had a steady, glassy look and there was a pulse beating fast on his temple. He seemed to be having some trouble focusing on me and I could see that his pupils were almost completely dilated. He raised his right elbow and the fingers of his left hand went pale as he tightened his grip on the barrels. His head came down as he made sure of his aim. I was looking right down the barrels at him.

"Don't shoot me," I said, in a firm voice.

He didn't shoot me but just stood there with the gun pointing at me and his right forefinger tight against the trigger. Mel was frozen on the sofa, her eyes on the gun.

"Put the gun down," I said.

He swayed back on his heels a tiny bit and his eyes lost their focus on me. The gun wavered slightly and I thought for an instant that he was going to put it down.

"No," he said, frowning. "I'm supposed to kill you."

He deliberately steadied the gun and squeezed the trigger.

The tight cluster of pellets passed through the air where my head had been and carried on through the double-glazed window. The sound was shocking in the confined space. He turned deliberately towards Mel, his finger moving back to the other trigger. I tried to get my hand to it to push it up as I lunged at him but I missed and the second crash came as I hit his soft body with my shoulder.

He was appallingly heavy and it seemed as if he absorbed my force, rather than was moved by it. My feet dug into the carpet and I thrust with all the power of my thighs, pushing desperately at his flesh. He started to go and then he went, taking half a step back to keep his balance but not enough, and far too slow.

His head hit the door jamb and he bent at the middle, slumping down and ending up sitting there like a massive rag doll. I grabbed at the shotgun though it was empty now and then turned to look for Mel. She was on the floor. She looked at me with big, shocked eyes and then sat up. She seemed to be okay. The sofa wasn't though.

"Fuck," I said. The word was louder than I expected in the ringing silence.

I threw the gun onto the sofa and looked at him. His eyes were open but he didn't seem to be seeing. The pulse beating on his temple was no longer beating.

I got up, squatted next to him and put a finger on his neck. My hands were shaking slightly and it took me a minute to be sure, but he had no pulse that I could feel.

I went over to Mel and helped her to her feet and put an arm round her.

"How're you doing?" I said.

"How the fuck do you think I'm doing," she said.

"Excellent answer. In which case I think perhaps we should leave right about now," I said.

"He was going to kill us," she said.

"I don't think it was personal," I said. I took one of the antimacassars off the arm of the sofa, used it to wipe my prints off the gun, and then put it back.

I took hold of her arm and pulled her out of the room and out of the house. There were a couple of neighbours, a man and a woman, outside the house opposite, and another man looking at us from further down the street. I waved at them, took Mel's hand and walked her towards the car. The woman held her phone up in front of her, taking our photos presumably. It had completely stopped raining while we'd been inside.

Mel got a bit more with it and we made it into the car at a good speed and left the scene.

"How're you doing?" I said.

"You seem to be all right," she said.

"He missed me," I said.

"But he might have killed you."

"And you too."

"Yes, and me too."

"I'm sorry about that. If I'd known, I wouldn't have let you come."

"Fuck."

"Listen, Mel. We're in a bit of trouble now. I think you should disappear for a while. Can you do that?"

"Don't worry about me."

"We'll go back to Polly while we still have the chance, and then scarper. Okay?"

"Fuck."

A couple of blue lights passed us going the other way but there's no saying that they were anything to do with number 24a. It seemed to take a long time to drive back to the docks.

I put the car in my reserved space in the car park and we walked through into the docks. The beggar's umbrella was down, covering him and there was an empty bottle of scotch on the ground. One way to deal with things, I suppose. The dog looked a bit anxious, so presumably he hadn't been included.

Thankfully, the journalist had fucked off. Perhaps something more juicy had come up. Possibly, up the Mile End Road.

Inside Polly, I made haste to empty the contents of my safe into a bag and added my Sig and a longish knife in a sheath. Mel sat at the table and watched me.

"Fucking hell, Si. I didn't take any photos," she said.

"You're feeling better then. I'm going to change into some different coloured clothes. You should do the same." I pulled my shirt off over my head and emptied the pockets of my trousers. "And then we should get out of here."

"I will," Mel said, not moving.

I had a thought.

"Where did you leave your bag during the party, Mel?" I said.

"On your bed. Why?"

"I think we've been very careless and very stupid," I said. "I think he was waiting for us and that means someone knew we'd be going. You didn't tell them…" She was looking at me oddly, I didn't blame her, "and I didn't tell them, so I think they read your notebook last night. But how…"

"Shit."

"… it's quite possible there's a tracker in your handbag, or phone or something… Are you getting me?"

"No, I mean, yes…" She was still looking at me strangely.

"I think we were distracted while someone put something in Susie's glass and then Susie's swim provided another distraction while they searched our things."

"What's that on your back, Si?" she said. She got up to look.

"What?" I said.

"Those scratches. Who did that to you? It wasn't me."

"It doesn't matter. This isn't the time."

"This is fresh. You've fucked someone."

"Mel…"

I turned to look at her. Her face was very still and she looked hurt. Very hurt.

"It was that girl, wasn't it," she said. "The red-head. I saw the way you looked at her. She was here, wasn't she?"

"I'm sorry. Just hang on a…"

"Fuck you, Si. Just, fuck you. I knew it…"

"Mel. Look I'll explain, but can we just get out of here first. Give me…"

"Fuck off. Just fuck off. I should never have…"

She picked up her bag and walked out of the door and stepped off Polly and went. Her face set.

"Oh, fuck," I said to myself. "Si, you can be a real prick sometimes."

I watched her walk along the walkway and go out of sight.

My phone rang. It was Bill.

"Si." He sounded weary and fed up.

"Hi, Bill."

"Were you just in Tower Hamlets?"

"Yes." I went into the bathroom and lifted my toothbrush from its holder.

"Thought so. Are you at the docks now?"

"Yes." I went through into the main cabin to get some clothes.

"You need to leave now."

"I know," I said.

Anja was there, sitting up in the bed, her head leaning back against the bulkhead. There was the haft of the fid that I use for splicing rope sticking out of her left ear, and on the little table beside her, was about half a kilo of cocaine.

"Sorry, Bill," I said. "I think I've really fucked this up."

25

RETURN OF THE NATIVE

I gently touched Anja's forehead. It was cool but not completely cold. The pallor of death had added itself to her natural pallor and as I looked at her, she was unreal, like a sculpture. And as I looked at her more and saw a tiny scar by her eyebrow and a mole on her throat, she was perfectly real and dead. Her life had always been fragile and I had ended it. And made her child motherless. I looked at her and made myself look at what I had done to her. And that made me angry with a slow anger that was directed mainly at myself, but for which I intended others would pay.

Her blue eyes were staring ahead as if unaware of the metal driven into her head. I thought, and hoped, that that was how it had been. On the bed beside her was the wooden mallet that I keep in the tool locker. Someone had been making themselves very much at home on my boat.

I had a look out of the window. Two uniformed policemen were walking along the path towards the security gate. What a surprise.

I got on with making sure I had everything I wanted and had left nothing important. Then I stopped and got the Sig and the knife out of the bag. I weighed the gun in my hand, feeling it's familiar heaviness. It was no good; my problem right now was the law, not the bastards who'd killed Anja, and these would only make matters worse if they caught me. Reluctantly I put the gun back in its hiding place and the knife back in the locker.

When I looked again, one policeman was by the gate and the other was returning with the dock manager. The chap with the camera was back, and was standing near them trying to overhear what they were saying.

I made sure that the door from the cockpit into the saloon was partially open and then went forward and shut the intervening door and turned the key.

A few minutes later, one of the policemen banged on Polly's side and called out, "Ahoy there, Mr Ellice. This is the police. We need to speak to you."

They waited a bit to see what would happen and I quietly undid the clips on the fore-hatch and fetched out one of the several plastic-coated cable bike-locks that I keep in one of the foc'sle cupboards for securing things to the ship in doubtful ports.

"Come on then, let's not piss about," one of them said, and started coming aboard. They both stepped over the railing and down into the cockpit.

"Look here, John," the other one said.

"Door's not properly secured," the first one said. "We'd better investigate."

They opened the door and came down into the saloon.

"Hello, Mr Ellice. This is the police. Show yourself, please," one of them called out.

"What now, Sarg?" the other one said.

"Suspicious circs. We look about and see what we can see, laddie."

I silently opened the hatch and climbed out.

The young man from the harbourmaster's office saw me and was about to call out but I put my finger to my lips, motioning him to be quiet. I wasn't far from him and the look in my eye seemed to convince him that it was his wisest course. I stepped as lightly as I could over the side but I couldn't help moving her a little and there came shouts and the sound of doors opening inside.

The young man backed away from me and I passed him with a smile. I opened the gate, swung it shut behind me and applied the bike-lock. It snicked closed satisfactorily and the young man, realising that I could no longer get at him, started shouting.

There was no need; the coppers were coming after me as fast as their bulky jackets and unfamiliarity with boats would let them.

I heft my bag and, ignoring the shouts behind me, walked away at a steady pace. I didn't get far; the young man with the camera was in front of me, taking pictures and looking happy and enthusiastic in his work.

"Afternoon, Mr Ellice. This is making my day, you know that?" he said.

"I'm glad for you," I said, closing the distance between us and giving him a shove that expressed some of my feelings towards him. He travelled the few yards of intervening walkway with flailing arms and disappeared into the dock.

There was a lot of shouting going on by now and everyone in the vicinity had stopped what they were going to watch. Everyone except the beggar with the dog. When I got to him, I knelt down beside him and stroked the dog's head. It looked relieved and wagged its tail a bit.

"What's up, old fellow?" I said. He seemed pretty clean for a street dog. He looked at me and then at the man. I glanced behind me. People were looking at me but none of them seemed keen to approach me. There was a lot going on that seemed to be focused on the chap in the water. Perhaps he couldn't swim. I hoped so.

I turned back to the beggar and gave his leg a nudge. Nothing happened. I moved in a bit closer. There was none of the rank smell of a person who seldom washes and his hands were clean, his nails neatly clipped. I gently pushed up the hat. There was a small wound on the side of his neck, barely a centimetre long. He was quite dead, but not completely cold.

"Sorry, old thing," I said to the dog and pulled the hat back down.

I scooped up the little dog, who seemed more than willing to be so scooped, and carried on walking away. Not slowly but not rushing either.

I blessed the god of taxis and stepped into one which was just dropping a couple off on Thomas More Street, and asked to be taken to Whitechapel.

"What's his name?" the driver said.

"Sorry?" I said.

"The dog. What's his name?"

"Dunno."

"Isn't he your dog, then?"

"No."

The dog sat on the seat beside me and shivered slightly. I stroked his ears and thought about things.

I got a phone out, didn't make a call and held it to my ear.

"It's done," I said. "No, no problem. I'll drop it off first. Tell Grant."

I listened to the sound of silence.

"…no…no… just tell Grant. If he's not there, tell Leila. They'll want to know now. Okay. Later." I put my phone away.

"Where d'you want to be, mate?" the driver said, looking at me in the mirror.

"Further up on the left. There by the Red Dragon."

He pulled up in a bus stop.

"That'll be twelve to you, mate," he said.

"Let's call it a ton," I said, getting money out.

"Hang on, I don't …"

I put two fifties into his hand.

"I'm not telling you what to do. You can make your own decisions, okay?"

"I dunno…" he said, but he still had the fifties in his hand.

I got out and walked off down the street with my bag in one hand and the dog under my other arm. I was going to need some kind of dog lead.

I went into Valance Gardens, sat on a bench and put the dog down. He went off to one side and had a pee. Then he came back and sat looking at me. I phoned Mel. She didn't answer so I left a message. It wasn't a happy message to leave and I ended it by telling her to get rid of her phone and carefully search her handbag and everything else.

Then I took the battery and SIM card out of the phone that I'd been using that wasn't the one Bill had given me. I bent the SIM card until it looked broken and dropped it in a bin.

"Come on then, dog. Let's get the fuck out of here," I said.

We took the tube to Waterloo and shared a couple of sandwiches while we waited for a train. He lapped up some water from an old paper coffee cup and then put his head on my foot and appeared to go to sleep. Neither of us was having the easiest day. A couple of uniformed officers wandered past us, chatting. They didn't look at us.

On the train, I put my bag onto the overhead shelf, settled back into my seat and closed my eyes. The dog, curled up on the carpet under the seat, began to snore.

When I opened my eyes, the city had given way to the countryside. The sun was getting low ahead of us in the west. It would be the longest day soon. I looked for Roe deer in the fields and it wasn't long before I saw some.

We got off at Salisbury, though my ticket would have taken us to the end of the line, and walked out into the town. We got supper, and a tip for where to stay, at a chippy and checked into a rather run-down inn on a busy road.

I climbed gratefully in between rough sheets and the dog jumped up onto the bed. I looked at him and decided I didn't mind.

I woke up feeling better than I had the morning before, made myself a mug of unpleasant tea, and phoned Bill.

"Si, thank goodness. Where are you?" he said.

"Gone back to my native soil. Catch me up on the news, will you."

"It's a mess. I'm currently part of a man-hunt for you. The girl, Anja, had cigarette burns in places you don't want cigarette burns. If it's any help, she wasn't conscious when that thing was beaten into her head. More Etorphine, according to Mac. A man more or less answering your description, and claiming to be you, turned up at the safe-house where she was staying. She went out to meet him in a nearby café and wasn't seen again."

"What about Mr Herbert?"

"Full of scopolamine. He had a heavy dose of that, and enough speed and cocaine to off an elephant. You didn't kill him."

"I wouldn't have minded if I had. I'm not so happy about the girl."

"You weren't to know."

"Yes, I was. What else?"

"I'm afraid we've got a complete fucking media storm now. They've got photos of you from the night of the charity auction. And from the party on your boat. And from the dock yesterday. CCTV and private footage. We're wasting a massive amount of manpower looking for you."

"Shit. Was that a private detective who was watching me? Pretending to be a street-person. Who killed him and who left Anja on Polly?"

"Yes. Chap called David Rowe. He was working for Mr Chesterfield. The dock cameras show two men in overalls delivering a heavy sail-bag. They wore baseball caps and kept their heads down. They knew the combination to the gate and where the cameras were. Presumably, they must have had keys to your boat too, or been good at picking locks. We've got some footage of someone in a hooded top bending down to speak to Mr Rowe. We can't see what he or she did, but he didn't appear to be suspicious. Neither did any of the people passing. Single puncture wound through both carotid arteries. Bled out internally. Very neat indeed."

"And very confident. What else?"

"We've impounded your car."

"I don't suppose I'll be needing it for a while."

"What are you going to do?"

"Keep my head down."

"Probably best. One of my colleagues is giving the cabby who picked you up a hard time at the moment but he isn't being very helpful. What did you do to him?"

"I might have given him the impression that I was working for the Greens."

"That might explain it."

"Have you ever seen a rabbit that's been killed by a stoat?" I said.

"Strangely enough, no."

"It'll have two neat puncture marks in its neck from her canine teeth, that's all."

"What's that got to do with anything?"

"I don't know."

"Well, don't get bitten by any stoats."

"Thanks."

I couldn't stand the sausages that came with my breakfast but the dog wasn't so fussy. The coffee wasn't great either. I packed up, I paid in cash, and the dog and I went out into the town.

Charity shops seemed to have proliferated and I had no trouble buying an old tweed jacket and a felt hat. I didn't see a pet shop but I came across a hardware store and got a bit of string for the dog. I got work boots, trousers and a couple of check shirts in a discount shop, and changed in a toilet cubicle at the bus station. It would take ages for the second of only three busses to where I was going to turn up, so I bought a newspaper and drank tea in a café. The girl who served me said I should get a proper lead for him. I said he didn't seem to mind. She looked sorry for him, and possibly me too, and brought him a bowl of water.

They'd used a photo of me talking to Susie in the paper. It was on an inside page. The main headline was about the missing girls. Suspected drug dealer sought in connection with girls' death linked to the disappearance of beautiful debutants. There was no mention of me being in the company of a dog. I left the paper on the table and caught the bus.

It went about in its circuitous way from hamlet to vale, including my village. I looked at the achingly familiar landscape and then, in my mind as me as a boy cycling by, I looked at myself on the bus. The boy thought it was all very amusing. The little bastard.

I got out at Walter's Cross, where you can wait and catch the Winchester bus, waited until it was out of sight and hopped over the gate into the field.

I let the dog off the string and the poor chap did a massive shit. Much lightened, he ran madly round in a circle three times and then stood there wagging as much tail as he had at me.

"Come on then, dog," I said. "Let's you and me go hunting."

We crossed the expanse of springy old pasture and pushed our way through the hedge opposite. I used the hat to keep the thorns from scratching my face. The dog put up a rabbit and disappeared after it. I considered calling him and thought better of it; if I had to worry about where he was, he was on his own.

He caught up with me halfway across the next field and passed me without pausing to say hello. He seemed to vanish into the next hedge without slowing down and then reappeared madly chasing a Muntjac. He was having a good day.

And after a bit, so was I. The grass was nice under my feet and the sights, sounds and smells of my boyhood landscape made me feel light-hearted and hopeful in spite of myself. There was a herd of young bullocks in the next field. They took our arrival as an invitation to a game and came charging towards us, ringing us round with their inquisitive noses and bucking their hindquarters.

They snuffled at us, their tongues sometimes licking up into their nostrils, and dared each other as to who was going to get the closest. The dog stood it for a bit, keeping by my feet, and then launched a feint at them, barking furiously. His bark was deeper than I expected.

The sward looked tempting so I lay down on it and said, "Come here, dog."

He came to me and stood beside me trembling. I put a hand on his behind and said, "Sit." He sat. The cows crowded round us, narrowing the horizon to a circle of heaving and jostling, dark flesh. One of them experimentally licked my boot.

I let my head lie back on the grass and looked up at the nearest beast. They have the most lovely eyes with long, delicate lashes and they smell sweet and friendly. Now that we weren't moving, they settled down and stood, heads down, waiting to see what we would do next. I felt the calmness, the slowing of my heartbeat that comes from the proximity of large herbivores. The dog may have felt it too, he settled down onto his belly with a growl that was also a sigh.

I put a hand on the grass beside me and worked my fingers into it a bit. The world of beautiful girls in dresses and dead girls in unpleasant flats and dead girls in mortuary drawers and dead girls on Polly seemed as unreal as school had used to seem unreal in the holidays. I beat my heels on the grass and felt the turf give a little. The movement made the bullocks by my feet start back a bit.

"Come on, dog. We've got things to do," I said.

I got to my feet, causing them to shy and back, widening the circle, picked up my bag, which now had some slobber marks on it, and headed for the far hedge, driving them ahead of me.

We struck the green lane that I'd anticipated, and the dog shot off down its penumbral, underwater interior. I followed on with a quicker step. The floor had been driven recently and the crushed grass stems were pointing the way we were going. The leaf-litter was soft and silent underfoot. The leaves on every hazel branch leaning in were full size and perfect in every detail; not yet tattered by insects. The dog danced frantically under a hawthorn bush from which a grey squirrel was chattering at him, he bounced ineffectually up and down on his hind legs. The squirrel saw me and ran up to the top and leapt for the next one, the dog following on below.

The lane eventually delivered us to the back of the church at Acton. I took the way past the school and the pond, turned up the lane and walked the half-mile or so to the Dower House.

I entered the kitchen and found Giles doing some washing up at the sink. He didn't seem surprised to see me.

"Good morning, Sir. Would you like some tea?" he said.

"Would I ever," I said.

"You seem to have acquired a companion, sir."

"I do, don't I."

"Does he have a name, sir?"

"Not that I know of. Any suggestions welcome."

"I'll think about it, sir. Their Ladyships are in the orangery. Go through."

"Their ladyships?"

"Yes, sir."

"Oh. Thanks."

Grace was in her usual seat and next to her, was Mel. The two Danes were lying flat out on their beds by the door to the garden. They raised their heads to look at me and at the little dog, but didn't find us interesting and put their heads back down. He went stiff-legged and moved off to sniff something important as if he hadn't noticed them.

"Come and sit down, Simon," Grace said.

I took the chair opposite them and the dog sat under it. I've faced military boards of enquiry that seemed more friendly. Mel's notebook was on the table and there were pens and a sheaf of typed papers under a paperweight in the shape of a moon-gazing hare.

"Hello," I said.

"Hello, Si," Mel said. It was her speaking, but from a distance, and not a friendly one.

"We are glad to see you," Grace said. "Mel thought it likely that you would come here, and I'm glad that she was right."

"Nice to see you too," I said.

"Unfortunately, this has not gone well. The whole thing is now being talked about and you are a hunted criminal. I am sorry." By which she clearly meant, disappointed. "However, you undertook this on our behalf, so we are going to help you leave the country. Your arrival is timely."

"I see," I said. The vase on the pedestal had flowers in it now, but the oak twig was still there.

"I'm sorry, Si," Mel said.

"Has all this hanging about drinking with my son shed any light on the matter?" Grace said. "Has anything useful actually come of this, to your knowledge?"

"What is it you intend to do?" Mel said. "You said you had things to do. You must tell me what you haven't told me now."

"That's a good question," I said. Actually, it was a fresh twig from an oak tree.

I don't know if it was the fresh air and exercise, or the translocation; seeing it all from another direction, but finally it all began to make a little sense. Not actual sense, but the first dim stirrings of the shape of it. I must have smiled as Grace said, "What is it you find amusing, young man?"

I looked at them again; two strong, attractive, intelligent female faces, and then at the moon-gazing hare on the table. It was very simple, but very good, with a powerful presence. It was dark and I'd assumed it was cast in resin, but it wasn't. It was finely-figured wood; possibly oak, but if so, very, very old. I started to realise that I was staring at it.

Luckily, we were interrupted by Giles bringing more tea. As he put the tray down, I noticed that his shirtsleeves were rolled up, showing surprisingly muscular forearms. His hands looked like they wouldn't have too much trouble cracking the odd walnut, and while I'd been in the habit of thinking of him as old, that was because of his manner, not his actual age.

"Thank you, Giles," Grace said, as he refreshed their cups from the pot and then poured some for me.

"My pleasure, my lady," he said.

I sipped my tea and hoped that the civilised routine of drinking it would go on for a bit. About a week would be good.

"Well, Simon?" Grace said.

Apparently not, then. Ah, well.

"I think I may just started to see the shape of the thing," I said. "Just then. That's why I smiled."

"What have you seen?" Mel said, and now I felt she was looking at me, not through me.

"It isn't clear yet, but it will be," I said, to Mel.

"Who is it?" Mel said. "You know who it is, don't you? I can see it in your face."

"I've remembered something Avus said to me," I said, to Grace.

"His grandfather," Grace said. "And what was that?"

I thought of him, of us, together in his gun-room; the smoke curling up from his pipe, him talking in the easy, meditative way of his. I think he must have known that his words were planting seeds. Perhaps his grandfather had done the same for him. We were looking at the portrait over the fireplace. The face of a woman I'd never met, but a very familiar face, nonetheless. I was silent for a moment, looking from Mel to Grace, remembering. They must have understood some of what I was feeling as they were content to let me do so.

When I was ready, I said, "Ladies, I undertook to do a job for you, I'd like to finish it, please."

"Can you, though?" Grace said.

"You said, please," Mel said, thoughtfully.

"Also, I've just got a rather lovely woman killed," I said. "I suspect you aren't too bothered about that, but I am. I intend to do something about that, unless you prevent me."

"That may not be possible," Grace said, looking at Mel.

"If you let me go, I will go and do what needs to be done," I said. "You should trust me now. I understand why you didn't tell me what you didn't tell me." I looked directly at Mel. "Or, at least, I think I do."

"I see," Mel said.

"You have failed so far, why should we give you a second chance?" Grace said.

"That isn't accurate," I said. "I didn't fail, I've been beaten. It's not quite the same thing, and it tells me that I was looking in the right place, and in the right way. Or rather, we were." I looked at Mel again.

"Who?" she said, again, frowning.

I looked back at her, letting her see that I wasn't hiding from her and hoping that she would trust me. "I'm only offering to be myself, Mel," I said. "But you do know me."

"You stupid bastard," she said.

There was no arguing with that.

"And you did fail me," she said.

"No, I failed Anja. I haven't failed you. Not yet. Not in my terms, anyway."

"Your terms are not…" Mel said.

"They are to me," I said. "I believe I have that right, even if you don't."

The two of them looked at me as if I'd just crawled out from under a stone. I didn't care.

"So," I said. "If there's nothing else, I'd like to take that gun and go and get on with it now."

Grace looked at Mel. Mel looked at me, and I could see she was still furious, but I was still me and we'd known each other for a long time.

"The bastard is probably right," Mel said. "We will let him go."

A little while later, I walked through the garden gate to the field with Thomas in a gun slip and a heavy bag of cartridges added to the burden of my bag. The dog ran out into the field as if released from near certain death. He raised his leg against one of the big round bales, which were still there. I resisted the urge to do the same and sniffed it instead. It was just as good.

We crossed the top of the long meadow and entered the outer yard of Home Farm. The piglets seemed to have grown considerably. The dog passed me at a run in the direction of the hay barn. I went through into the inner yard and looked up at the swallows doing their thing in the soft evening light. It still felt like coming home.

Return of the Native

Lizzy answered the door and stood there looking at me, with her hip cocked as usual. She looked tired and smelt of the disinfectant you use in milking parlours. One side of her face was speckled with something that might have been mud but was probably wet cow-shit.

"Oh, it's you," she said.

"It's me," I said.

"And this time, you're carrying a bag."

"This time, I'd like to stay for a few days," I said.

"Oh, you would, would you," she said, and then she smiled.

26

A DIVING EAGLE

"You've got a dog," Lizzy said. He'd appeared and was standing in front of her, attempting to make himself appealing. Apparently, it was working, as she squatted down to talk to him. "What's his name?"

"His name's... Jake," I said.

"Hello, Jake." She stroked his head and he responded by wagging his stump enthusiastically. "Come on then, I'll show you your room."

"I get a room?" I said.

"No, your dog does. It's up to him if he lets you share it."

Jake followed her into the farmhouse, and I followed him.

"You can sleep in the attic," she said, kicking off her boots and starting up the stairs. "If that's okay?"

"I'm quite certain it's perfect."

"Good, then follow me."

A Diving Eagle

"No, dog. Not you," I said, pulling off my boots too.

"I don't mind," Lizzy said.

"I do. If you don't mind me minding?" I said.

"No, I don't mind you minding."

We walked up the tired stair carpet on the worn elm stair treads and she opened an old brace and ledger door with a rattly catch on the first-floor landing.

"This is the bathroom."

It was a bathroom alright. It even had a bath in it.

"Does it have running water?"

"Yes, but not much hot running water. There are towels in the airing cupboard on the landing. This way."

She took a sheet and duvet cover out of said airing cupboard and then took me to a wooden door off the landing that I'd taken for another cupboard. Open, it revealed more stairs. Old and narrow and steep. I had to duck my head as we went up.

My room was the whole attic of the house. It was flooded with the evening light from four dormer windows let into the pitch, two on each side, which gave light and more head space. On the bare elm boards was an old rug and on it a single iron bedstead with a horse-hair mattress. At the far end of the room was a collection of trunks, boxes, hat-boxes, a rocking horse, three small chairs and an angry looking stuffed goose. I put my things down and went to look out of one of the windows.

From up there, we could see over the near sheds and down the long meadow towards the wood. On the right, the walled garden was laid out in its beauty. Cal was wheeling his barrow into the yard. The swallows were passing below me and rising up to eye-height and passing close, close as if I might reach out and catch one.

"Will it do?" Lizzy said.

"Will it do?" I said.

"The room," she said.

"The room is better than the best bedroom I ever had when I was a boy. I can lie on the bed and watch the swallows."

"Oh. Okay." She smiled at me. "How're your hospital corners?"

"They should pass," I said.

We stood on opposite sides of the bed and made it up. Pulling the sheet tight between us, folding it and tucking it under. My corners were better than hers.

"The army?" she said.

"Yes," I said.

"You can go and help Julie take the cows back out and then we'll go to the pub. Okay?"

"The pub?"

"The Barrel. In the village. I've had enough of this day, and you'll make a reasonable excuse not to cook supper. Okay?"

"Definitely."

"Good."

She went, leaving me in the room. I tipped the contents of my bag onto the bed, pulled my laptop and a few other things out of the pile and hid them in one of the trunks. It was full of old dresses and smelt of mothballs.

Jake was waiting for me at the bottom of the stairs. I told him he was good for waiting and stroked his ears. Then I went into the kitchen, put Thomas gently standing up inside the long-case clock and said, "Come on then, dog, let's go and move some cows."

We went out into the yard. There was a distant sound coming from behind one of the doors in the building opposite the house, so I opened it and went in. It was a simple office with an old computer, a filing cabinet and a desk with a few piles of paper and several copies of the *Farmer's Weekly*.

Through the doorway at the back I could hear the gentle lowing of cows and the suck and hiss of milking. I followed the sounds and found a room with a big stainless-steel storage tank. Through another doorway beyond, was the parlour itself. It wasn't big but looked new and clean and had the distinctive smell of disinfectant. About twenty beautiful, big-eyed, wet-nosed Jerseys were munching away at their cake ration while Julie went amongst them.

I leant against the wall and watched. She slapped them, leant on them, calling them by name, going along the row removing the clusters of teats from their udders with rough and gentle familiarity. They stood calm and elemental, chewing unhurriedly, rumbling internally and occasionally sending inconceivable volumes of pale, steaming piss onto the floor behind them.

A shadow passed through the light from the doorway and Lizzy was standing beside me. Because of the noise, she had to stand close to me to be heard.

"Do you want to try some?" she said.

"Yes please," I said.

"Come on then." She rinsed out an enamel mug at the sink and held it under the tap at the bottom of the cooler. A stream of white liquid ran down into it, frothing slightly. She gave it to me and I drank it down, discovering how thirsty I was. It was still warm and rich, much richer than milk usually is, refreshing and, though liquid, much more than just a drink. It was wonderful, and I said so.

"Good. So, you came back then," she said.

"You look tired," I said.

"I'm fine. Go and help Julie now,"

"Yes, boss."

In the parlour, the cows had finished their ration of cake and Julie was unhooking the last of the clusters from the furthest one. "Come on then, old girl. Time to go," she said, sliding back the bar that prevented the cow from withdrawing her head. The beast backed out without any further instruction and began to head towards the far door in her stately, unhurried way. Julie went to the next one and released its bar.

"I can do this," I said, stepping up beside her.

"Fuck! Oh, it's you," she said.

"Go on," I said. "I'll get this."

"Oh. You sure?"

"I'm sure," I said. "We're going to the pub, according to the boss."

"Oh, okay. They know the way. Just keep them moving. Cal's gone to open the gates."

"Will do."

I stepped in beside the next cow and released it. I put my hand on its flank as it backed past me. It was warm and smooth to the touch. Julie stood for a moment, watching me. She must've been satisfied, as when I next looked, she was gone.

They all came out without fuss except the last one who seemed to think she should move up one in the line. She barged into the girl before her, trying to push past her. I slapped both their rumps and sent them on together.

Beyond the wide metal door was a concrete apron with a slurry tank and beyond that a green lane with tall borders of cow parsley. Ahead, Cal waited to turn them through a gateway into a field. They swung their heads to take mouthfuls from the verge and would have stopped if I hadn't kept them on. Their tails swished at the evening flies and they moved on, through the gate and into the field with the steady, eternal rhythm of the contented bovine.

"Oh, it's you," Cal said, shutting the gate.

"Seems to be," I said.

Jake passed us at his usual speed, on some urgent matter.

We walked back towards the house. Part way Cal said, "Was that a dog?"

"Think it was," I said.

When we got to the yard by the house I sat on the wall and watched the swallows. Cal sat down too. After a bit, he said. "So, what you doin' 'ere, then?"

"Just waiting for the girls," I said. "I believe we're going to the pub."

"Ah. They'll be making theirselves beautiful," he said, as if he was wise in the ways of women.

Jake reappeared with a rat in his mouth and, unmistakably, a grin of self-satisfaction. He lay down and started to eat it.

Julie and Lizzy came out of the house. Julie was wearing a light cotton dress and Lizzy had put on tight jeans and a t-shirt. They had washed their faces and put their hair into some order. In Lizzy's case, not much.

"There's a dog 'ere," Cal said.

"And a rat," Julie said. "Or at least, part of one."

"Wha's'isname?" Cal said, bending down to stroke him.

"His name's Jake and you might want to let him finish his rat before you do that," I said.

There was a low growl from the direction of the dog and Cal withdrew his hand.

"Reminds me a bit of Minnie," Julie said.

"Who?" I said.

"The Keeper's dog," Lizzy said, walking to the old Landrover parked by the wall.

"Come on you," I said, putting the dog in the back of the Landy, rat and all, and then getting in after him. Cal joined me, and the girls got in the front, Lizzy driving.

The Barrel looked like it was supposed to look in my mind; low and steep-roofed and friendly. It brought back the memory of my first evening in a similar pub not so far away, and the girl who had served us pints of cider, though she knew very well how young we were.

The door stood open and light and the sounds of people talking spilled out. I followed the others to the bar where a barmaid with dimpled cheeks and a low-cut top was pulling pints. If I interpreted the fleeting expression on her face as she saw Lizzy correctly, she wasn't pleased to see her. The room was about half full, mainly men, Morny among them.

"Evening, Sharon. Tell me we've made it in time for food?" Lizzy said.

"I'll ask Steve, hang on." She disappeared into the back and a solid, steady looking chap in his early fifties came out.

"Ah, it's Lizzy and Julie. What would you like?"

"Hi, Steve. We've had a bit of a late one and we're starving," Julie said. "This is Simon, by the way."

"Pleased to meet you, Simon." He extended a hand over the bar and we shook hands. "I've some pie left and there's some sausages and the fryer's still hot. Any of that grab you?"

"I'll have sausages and chips, please," Cal said.

"Right you are, Cal," Steve said, making a note on an order pad.

"Pie for me, please," Lizzy said.

"And me," Julie said.

"Me too, if there's enough. If not sausages would be fine," I said.

"Leave it with me, I won't be long."

"So, who's your friend then?" the barmaid said, looking at me.

"Sharon, Simon. Simon, Sharon," Lizzy said. "Mine's a pint of gold please and Julie'll have the head."

"Nice to meet you, Simon." She put out her hand, it had short nails painted red, took mine and held it. "What would you like to drink?" She was really quite pretty.

"Something brown and strong please," I said.

"That'll be the head then."

"I'll have a pint of head too please," Cal said.

She didn't bother acknowledging that but let go of my hand and got on with pulling pints. I got some notes out of my trouser pocket and had a better look at the other customers.

There was a group of young men further down the bar, standing, holding their pints and talking. I thought one of them, a big lad, gave me a loaded glance. Morny was at a table playing chess with a studious looking man in an old tweed jacket. They were deeply absorbed in their game. There was a couple at one table having supper together, another table had four men, and another had a group of teenagers, some of whom were definitely under sixteen.

"I'll get these," Lizzy said, pulling a small purse out of the back pocket of her jeans. I'd noticed it there, outlined by the tight fabric across her bottom.

"Why don't you get the next one; I owe Morny a pint anyway," I said.

"You owe Morny a pint?"

"Yeah, he didn't shoot me when he found me in the White Wood the other day. Can I put one in for Morny, and will you have something yourself, Sharon?"

"I don't suppose he'll mind that, and I'll have a pint, thank you very much," she said, taking my money.

"I'm just going to go and talk to them," Cal said, indicating the men at the bar.

"I thought you would," Lizzy said.

"Here you are, sweetheart. Will you be staying long?" Sharon said, giving me my change.

"Depends if Lizzy sacks me or not," I said.

"You working at Home Farm then?"

"Yup."

"She won't sack you, darling. Bloody lucky to have you." She moved off to serve another customer and I followed the others to a table.

"You know what villages are like?" Lizzy said, perching neatly on a stool.

"Is Cal telling those lads about me?" I said, settling Jake under the table.

"Yup, and what he doesn't know, he'll be making up," Julie said.

"What was that about Morny not shooting you?" Lizzy said.

"I took a walk with a gun down the long meadow and into the edge of the White Wood a few days ago. Next thing I know he's standing there giving me the eye."

"He does that; the man's half cat."

"And he remembered me from when I was about fourteen or so. He caught me poaching roosting pheasants with a .22 and gave me a fairly reasonable kicking. He didn't tell on me though."

"Men and their pride," Lizzy said, smiling.

"Well, Mr Wandering Whateveryouare," Julie said. "Cheers." She raised her glass, and we touched glasses and drank.

"Hm, that's better," Lizzy said, easing her shoulders and visibly relaxing.

"Now then, Si," Julie said, looking at me with intent." As you've moved in, you should tell us a little about yourself."

"Should I?" I said.

"Yes please," Lizzy said.

I looked at her and it seemed only fair.

"Okay. What do you want to know?" I said.

It was a gentle enough inquisition and I told them no lies of fact, only lies of context and omission. I talked about growing up in Aldermark and then not in Aldermark because I was at school and in the no-mans-land between. I told them a little about my time in my father and grandfather's regiment and how that didn't work, and then that I'd been crewing yachts."

"None of which actually explains why you're here helping out on a farm," Julie said.

"What about you, then, Lizzy?" I said. "You're not from round here, are you?"

"No, I'm from London town. Well, Essex. But I love the life," Lizzy said, stretching and rubbing her face with her hands. "This is what I was born for. And on a farm like this; it's a dream."

"So, you'll be marrying a lad from the village and settling down here," I said, smiling.

"I might," she said.

"You won't," Julie said, glancing towards the bar. "You'd drive him mad and he'd kill you."

Steve brought plates of food and put them down in front of us. Simple but good.

"I expect Cal would like his over there," I said.

"Right oh," he said. "Shall I send Sharon over with three more beers?"

"Yes please. Now I know why they say this is the best pub in the village," I said.

"This is the only... Oh, yes. Beers coming up."

Sharon spilled a bit when she put them down on our table but it didn't matter.

"I think you're having a romance," Julie said, between mouthfuls of pie.

"How do you mean?" I said.

"The illusion of return to childhood," she said. "The English rural dream. The cottage with roses round the door. The sound of church bells carrying across the meadows..."

"The quaint English inn with the buxom barmaid..." Lizzy said, glancing towards Sharon and smiling.

"The thwack of leather on willow, the children paddling in the duck pond. I'm running out of clichés, but you know what I mean," Julie said.

"Those blue remembered hills," I said.

"And them," Lizzy said.

"Exactly," Julie said.

"Yes, but aren't we all?" Lizzy said.

"Don't let him off," Julie said. "Either that, or he's hiding from something."

"Well, let's just get some work out of him while he's here," Lizzy said.

"Amen to that," Julie said.

"I can't tell you how long I'm staying," I said." Because I don't know. But while I'm here, I promise to earn my keep. What is it you'll be wanting me to do, mainly?"

"Everything," Lizzy said.

"Oh, and I promised to meet a friend for an hour or so tomorrow morning. I hope that's okay?"

"I suppose I'll allow it." She smiled. "I think we might use your muscles to get ahead of the fencing a bit. The weaners are overdue to come out. And the sheep need moving… and there's a thousand other things."

"And there's the village fete on Friday too," Julie said.

"At the hall?" I said.

"Yup. Always on the solstice. Has been since forever, apparently. We'll be helping set up on Friday with everyone else, and it's one of our pigs'll be on the spit and a lot of what's eaten will come out of the garden too. I take it, you can drive a tractor?"

"I learnt to drive on a tractor," I said.

"Well, Si," Lizzy said, "I can't say as I exactly know who or what you are, but you do seem to have a knack of turning up just when we need you."

Morny, standing at the bar, caught my eye and jerked his head to indicate that I should join him.

"Won't be a minute," I said.

"Sharon, I expect the man'll have another pint of Head," Morny said, when I joined him.

"Probably a good plan," I said. "And what the girls are having too please."

"You heard the man, Sharon," Morny said.

"As you say, Morny," she said.

At our feet, the dogs introduced themselves in a manner that didn't sound very polite. We looked at them. They were standing stiff-legged, teeth showing. Their tails were up though; it was the beginning of a game.

"She's a tart really, though she doesn't look it," he said. "If you get rowdy, I'll not stand for it," he said to Minnie.

"Same to you, dog," I said.

They wagged their tails at us briefly and went back to what they were doing.

"Here you are, my love," Sharon said passing me a pint of beer.

"Cheers," I said, taking a sup.

"And to you, Simon," Morny said, doing the same.

"What is it you all see in that farm-girl?" Sharon said, looking towards Lizzy and Julie. One of the lads from the bar had gone over to talk to them. Or rather, to Lizzy.

"She means Lizzy," Morny said, lowering an eyelid in my direction.

"She's skinny and funny always wears nothing but jeans and a t-shirt and not so much as lip-gloss," Sharon said.

"Ah, but she's got a sweet, wild spirit, and there's not a mean bone in her body," Morny said. "There's something about her that's like a young colt. A bit gangly, but kind of exciting."

Sharon and I both looked at him.

"What?" he said. "I'm old and ugly, but I'm not blind, nor a gelding."

"Men!" Sharon said, and went to serve another customer.

"I see you're in disguise this time," Morny said. He looked at my clothes.

"No idea what you mean," I said, smiling.

"Nothing changes, then," he said. "Hm. Well, don't worry, I didn't tell on you then, and I'll not now. Just see you don't bother my preserves, is all."

"Thanks. I don't think I'll have time for any mischief, given what they've got planned for me," I said, looking towards the girls.

"It is busy season, right enough," he said.

"Come and join us," I said.

"Don't mind if I do," he said.

The lad from the village who had been talking to Lizzy gave me a dark look as he passed me, heading back towards his friends.

"Is he giving you any trouble, Lizzy?" Morny said.

"Jimmy? Not really," she said. "Just the usual."

"Well, let me know if he does, and I'll put him back in his box," Morny said.

I looked at Morny, who's not a big chap whatever else he is, and at the lad, who was built along the general lines of a brick out-house, and wondered. Neither of the girls seemed to find what he'd said at all surprising though.

"Jimmy's got a bit of a thing for Lizzy," Julie said.

"Jimmy's alright," Lizzy said. "He just…"

"A fucking idiot," Julie said. "Well, never mind him. So, Morny, you know this man here, do you?"

"I knew the boy, I can't say I know the man," Morny said, with a twinkle in his eye. "I expect, somebody will probably be wanting him to do something in the nature of a real job; something in an office, or something."

"I'm just not cut out for wearing a suit," I said, with a shrug. "They keep trying to make me, but it's not happening."

"I can understand that," Lizzy said.

"And me," Julie said.

"Whereas I'm bitterly disappointed I never made it into accountancy," Morny said, raising his glass.

We all touched glasses to the thought.

"Seeing as you didn't, are you coming over with Toby about five tomorrow?" Julie said.

A Diving Eagle

"I believe I am. The little bugger's got to earn his cartridges…"

There was the nice, easy comfortableness between the older man and the two women, of people who are safe with each other and share a way of life. They fell into talking about village and farming affairs, mainly the coming village fete. I half listened, feeling happy just to be there, and let my eyes wander about the bar.

"What gets me, is the way they go around in their tweed jackets talking to each other as if we can't hear them," Julie said.

"It's one of those occasions where the rich and the rest of us are in one place doing more or less the same thing and pretending the other party doesn't exist," Morny said. "I find it amusing, most of the time."

"It's the way they clog up the lanes and expect me to back up with a trailer on that annoys me," Lizzy said.

Steve, the landlord, went over to the table of teenagers and collected some empty glasses. They spoke to him, being very polite, letting him know that they were being no trouble. He put the glasses on the bar and went to the table of four men to get theirs. He spoke to them, and they replied in a friendly way, but I didn't think they were local people. One of them had a tattoo on his forearm. I couldn't see what it was.

"You're not shooting then?" Julie said.

"Shooting?" I said.

"No. They banned me last year," Morny said. "Said it wasn't fair. I said it wasn't fair they banned me. Not my fault if everyone else has two left eyes."

"There's clay pigeons as part of the fete," Lizzy said. "It got boring because Morny always used to win, so they used to make up two hampers, one for Morny and one for the runner up, who was the real winner, if you see what I mean."

"Until some rich chap complained," Morny said.

"What rich chap?" I said.

"I don't know. One of the Earl's friends," he said.

"Oh?" I said.

"What we were just talking about," Julie said. "The fete. It isn't just the village, there's also all of his friends too. They bring a bit of money, I suppose, but they tend to get in the way."

"Some of them can shoot a bit," Morny said. "Only a bit, mind, but not too bad for city people."

"He has some kind of dinner for them in the evening," Julie said. "I mean, there's a massive wild hog from the Frankoms and lamb from us and more veg than I can get into the Landy for one trip. Brings in outside caterers and waiting on staff and everything. I've been working up to it for a fortnight. The salad's as good as can be, though I say it myself."

"About how many?" I said.

"Oh, at least a hundred," Lizzy said.

"All of that," Morny said.

"So, rich city people come to the fete on Saturday?" I said.

"Quite a few of them have a go at the shoot and then they stay on for the Earl's party after," Morny said. "It's been an annual thing since the new earl took over. He's a city type, as they say, and he's entitled, I suppose. A lot of the same faces come back for the pheasant shooting, come October. Can't say I like them generally, but it's my job and there it is."

"Those men over there," I glanced at the four men, "do they work at the nut house?"

"How'd'you know that?" Julie said.

"Just a guess," I said.

"Poles mostly," Morny said. "No harm in them. Don't get into fights leastways. Unlike that lot," He looked at the group of lads by the bar.

"'scuse me a minute," I said and got up, "and I don't mean to be a lightweight, but would it be alright if we went home soon? I've got some sleeping to catch up on and I'm expecting to be working a bit tomorrow."

"Damn right you are," Lizzy said, smiling. "Yes, meet you out there in a minute."

I walked out through the bar and as I went, I gave the lad called Jimmy a wink.

The gents was outside at the back, facing onto the open field. It was basic and benefited from a lot of fresh air. I did what needed doing and came back out into the very last of the long soft evening, with my head full of many thoughts.

Jimmy and two of his friends had come out of the pub and were stood there looking at me. Cal was behind them.

"I want a word with you," Jimmy said.

"Watch him Jimmy," one of the others said, "he's quite a big fucker."

"The bigger they are…" Jimmy said.

"What's the problem?" I said.

"You gave me a wink," he said.

"No, I didn't," I said.

"Yes, you did. And you're to leave that girl alone," Jimmy said.

"Lizzy?" I said.

"That's the one," he said. "And bugger off now."

"No chance," I said.

"You don't belong round here, you fucker, and I'm telling you to fuck off," he said, and came up within finger poking range of me.

"Nice to see you country people have still got sophisticated vocabularies," I said, smiling at him nastily and backing off a bit.

"You pussy. Go on, fuck off. Fuck off now," he said, closing the gap again and measuring distances with his eyes in readiness, his anger rising.

I looked past him, His two friends weren't far away, but Cal had disappeared.

"Is this going to be just you and me, or all three of you?" I said.

"I'm going to fill you in and I won't need any hel…"

My punch to his stomach cut the word off but didn't wind him as much as it should have. He had fists like hams, and had no doubt spent most of his life heaving heavy things about. The blow that he'd started, missed my nose by a fraction and I got a block under it and turned him enough to give him one hard and short in the kidneys. That made him grunt and gave me time to back off a little.

He came on, hands up, more cautious now, but determined and confident. I took another step back to encourage him, and then another, making him come on faster. Then I feinted right, stepped out left and tripped him with a kick to the ankle. He went down on one knee, lunging out to take me with him, and getting a hand to my shirt. I pulled away and luckily the fabric tore, giving me enough space to hit down at his wrist. He grunted and let go, rising and pivoting towards me. I gave him one hard, but not too hard, to the throat with my right, which stopped him. That gave me time to set my feet and hit him properly.

This time I gave him everything I had to the solar plexus, driving from the ground, through my hips, into the space behind him. He folded and went down onto his knees, holding himself with one arm and preventing himself from going completely face down with the other. I set my feet again and debated using my left to finish him. His friends stood there watching me, not knowing what to do. There were a lot of other people behind them now.

"Stop! Don't hurt him, Si," someone said. It was Lizzy. She, Julie, Morny, had come out of the pub too. Lizzy looked pale and frightened. So did Julie, but not so much. Morny looked amused.

"Let them be, girl. Jimmy's got to learn," Morny said.

"Jimmy, you've got no right," Lizzy said. She looked pale and her voice had a tremble in it.

"Okay," I said. I dropped my hands.

One of the teenagers, said, "Fucking hell, mister. You've killed Jimmy."

A Diving Eagle

"No, he hasn't," Morny said, joining me and looking down at the big man. "Probably done him a bit of good, on the whole."

"Are you okay, Si?" Lizzy said. She and Julie were there too now.

"He clearly is okay," Julie said, looking at me thoughtfully.

"Sorry about that," I said, holding up the dangling flap of my shirt. "I tried not to hurt him, honestly."

The rest of the customers from the pub were standing there looking at us now, including the four men from the Abbey. I didn't look at them.

"Yeah, right," Morny said to me, under his breath.

27

THUNDER CLOUDS

"Jimmy's an idiot," Julie said. We were standing outside the Barrel. Jimmy had revived enough to be led away by his friends and it was becoming time to do something else, like go to bed.

"I hate it when you men…" Lizzy said.

"Don't fret, girl. No harm done," Morny said.

"He knows how to hold a grudge, mind," Julie said.

"With any luck the other two'll make him see sense. I might even have a word myself," Morny said.

"I'm sorry, Si," Lizzy said. "You didn't do anything to deserve that."

"I don't mind," I said.

"Well, you should," she said.

"He doesn't though," Morny said. "Forget it. It's nothing. Now, I know it's early but I'm an old man and need my sleep."

"Yeah, right," Julie said.

"Go home, you three. We've all got a busy day tomorrow," he said.

Thunder Clouds

"Shall I drive?" I said, holding out my hand for the key.

"If you want," Lizzy said, giving it to me.

She got in the front and I passed her Jake. He sat on her lap and she put her head down to smell him and then stroked his ears. Julie got in the back. I shut her in, started up and drove us home. The last of the light of the long day faded past dusk and into night. Moths fluttered in the weak beams of the headlights. In the outer yard, a cat's eyes were bright for a moment and then went out as it turned its head. I pulled up in the inner yard, turned the engine off and we got out into the black stillness of the countryside at night.

Lizzy went into the house and turned on the light in the hall. It was hard and white after the darkness.

"I'm going up," she said. She went straight up the stairs and I heard the bathroom door shut.

"Julie, will you help me with a bed for Jake?" I said.

"Come with me," she said, going into the front room and turning on the light. She took an old blanket out of a trunk behind one of the sofas and gave it to me. "Here, he can have that."

"Thanks. I'll just take a turn round the yard with him and then settle him down in the kitchen," I said.

"I'll go up myself. Don't worry about being quiet or anything. Make tea or whatever, if you want."

"Thanks. I'm sorry if... I didn't mean to upset anyone."

"Forget it. It'll be okay in the morning."

"Good. Goodnight, Julie."

"Goodnight, Si."

I put the blanket down on the kitchen table, lifted Thomas out of the clock, slipped a couple of cartridges into her from my pocket, and went out into the night. It was black dark after the electric light so I walked carefully, sliding my feet and giving my eyes time to adjust. Jake had no such issues and disappeared into the darkness.

In the outer yard, I smelt the warm brown smell of the manure and the fresher smell of the hay. I had a pee against the muck-heap and bats became visible, flickering against the stars.

"C'mon dog. That's it for the day," I said, and turned back to the house. There were lights on upstairs.

Jake didn't appear until I'd got back into the kitchen. I turned the key in the door to the back garden and worked a little cooking oil into the bolt on the front door until it would slide home easily.

I folded up the blanket and put it by the Rayburn and gave him a bowl of water for the night. I found a rather nice and surprisingly sharp, kitchen knife in a drawer and used it to cut him a piece of cheese from the fridge and made him sit and take it properly. I wished him goodnight and told him to stay put, he seemed to understand.

I left the knife wrapped in a tea-towel stuck in one of my boots by the door and trod the stairs in socks, looking for creaks, and found a few. Both bedroom doors on the landing were closed. I brushed my teeth and ascended to my room without turning a light on. The starlight was delicate on the boards and the smells of dust and mothballs and the freshness of the washed linen and blankets were stronger in the darkness.

I set my phone to vibrate an alarm for bloody early, and lay down with Thomas loaded, but not cocked, beside me. The bed-springs creaked as they took my weight. I closed my eyes and set to counting my breaths, forcing stillness on my mind and body so that I was resting as much as I could without sleeping. The house settled and quietened below me, and the moon rose, making shadows from the bedstead on the wall.

I went down in time for Lizzy to find me buttering toast at the kitchen table as the clock was chiming five-thirty. Her hair was in the delightful tangle of the night, and she was yawning and rubbing her eyes. I poured a mug of tea from the pot and held it out to her.

"Oh," she said, tightening her dressing gown. "You're up already."

Julie came in, saw me, and said, "Bloody hell."

"Morning," I said, pouring tea for her too. "Sleep well?"

"Fuck yes," she said, grasping it. "Thanks."

"Julie!" Lizzy said.

"Sorry," Julie said, "it's just…" she waved a hand at me.

"Toast and coffee?" I said, smiling.

"I know," Lizzy said, smiling. "Me too. Yes please, Si. Toast and coffee would be lovely." She pulled out a chair and sat down. Julie did the same.

There was the sound of scratching at the front door. I opened it and let Jake back in. He went straight to Lizzy and looked up at her, wagging his stump. She bent down and stroked his head with both hands. He was clearly in heaven. I would've been quite willing to swap with him.

"So, you say you can drive a tractor?" Julie said, looking at me.

"Eh?" Lizzy said, looking up.

"Should be able to," I said.

"Are you thinking what I'm thinking?" Julie said, looking at Lizzy.

"I am now," she said. "I'll get him started and then do the milking, you get Cal to help in the garden."

"Yes, boss," Julie said, grinning.

"You won't have time to shoot anything," Lizzy said, as she and I walked out into the yard, some coffee, food, and a quick brush with the bathroom later.

"Sorry, force of habit to bring it," I said. "I take it, you don't let Cal loose on the heavy machinery?"

"Last time he got on a tractor, we had to rebuild part of the dairy."

"I think you'd better talk me through the controls," I said, looking up at the big green John Deere in the yard. "I'm somewhat more used to that kind of thing." I pointed at the little Fergy that was sitting by the hay.

"I see. Does Jake know not to get run over?"

"No idea."

"Get him. He can sit in the cab."

I called him and he came to me and I picked him up and followed her up into the cab. She took the driver's seat and I took the smaller passenger seat beside it. I hadn't known that tractors could have passenger seats. I put the dog on my lap and held onto him.

"I suppose this thing has air conditioning?" I said.

"And a dock for your iPod."

"I don't have an iPod."

"Me neither."

She started the beast and took me quickly through the controls, not repeating herself, expecting me to keep up. Her slim, hands were quick and little creases appeared above her nose as she concentrated.

"Your turn."

She nimbly climbed up onto the seat and accepted the dog, who seemed perfectly happy about the situation, and then stepped behind me as I moved over. I found the lever under the seat and moved it back so that I could get my feet to the pedals. She sat down on the passenger seat and began stroking the dog's ears.

I was surprised by the massive torque of the engine as I let in the clutch and had to de-clutch and brake quickly, making us leap forward and then bounce to a halt suddenly.

"Not used to so much power then?" she said.

"You could have warned me," I said, and tried again.

This time I managed the power, and soon had the grab on the fore-end loader working smoothly.

"Good. Think you can pick up the trailer, take it out, drop it, load it and bring it back?" she said.

"Yes boss."

"I'll see you there in about an hour then."

"An hour?"

"I'm making allowances for you being a bit slow."

"Oh, are you."

"Don't try turning a corner with the diff lock on. It won't happen," she said, opened the door and climbed down.

"Yes boss."

"And don't break anything."

"No boss."

I watched her striding off across the yard in her loose-hipped, fluid way.

"Right then, dog. Let's you and me, do this," I said, and let in the clutch carefully. I backed up to the big four-wheeled trailer, found the right lever to raise the hook to pick up its towing eye, and trundled off to the long meadow.

I didn't make it back in an hour, but I wasn't far off. Catching up the big round bales and stacking them on the trailer required a certain delicacy of touch which it took me several goes to acquire. It was harder than I thought, but I put my mind to it. Jake sat in the passenger seat, got bored, curled up and went to sleep.

When I got to the yard, I found that Lizzy had connected a bale wrapper onto the back of the Fergy and manoeuvred it into place towards the rear of the space. I backed the trailer in, parallel to the open side of the barn, dropped it off, spun the big tractor round and climbed down. Jake woke up and jumped down too. It was a long way for a little dog but he just took it at a run and went off somewhere for some reason.

"You can back a four-wheeled trailer then," Lizzy said.

"Can't everyone?" I said, grinning.

"Think you can put one on the bed of the wrapper without breaking it?"

"I might. Where are they going?"

"Over there by the wall." She pointed. "If you damage the film it'll spoil."

"You don't say."

I got back up, lifted the first bale and placed it with great care into the bed of the machine. She stood to one side with the remote control and spun the black plastic sheeting onto the bale like some monstrous silk-worm cocoon. I lifted it carefully out and delivered it to the space beside the wall. One done.

We worked through the load, eighteen bales wrapped and stacked, and met on the ground.

"Want to stop for a cuppa?" she said.

"I do, and I don't," I said.

"No problem." She poured a mug-full from a thermos and handed it to me. "Go on then, what're you waiting for?"

Inevitably, the tractor had a cup holder, so I put my cup in it and got on with the job. And I worked; constantly figuring out the most efficient place to put the trailer and the quickest way to pick up the bales. I got my time for a load down to three quarters of an hour and I knew I would get a bit more as I got smoother. Each time I got back, Lizzy appeared and we wrapped them together. I saw no one else at all, either in the field or in the yard.

On my fourth time, she looked at the growing pile of wrapped bales and said, "You can take a break if you want to."

"Okay. I might do the rest of them tomorrow," I said, watching her face. "Only kidding," I said, quickly getting back in the saddle.

By the time I'd put the last bale on the trailer I was throwing that tractor about like a toy and I'd learned to use the independent brakes and the diff-lock to make the most of its grip and turning circle. I raised the hook at the back to pick up the trailer and headed out of the now empty field with the last load. It was going on for one and I'd been working hard for about seven hours with nothing to sustain me but a mug of tea.

Lizzy was waiting for me, sitting on the wrapper. I didn't stop to speak to her but just dropped the trailer and went for the first bale. She caught my mood and we went through the load together at pretty good pace. Soon it was the last bale and then the trailer was empty. I put the loader down to the ground, turned off the engine, grabbed my empty mug, slung Thomas in her gun-slip over my shoulder, and climbed down. Lizzy stepped up to the Fergy, reached over and killed that too. There was silence. A wood pigeon began its song in the orchard and the air smelt deliciously of manure and earth and summer and diesel and warm machinery.

We stood and looked at the small mountain of winter feed that we'd created. Three high, four deep and going almost from the barn to the pond in the corner. I stretched and yawned and shook myself to get some of the creases out. Lizzy was grinning. She smelt of disinfectant again.

"Bloody hell, Si. It's done," she said.

"What's next, boss?" I said, saluting.

"Lunch. Lunch is definitely what's next."

Julie and Cal stopped work too and we ate bread and cheese and tomatoes and salad leaves at the table the in front of the house. The cat was back on the mounting block and kept a good eye on Jake without seeming to. The dog lay on his back in the dust, put all four legs up in the air and squirmed about with happiness. Then he sneezed and lay on his side with one eye on the cat.

"Don't you dare," I said.

"Have you been bird-nesting again, Cal?" Lizzy said.

"Not me," he said. "I haven't since you tol' me you'd sack me that time."

"So, why's the two-piece ladder not in its usual place in the barn?" She looked at the tall stone wall that led to the walled garden, and sure enough, there was the ladder leaning against it.

"'Cos I haven't put it back, I suppose," he said.

"Yes, but why wasn't it there in the first place?"

"Dunno. Some bloke came in with it."

"What do you mean, some bloke came in with it? Why?"

"Don' ask me. He jus' walked in with it an asked if it was ours. I said it was, and put it there. He said he found it somewhere."

"That's odd. Where?"

"I dunno."

"You didn't ask?"

"No."

"Could be the Carter boys," Julie said. "They're getting to the age when they're up to all kinds."

"Could be," Lizzy said. "What bloke, Cal? Who was he?"

"Dunno. Just a bloke."

"Cal, you're as good a detective as you are a tractor driver," Julie said.

"Am I?" he said.

"So, what're we doing this afternoon?" I said.

"I think it's going to rain," Julie said. "There's a heaviness about the air."

"I think so too," Lizzy said. "I'll bet it stops before evening. Si, you'n me'll go and fix the fences down in the wood at the bottom of the five-acre. Julie, you and Cal can finish off in the garden and get the cows in for milking."

"Works for me," Julie said.

"And by then, Morny and his boy'll be over and we'll load up and get off to the hall and help set up for Friday. If you've got any strength left." She looked at me.

"I'll do my best, boss," I said.

As Lizzy and I trundled off in the Landy with posts and a roll of wire and tools in the back, there were the first rising plumes of clouds that were becoming thunderheads in the sky to the south, and the air felt uneasy. Jake sat on Lizzy's lap.

We went down the track behind the milking parlour and crossed two fields to an acre or so of scrubby woodland enclosed in fencing. One half of it was a bomb-site and a massive sow was asleep in a wallow under a tree. The other was full of nettles and thistles and burdock and needed its fence putting back together badly.

I put the gun on the bonnet of the Landy with its slip partly unzipped so that I could get to it quickly. Jake went off to see what he could catch and kill, and Lizzy and I started work.

I drove in the new posts where they were needed and took tension on the wire and backed up the post while she hammered in the staples. She swung the two-pound hammer with practiced ease, not letting it jar her. She was always ahead of me; notching posts to take bracers with a bow-saw, picking the line and starting the ground for the posts with a heavy iron bar.

I picked up a fair collection of burdock burs in my shirt and my forearms and hands were soon pink and slightly swollen from nettle stings but the work was good.

The ground was hard and dry, so it was heavy work. It was good to be using my shoulders on the post driver, swinging through to drive them well in. We stopped for a break when we'd done one side of the pen. The line ran true without any sagging and the wire was taught enough to twang. Stock fencing at the bottom and two lines of barbed wire at the top.

"At this rate, we might get those weaners out tomorrow," she said, passing me tea from a thermos.

Some pigeons clattered up from the White Wood in the distance and I watched the top of a van pass along the road towards the Abbey.

I got up and sat on the bonnet of the Landy and she got up beside me.

"You look far away," she said.

"I was just wondering what disturbed those pigeons," I said.

"Morny probably. He's always in that wood when he's not somewhere else. He leaves his Landy by the pens on Lakey Rise and walks down behind the hedge. It never completely dries out down there and I know it's him because Minnie's missing a toe."

"So, there's a back way into the White Wood?"

"I've never been that way, but there must be."

A magpie made its alarm call not far from us at the end of the copse.

"I'll just walk down and see what's moving down there," I said.

"Okay, but don't be long. Let's get this done before the weather breaks."

"Yes, boss."

"With me, boy," I said to Jake. "No. With me. Don't run off."

I slipped a couple of cartridges into the gun and thumbed the hammers back and we walked down the edge of the straggly bit of wood that was an out-crop of the White Wood. I didn't see anything, but it was too quiet. No tree-creepers crept or nuthatches flicked about. Something, or someone was in the trees and had only just arrived. Jake thought so too. We turned back and I phoned Bill. He didn't answer, but called me back a minute later.

"This is weird," he said.

"What?"

"I've just come from a briefing that's all about finding you, and now I'm talking to you."

"I'm sure you'll cope. Where's Freddy?"

"Hereford. Why?"

"I'm lonely."

"We still don't have a warrant or any way to get one."

"Don't worry, you will. Just get me Freddy, will you. I mean, right now."

"How will I get a warrant? Or don't I want to know?"

"You don't want to know."

"Oh, fuck. Where, exactly?"

I told him, and then went back to work with Lizzy, but I kept the gun in its slip near us and I left the cartridges in it, which I normally never would do.

We worked on around the pen, increasingly in sync with each other. I always moved the Landy so that it was only a few feet away. We hadn't brought enough new posts so we re-pointed some of the old ones and made good progress. Jake sat not far away, looking towards the wood, as if he knew he had a job to do.

The clouds built up above us. There were only two more posts to drive when the first fat drops began to fall.

"Ah, well. Nearly made it," she said.

"You want to stop?" I said.

"You don't?" she said.

"I don't care," I said.

"Okay, Mr. If you want to finish it, let's finish it."

We finished it and the rain washed her hair into streaks and made her t-shirt stick to her body. It hit the dry earth and quickly made it wet. There was that smell of rain on dry earth when it hasn't rained for a while. The air was full of it. When I'd driven the last post and she had driven the last staple I put my face up into it and let it run into my mouth. It tasted soft and good and not that cold.

"I love the rain," she said and shook her head so that it flew off her hair.

She was standing in front of me, looking at me. I was completely wet and so was she and our wetness was like nakedness. It didn't seem wrong to kiss her and she must have felt the same as she met me half way. Her face was wet and for a moment there was only our lips touching, me kissing her and her kissing me back. I moved forward and put my arms around her to draw her body to mine.

"No," she said, putting her hands on my chest and pushing us apart.

I didn't want to stop so I kept my hands behind her back. She was slim and light compared to me and her pushing made no impression on me.

"No, no, please," she said, pushing harder and trying to wriggle out.

"What's wrong?" I said, shifting my grip so that I had a hand higher up behind her back so that I could pull her closer to me.

"I'm sorry... I..."

It wasn't just rain on her face.

"Sorry, I didn't...." I let go of her.

Not just unhappy, scared.

"We should go back," she said, stepping away and not looking at me.

"Lizzy, I didn't..." I said, but she wouldn't look at me and walked away.

We collected up the tools and the broken posts and I wound up the old and damaged wire and we put it all into the back of the Landrover. The rain was cold and wet now and picking up the wet things wasn't so nice. She looked small and bedraggled when she tried to lift the heavy post driver onto the pile in the back of the vehicle. She struggled herself, rather than waiting for me to come up so that we could do it together.

We drove back in silence in the steamed-up, wet cab. Cal was in the yard when we got there.

"You're wet," he said, staring at Lizzy's breasts which were revealed by the wetness of her t-shirt.

"Go in and change," I said to her. "Cal and I'll sort this out."

"No. I'll manage," she said, going to the back of the vehicle.

"No. Go in and change," I said, putting a hand on the door and opening it myself.

She looked at me now, becoming angry.

"You're very wet," I said, letting my eyes flick downwards for an instant.

"Oh."

"I'm sure Cal knows where everything goes," I said.

"Yes. Okay." She turned away and walked straight into the house.

"Did you see her…?" Cal said moving beside me.

"Shut up, Cal," I said.

"Yes, but did you see…"

I took a handful of the front of his overalls and lifted him a bit.

"Shut up, Cal," I said.

"Oh, right then," he said. "I'd best be quiet then." He looked at me with a wary, knowing eye.

"You know where this old wire should go?" I said, putting him down.

"We puts it on the metal heap behind the hay barn just beside the old trailer that's got a flat tyre. When it builds up Lizzy phones someone and a man comes with…"

"Go and put it there. I'll do the tools," I said, pulling a pile of it out, bringing a lot of other stuff out with it.

"Okay, I'll do that then," he said. He took hold of a strand of it and started dragging it away.

I put the tools away in the tool-room and gave the fencing pliers a squirt of WD40 from the can on the shelf near the door. I piled the old bits of fence-post into a wheelbarrow and left that for Cal to deal with. I took the gun in its case and went into the house. Jake lay on his back on his bed and wriggled and rubbed, drying himself. I went upstairs for a quick wash and some dry clothes.

When I got back downstairs, Julie was sitting at the kitchen table. She looked tired and wet but happy.

"Hey, Si. How goes it?" she said.

"Isn't that good rain?" I said.

"I've been praying for it."

She got up and went to the back door and opened it. The sound and smell of the rain came into the room.

"The sky is lightening," I said. "I think it's going to stop soon."

"That's okay, it's done its job. It can stop now, if it likes. How did you two do?"

"The fencing is fenced."

"Wonderful. I shouldn't say this, but it is nice having a man about. And his dog." she bent down to rub Jake's belly. "Have you actually fed this animal at all?"

"He seems to be feeding himself."

"That's not fair. There's some old bones and scraps in the freezer in the tool room that he could have."

The little bugger seemed to understand that and sat up and looked at me.

"Okay, I'll go and have a look."

"You do that. I'll put the kettle on and we'll have some of the cake."

I went into the tool-room and started ferreting about in the bottom of the chest-freezer standing against the back wall. Thomas came with me. She could do with a good rub down with a dry cloth.

I'd piled up a few bits and pieces of frozen meat that looked suitable; some of the labels had come off and it was partly guesswork, when the doorway darkened. I turned to see who it was. It was three heavy-set men with short haircuts and the sort of presence that's usually bad news for someone.

"Good evening, Mr Ellice," one of them said, in good English.

There didn't seem to be much point in denying it, so I said, "Good evening," and picked up Thomas and thumbed back the hammers.

They came in, shut the door, spread out, and conferred briefly in Polish. I pointed the gun at the middle one.

"You won't use that," the one on the right said.

"I will, you know," I said.

"No, you won't," he said. "You'll come with us. We won't hurt you, but you've got some questions to answer."

"Strangely enough, I have some questions for you too," I said.

They began to move forward, getting as much around me as they could. The one in the middle started to move his hand around behind his back. I put the contents of the right-hand barrel into the centre of his chest.

28

A WOUNDED BIRD

Shotguns are loud things. The crash of the shot was given back hard by the bare concrete walls. I'd opened the gun, flipped out the used cartridge, put another in, closed her and got the hammer back by the time the man had finished collapsing backwards onto the floor.

The other two had been stopped by the shot as much as the dead man. We all stood there and looked at him. The hole in his chest where his heart had been didn't go all the way through, but nearly. He wasn't bleeding as much as if he had had a heart to keep on pumping.

I pointed the gun at the one on the left. He was looking at what was on the floor. So was his friend.

"Now there are two of you and two cartridges in this," I said. "Do you think you can get to me in time?"

They looked at me, wanting desperately to get at me but physically stopped by the gun.

"Bend from the hips and untie your boots," I said.

"Why should we?" the one on the left said.

"You don't have to," I said. "But if you don't, I'll shoot you and do it myself. You're just as useful to me dead as alive."

"Do kurwy nędzy," he said.

"Same to you," I said.

This time they believed me. I made them undo their boots and kick them off, and then drop their trousers, step out of them and kick them over to me. And then their shirts and underpants. They didn't look any less dangerous standing there naked. They also had tattoos; the diving eagle clutching a lightning bolt.

I made them turn around and lean against the far wall at a steep angle, while I removed knives, keys, phones and various other things from their trouser pockets. Then I did the same for the dead one. He had a short-barrelled Walther tucked into his trouser waistband. I dumped all this into a used carrier-bag and added Jake's meat on top.

"Now then you two, there'll be someone along to let you out in a bit. Until then, you are to sit down and be quiet. If you don't, I'm going to lob a can of petrol through the window followed by a match. And then I'll stand outside and shoot anything that manages to make it out before it all burns down. I'm done with this place now and I don't mind making a start on the tidying up."

"I don't believe you, Mr Ellice," the leader said.

"That's your privilege, old thing. Now, you must excuse me, I've got a dog to feed."

I backed out carefully and shut the door. There was a small, worn padlock hanging open on the hasp. I snicked it into place and phoned Bill. He went a bit mental, but he got the point. I tucked the carrier bag under the bench by the table and took the meat with me into the house.

"Get lost, did you?" Julie said. Lizzy was sitting by the Rayburn cradling a mug and talking to Jake. She didn't look up as I came in.

"Sorry, got distracted by a rat," I said.

"I thought I heard a shot. Did you get it?"

"Yup." I put the bag on the draining-board and fished out some frozen meat for Jake. He took it respectfully from my hand and went to work on it in his bed.

"That's still frozen," Lizzy said.

"Think of it as an ice-lolly for a dog," I said.

"You seem to be very attached to that gun," Julie said. "I don't think I've seen you without it since you got here."

"There's a reason for that," I said.

"Go on," she said.

"It's my grandfather's; I've been thinking about him a lot lately." I helped myself to a big slice from the cake in the tin.

"I thought you looked serious when you came in," she said.

"You're right, serious is how I feel," I said. "The rain has stopped and I think the sun is going to come out. Shall we go and do what's next?"

"Reckon, we should," Lizzy said.

The outer yard was wonderfully fragrant after the rain, and the surface of the dirt, soft and no longer dusty. I picked up the hay-trailer with the John Deere and backed it into the barn beside the small-bale straw. Morny arrived in another battered Landrover with a trailer full of clay-pigeon traps. With him was a well-grown youth of fifteen or so who was introduced to me as Toby. He would soon be bigger than his father.

Between us, we made short work of loading forty bales onto the bed of the hay-trailer. Lizzy and Julie appeared in the farm Landy, loaded down with veg from the garden and we set out in convoy for the hall. Cal rode on the trailer for hygienic reasons and Jake deserted me for the superior attractions of Lizzy. I had Thomas for company though. Behind us, as we left, nothing happened; no one hammered on any doors, or started shooting anyone.

A Wounded Bird

The lane took its wandering way to the junction with the road to Effington. We turned onto that and almost immediately the walls of the park appeared on our left. Being so high up I could see over, so I looked for the Fallow deer that should be there, but didn't see any. A bit further along, a gang of three men were re-making the wall where the roots of a chestnut tree had heaved it into disrepair. They were making a good job of it.

The pillars of the main gates had been re-pointed too and the ironwork shone with fresh paint. We turned in and started down the dead-straight avenue of three-hundred year oaks that led to the north elevation of the house. The deer were grazing on the sweep of parkland that led down to the lake. On the other side, dozens of cars, lorries, four by fours with trailers were parked in organised rows. There were people and dogs everywhere.

We didn't go as far as the oval of gravel in front of the house but turned right, onto the road that led round the west side. A white butcher's van pulled onto the grass to let us pass. Lizzy and Julie turned into the yard between stables, but Morny waved to me to follow him off the road and down between the trees. To our left, the big sweep of land between the south face of the hall and the lake held several marquees and other tents and stalls and all the things of a country fair, and was full of the bustle of getting ready.

We drove slowly to the glade flanked by copper beeches in front of us and stopped. There were a few other vehicles and men already there. I got down and went to join Morny, who was standing looking at the space thoughtfully. The other men came over too and greeted him. One of them was one of the men who had been with Jimmy in the pub the previous night.

"Right then," Morny said. "What we'll do is quite a lot like last year, but let's have a couple of crossing birds over by there and…"

He directed us and we drove posts to make shooting stands, set out traps to throw the clay discs and sheltered them behind walls of straw. It took a while and it was a good job there were that many of us. We fell into working easily together, as men who are used to doing physical work with other men, will. Toby was as strong as most of us, and fully one of the team. It occurred to me that by the time I finished for the day, I would have had plenty of exercise; it felt good.

"You got your gun in the cab?" Morny said to me.

"As it happens," I said.

"Thought so. Go fetch it; we'll give it try, and then go and appraise the beer tent. Suit you?"

"Suits me," I said, and fetched Thomas.

"Pull!" he said.

A couple of clays flew out and I got the gun up in time to miss the second one.

"You awake now?" he said.

Second time, I got them.

"Too easy. 'Ere, lad, you move 'im round so it's more of a going away bird. Ready?"

"Pull!" I called.

I got them, but only just. We went on round the course with me shooting and him looking over my shoulder and calling out changes. The result was hard but fair. Except perhaps the last pair, which were bastards.

"Got to have something to separate the men from the boys," he said.

"I could hit 'em," Toby said.

I passed him Thomas. He looked at his dad.

"Go on then," Morny said. "You said it, now do it."

The lad stepped up, gave the gun a bit of an experimental heft, called 'pull', and made dust of both clays. He passed the gun back to me, grinning in spite of himself.

"I've seen worse," Morny said, with an almost straight face. "Now then, who wants a beer? This'n 'ere is buying." He jerked a thumb at me.

"Oh, am I?" I said.

"Yup."

"Why?"

"In gratitude for the practice," he said.

"Practice for what?" I said.

"How should I know," he said. "But you in't carrying that thing around for no reason, is you?"

We walked down into the purposeful bustle of preparation in the main area and found that the beer tent was indeed open and serving. Some thoughtful soul had also ordained that there should be a good quantity of bacon rolls available to the workers. We all received both with enthusiasm and there was a good feeling of life and activity shared; including Jimmy's friend, who seemed to have forgotten that I was the enemy for the time being.

Julie and Lizzy found us there, and accepted sustenance, but they were clearly tired, and the light was fading.

"Longest day tomorrow," Lizzy said.

"This one's not been that short," I said, yawning.

"Drink up, you lot," Julie said. "If we don't leave now, one of you is going to have to carry me to bed."

There were plenty of offers to do just that from the men, and Lizzy smiled at her friend. We put our glasses on the bar and headed home, pulling onto the grass of the avenue to let a familiar phantom sweep past us. The lord and master was back in his seat.

I parked the big tractor in the outer yard without unhitching the trailer; I would do that in the morning, and walked through into the inner yard as the girls were parking the Landy. It was almost fully dark but there was just enough light to see that the padlock on the tool store was now missing. I refrained from going to have a look and opened the front door of the house, Thomas casually held in my right hand. The house was its usual homely self, and quite free of tattooed thugs.

"Fuck, that was a long day," Julie said, coming in behind me and pulling off her boots.

"And a good one," Lizzy said, looking at me and smiling shyly.

"Anyone seen my dog?" I said.

"He's in the yard," Lizzy said. "He found an interesting scent to follow."

"I'll go and find him and make him go to bed," I said. "I need some sleep now."

"Amen to that," Julie said. "See you in the morning, Si."

"Sleep well, Si," Lizzy said.

"And you," I said, going out and closing the door behind me.

I walked out into the outer yard and listened to the busy silence of the night. It wasn't that busy; there were bats flying but they don't care what's happening on the ground. Part of the darkness of the shadows under the big hay trailer moved towards me.

"Don't point that antique at me, son," it said.

"Nice to see you too, Freddy," I said, letting the hammers down and breaking her.

"Here we are, clearing up your mess, as usual," he said.

"Glad you've finally found a way to make yourself useful. What've you done with them?"

"The dead one got discovered by local plod half an hour ago. There was an illegal firearm and a bag of coke on his person and he's been provisionally identified as one of the staff of this nut-house. His prints set off a few alarms too. Bill's bothering a judge for a warrant now."

"What about the breathing ones?"

"In the back of a van not far from here. Being a bit stubborn."

"They are that type. You bunch of fairies ready to do some work tomorrow then?"

"Oh nine hundred."

"I take it, you're going in fancy dress?"

"You're not coming."

"Yes, I am, you might fuck it up. What're you doing now?"

"Watching over your sorry carcass, apparently."

"Excellent. I could do with a nap. Don't suppose you've seen a small dog?"

"This one?" the bulky shape that was Captain Tom 'Freddy' Fredrickson beckoned and another piece of the night detached itself from the deep shadows in the barn, approached and offered me a bundle that turned out to be an angry little dog with tape around his muzzle. I received him and he stopped struggling.

"I'm just going to have a walk in that field over there." I pointed in the direction of the long meadow.

"If you say so. Want me to make sure someone doesn't make off with you?"

"No, I want you to just exactly not do that."

"Whatever."

When I'd got sufficiently far into the field, I untaped the dog and put him down. This time, he didn't disappear into the darkness, but stayed near me. I walked steadily across the stubble until I wasn't far from the gate into the Dower House garden. I stood there and waited.

Jake gave a low growl and moved behind me. A distinctively feminine form walked out of the darkness and said, "Si."

"Hi Mel."

"Who is it, Si?" she said.

"I'm not sure," I said. "But I think I know where they are. The girls."

"Jane?"

"And Natasha, yes."

"Where?"

"In the abbey."

"What abbey?"

"This abbey. Or, what's left of it."

"Noor Abbey?"

"Yes."

"But you said…"

"I lied."

"Bastard. Oh, my God. You're sure?"

"No, but I think I may have seen them and it's staffed by ex-members of GROM. And it has at least one silver-grey transit."

"What's GROM?"

"Polish Special Forces."

"Why didn't you tell me?"

"I am telling you. And I think I may know why the Greens called themselves the Greens."

"Why?"

"All roads lead back here, one way or another… Don't they?"

"Do they?" she frowned.

"I think they do. I've brought some friends with me and we're going to have a look inside the abbey at ten tomorrow morning."

"Oh, are you? We'll see about that."

"And you're going to let me. We'll see that no one comes out the front, but I think it's very likely that they have a back door somewhere. And if they do it would presumably come out…"

"Into the White Wood. Oh, I see."

"But we're not going to go into the wood. Okay with you?"

"Yes."

"They might get away that way," I said.

"They won't." There was no doubt in her voice.

"That's what I thought. Good hunting to you tomorrow."

"And to you, you bastard."

I walked with a weary, relieved step back to the house, keeping Jake near me as we passed through the yards, and closed and bolted the door. Thomas went into the clock, some cheese went into an equally tired dog, and I went thankfully to bed.

A Wounded Bird

By the time I'd brushed my teeth and undressed, the moon had risen and its pale light was streaming in through the attic windows. I lay down and pulled the duvet over me, letting my body sink down onto the ancient mattress, intending to sleep properly for the first time in several nights.

"Si?"

I almost missed the hesitant sound.

"Lizzy?"

"May I come in?"

"Yes. Come in."

She came in. I sat up in the bed. We looked at each other. She was wearing a silk nightdress which only just came down far enough.

"Come here," I said.

She came forward into the moonlight. Her eyes were bright with unshed tears and she looked tense and drawn. I made space and she sat beside me on the bed. I put my arm around her and discovered that she was trembling. She put her face up to mine and kissed me. I held her and kissed her. She pushed me back onto the bed and lay on top of me, kissing me and still trembling.

"Wait," I said and I put my hand up so that I could cradle her head and I turned us over so that she was lying beside me and I held her tight and still. The trembling became a sob and then another and another. I held her close against me and spoke gently to her, saying I don't know what. She buried her face into my neck and my neck became wet with her tears, and I held her tight and stroked her hair and spoke to her until the worst was over.

Before sleep claimed me, I pulled the duvet properly over us. She was breathing evenly now and her taut flesh had become soft and smooth and we went down into sleep together; heart beating next to heart.

29

HERE, BOY, PASS ME MY ASSAGAI

In the morning, she was gone. A sparrow fluttering against the window woke me. It darted repeatedly into the top of the frame, its wings brushing the glass, and then came down with something in its beak, paused holding onto the sill and took off with it, presumably to feed its young in one of the many nest-boxes that someone had thoughtfully put up about the place. Lizzy, presumably.

My phone said that it was after eight. I sat up, rubbed my head a bit to help wake me up, and went to look at the world from the window. The swallows were catching their breakfast and everything I could see looked pretty much as it should. I put my clothes on, and went to see what was happening downstairs.

Jake got up from his bed to say good morning to me. Julie looked at me like I was a slug she'd found in a lettuce. Lizzy looked at me quickly and then looked down at her plate. The old laptop was open on the kitchen table.

"Morning," I said.

"I knew you were too good to be true," Julie said. She had her phone in her hand.

"Ah," I said, pouring myself some coffee from the caffetier and sitting down.

Julie turned the laptop round. There was the photo of me diving over Polly's rail. The headline read, 'Playboy Killer On The Run'. There was also a headshot of me from the night at the *Umbra Villus*. It was definitely me.

"That's why you never put that gun down," Julie said. "And why the door was bolted this morning. Isn't it?"

"Er, sort of," I said. "Thanks for letting me have breakfast." A place had been laid for me.

Julie gave Lizzy a look.

"I'm going to phone the police, but she made me promise to hear what you have to say first," Julie said.

"Is it true, Si?" Lizzy said, looking at me. "Did you kill that girl?" She was holding herself together but I could see the effort it cost her.

"Yes, in a way. I didn't mean to, if that helps. I didn't kill her, but I did get her killed, which is near enough the same thing."

"What happened?" she said.

"Does it matter?" Julie said.

"Yes, it does. Tell us about it, Si."

"I… er," I looked at the clock. "I don't think I have the time just now…"

"You have to go to the police, Si," Lizzy said. "I'm sure if you go to them, rather than have them find you, it'll help. Have some breakfast and tell us about it, and then we'll go together."

"Or, I can give them a call now," Julie said, brandishing the phone. "Up to you."

"Fair enough," I said, sitting down.

"I'm sorry, Si," Lizzy said.

"Why are you sorry?" Julie said. "He's the one who should be sorry."

"To be honest, you phoning the plod wouldn't be a great idea," I said. "How about if I do it instead?"

"What do you mean?" Julie said.

"Hang on a sec," I said, taking out my phone and calling Bill. "Ah, Bill. Good morning."

"Si. Good morning. Are you ready?"

"Nearly. Come in a minute, will you. Oh, and you can bring my fancy dress."

"Don't be an idiot. I'm not going anywhere near you."

"I've been made," I said. "Just come and flash your badge. Or I'll have to kill them." I smiled at Julie.

"Oh fuck. Okay."

Four minutes later an average looking saloon car pulled into the yard and there was a knock on the door. I went to answer it, and let in Bill with a large hold-all.

"Are you mad?" he said.

"Give me that and show them your warrant card," I said, taking the bag. He followed me into the kitchen.

"You look like a policeman," Lizzy said.

"I am a policeman, miss, and I really shouldn't be talking to you," Bill said, presenting his credentials.

"Would you like some coffee?" she said.

"Ah, er, yes. Thank you very much. Now, er, the thing is…"

"The thing is," I said, putting on the black jacket that was in the bag and zipping it up, "if anyone ever finds out Bill and I know each other, it'll be really bad news for me. And probably him too."

"We know how to keep secrets," Julie said.

"Good," I said. "We have to go now, but I'll be back later, and in the meantime…"

"Just carry on as normal and don't say a word to anyone?" Lizzy said, smiling at me sweetly.

"If you wouldn't mind, miss," Bill said.

"Are you actually going to tell us anything?" Julie said.

"No idea," I said. "Maybe later. I will definitely be back though, whatever." I pulled the black balaclava with eye-holes over my head and put the strap of the MP5 submachinegun over my shoulder.

"Fucking hell," Julie said.

"Don't swear, Julie. It's okay, really it is." Lizzy said. "I know he's not a bad man. Not really. Now, stop looking cross, and let's get on with the day so that we can go to the fete."

"Thank you," I said. "Come on, Bill. We don't want to be late for the party, do we."

"Be careful, Si," Lizzy said. She bent down and scooped up Jake, put him on her lap and gave him a gentle hug. "And come back and tell us about it. Okay?"

"Okay," I said.

Noor Abbey secure mental health facility looked as much like an expensive and exclusive country hotel as anything else. They'd made an effort with the façade of the new building; it was a long sweep of arches in engineering brick and glass in a curve from one side of the surrounding wall to the other. It made a courtyard between the building and the massive gateway in the surrounding wall and its attendant gate-house. This courtyard was now full of the police vehicles and Range Rovers that we were all getting out of.

We spread out a bit and took up casually defensive positions. There was no way into the garden beyond except through the building itself, no easy way over it, and several cameras looked down at us. The high arched gateway, through which we'd driven, had new oak doors in it, the wood glowing golden in the morning light. They were standing open, but if the attached hydraulic rams closed them, the place would do fine as a killing jar.

"Nice place, eh, Freddy?" I said, over coms.

"Stick a car in the gateway, someone," he said. "Don't want anyone up our arses, do we."

"Are we all ready?" Bill said.

"Let's go see who's home," Freddy said.

Bill went up to the main door and held the key-card that I'd found on the man I'd killed to the entry system. There was an audible click and it eased open a little.

"Well, what do you know," he said.

"Freddy Troop, Go, Go, Go…" Freddy said.

Freddy two and three went in right and left. Four and five after them, pushing further in. Freddy and I last, taking the centre of the space. Big and bold, all in black, ballistic vests, black balaclavas with eye-holes, guns up and don't fuck with us writ large.

The impression of the place being some kind of hotel was reinforced by flowers on a table, a beautiful rug on the floor and a sufficiency of mahogany and oil paintings. There was a sort of squeak from the attractive woman in her thirties who was behind the reception desk.

"Clear." "Clear." "Clear." "Clear." "All clear, come on in, noble leader."

Bill strolled into in the spacious lobby and addressed the mildly traumatised receptionist.

"Good morning, miss, my name is detective inspector William Smith of the Metropolitan Police, and I am executing a search warrant of these premises. Will you please inform your superior?" He held up a piece of paper, which may well have been the said search warrant.

"Yes, yes, right away, sir." She grabbed the phone off its cradle and pushed a button on the base unit.

"Thank you. You can tell them that we will start with the staff accommodation block."

"This way," Freddy said, indicating a door on the right.

Bill held the key-card to it, but nothing happened.

"Bugger," Bill said.

"Centrally locked," I said, looking up at one of the cameras in the corner of the ceiling.

The receptionist spoke urgently in a low voice to someone on the phone.

Bill waved in the young DC and ten uniforms who were waiting in the courtyard. They all came in and one of Freddy's men went back out to guard our rear. I walked over to one of the windows looking out into the gardens. It was partially open, but fixed in position so that there would be no chance of getting through it. I could see that my previous prejudice against the architecture had been a little unfair. From here the buildings set around the fine central lawn looked functional, but modest; playing a secondary role to the gardens, the fine brick wall, and the trees of the surrounding wood.

"Excuse me, miss," Bill said. "We are exercising a lawful warrant and we have the right of immediate access to this building. If you don't open this door at once, we will use force to do so."

"They could be bussing them out at the back by now," Freddy said.

"That's okay," I said.

"If you say so. Freddy Four, fetch a whizzbang, will you?"

There was a buzz and the door clicked. A man came through. Freddy Two caught the door so it wouldn't close.

The man, who was a head taller than Bill, was looking at us in the kind of way you generally look at something before you kill it.

"What do you want?" he said.

"Police executing a search warrant," Bill said. "And you are?"

"Gustav Komika, head of security."

"Well, Mr Komika, if you would be so good as to take us to the staff accommodation block first, we will start there," Bill said.

"That is not possible," the man said.

"It's going to happen though," Bill said. "If you attempt to prevent us from carrying out our lawful duty, you will be arrested."

"That place is private. You have no right."

"Yes, we do. And, I'm afraid we are going to search it," Bill said. "Whether you open it for us, or we open it for ourselves."

"Ugh. Jestes obciaqeneim gowna," the man said, looking round at us.

"Przenies dubek," Freddy said.

"Okay," he said, "What the fuck. This way."

We passed quickly down the corridor, Gustav waving his electronic pass key at intervening doors, flanked by Freddy and Freddy One.

I was sure that the quickest way there should be straight on, but the man led us past the kitchens and out of a back door into an alleyway. This part of the estate was more functional, but still well-maintained and orderly. The path curved round to the entrance of the three-story accommodation block; the building in whose windows I'd seen the night-watching girls. He let us in through a door into a lobby and closed it behind us. There was a central corridor with doors leading off, running away from us, and a stairwell leading upwards.

"What now?" Gustav said, looking at Freddy with an expressionless face.

"Just start opening doors, please," Bill said.

"Very well." He knocked on the nearest door, waited briefly, then opened it with his key-card and stood aside for us to enter.

We were without doubt intruding on a private living space. There was a sitting-room with sofas, a TV, table and chairs, and a dormitory with two sets of bunk beds. There were used mugs, books, magazines, a pair of glasses, makeup and hair-clips. A pair of tights hung from a drying rack and there was a poster of horses galloping on a beach blue-tacked to a wall. It was basic, but in its way, homely and perfectly nice.

"Satisfied?" Gustav said.

"And the rest," Bill said.

"If we must."

By now I was sure it was pointless, but we went into the thirty-odd other rooms anyway. They were all pretty much the same and they were all empty. Our inspections were cursory. In one, I went to the window and looked out across the grounds. When the others moved on, I paused to check my phone and Gustav had to come back and swear at me to make me keep up. The DC and two officers took possession of the room which Gustav said was the dead Pole's. The rest of us went out and stood on the central lawn and generally milled about and looked at what there was to see.

"Bill," I said, over coms, "Can you get them to get DNA from room 321 too?"

"Will do."

From my vantage point up a ladder outside the wall, looking down into it, I had mainly noticed the rooves of the buildings, but now that I was in it at ground level, it was the lawns and the flowerbeds and the flower-fringed pathways that dominated. The effect was definitely of an expensive boutique hotel verging on a retirement home.

The buildings, though modern, were never more than two stories high and were well-integrated into the gardens with trellising and shrubberies so that often they seemed to have their own piece of garden. And often, unless I was mistaken, these bits of garden were tended by the occupants, as much as by the staff. The only taller building was the accommodation block, and that was set back behind the rest so that it didn't intrude.

"I think we've missed them," I said, over coms.

"If they were ever here," Freddy said.

"Oh, they were definitely here," I said.

"In which case, they must still be here," Bill said.

"You find them, and I'm buying," I said.

"You're buying anyway," Freddy said.

"If only," Bill said. "Now we're going to do what I told the judge we'd do, which is to go over every inch of this place and interview every member of staff."

"Including the nutters," I said.

"I think you should do that, Si," Freddy said. "You're far more likely to get on with them than the rest of us."

"Actually, I think you may be right," I said, looking at an old gentleman in a wheelchair who was regarding us from under the brim of an immaculate straw boater. "I've a feeling some of them are intelligent and cultured human beings."

"Go fuck yourself," Freddy said.

"You make my point for me," I said.

"Heads up," Freddy Two said. "Local brass at three o'clock."

The receptionist was approaching us across the lawn and there was a man with her. He wasn't an impressive specimen; his lank, black hair was too long and his shoulders were high and he stooped slightly. He wore a tired brown corduroy suit and a thin black tie.

When they got to us, the man looked at us in turn with dark eyes without speaking for a moment, and then said, "Gentlemen, my name is Dr Simm. I am the managing director of this facility. I understand you are exercising a search warrant." His accent hovered in the general direction of German, but I wasn't certain.

"Pleased to meet you, doctor," Bill said. "Yes, I'm afraid we are. We won't take up any more of your time than we have to, but we have to interview your staff and patients and search the premises."

"You understand that this is a secure facility and that some of our clients can be dangerous?" he said.

"Of course," Bill said.

Here, Boy, Pass Me My Assagai

The young DC and the uniforms appeared and joined us, she shook her head.

"So, officer. Can you tell me what you are looking for?" Dr Simm said.

"No, doctor. That's not for me to say, I'm afraid."

"In which case, can I ask why you are doing this?"

"You may. I'm sorry to have to inform you that a gentleman by the name of Kowalczyk was found dead not far from here earlier today. He was a member of your staff, I believe."

"Not that I know of."

"Your head of security has just shown us his room."

"In which case, it seems I was mistaken."

"So it does. Someone shot him, I'm afraid. An electronic key-card that was found on his person, opened your main door."

"That is unfortunate, but even so, I do not understand why it is necessary for you to search the premises."

"The dead man had on his person an illegal firearm and traces of illegal substances and we have reason to believe that he was an ex-member of the special forces of a foreign power," Bill said.

"And that is why you have these men with you," Dr Simm indicated Freddy Four and Five, who were standing not far away, with a dismissive gesture. "They will not be needed. I have given Shirley a master key. She will give you access to all the facilities and I myself will accompany you to interview the residents."

"Let's you and me, go visit the nutters Bill," I said, over coms.

"Thank you, doctor, that is good of you," Bill said. "We will split up into teams…"

He disposed of us, sending the DC and one uniform to a room in the office suite to start the interview process with the assistance of Shirley and the rest of the uniforms were divided up into teams, each with a member of Freddy Troop, just in case, to do a physical search of the rest of the buildings.

443

"And now, doctor, if I may, I'll take you up on your invitation to accompany us to visit your patients," Bill said.

"Very well. Follow me. Gustav, you may go and help that young policewoman with her interviews. I expect you will know where to find individual members of staff better than anyone else."

"Yes, doctor," the man said, and went. It was nice when he'd gone.

"Ask him about the nutters," I said, in Bill's ear.

"Forgive me, doctor, this came up very suddenly and I haven't had time to find out much about your facility; what kind of people are your patients?" Bill said.

"We call them clients, or more often guests," the man said. "Here at the Abbey Noor we specialise in the care of those who are deemed to be resistant to treatment. Our primary function is to enhance their quality of life, while maintaining their safety and the safety of others. If Mr X decides to regard this place as, let me say, a hotel, and the staff here as his servants, we do not find it necessary to disillusion him."

"I see," Bill said. Hm, perhaps I do too, I thought to myself.

"This way. We will go and pay a visit to Miss Aurelia Hampton first. If she offers to shake hands with you, do not do so," Dr Simm said.

Miss Aurelia turned out to be a tall lady, possibly in her late seventies, though it was hard to tell, who was dead-heading the roses outside her patio doors. She had the kind of accent that the aristocracy used to have before it became self-conscious about accents, and the room beyond was clearly furnished with her own furniture; rather too much of it.

She greeted Dr Simm with an airy courtesy and looked at the rest of us with a fine hauteur. The secateurs in her right hand continued clipping roses in the air while she talked to us. I looked into her eyes and saw there malevolent intent made corporeal. I had no desire to get my hands anywhere near those secateurs. Bill tried showing her a photo of the dead Pole, but she just looked down her nose at us and pretended not to have heard such an impudent question. We departed in poor order.

There was a certain amount more of this, and if it achieved anything, I couldn't say what. Except perhaps, that I could see that all the units of accommodation were grouped into sections, each with its own access and screens of planting between. I would bet that all the doors were electronically operated from a central command station and that each section, probably each room, could be individually secured. Oh, and that the customers all came from a fairly narrow section of society.

There was a retired general who was still fighting the natives; possibly the Mau Mau. A pale youth whose bright chatter seemed perfectly normal; we had to visit him inside as he wasn't allowed out without restraints. One woman lay amongst a litter of magazines and makeup and gave her dressing gown, her only item of clothing, to Bill to hold while she made eyes at him.

There were twenty-two in all. Perhaps, in some, it was mental illness, but to me it looked like madness; well-appointed and well organised, but black and frightening. I could see that you would very quickly get used to it though. We looked briefly into their individual sections of accommodation, each one reflecting their personalities, and it was obvious that our girls weren't hidden there either.

Everywhere we went, there were staff in attendance or nearby. They were all dressed in simple blue and white uniforms and looked calm and contented with their work. None of them were the girls we were looking for. Some of those we heard speak, had Polish accents, but not all.

We followed the doctor out onto the lawn between two sections. I noticed that what had at first glance appeared to be an ornamental ironwork structure supporting a splendid clematis, was cleverly designed to be almost impossible to climb.

"I have to say, doctor, that this is all very impressive," Bill said.

"It is good of you to say so, officer," the doctor said.

"And no doubt expensive. For the guests, I mean."

"Our customers value what we do for them," he said.

Or at least their families value you keeping them, I thought. In the case of mad relatives, deep pockets can buy easy consciences.

We turned over all the stones and looked in all the corners. When it became clear that there were no threats to life and limb in any of the buildings, Freddy troop, and their unofficial supernumerary, me, left them to it and had a good look at the grounds. That didn't tell us anything either, except how high the surrounding wall was, and how devoid of exits. It wasn't long before we'd looked in every place which could possibly have hidden anything much bigger than a cat.

An anxious looking Bill went off to assist with the interviews and the rest of us started wandering about wondering what we'd missed. It was another warm day and I nearly pulled my balaclava off before I remembered.

I followed one of paths between beautifully planted borders and high box hedging to the hexagonal summerhouse I'd seen from up the ladder. I opened the door and went in. It smelt of geraniums. There were glass doors opening onto each of the box-lined walkways that led to it, and there was a bookcase full of books on one of the walls. I studied the backs of the books to see if there was anything interesting. I pulled one of them out. There were deep, cushioned seats around the edges and a rocking chair and several deck-chairs. I sat on one, leant back, and phoned Mel.

"Well?" she said, picking up after almost half a ring.

"Oh," I said. "Nothing. You?"

"No."

"No?"

"No."

A spider was weaving her web up in the apex of the wooden roof.

"Were you wrong again?"

"No, they were here. Or are here. I don't know which."

"Then, where the fuck are they?"

"No idea."

"What're you going to do?" Mel said.

"Right now, I don't know," I said. The spider, apparently satisfied with its work, retreated to the centre of the web. "Think about it, I expect. I'll call you later."

"Yes, but what…"

"Sorry, I've got to go…"

"Si…" I disconnected.

I went to the door and looked at the trees of the surrounding wood. I'd be willing to bet that at least one of them contained watching eyes.

"Freddy Spare, come in. Freddy Spare, report to main entrance." It was Freddy's voice over coms. Time to go.

"Oh, fuck, fuck, fuck," Bill said, in the car. Freddy was at the wheel and I was in the back. The real policemen were getting into their crew-bus and the rest of Freddy Troop had buggered off out of sight in Range Rovers.

"What's up?" I said. "Apart from the obvious."

"I'm now deeply in the shit," he said. "A lot of man-power used, and no hint of an arrest. And I've got one dead body and two inconvenient live ones to account for."

"So, it wasn't the right place," Freddy said, shrugging. "Whoever thought this prick would be right anyway?" We passed through the gateway and he pulled his balaclava off and smiled at me.

"Oh, he's right alright," Bill said. "But what the fuck are we to do about it? And where the fuck are they?"

"Say why," Freddy said.

"There was no one in the accommodation block," I said, pulling my own head-gear off with relief.

"Yes, we saw that," he said. "So?"

"The place runs 24/7; there should've been the off-duty lot sleeping."

"Oh."

"One of the coffee mugs was still warm, and this," I pulled a book out of my trousers, "belongs to Jane Hamilton. I found it in the summerhouse."

"How do you know that?" Bill said taking it. It was a copy of *Extragalactic Cosmology* by somebody or other. It had the corners of several pages bent and there were scribbles in the margins. "Oh, yes. She is, was, doing a PhD in astrophysics. Well remembered."

"Not general reading," I said. "They're in there somewhere. Or they were when we got there. I've no idea where they are now."

"I agree," Bill said, "And there were too many rooms for the number of staff who work there, and most of the things in the rooms were female, but more than half the staff we saw, were male."

"That's true," Freddy said. "And actually, you're right for another reason."

"Oh?" I said.

"Yon Gustav chap is a real nasty hard bastard, or I'm the fucking tooth fairy," he said.

"This feels familiar," I said.

"You making a tit of yourself?" Freddy said.

"Basically, yes," I said.

"You poor thing," he said.

"What the fuck do we do now?" Bill said.

"Tea and cake," I said.

"Tea and cake?" Freddy said.

"Yes, at the farm."

"Why?" Bill said.

Here, Boy, Pass Me My Assagai

"I've got a bad feeling. Freddy, do you have to drive like an old woman?"

"Here we go again," he said, grinning and giving the car the benefit of his right boot.

There was no one in the outer yard, or the inner, though the Landrover was there. I went into the kitchen. It was empty. Bill and Freddy came in behind me.

"They'll be at work somewhere about the place," Bill said.

"Or they'll have gone to the fair," Freddy said.

"They didn't lock the door," Bill said.

"I don't think they do," I said. I filled the kettle and clicked it on.

"Well, Si. I hope you know what to do, cos I've no fucking clue," Bill said, sitting down. "You realise that whoever this is, know's you're working for me now?"

"That just means we need to catch them and kill them," I said, going to the fridge.

"Kill who, exactly?" Freddy said.

"Well..." I said, looking for the milk jug and finding something else, "... I think this may be a clue."

I lifted out a small rolled up piece of paper and took it to the table. I unrolled it and there was a finger lying on the table. A girl's little finger, small and delicate, but also hardened from work and with dirt under the neatly clipped nail, snipped off below the first joint. There was writing on the paper. It said simply, '20.00'.

"Fuck. You really are dangerous to know, Si," Freddy said.

"What does it mean?" Bill said.

"That's an invitation," I said. "An invitation to a party."

30

A RABBIT ON A GREEN FIELD

There were things to be done and plans to make and it didn't help that Mel still hadn't forgiven me, but as usual, I told everyone what to do, and, as usual, they did it, and when the appointed time arrived, I put Thomas and a bag of cartridges into the back of the old Landy and took it along the lane to the hall.

There was a tide of departing cars flowing the other way as families and ordinary mortals left the fete to go to their barbecues and so on. I stopped at the tape across the road that diverted cars into the temporary car park on the grass and a cheerful chap in a hi-vis jacket came to have a look at me.

"I believe I'm expected," I said.

"Mr Ellice?"

"Yes."

"Go on down, sir." He removed the tape for me and I went on down to the oval of gravel in front of the north entrance. It was full of cars; well, Range Rovers mainly, and a few Mercedes and a couple of Rolls. There was the crackle of shotgun fire from the direction of the clay-pigeon shoot and a peacock looked down at me from the old cedar of Lebanon.

I walked up the steps to the palladian portico, past a gentleman who wasn't bothering to look like he wasn't a guard; he nodded to me casually; and through the wide double doors. The massive building imposed its will, as it was meant to, claiming my senses. The world without receded as I crossed the wide black and white marble tiles of the foyer towards the great hall. There was the ripple of a piano in the far distance.

I went through into the ancient banqueting hall and discovered a scene of great activity. The immense runs of table were already swathed in brilliant white table-cloths and the candle-sticks were out. A fierce looking woman was standing in the centre, watching as two white-gloved men laid places and several others carried in the oak chairs from one of the storerooms from the lower level and placed them carefully.

The two massive candelabra had been let down from the ancient beams on their chains and were being polished and set with long bees-wax candles. From behind the tapestries that draped the front of the minstrel's gallery on the south side, came the hum of a vacuum cleaner. The smell was the smell of polish and stone and space large enough to accommodate ancestors and a good number of the animals they had killed. The armour had been cleaned and the gilt on the frames of the portraits shone, but the fifth earl still looked like an angry ferret, and the boar over the fireplace was still missing a tusk. On some level, it felt like home, as it always had.

"Good afternoon, sir." A man put down his magazine and got up from one of the chairs by the door to the yellow room. As far as I could remember, there was no gorilla in the hall's taxidermy collection, but he was a good candidate for the role. "Can I help you?"

"Seen Berry, have you?" I said.

"And you are?"

"Ellice."

"I believe you'll find his lordship in the library." No shit.

A waitress, in a neat black and white uniform, came out of the door he was guarding and passed us. I turned so that I could watched her go. It was worth it.

"Thanks."

I passed through the yellow room with its tableau of stuffed mockingbirds and entered the festival of mahogany and leather that the sixth earl had constructed for ignoring the family's remarkable collection of books in. The doors to the terrace were open and the distant sounds of the summer day competed gently with the one of Schubert's sonatas. It was indeed Berry who was strumming the ivories of the grand. Maisie was spread decoratively across a nearby chesterfield.

He looked up, saw me, and smiled. He dropped his head, abandoned Schubert and flowed smoothly into a rendering of his song. Maisie leapt to her feet, kissed me and ruffled my hair with her fingers. "So glad," she said. "So glad."

"Hi Maisie."

Berry let the music peter out and lifted a coffee cup and saucer from the top of the piano and took a sip, looking at me thoughtfully.

"Si," he said.

"My lord," I said.

"How wonderful. Have a pew, do."

I sat down on the sofa next to Maisie, who, for once didn't drape herself over me.

"I got your invite," I said.

"Oh, good. Can I offer you a drink?"

"I'm fine thanks," I said.

He looked at me and I looked at him and the truth was that we knew each other very well. It didn't need saying really, but I was going to say it anyway. I could feel Maisie's attention on us.

"Cony on vert salient, preyant, isn't it?" I said.

"No. Vert, a cony salient, preyant, sable upon a child waddled gules."

"Vert, yes. But it's not a rabbit though is it?"

"No, it's a hare."

"Thought so. You always did like a good pun, didn't you?"

"A pun?" he said.

"As in, canting arms, I mean," I said.

"Ah, as in that. Go on."

"In French, hare is lievre, which is your family name. And I expect Lievre was originally Vert, or Le Vert, as in green. Am I right?"

"Yes. I imagine it was easier to draw a hare than to find some green paint. Back in sixteen whatever-it-was," he said. "If you didn't have any green to hand, you could draw a hare on your shield and everyone on the battlefield would know you belonged to us."

"Lievre, le vert, green," I said.

"Exactly," he said.

"Neat. Works either way, just like hare and hair." I put a hand to my head.

"Oh, hare and hair?" he said. He was sitting upright now; giving me his full attention. And for once Maisie wasn't looking like a vacant space in the universe.

"The *Sea Hare, Caesars, Umbra Villus, Sub Vello* and *Coma Club*; they're all words to do with hare. I mean, hair."

"Good heavens, so they are. Gustav, Jakub, will you…"

"You two are the Greens, aren't you?"

Berry didn't answer that, but just watched me patiently. The oversized thug from the Abbey and another man, who I was pretty sure was one of those who'd chased me through the wood, stood up from two of the big wing chairs with their backs to us and took up station behind and in front of the sofa.

"Get up and come over here," Gustav said, indicating a clear space.

I did, and they both moved so that I had no chance of taking any advantage.

"Feet apart, arms up, if you try anything, I assure you it won't work and you will get hurt," he said. I believed him.

They searched me with the thoroughness of those who are really looking, not just going through the motions. They found nothing in my pockets, I'd emptied them before I left, or in my boots, or the hems of my clothes. Gustav tore my shirt open and pulled down my trousers. Berry sipped his coffee and Maisie watched with interest.

"Nothing," Gustav said.

"You thought I might try recording you?" I said.

"No, dear heart, I didn't think, but I do like to check. You can pull your trousers up and sit down again now, if you like."

"How kind of you." I did that and the thugs moved away a bit, but not far. Gustav took a silenced automatic of some kind from behind his back and cradled it in front of him, just in case.

"Well, Si, here we are then," Berry said.

"I did always like you, Berry, but then you never fucked me about like you did other people."

"That's because you'd've beat my head in, if I had."

"Of course."

"Why did you come?"

"Because you invited me. And if I didn't, you'd just keep sending me parts of the girls, wouldn't you?"

"Of course. But why do you care?"

"I don't entirely know."

"I knew you would though. How long have you known?"

"Only since last night. I've been rather slow."

"I did practically tell you."

"That night at the Friars. And you offered me a job."

"Would you have worked for me? I hoped you would."

"No. Not under any circumstances. Why?"

"Why have I done all this? Money, of course. Some generations have it to spend, and some have to make it back; I've happened to be one of those. Had to do something to keep the party going."

"Can you imagine Berry being poor?" Maisie said. "That would be so boring, darling. Wouldn't it?"

"When you say it like that, it's obvious. It's you who runs the clubs, isn't it?"

"I have a talent for it, haven't you noticed?"

"You do, darling," Maisie said, "You really do."

"Berry, who we all know and whom no one takes seriously. But wherever I've met you, people run around after you. You always get exactly what you want when you want it. The managers of the clubs come and talk to you and the staff serve you before anyone else. If you ignore all the party animal stuff, you look like the boss."

"As soon as you turned up, I knew there'd be trouble," he said.

"It was you who put something in Susie's drink, wasn't it, Maisie?" I said. "When Berry's singing distracted us all."

"Yes, that was me," Maisie said, raising a thin pale arm and waving it in the air. "I did it."

"When I start to sing, people pay attention, you know," Berry said. "Always do."

"Why the girls?"

"Why which girls?"

"The posh ones. Jane and Natasha and Susie and all that."

"You don't know?"

"No."

"Good. I didn't think you did. That was you up a ladder the other day, I take it? And no doubt you were one of those black-clad idiots bumbling about this morning? Find anything, did you?"

"No. Where are they?"

"It's not important. That man, Smith, is a genuine policeman. So, you're working with the Law, are you? Poacher turned gamekeeper. Quite literally, in your case." He didn't smile.

"Let's say, it's a loose association."

"I assume they'll be turning up sometime later; when the party's in full swing and we're all a bit drunk. Probably through the passage behind the fireplace in the hall. Is that right? Or, something like that."

I kept my mouth shut and did my best not to let my face show what I was thinking.

"Well, good luck with that. And you've trotted along as instructed so that I won't carry on chopping bits of that farm-girl in the meantime."

"I'd still like to know about the girls," I said.

"I put up a lot of bird boxes, did you know that? All over the estate and Home Farm. First thing I did."

"So?"

"Half of them have cameras in them. I like to know what's going on on my land."

"Ah. I see."

They put a bag over my head, forced my hands behind me and bound them. And then my ankles. And then they carried me for a bit and put me, without much care, on another bit of floor. The bag smelt of someone else's unwashed socks. For a while I thought I was going to die of suffocation, but I didn't.

When it had been silent for a bit, I tried wriggling to see if I could sit up or something. A small cart-horse kicked me in the belly, so I didn't do that again. Time passed like fingernails across a blackboard and the ropes bit into my wrists and ankles until it seemed probable that my hands and feet would shrivel up and fall off.

Eventually, they picked me up again and carried me away. There was the sound of many people and talking and laughing and the clink of cutlery and glass. Fiddles and a flute in the background. They cut my wrists free and two mechanical grips, or similar, held my arms and sat me down in a chair. It was hard and smooth against my trousers.

They held my forearms against the arms of the chair and there was the distinctive sound of zip-ties and the pressure on my wrists returned.

"Well, Mr Ellice," a voice said, from a distance.

I lifted my head and turned towards it.

"Take the bag off," another voice said.

Rough hands loosened it from around my throat and lifted it up. I took in a flash of the scene and then shut my eyes against the brightness of it, and then opened them a bit again and it got easier.

"Let's have a look at the fucker," the first voice said. It was a lot closer now the bag was off, unpleasantly so.

I was in the banqueting hall and, standing in front of me, were two men. One of them was Tony and the other was the fighter from the boxing club. Both were in evening clothes. Behind them, the room was full of people, mainly at the tables, but also milling about. A number of them were looking at me too.

"Nice to meet you again," Tony said. He was looking very pleased with himself.

"You too," I said. "If you'd care to let me get up, I'll break your nose again, if you'd like."

"Don't worry, there'll be plenty of time for that," he said, showing me his teeth.

"Hello, Simon," the other man said. "My name is Kem. I don't think we've met. Kem Lorel." He was smiling at me with a gentle, thoughtful expression. It was one of those kinds of smile that are more worrying than a reasonable amount of heavy ordnance.

"I would shake your hand," I said, shrugging my shoulders as best I could.

"You may get the chance of that," he said.

"I look forward to it," I said.

"Little you know, you stupid fuck," Tony said, grinning at me.

"Is your friend house-trained?" I said to the man with the strange name. "I think he's just wet himself."

"Fuck you, you…" Tony raised his arm to slap me hard across the face but the man's hand caught his wrist as it came down, stopping it dead a few inches from my left eye.

"No, Tony," Kem said, turning the man to face him with no apparent trouble. "Not yet."

"Did you like what we did to your friend, shit-head?" I could feel the spittle on my face. "That Russian bitch. What do you think we're going to do tonight? Eh?"

"Enough, Tony. Go and get the girl now." Kem released Tony's hand and gently rested a finger against his chest.

"Okay, Kem. It would be a pleasure." The bastard was smiling again. If you could call it that.

"But gently; no damage," Kem said.

Tony went, giving me a nasty leer as he did so. Kem checked the zip-ties that were holding my wrists and then his hand moved to his back, under his jacket, and reappeared with an eight-inch knife that looked old and very sharp. He squatted, reached forward and I felt the pressure on my ankles release.

"Thank you," I said.

"We don't want you going lame, do we," he said, smiling again.

"I suppose not," I said, rubbing my feet against each other in an attempt to wake them up.

"It would be better not to get up and walk about while I'm gone," he said. "If you do, one of these gentlemen will shoot you." He glanced towards the nearest group of people. Looking at them, I thought they might shoot me anyway.

"I see your point," I said.

"Good. I'll see you in a bit," he said, and went.

I watched him walk away; graceful and purposeful, and then started to have a proper look at my situation. I was at the back of the hall, not far from the main entrance, but towards the wall, out of the way. I was tied to a heavy oak chair and there was a similar chair next to me. The two massive suspended candelabras were lit and occasionally dripping wax onto the floor. Tall silver ones graced the tables, and were supported by lamps in all the sconces on the walls. The only electric light seemed to be a bulb that someone had put inside the suit of armour and the lamps that lit Berry's glowering forebears in their heavy gilt frames. Everything shimmered in the soft light.

There must have been at least sixty people in the room, and an interesting crowd they were. Hard faces; the men and the woman. More testosterone and street-smarts than formal education. Loud and cheerful voices; excitement contained. Accents from Glasgow, Manchester, Liverpool, Birmingham, other places I wasn't so sure of. The wine was flowing and the familiar pyjama-clad waitresses were moving constantly among them, taking orders, filling glasses, offering canapés. I looked for faces I knew. I looked for my noble host, and failed to find him.

Tony returned with a girl slung over his shoulder. He dumped her in the chair next to me. Her head hung down, her face concealed by her tangled hair, conscious, but letting whatever was happening, happen. He zip-tied her wrists to the arms of the chair and her ankles to the legs, showed me his teeth again, and departed. She kept her head hung down, not paying any attention to anything. There was a bloody bandage on her left hand.

"Hey, Lizzy," I said.

Nothing.

"Hey, Lizzy. It's Si. You can look up, it's okay."

"Si?" she turned her head a little so that she could see past her hair.

"How're you doing?" I said.

"Si. Oh, my God. Are you okay? Did they hurt you?"

"I'm fine. Did they hurt you? Apart from your finger."

"No." She sat up a bit. "Well, not really hurt me. These men... And a woman... We were just getting ready to..." She took a couple of sharp in breaths and then bit her lip to stop herself crying.

"It's okay," I said. It wasn't, but there was no use saying that.

"Sorry," she said, holding back the panic.

"That's okay," I said. "Tell me about it. It'll help."

"They put bags over our heads and carried us."

"Yes, they did the same to me. You said there was a woman?"

"Yes. I was surprised."

"Did you know her?"

"No."

"What did she look like?"

"Oh. Dark glasses. I think that was a wig, under the hat. Thin though. Fine hands. Poise. She definitely had poise." She shuddered and then sat up a bit more, squaring her shoulders. "And she seemed to know us."

"Oh. That's interesting."

She was silent for a bit, and so was I, thinking.

"That policeman? He was a real policeman?" she said. "Your friend."

"Yes, he is. What did they do with you? Where's Julie?"

"Where are we? Is this the Hall?" She looked cautiously at the people nearest us and then brought her eyes back to mine.

"Yes, we're in the banqueting room at Leigh Hall."

"I thought so; I came in here once. But that doesn't make sense. Lord Beresford can't know about this, can he? What's going on?"

"How did you get here?"

"A van, I think. They put us in the back of a van. Julie's downstairs. They had us in the laundry. Why is this happening, Si? What have you done?"

"What I have done, Lizzy, is get you caught up in my mess and put you in very great danger. I'm very sorry."

"I don't expect you meant to."

"No, but I'm not sure that counts for much."

"It counts for something. And you'll just have to get me out of it. Won't you?" She looked at me as if she was expecting me to do that, which was a pretty remarkable thing under the circumstances.

"I'll try to," I said.

"I know you will. What do you think is going to happen to us?"

"I've got a nasty feeling we're the after-dinner entertainment in some way or another."

"Oh." She apparently decided not to pursue that one. I didn't blame her.

More people had come into the room now and the intensity of the noise had increased. A group of men were standing in front of us, clearly talking about us. The way they were looking at Lizzy made it hard for me not to try to break the chair and get at them.

"Did you see any other girls down there?" I said, partly to distract us. "In the laundry. Apart from you and Julie?"

"No, I don't think so," she said.

"Okay."

"Si?"

"Yes, Lizzy."

"Will you tell me about all this now please?"

"That might get you into more trouble."

"More trouble?" She smiled at me and raised her head some more. I felt that I had a new definition of courage to think about. If I ever had time to think about it.

"Fair point. A friend of mine asked me to look for some missing girls..." I told her about it. Briefly. While the anticipation rose in the room and people started to take their places at the tables. It was good for both of us to have something else to think about. Her face softened as I told her about Natasha, Hillary, Imogen, Jane, and the others.

"Oh, my God. That's terrible," she said, when I came to finding Anja dead in Polly. "And she has a daughter?"

"Yes. A daughter who doesn't yet know she's lost her mother. So, you still think my good intentions count for something?"

"You have to find her," she said. "You just have to."

A man in a dinner jacket and white gloves walloped the gong by the door a good one, followed it up with a brief tympani with the drumstick and then caught the beaten brass disk, stilling it. Silence fell. Everyone turned their heads up to look at the gallery, so we did too.

"Good evening, everyone," a clear, light, but carrying voice said. "Welcome to our midsummer ball." It was a man, complete with hat and dark glasses. And beside him, a woman, similarly disguised. Grant and Leila Green, presumably.

They leant on the heavy oak railing and looked down at us, their subjects. Everyone seated beat the table until the glittering glassware shook, and whistles and shouts and a general 'hurrraaaah' rang through the hammer-beams above us. They smiled at us, and Leila moved her hands for quiet, and there was quiet.

"In a while," she said, in an equally strong voice, "we will have speeches and toasts and there will be some entertainment." She looked down at me and I felt the force of her gaze through her dark glasses. "But now, we are hungry, so let our midsummer begin. A boar! A boar! Bring on the grizzly beast, and let us feast!"

From the doorway, trumpets rang out and four men trotted smartly in bearing a table on which lay, resplendent, a wild boar couchant, and well roasted, apple in mouth and all. Behind them flowed a river of pyjama-clad girls bearing silver dishes piled high with food, stacks of plates, jugs of gravy and all the things that one's heart could desire to go with a fine roast pig. The man who'd banged the gong, now brandishing a carving knife that would double as a small sword, bowed before the gallery, received a nod from Grant, and set to carving with a will. I discovered that in spite of everything else, I was bloody hungry. The assembly, and those who were serving them, settled to the task of filling their plates without giving us a thought.

I turned to Lizzy and shrugged my shoulders. What could you do.

"Who are they?" she said, perhaps less affected by smell of roast pig than me.

"That's a very good question," I said. My eyes were on the gallery, where Berry and Maisie had taken their seats with Grant and Leila.

31

THE GREENS

"This world you seem to live in, I mean, you don't even seem that worried," Lizzy said.

"I have other things to think about at the moment. You always trust your feelings about people, don't you?" I said.

"Yes. Don't you?"

"Sometimes I get confused by the facts."

"Feelings are facts too."

"I suppose in a way they are. You're quite right; I am different to you," I said.

"Yes." She said it simply, matter of factly, as if it was a simple, obvious thing.

"Yes. So, my feelings are from a different point of view."

"Of course."

"Do you know, sometimes I'm an idiot."

She smiled at me a smile that helped. Or would have done, in more normal circumstances.

"Yes, but why are you an idiot this time?"

"Because I've been looking for someone who looks like something, when I should have been looking for someone who feels like something."

"Feels like what?"

"Like me, actually."

"Quite nice then?" She smiled at me.

"Perhaps. I mean, thank you, but no. I mean, who feels like they're my kind, to me."

"I think I understand."

"I'm glad you do. The thing is, the person who I know it is, doesn't feel right and the person who I know it isn't, does."

"Is what?"

"The person behind all this. I believe they're quite a lot like me."

"Not entirely like you," she said, looking at me with perfect serenity. "Though you do tend to use others."

"I do, don't I. Lizzy?"

"Si?"

"When you buy new heifers for the herd how do you choose them?"

"I look up their pedigree of course. Why are you thinking of that now?"

"I think I know why these particular girls were taken."

"Why?"

"They're bloodstock."

"But they're people."

"And therein lies the difference."

We sat in a strangely comfortable companionship while organised crime from the major cities of the country feasted and talked and traded stories. Someone had set place cards and spread the members of the families and organisations through the room;

preventing islands of power and possible conflict. I thought that would break down later as people started to loosen up and move seats.

After a long hour and a half of steady eating, and more than steady drinking, Grant rose to his feet, tapped his glass and elegantly thanked his guests for their support in the year. Support, as in custom, presumably. An older man with a strong cockney accent rose and responded with breath-taking crudity and wicked humour, and then gave way to a woman in her forties, I think; it was hard to tell, in a suit with shoulder pads. They both spoke of investment and relationships and the strength or weakness of trade. I haven't had much to do with gatherings of businesspeople, but this was clearly one.

The band played in the background and the tide of conversation ebbed and flowed, as did the wine. The pyjama'd girls danced through it all, lovely and innocent seeming in comparison to those they served. The pig was reduced to a dilapidated remnant and was succeeded by a summer pudding of similar proportions and countless accompaniments. The pace of consumption, of food at least, slowed and more frequent glances were cast in our direction.

And then the chap who was acting as maitre d went and banged the gong again. He had to give it a bit of grief to get their attention, but those at that end of the tables caught on and shushed their neighbours. Grant and Leila got to their feet, glasses in hand.

"Ladies and Gentlemen…" Grant said.

"If any," Leila said, into the respectful silence.

"As I was saying, ladies and gentlemen," he said. "Now for some entertainment. There…"

"Will be charades as usual for those who wish to play…" His sister interrupted him again.

"… will be charades as my sister says, and this young lady here," he pointed towards Lizzy, "is tonight's prize. She…"

The Greens

"May look like a draggle-tailed little slag, but I assure you, she'll clean up very well..."

"But before we..."

"Should you wish to bother to clean her up, of course..."

There were coarse cheers from some sections of the audience.

"As I was saying," the man over-rode her again, "we will have charades as usual, but before we do, this gentleman here..." He pointed to me.

"Handsome young fellow that he is," Leila interrupted again.

"A chap by the name of Ellice. Simon Ellice, who..."

"Is currently being hunted by the forces of her Majesty's plod for various crimes, including..."

"Annoying us..." Grant turned and was looking at his sister. "Am I doing it?" he said.

"No, I'm doing it," she said.

"So I see," he said. "Go on then."

"Annoying us. So, we thought we'd help them out a bit. Tonight, *Sub Vellos* comes to the summer ball..."

She raised both hands and the assembled throng cheered again.

"Master of ceremonies, if you would care to..." her brother took control again.

"Start proceedings, please do so," Leila said, clapping her hands sharply.

Four men grabbed the table with the remains of the pudding on it and bore it away. Two more with wide brooms swept the floor clear of the droppings from it.

"Oh, Si," Lizzy said, under the thunder of applause and cheering.

"Hang in there, Lizzy," I said, watching the door.

Tony and Kem appeared one either side of me and took my arms while the maître d' cut my bonds. Then they lifted me up and half dragged, half carried me into the centre of the space between the two rows of tables and let go of me.

I tried moving my feet and they seemed a bit numb, so I stooped to massage them. There was the sound of whistling and calling out and everyone's attention was on us. Tony put a hand on my arm and started heaving me to my feet. I came up reluctantly, my feet not coordinating, being turned to face him by his pulling.

"Get on your feet, you fucker. Your time has come," he said.

"I don't think I..." I said, stumbling slightly and moving my right arm back to help me keep my balance.

"Come on, you..." He tightened his grip on my arm and leant forward, bring his other arm up to slap me. My stumble turned into a quick shuffle, getting my feet well under me, and my right arm completed the circular motion. Now driving from my hips, my left arm pulling back and opening him up.

I tightened my fist at the last instant and struck into his throat with the intention of coming out the other side. And then snapped back, stepping left, away from where Kem was.

He was no longer there. He was looking at me from a pace away and he was smiling again. Tony's head hit the floor with a satisfying crack. I rearranged my feet and got both hands up and in front of me. The room had gone quiet.

"I believe you've smashed his larynx, bust a few blood vessels and cracked his skull," Kem said. He was looking down at Tony with interest.

"That's about what I meant to do," I said.

"He's going to die. Probably in about ten minutes," he said.

"Good."

"Indeed." He peeled his shirt off over his head.

A chant broke out in the room, "Fight! Fight! Fight! Fight!..." People were banging their fists on the tables.

Kem walked to the table, poured water from a jug into a spare glass and brought it to me.

"Thank you," I said. It revived me a bit and I kept firm hold of the glass.

"You're welcome. Are you ready or would you like a bit more time?" He was speaking quietly and looking at me steadily. Although we were surrounded by people, there was no way we could be overheard against the uproar.

"No, I'm fine."

"Good," he said, smiling. He stepped aside loosening his shoulders and starting to move his feet in a graceful dancing sidestep.

I sent the glass as hard as I could at his head, but when it passed through that space; his head was no longer there. It hit a candelabra on the table behind, scattering candles and hot wax. People shouted and some cheered.

"There is no umpire. We are to start when we are ready," Kem called out, keeping his distance now.

"I know," I said. I unbuttoned my shirt and took it off and then started to move about a bit to get warmed up myself.

"By the way, I'm ready," he said.

I stopped moving and made myself tight and then loose, feeling the feeling of punching from the belly and moving from the hips. I flexed my fingers and made a fist, feeling the feeling of weight in my hands that means you can hit hard and not get broken. I looked at Kem and the world narrowed and time slowed down. I found that I was smiling.

"And I see you are ready too," he said.

"Yes, I'm ready," I said.

We trod the boards, moving around each other. The space between us like a physical thing. I was very aware of his body; the slide of his muscles under his skin and the way he carried his head. We started to feel each other out, trying a blow here and there, searching for the indefinable connection that lets you be inside the other's guard before he knows it.

When he hit me the first time I leant into it and followed it, one, two to his body and head and put him back, and then back. The pain was good and settled me, and the salt and wet blood in my mouth took me further into the fighting place.

I hadn't hurt him but I had connected and I wanted more. I moved in and moved in again, remembering his feet and coming on, but refusing to be drawn beyond my balance, and finally felt the solidness of his face against my hand as the world stopped and my legs didn't feel right and the next breath wouldn't come. He had come straight through my guard and taken my breath from me.

I swung out with my right reflexively and that saved me from his hook, and I got back and the breath started to come again. I was still up, but that exchange was his. I hadn't seen his jab to my body and it was a sign. Not a good sign.

He came in and I met him to block and counter and we were into a standing exchange, fast and free-flowing and it finished as he danced back away from my right cross and there was blood flowing down into my left eye.

There was more knowledge between us now and we were moving into some rhythm, each of us breaking it and the break becoming part of it and the sweat started and my breathing was no longer even. We traded a bit and he was faster but I was fast enough and strong enough that he couldn't walk in. But only for now. The first real damage would probably be the last.

In the break that happened, that always happens in fights, when we stood back by accord for a moment, I heard the shouting of the crowd and saw him clearly enough to see that he was bleeding too and smiling. I was smiling and my left forearm seemed to be numb and I didn't care about anything and if I could survive being hit long enough to get a real one in, it would be okay.

I moved again but he was before me but not in front of me and I moved sideways into him in time to take his kick on the thigh, not the knee, and that hurt much more than my face had. I tried to go into him, searching with a long right and a long left but my leg hadn't moved like it was supposed to and he wasn't there. And then he was in front of me and my head went back like I'd run into a sledgehammer.

I tried to block what was coming but I couldn't see it. Everything was black and out of line and I felt like I was floating and I knew that I'd lost and the next one would be the last one.

But it didn't come, and instead there were soft, white clouds rolling up from under the tables and my eyes began to water and my throat began to close.

32

STOAT'S NEST

A nightmarish creature with huge eyes in a black face appeared in front of me and pushed a squashy, rubber thing against my face. I eventually caught on and helped pull the rubber hood of a gasmask onto my head and things stopped getting worse. My eyes were still streaming and my head felt like it was in the next county, but I blinked away enough tears to begin to see. The figure in front of me was wearing pyjamas and, by the eyes, which was all I could really see of her, was Susie.

The room was full of coughing and retching people amid the swirling teargas. A figure passed me, leaping onto the table. It was Kem. He plucked up a chair and kicking things out of the way to make space, set it on the table, put a foot on the seat, then the back and launched himself at the wooden railings of the gallery. His left hand caught one of the spindles and he pulled himself round and handed himself up it as easy as walking.

Susie was behind me now, pulling on the straps of the mask, making it secure. She slapped me on the shoulder, letting me know it was okay and I turned and looked for Lizzy. She was still strapped to the chair but another girl in pyjamas had put a mask over her head and was bending to cut her free.

The white smoke was beginning to thin and settle now, falling towards the floor. More figures in masks, this time heavy male ones all in black were appearing in the doorway and taking possession of the coughing and retching people struggling for the way out. I looked up and could see figures moving in the gallery. The shock of the punch from Kem and the chemical attack on my eyes and throat and lungs was passing now and my brain was clearing. Berry. The Greens. A surge of energy came into my body and I launched myself at the table and the chair on it.

The chair tipped wildly under me as I pushed myself up from it, but I caught a bit of the woodwork and pulled myself up and over. At this height, the air was clearer and the other people there seemed to be fine without masks, so I fumbled at the straps and pulled mine off. I dropped the mask and wiped some of the mucus off my face.

"She's okay," Kem said.

"Yes, I'm fine," one of the pyjama girls said. She shook her head and her long black hair fell out and I saw that it was Mel. She looked a bit pale, but otherwise perfectly normal and cheerful.

"Glad to hear it," I said. "So am I, I think."

"Kem would've killed everyone in the building before he let anyone lay a finger on me," she said.

"I would indeed," Kem said, smiling again.

"Do you drive a dirty-white Land Rover, by any chance?" I said, looking at him anew.

"Sometimes I do. Yes, you are right; my family have served them for more generations than we know." He said it with pride and he was looking at Mel as if she were above and beyond all other mortal beings; a circumstance she seemed to find quite normal.

"Well, bloody hell," I said.

"Oh fuck," Berry said. "You're one of them. I should've known."

I looked at him for the first time. He was still sitting down which seemed odd. Then I noticed that there was a slim metal spike sticking out of the back of his left hand, pinning it to the carved rail of the balustrade. The knob on the end of it was in the shape of a beautiful gold and silver hare curled up. Maisie was on the chair next to him and was just sitting there with her chin on her chest. Her eyes were open, but I didn't think she was taking anything in.

"Is that your hairpin, Mel?" I said.

"Yes. He mistook me for a girl." She laughed.

"I feel we're missing a couple?" I said, looking at the doorway that led to the entrance from the landing on the main staircase.

"No, they went this way," Kem said, lifting one of the tapestries on the wall and revealing another of those low doorways with a solid, old looking, oak door in it. "Tricky sort of a house, this. It's locked, unfortunately."

"Ah."

"What can I say; we're one of those kinds of families," Berry said. "Si, you wouldn't just remove this splinter for me, would you? For old time's sake?"

"In a bit," I said. "There's no rush now." There was a small table against the back wall and it had plates of food and glasses of wine on it. I gave it some attention.

"Never mind all this," Mel said. "We don't care about all that. Where are the girls? If the Greens have them and he is the Greens," she looked at Berry, "then where the fuck are they?"

"Good question," I said, after swallowing a mouthful.

"Can you get us out of here, Si?" Kem said. He looked down at the banqueting hall below us which now contained Freddy's team in full black kit, gasmasks and MP5s, as well as the assembled retching and staggering throng. "I want to talk to Berry somewhere where no one can hear him scream."

"If they aren't at the Abbey, they have to be here somewhere, don't they?" Mel said. "If he is the Greens."

"Ah, but I'm not the Greens," Berry said. "I never said I was."

"But, you and Maisie, that was a pair of actors or…" Mel said, looking at me.

"No," I said. "Berry is just Berry. Maisie is just Maisie. The Greens are real and that was them."

"But you said he was it, them I mean," Mel said.

"Yes, but I was wrong again. It's been happening a lot lately."

There was the sound of fumbling from behind the tapestry and Kem lifted it up. His knife appeared in his hand. The door opened and the cheerful, weather-beaten face of Morny looked at us. He nodded to me and stepped in, revealing Susie. She was smiling and looking very alive and very beautiful.

"Si!" she said, and leapt into my arms and held me rather uncomfortably tight. "What a fight. I thought…"

"I wasn't actually going to kill him," Kem said, smiling. This time it was the kind of smile that didn't portend Armageddon.

Sophie Mole, Tamara Asty, Julie Whitsmith and Becky Rice came out of the small doorway too and went to stand behind Mel. Like Susie, they'd all changed out of their pyjamas into jeans and t-shirts. The narrow gallery was starting to seem quite full.

"You too?" Berry said, to Morny.

"Since the fourth generation, my lord," he said, touching his cap respectfully to the peer.

Berry turned round enough to look at the assembled girls, and then turned back to look at me. His face was set and I could see that it wasn't just the blade in his hand that was troubling him.

"You were right," Susie said, releasing me enough so that she could get a better look at me. "A girl in pyjamas, is just a girl in pyjamas."

"We all tend to see the uniform, not the person," I said. "Well known fact. Kem, do you have my gun, by any chance?"

"Yes, I have your gun," Kem said. "You look like you want to use it."

"I do. Care to do something with me? I think my friends are busy." I looked down at the main room where people were now being systematically led out by uniformed officers.

"What would you have me do?"

"Come hunting with me. And you, Morny, if you will?"

"My Lady?" Kem said, looking at Mel.

"You know where the girls are?" Mel said, looking at me.

"I think so," I said. "But there's no time to talk about it right now."

"Go with him," Mel said. "We will deal with this." She rose to her feet and the way she was looking at Berry wasn't any version of the girl I knew. The other girls were looking at Berry and Maisie too.

"Lead on, Si," Kem said.

"Count me in," Morny said.

"Si?" Berry said. He was looking genuinely frightened now.

"Sorry," I said. "You let them kill Anja."

"A girl?"

"Yes, just a girl."

I put the gasmask back on, and walked out onto the wide landing of the grand staircase. One of Freddy's men was standing in the hall, all in black and with a similar respirator, but also an MP5. He was watching two uniforms drag a woman in the remains of a ball gown out of the building. She was trying to scratch and kick them. I could tell that he was enjoying himself. I walked down to join him.

"Thought that was you," he said, rather indistinctly. "What a fucking tea-party."

"Is that you, Freddy?" I said.

"Who else would be here digging you out of the shit? As usual."

"Tonight, Titania, queen of the fairies. Seen Bill?"

"Up to his bollocks in it, processing. Out the front."

"Don't work too hard, will you."

"Fuck off."

I walked out into the soft summer evening. The last of the light was going out of the air, the coach-lights on the walls were throwing shadows from the many vehicles, and the trees of the parkland were looming black shapes.

The Range Rovers had been joined by a fleet of police cars and vans and there was a lot of coming and going by uniformed officers. Bill was walking in circles talking to his phone. I went and joined him and he waved away a couple of burly uniforms who had noticed me and were looking inclined to find out who and what I was.

"Fucking hell, Si. I've just arrested one chief constable and two fucking deputies," Bill said, putting his phone away. "And a lot of this country's organised crime I knew about, and a lot I didn't. Tony Beach and his team are in a chopper headed this way now. What I don't know is, what I'm going to charge them with?"

"People trafficking," I said.

"What people?"

"Give me a Range Rover and a phone with your number in it, and I'll call you in a bit."

"Anything you want, Si. Anything at all."

I drove straight through the low chain that separated the parking space from the immaculate grass. It was stronger than I expected and I heard some of the plastic bodywork of the Range Rover breaking, but it wasn't my Range Rover. I carried on round the house and stopped by the side entrance, off the terrace walk. The back door opened and the heavy car sank on its springs as two large dogs leapt into the boot. Morny got in the back and Kem in the front.

Correction, three dogs. A small, rough tongue was licking my arm and a stumpy tail wagging for all it was worth. I took my hand off the wheel long enough to ruffle Jake's ears and then stamped on the accelerator and we were off.

The quickest way was through the parkland and then the fields to the south of the White Wood, so that was the way we went. We didn't stop to open the gates, but, as I said, it wasn't my car. I turned the lights out when we got to the road but the moon had risen so I gave it the beans down the straight towards Effington and coasted onto the wide grass verge a hundred yards before the gateway to the Rectory.

Both Kem and I were wearing trainers and the loudest sound was the patter and scuff of three sets of dogs' paws on the smooth tarmac. Morny didn't count. When we got to the stone pillars at the entrance, we stepped quickly onto the gravel drive and then quickly off it onto the soft, mossy grass inside. We crossed the space to the cedar in the centre of the front lawn and crouched down in its shadow, cast by the light flooding out from the building.

All the windows of the Rectory were all lit up and the front door was wide open. All the curtians were open and we could see into the rooms. No one moved inside.

"They are waiting for us," I said. "Or at least, for someone."

"Why do you say that?" Kem said.

"The lights are on so that they can use the CCTV. I think someone, in an office with a steel door and banks of monitors, is quickly transferring money and gathering valuables. Destroying records. I'd like to stop them if I can."

"Are you waiting for something?" Morny said.

"Yup, I'm waiting for you to sneak off round to the back so that we've got them between us," I said. "Or would you rather have a nap first?"

"The youth of today," he said. "Got no respect." And then he was gone.

We gave him four minutes and then Kem and I got up and walked into the brightly lit hall. I had Thomas in my hands, hammers back, and the bag of cartridges over my shoulder. Kem was carrying what looked like a boar-spear and his dogs were at heel. We looked quickly into the adjoining rooms, a library and sitting room, but they were empty. The broad stone stairs wound up to the right and a wide, panelled passage led towards the back of the house. I was just about to go that way when we heard steps on the stairs above us.

Francesca Dutton was walking down. She was in an elegant but functional trouser suit and was carrying a good-sized handbag. She seemed perfectly composed and in no hurry. She had one of those small mirrors that women carry in her hand and she shut it and opened her bag to put it away.

"Good evening. Can I help you?" she said.

There was something wrong about it; she hadn't reacted to our weapons and her voice was too loud. I turned as fast as I could and put the right-hand barrel into the shoulder of a man coming from the passage, at the same time as he opened up with an MP5. His shots smashed the hall windows behind us as he spun round and fell down, none of them hitting us.

"That'll do girls," Kem said.

The remains of Francesca Dutton had slid to the bottom of the stairs, her long, pale legs lying awkwardly on the bottom two. Her throat was gone so far back that the pale bones of her vertebrae were visible through the welling blood. One of the dogs spat out a bit of her and they both moved daintily away from the pool that was spreading on the floor without taking their eyes off her. There was a long-barrelled small-calibre automatic on the floor beside Kem's foot.

The man with the MP5 was still alive, but no longer relevant. I considered taking it from him, but decided to stick with Thomas; it was that kind of evening.

We went up the stairs and through the next two floors at speed with the dogs doing most of the work. If they didn't think there was anyone there, then we believed them. There wasn't any kind of office of the sort I was expecting.

"Down again?" Kem said.

"No. We've missed something," I said.

"What?"

"There's the Victorian bit through there," I pointed to a wall, "it ought to connect. I don't see why it doesn't."

"These are tricksy kind of people," he said.

"Aren't they just."

I went back into the room that we'd just come out of. It seemed to be a little-used spare bedroom. There was a nice mahogany bookcase against the wall and it wasn't sitting right. I touched it and pulled. It swung easily towards me, revealing on the other side of the thickness of the wall, a solid steel door, six inches ajar. Charlie Dutton was looking at me through the gap. Not the Charlie I'd met before, but the real one.

There was a long instant while we held each other's eye and then I was trying to get past the bookcase and get Thomas lined up and he was heaving on the door.

I didn't get a shot but I got the barrels into the gap as the door slammed onto it, jarring my hand. I was heaving against its weight and so was Kem and the dogs were trying to get past us. It swung and the dogs were through ahead of me. I saw his back as he reached the end of the corridor and swung through a doorway. I shot over the dogs' heads and saw the safety glass in the fire-door beyond star but not break.

"Morny will get him," Kem said.

We were standing at the closed doors of the lift. The motors were humming.

"What is this place?" Kem said.

We looked and found an operating theatre and rooms with hospital beds; three of them occupied. A couple of women in nurse's uniforms cowered behind a desk, watching us with frightened eyes.

"Ah hah," I said.

"What?" Kem said.

"I'll tell you later," I said, putting my foot against the door to the stairwell with everything I'd got. It splintered and split at the lock and crashed back against the wall. We sent the dogs racing down and Jake went behind them, though I wasn't sure what use he could be. We followed and came out at the bottom of the lift-shaft. The lift stood there empty, with its doors locked open.

"I think we should be careful going out there," I said, indicating the doorway to the back courtyard.

"Wait," Kem said, to the dogs. He opened the door with the point of his spear and I stepped into the gap. There was nothing moving. The Mercedes van was parked to one side and the door to the boiler room was open. I didn't like it.

"We'll use the girls," Kem said, moving so that he could see too.

"Good," I said.

"Go to it," he said.

The dogs moved out across the cobbles, looking about and raising their noses to smell the air. Jake went a few feet behind them, sniffing the ground. Kem and I went after, moving apart so that we weren't one target.

"Psy! Psy!" someone shouted from my right.

I turned, too late, to see the muzzle flash from an MP5 coming from the door to the boiler room. There were other shots but I ignored them and put one through the door and followed it fast, stepping sideways out of the opening.

The shattering noise of a twelve gauge at short range had shocked him, even though it had missed him by feet, and his burst was slow and missed me by inches. I'd expected him to be taller, so my second barrel took the top of his head off, but that would do.

There were more shots from the direction of the kitchen and from behind the van and then a scream. I reloaded and went out to see.

Morny walked out of the kitchen door. Kem came out from behind the van looking grim. One of his dogs was with him. The other was in the middle of the yard, her hindquarters twisted under her, her forepaws trying to raise her. Not making a sound.

He went to her, sat down beside her and pulled her head gently onto his lap. He spoke to her and she stopped trying to get up and lay against him. I turned away and went to see what was what.

There was one ex-GROM dead in the boiler room and one behind the van. The one behind the van bore the signs of an encounter with a dog. A woman came out of the kitchen supporting a man who looked grey and holding himself as if he was in great pain. They were leaving a trail of blood as they moved. I kept the muzzle of Thomas pointing in their general direction but I don't think it was necessary.

"How're you doing, Si?" Morny said.

"Pretty good. You?"

"Best day I've had for ages."

Jake was standing by the other door. He looked at me and whined. He was shaking a bit. Actually, so was I. I went to have a careful look. It was the staff room where the Pole had been rude to me a few days earlier. He was past that now. He sat in his chair with another MP5 and an un-drunk cup of instant coffee in front of him on the table. His head hung forward over his chest and blood dripped from his open mouth. Kem's spear was growing out of his chest.

Jake went round the room sniffing and then came to me. He seemed disappointed. Back in the yard, Kem was standing up now and the dog was lying on her side not moving. I got the phone Bill had given me out of my pocket and rang him.

"Si, where are you?" he said.

I told him where. "You might want to bring an ambulance or two and a doctor if you can lay your hands on one, and soco."

"What the fuck have you done?"

"Found my stoat," I said. "You can send Freddy back to the Abbey now. Tell him to get ready to open the front door."

"But we have the key?"

"He'll know what I mean."

Kem and Morny were standing there looking at me. I stood there looking at them, thinking. I went back to the staff room. They followed me.

"Morny, we're on chalk here, aren't we?" I said.

"Not exactly, no," he said.

"The Fyne brook is a chalk stream."

"So it is. The chalk breaks through there. There's a layer of hard lias on top."

"But the lias isn't that thick?"

"Only a few feet in places."

"When I came in here before there were a lot of coats hung up there," I said pointing to the coat rack. "But it was a hot summer day."

I stopped talking so that I could concentrate on the room. There was a figure carved into the keystone of the mantle-piece. It was a hare; a very familiar hare.

"That's what they call hubris, isn't it?" Kem said. He was wiping the blade of his spear on one of the spare coats.

"If we can find the way in, it might be," I said.

I stooped into the fireplace. There was no ash, it had been cleanly swept. I couldn't see much, so I got the phone out and used it as a torch. There was nothing to see except blackened stones and a bread oven at the side. I put my hand into that and felt a stone sticking out into the space. It was clean and smooth as if from much handling. I tried pulling it and pushing it and wiggling it and then lifted it and the whole of the back of the fireplace swung open to reveal a set of steps leading downwards.

33

GOOD EVENING, MY LADY

I could see why people liked to take a coat. I hadn't even got a shirt. It wasn't far underground but it was distinctly cool and rather gloomy. I looked up at Kem and Morny looking down at me, and said, "We could do with a torch. I don't suppose there's one up there, is there?"

"Why don't we turn the lights on?" Kem said, pointing to a new looking waterproof switch on the wall at the top of the stairs.

"If I put new wiring in my secret tunnel, I'd have it let me know when someone used it," I said. "Wouldn't you?"

"Strangely enough I've never thought about it, but you may be right," Kem said.

"It's not much, but how about this," Morny said, turning on a small hand torch and shining it down at me. "I keep it on me for odd things."

The weak light didn't carry far but it was better than the phone. I pointed Thomas where I was going, clamped the torch against her with my left hand, and began to run. There were the sounds of the others running with me.

The passage wasn't quite full height, at least not for me, and the floor was uneven. Occasionally, rough brickwork supplemented the chalk through which it had been cut. As far as I could tell it was dead straight and went on for a long way. Anyone at the other end with an automatic weapon could have turned us into a pile of bodies very easily so it seemed wise not to hang about.

The end came suddenly, rough steps cut from the rock leading up into darkness. I shone the light upwards and saw thick metal bars apparently bolted into a slab of rock above me. I went up and Kem was beside me. I pushed and he pushed and the slab swung upwards surprisingly easily, another massive piece, a counter-weight, coming down beside us.

I put my head and the gun up together and looked into the well-lit crypt of the old Abbey. It was massive, more than big enough to hold the forty or so young women who were sitting there on cheap plastic chairs, looking at me apprehensively.

I swung my legs over the edge of what appeared to be a sarcophagus and went quickly out. The others followed. It was a square space of many interlocking vaults; thick pillars of stone supporting the roof, and cut blocks lining the walls and floor; three, maybe four tennis courts worth. I kept Thomas level and looked at the girls.

"Don't I know you?" one of them said. She was looking at Kem.

"Yes, my lady," he said, going to her and kneeling. "My name is Kem Lorel."

"Herbert Morningstar, mam, mam," Morny said, touching his cap.

"Then you are…," the girl said. "Yes, you are. Does this mean that we are safe?"

"Yes, I believe so, my lady," Kem said. "We will make sure, and do you know what day it is?"

"Yes, we do… Tonight, of all nights. Ahh, thank the good…" Her shoulders relaxed with and she smiled with an inner happiness that transformed her.

"Leave it with us for a little, my lady," Morny said, rising.

"I think you're Jane Hamilton?" I said.

"I am, but I don't think I know you?" she said.

"We've never met," I said. "And you're Natasha Wilkinson, aren't you?" I said, to the girl sitting next to her, who was also looking beatifically happy.

"That's right," she said. "And who are you?" She had the long dark hair and pale complexion of the drugged girl in *Umbra Villus*, but now looked the picture of health.

"I've been looking for you," I said. "But I'll let someone else explain another time."

"Strange," Jane said, looking at me.

"I think we may be being watched," I said, waving Thomas in the direction of a cctv camera attached to the roof.

"Then, let's go and talk to the watcher," Kem said. He was smiling his smile again.

"I've heard about this, but I didn't think I'd ever see it." Morny said. He was looking at the some of the many sarcophagi that were set in rows on the floor. Some of them had cushions on them to make them comfortable to sit on. There was also couple of trestle beds, a water cooler and a bookcase full of books.

I followed the wires from the camera to one corner of the crypt and found stairs turning upwards into darkness. Kem and Morny joined me and I walked up them.

The torch had given out completely, so I put my hands up and felt wood. I pushed and it lifted, and faint moonlight came in. I seemed to be in another sarcophagus but this time it was a big wooden box. I pushed the lid fully open and climbed out into the pretty little summerhouse in the Abbey gardens. There was a big pile of cushions for the garden furniture on the floor.

I turned back to those coming up behind me and put my finger to my lips to indicate silence. And then realised that this was quite unnecessary. Kem's dog leapt easily out and stood waiting. Morny gave Jake a hand and he took his place at my feet.

We crouched down at the entrance of the summer house and looked out into the moon-washed garden. It was silent and empty. There were lights on in a few of the windows, including the accommodation block. Kem knelt beside his dog and they both looked at the empty lawns with the same misgiving I felt.

"We could go that way," Morny said doubtfully, indicating the door that opened towards one of the box walkways.

"Let's do both," I said, "But hang on a minute."

I got the phone out and sent a text, 'now', to the one number in it. There was a pause and then a good solid 'crump' from the direction of the offices. A figure rose from behind a big hebe bush about fifty meters from us and ran towards the sound. It was carrying what looked like an AK47. "Tsa!" Kem said, and his dog was after it.

Morny went out the back like a black shadow on skates, and Kem and I went after the dog, going left and right, racing for cover. There was the sound of automatic fire and muzzle flash from the office-block and then the disciplined tap-tap of someone answering it. And then one barrel of Morny's twenty-bore from somewhere to my left.

Two dark shapes came out towards me from behind one of the trellis screens near the office entrance, both with AKs raised. I had Thomas swinging in to the first one, my finger on the front trigger, but a dark shape met it the air and pulled it down. I tried to get onto the second, knowing that I would probably be too late, and saw that a pale, wriggling shape was hanging off his arm, dragging it down.

I didn't have to find a shot. Kem's spear was there, lifting the man and turning him over to crash headfirst into the turf. When I got there, Jake was still worrying at the arm, his growls stifled by the mouthful of cloth and flesh. The wash of light from the windows showed me a pale face and I could tell that in the daylight, the man's hair would be ginger. Jules Dutton.

Kem checked the other one, but his dog had done its job and that patch of grass would be growing especially well from then on. No one I recognised.

There was no hurry then. Morny joined us, looking pleased with himself and he and Kem went back to fetch Jane. I told Jake to stop messing about and come with me and went to see what was occurring in the offices.

Bill was seated across the desk from the white-coated figure of Dr Simm. He had a compact Glock in his hand and a slightly dazed expression on his face. The doctor's right arm was hanging down and dripping blood onto the floor. He seemed to be in great pain.

"He was going to shoot me," Bill said, when he saw me.

"Hi Charlie," I said.

"Huh?" Bill said.

"Let's have a proper look at him, shall we?" I said.

I stood Thomas up against a filing cabinet and went over to the man. He looked at me as if he could see right through me and I meant nothing to him. I gave him a grin and pulled off his black wig and his glasses and then tore open his white coat revealing a loud waistcoat.

"Fucking hell," Bill said.

"Though I bet it's not Charlie, is it?" I said. "It's Ivan or something, isn't it?" I put two hands on his shirt and tore that open too. Sure enough, on his sternum was a tattoo of the diving eagle and lightning bolt.

"Ona cię dostanie," he said, straightening up and looking me in the eye.

"Come again?" I said.

"I said, she will find you," he said, smiling at me.

"Will she? Ah. Bill, how many nurses did you find at the rectory? With the patients there."

"One, I think. Why?"

"Dressing up is a family thing. Never mind." I went back to the other side of the room and repossessed myself of Thomas.

"Whatever you say," Bill said. "I need a cup of tea and a lie down, but I suppose I should read him his rights and we should…"

"Don't bother," I said. "But you might want to cover your ears." I put an ounce of number four shot through his chest where his heart should be, if he had one. When he'd fallen away, there was a considerable mess on the wall behind him.

34

IN THE HANDS OF WOMEN

I found Freddy in the courtyard. He'd taken his black balaclava off and was looking happy and as much disturbed by the turn of events as any oak tree would be. We had a brief chat about this and that, and he agreed to get his men to turn their backs for a moment.

I led Jane through the foyer, flanked by Morny and Kem, and we walked out onto the road and then turned right into the wood. Before we'd gone far, there was the sound of many sirens approaching fast on the road.

Mel herself met us in a small clearing not far in. She was wearing a long pale robe and was accompanied by two other girls, also in robes, and three men with long hair and boar-spears. I stopped in front of her. She smiled at me.

"Hello, Si," she said.

"Hi Mel," I said.

"You will be the only one to call me that tonight," she said.

"I know, my lady," I said, smiling.

"I had other plans for you, but…"

"After nine days abstinence?" I said. "I'm honoured."

"How did you know?" she said.

"Something you said. And I searched your things and found some pills."

"Yes. It doesn't matter now." She looked past me towards Kem, who bowed his head. "Under the circumstances, you may join us, if you care to?"

"I would be honoured," I said.

"Good. Come on then." She turned back and we walked together into the wood.

A while later, that seemed both a long time and no time at all, our faces bathed in the light of the three fires, I knelt in the clearing that was now as hallowed as any church. In front of me were at least a hundred women, all in pale robes, all our eyes on the three of them standing by the stone. Grace, Mel and Susie. On the stone was a long, pale shape and its head hanging down, had long black hair.

"Is there colour in the leaf?" Grace said, her face towards the east.

There was a long silence while the light grew perceptibly stronger and the world began to take on its colours again.

"Is there colour in the leaf?" Susie said, her eyes also towards the east.

There was more silence, the silence of perfect attention, and the light grew a little stronger.

"Is there colour in the leaf?" Mel said, her voice now slightly hoarse.

"Yes, there is colour in the leaf," the whole assembly said.

"Then this is the new day and we are done," Grace said. "Please put your vestments on the table and your bowls in the fire as you go. Your guides are waiting for you at the appointed places. If we don't see you on the moon, we'll see you here at the turning. Go well in her sacred, eternal name. Amen."

"Amen," rippled through us and we rose, released, and stretching and yawning and shaking off the otherness of it, and getting back to our normal, secular selves.

I was shivering by the time I got to the farmhouse, and Jake was dragging himself along too. Julie put a blanket over my shoulders and Lizzy took hold of my arm and led me to a chair. They both looked tired, but calm and happy. Lizzy had a neat, clean bandage on the stump where her little finger had been.

There was tea and toast and bacon and eggs, and Jake barely had time to finish his frozen bit of meat before he was asleep on his blanket. My head was nodding too, but it didn't matter, there was nothing that I had to do now. We didn't talk about it much; it was too soon for that yet.

"Does this mean we'll lose the farm?" Julie said.

"Not if I can help it," I said.

"I wonder where Cal is?" Lizzy said.

"Drunk in the hay probably," Julie said. "That's where he usually is on the night of the fete."

"What on earth will we tell him?" Lizzy said.

"Something about aliens," Julie said.

"You two both went to the women's walk-in centre in London, didn't you?" I said.

They looked at me.

"And Jess got you the jobs here?"

"Yes, that's right," Lizzy said. "How did you know?"

"In future, I'm going to try to remember to be suspicious of anyone I get on with too well," I said.

"You get on with us," Lizzy said.

"I do, don't I," I said.

There was the sound of cars arriving in the yard.

"I wonder who that is?" Julie said.

"Whoever it is, I think you should go to bed now, Si," Lizzy said. "Your dog has more sense than you do."

"That's okay," I said. "I'll sleep on the plane."

"You're leaving?" Lizzy said. "Now?"

"I must," I said. "I have a promise to keep. But I'll be back. Perhaps not for a while, but I'll be back."

I gave them both a hug. Julie ran up to the attic to get me a shirt and then I went out and got into one of the waiting Range Rovers and we drove away.

35

SOUP'S OFF

I didn't have enough hands, so I used my elbow to press the bell of my parents' flat in Holland Park. Mum opened the door and didn't know whether to look at me, or the sleeping girl in my arms. I solved the problem by giving her the girl and going into the kitchen to put the kettle on.

"I put her in your bed," she said, joining me at the table by the window a bit later.

"Her name's Irena," I said, pouring her some tea. "Her mum's dead and Bill hasn't been able to find any other family for her."

"I see."

I let it sink in and drank my tea and looked for squirrels in the trees of the square.

"You think we should?" she said.

"Yes," I said.

"Oh, my God. Can we?"

"No idea. What's to stop you?"

"Where's your father. I have to send him shopping now. Unless...?" she looked at me.

"Don't even think about it. I'm meeting him in twenty minutes. I'll send him home when I'm done with him."

"Si..."

"Mum?"

"Thank you."

"No problem." I left before she started to cry.

The gunroom had acquired another stool, so now there were three. Dad got off his and gave me a hug, which confused both of us. I sat on the third stool and accepted a mug of tea and a biscuit. Bill was working oil into a gunstock with apparent competence. He still looked knackered.

"Good flight, Si?" Dad said.

"Not bad. I'll be glad to get back to sea though."

"When are you leaving?"

"Not sure. This tide, or the next."

"Nat says hi," Bill said, looking at me properly for the first time.

"Say I say hi, back," I said.

"Do you want to know about it?" he said. "The girls and everything?"

"Egg donation and organ harvesting," I said. "Why have an ordinary child, when you can have a member of the British aristocracy? If you can't have your own, and if you can afford it. Like the Pogodins and the Wallaces of the world, can afford it."

"We've had a conversation with them, but we can't charge them," Bill said. "The Wallaces and the Pogodins and a few others. We found Francesca's laptop in a drawer and it had everything on it. The girls were held for a few months while their cycles were synchronised with the recipient and their eggs harvested. I expect the service came with an unspoken guarantee that there would be no more little darlings from that particular noble line."

"Which is why they killed them," Dad said.

"And each child came with its own personal pedigree on a fancy scroll, didn't it?" I said.

"Major Smythe is in our cells," Bill said. "Conspiracy to enslave. He's a disbarred member of the college of heralds. We've got all his records too."

"Cold-blooded bastards," Dad said.

"Yup," I said.

"And they collected girls from eastern Europe," Bill said. "They tissue-typed them and either kept them at the Abbey or sold them on to be prostitutes. When a recipient turned up, they were fetched back and their organs harvested."

"I assume Jules was doing the surgery?" I said.

"Yes. We found human remains in that furnace out the back," Bill said.

"And Jess and Berry were doing the poisoning between them. Berry at the private house-parties and Jess at the clubs dressed as a waitress. Berry ran the clubs and Jess and Jules ran the slave-trade, Charlie and Francesca ran the medical side. Very tightly organised. You know Charlie was ex-GROM?"

"I saw the tattoo," I said.

"But what happened to the tenth earl?" Dad said. "We can't seem to find him."

"You won't," I said. "But you don't need to. It's fine."

"Why did he do all this?" Bill said. "Apart from the money, I mean. They were his people, after all; all these girls."

"Not keen on women," I said. "It was to do with his up-bringing. He never felt he was good enough. Best not to pursue it."

"If you say so."

"Good. The hotel, isn't going to be doing so much business," I said.

"I expect it'll survive," Bill said.

"Any sign of the girl?"

"Jessica Dutton? No sign at all."

"Have you noticed that when someone has a very distinctive feature, like flaming red hair, if you get rid of that, with a wig or something, then they're much harder to recognise?"

"Quite a girl; pharmacologist, philanthropist, waitress and cold-blooded killer," Bill said. "No wonder you two got on."

"Thanks. You know she poisoned me once? Put me to sleep on Polly, searched her, and stole my spare keys."

"How did she manage that, I wonder?" Dad said, smiling.

"Don't ask. Used working for the women's shelter as a way to pick up any women that got away. I bet it was Jules in a wig who got Anja out of their secure accommodation."

"Speaking of things we don't know," Bill said. He hadn't really been listening. "Who was it who set off all those tear-gas canisters at the hall? And who killed all those people at the rectory and the Abbey? The ME said some of them died by dog bite."

"I've got pretty good teeth," I said, giving him a grin.

"You're not going to tell me, are you?" Bill said.

"No."

"Bastard."

"Let's just say that the Berry and the Duttons accidentally offended the Gods and suffered divine retribution," I said.

"What do you mean, offended the Gods? What Gods?"

"In this case, the female ones."

"I wonder where Henriques is?" Mel said, looking at the other tables over her menu.

"Gone on to other duties, I expect," I said.

"What do you mean?"

"Well he wasn't really a waiter, was he?"

"No, he was an actor."

"If you say so."

"What do you mean?"

"Nothing. What're you going to do now?"

"Oh. I thought I'd take a holiday."

"But aren't you in full flow now? I read your piece in the Guardian."

"No, you didn't."

"Okay, I didn't read it, but I knew it was there."

"Only because I sent you a text to tell you it was."

"Sorry."

"That's okay."

"Where are you going on holiday?"

"I've a friend who has a villa in the south of France. Not far from Cannes."

"Sounds nice. Will you be there for long?"

"I don't know. A while, I expect. A few months. Why?"

"About nine months?"

"No, longer than that. What're you going to do?"

"Just take a little cruise. Get some sea air and think about it all."

"I see."

"You don't sound like you believe me."

"I suppose you don't need your car then?"

"I suppose I don't." I took the key out of my pocket and gave it to her.

"Thank you."

"You're welcome."

A waitress came over to see if we were ready to order. Mel chose the soup, so I did too. With a pizza to follow.

"Stop looking at that girl's behind," Mel said, as I watched her walk away.

"It's a very fine behind," I said.

"Men," she said.

"How are all the girls?" I said. "After all that."

"Mixed. Nat's okay, but they took Jane's eggs…" we talked about it all for a while in a guarded sort of way. Being careful not to say the things that shouldn't be said. "Haven't seen Susie for a while though. Have you?" she said. "It's almost like she's avoiding me."

"I'm sure she's fine," I said.

"That wasn't what I asked."

The waitress brought the soup. It looked good and smelt excellent.

"Mel, will you do something for me?" I said.

"I might. What?"

"Wait there a minute and don't eat anything. Not even a tiny bit."

"Oh. Okay."

I picked up my bowl of soup and went where the waitress had gone; through the swing doors into the kitchen. There was no sign of her so I asked the lad washing up. He looked confused but nodded towards a door that said staff-room.

She was by an open locker getting changed, her head shrouded in the tunic that she was peeling off. I went silently up to her and put the bowl of soup on top of the next locker. When her head came free from the material, there I was and she was looking at me. She didn't seem surprised.

"Hi, Jess," I said.

"Hello, Si," she said.

"Nice to see you again."

"Nice to see you too. We didn't get to have our race, did we?"

"Perhaps we did, in a way, don't you think?"

"Who's going to win, do you think?"

"I think we both know that."

"Do we?"

"I do."

Soup's Off

There was no point waiting so I put my hand over her face and smacked her head hard against the locker. That quieted her enough, and the long thin blade that she'd been working out of her belt dropped to the floor. I held her nose, tilted her head back and poured some soup into her open mouth. Then I turned her to face away from me and clamped her mouth shut with my other hand.

She fought like a demented thing, twisting and writhing until I thought that she would break her own neck, but eventually she had to swallow. I let go and pushed her away. She slumped down to the floor, shuddering.

"Will it be quick?" I said.

She didn't speak, perhaps she couldn't, but just looked up at me, hating me. I could see from the way her eyes were changing that it would be quick.

I stayed with her while it happened, and then I put a finger on her neck to be sure. Then I left, taking the soup bowl with me.

At the table, Mel was waiting, looking annoyed.

"What's up?" she said.

"Soup's off," I said picking up her bowl and putting it inside the other one. "Actually, I'm not hungry. I think we should go."

"You, not hungry?" she followed me outside and watched as I dropped the two bowls into the dock. "Why?"

"Tide's going to turn soon. I think I'll make a move."

"Now? Right now?"

"Yes, right now." I pulled her to me and kissed her before she could stop me. Inside the restaurant someone screamed.

The gates from the dock out into the Thames took a long time to open but I was on my boat now and the world of the city was nothing to do with me. The muddy water surged around us and I stood at the helm and watched the currents and the other traffic carefully as the prop drove us out into the fat, flooding river.

There was still a half hour of tide to come and we would be pushing against it to go downstream, but after that it would turn and sweep us down to the sea. The old wharves and new office buildings and the sweep of the river looked fine. Ancient and new. I decided I liked the city, but that I wouldn't bring my girl into its dirty waters again.

"You can come out now," I said.

"Sure?" Susie said.

"Yes, come up here with me and learn to steer this boat."

She came out and stood next to me, with one hand lightly on the wheel, looking down the river, her eyes clear and untroubled.

"Well, my goddess?" I said.

"Well enough, Si. Well enough," she said, leaning back against me.

About the Author
Rod Humphris

In his office you will find Rod typing, flanked by two enormous dogs, and surrounded by the ephemera he has collected on his travels.

"I always read. Since I can remember. First Asterix, then Willard Price, then Conan Doyle, then everything else. I've had a paperback jammed into my back pocket most days of my life. I remember wanting to write a book when I was about 12 and wanting to put everything into it".

"I've read every kind of book, but the ones I love most are stories of adventure, so that's what I write. I've put thousands of hours into learning to do it well. It's taken me a long time, but I've developed my own voice and my own style. I spend so much time with Si, my main character, that he seems as real to me as anyone I know. In some cases, more so. I'm happiest and most productive when travelling about in my battered old truck with a canoe on top and a dog in the back."

Rod Humphris is the winner of N. N. Light Best Fiction Award 2016

The
Simon Ellice series

"Simon spontaneously appeals to the reader by embodying that dream of a man who fears nothing, dares it all, outwits his adversaries and abides only his own judgement!"
- Amazon UK reviewer

Charismatic, bold and a ruthless warrior, Simon Ellice slinks through the world like a shark in a limpid pool.

Known simply as Si to friends and enemies, he doesn't dwell on past traumas, passing through life with a dry sense of humour and a death wish.

"A bit of a psychopath, he lives by his own moral compass"
- Amazon UK reviewer

A magnet for danger, Si also inspires loyalty in those who follow him. He gives his all, so why shouldn't they? He can be egotistical, self-centred and irresponsible, but readers will want to know more.

Dead Ground

Simon Ellice series, I

In the mountains and passes of Nuristan, British forces hunt the Taliban. Trouble is coming, that is certain. Only Lieutenant Simon Ellice, with a clarity born of grief and anger, can see what must be done. Dead Ground is a story of the impossibility of the task assigned to British soldiers in Afghanistan. A tale of the heroism, loyalty and individual responsibility in the chaos of war.

"Immersive, terrifying and moving experience"
- **Martin Fletcher**

"Humphris is good on the range of emotions experienced under extreme pressure in an isolated base"
- **NB Magazine**

"When you get your hands on a copy of Dead Ground by Rod Humphris you won't be able to stop yourself from flicking open the cover, playing with the flaps and enjoying the tactility of the uncoated card stock used for the jacket. The fulll wraparound illustration is pretty striking as well."
- **Crime Fiction Lover**

Go Fast

Simon Ellice series, II

N.N.Light Award Best Fiction, 2016, Winner

Highly charged, action packed and intelligent, Go Fast is set in the vivid, exotic location of Morocco and is the first novel in the Simon Ellice series. On moonless nights Si runs hash from Morocco to Spain in his go-fast boat but soon discovers he's caught up in a tangle of illegal power and hidden love.

"It reminds me a little of Alex Garland's The Beach in its yearning for alternatives, its subversive, outlaw activities, the effortless, upbeat, driving momentum of its storytelling."
- **Martin Fletcher**

"Simon was fantastic. The flawed character of Sam reminds me of the character Bullseye in Daredevil. Gripping, action filled, brilliantly staged, surprises, suspense, humor *that made me laugh anyway* and now I cannot wait for the next book."
- **N.N. Light**

"I was plunged straight into the action and I loved the set-pieces at sea"
"too amoral" "a white knuckle ride of thriller"

Starlight

Simon Ellice series, III

Jamaica. Simon Ellice goes on a cocktail charged dally in Port Antonio. He brushes shoulders with the cloudy-eyed, over-sexed and deeply tranquillised Hollywood set. They become enamoured with him, and Si thus becomes embroiled when the ostensibly ostentatious wealth entices the exuberantly poor. Opportunistic thieves Stanley and Jason rattle Si's cage and go further than he was expecting. The question is, why?

"The pacing is clever, deceptively slow to begin with as the characters converse seemingly in a meandering unfocused way and then everything gradually crystallises when brutal reality intrudes."
- **Martin Fletcher**

"As the smell of marijuana drifts across a still bay and a murder plot unfolds, this 92-page novella gives readers the chance to dip into the author's work and sample his unique style"
-**Crime Fiction Lover**

Need more Si in your life?

Website:
www.ratstales.co.uk

Twitter:
@Rats_Tales, @Rod_Humphris

Rat's Tales Publishing Facebook:
https://www.facebook.com/ratstalespublishing/

Instagram:
@ratstalespublishing

Yes, we know. Simon Ellice is like marmite - you either hate him or love him, nothing in between. Whichever your take on this is, talk to Rod about it!:

talktorod@ratstales.co.uk